Tor Books by Glen Cook

An Ill Fate Marshalling
Reap the East Wind
The Swordbearer
The Tower of Fear

THE BLACK COMPANY
The Black Company (The First Chronicle)
Shadows Linger (The Second Chronicle)
The White Rose (The Third Chronicle)
Shadow Games (The First Book of the South)
Dreams of Steel (The Second Book of the South)
Bleak Seasons (Book One of Glittering Stone)
She Is the Darkness (Book Two of Glittering Stone)
Water Sleeps (Book Three of Glittering Stone)
Soldiers Live (Book Four of Glittering Stone)

The Silver Spike

The Ninth Chronicle
of the
Black Company

SOLDIERS LIVE

GLEN COOK

BOOK FOUR
OF
GLITTERING STONE

TOR®
fantasy

A TOM DOHERTY ASSOCIATES BOOK
NEW YORK

This is a work of fiction. All the characters and events portrayed in this book are either products of the author's imagination or are used fictitiously.

SOLDIERS LIVE

Copyright © 2000 by Glen Cook

A Tor Book
Published by Tom Doherty Associates, LLC
175 Fifth Avenue
New York, NY 10010

www.tor.com

Tor® is a registered trademark of Tom Doherty Associates, LLC.

ISBN: 0-812-56655-6

First edition: April 2001

Printed in the United States of America

0 9 8 7 6 5 4 3 2 1

For Russell Galen, #40, at a quarter century. It hasn't been a perfect marriage, but close enough to keep me smiling. Let's see if we can't make it to silver. (Diamond? Whatever a 50th anniversary is.)

1

An Abode of Ravens:
When No Men Died

Four years passed and no one died.

Not of violence or hazard of the calling, anyway. Otto and Hagop did pass on within days of each other, of natural causes associated with aging, last year. A few weeks ago one Tam Duc, recruit in training, perished of the overconfident exuberance of youth. He fell into a crevasse while he and his lance brothers were riding their blankets down the long slick slope of the Tien Myuen glacier. There were a few others. But not a one by an unfriendly hand.

Four years has to be a record, though not the sort often recalled in these Annals.

That much peace is impossible to believe.

Peace that prolonged becomes increasingly seductive.

Many of us are old and tired and retain no youthful fire in the belly. But us old farts are not in charge anymore. And though we were prepared to forget horror, horror was not as accomodating toward us.

In those days the Company was in service to its own name. We recognized no master. We counted the warlords of Hsien as our allies. They feared us. We were supernatural, many recalled from the dead, the ultimate Stone Soldiers. They dreaded the chance that we might take sides in their squabbles over the bones of Hsien, that once-mighty empire the Nyueng Bao recall as the Land of Unknown Shadows.

The more idealistic warlords have hopes of us. The mysterious File of Nine provide arms and money and let us recruit because they hope we can be manipulated into helping them restore the golden age that existed before the Shadowmasters enslaved their world so cruelly that its people still call themselves the Children of the Dead.

There is no chance we will participate. But we permit them the hope, the illusion. We have to get strong. We have a mission of our own.

By standing still we have caused the blossoming of a city. A once-chaotic encampment has become ordered and has acquired names, Outpost or the Bridgehead among those who came from beyond the plain and what translates as Abode of Ravens amongst the Children of the Dead. The place keeps growing. It has generated scores of permanent structures. It is in the processing of acquiring a wall. The main street is being paved with cobblestones.

Sleepy likes to keep everyone busy. She cannot stand a loafer. The Children of the Dead will inherit a treasure when we finally go away.

2

An Abode of Ravens: When the Baobhas Sang

Boom! *Boom!* Somebody hammered on my door. I glanced at Lady. She had stayed up late last night and so had fallen asleep while studying this evening. She was determined to discover all the secrets of Hsien magic and to help Tobo harness the startlingly plentiful supernatural manifestations of this world. Not that Tobo needed much help anymore.

This world has more real phantoms and marvellous beings hiding in the bushes and behind the rocks and trees and on the edge of night than any twenty generations of our own frightened peasants could imagine. They gravitate toward Tobo as though he is some sort of nightside messiah. Or amusing pet, maybe.

Boom! Boom! I would have to get off my butt myself. That looked like a long, hard trek over there.

Boom! Boom! "Come on, Croaker! Wake up!" The door swung inward as my visitor invited himself inside. The very devil of my thoughts.

"Tobo . . ."

"Didn't you hear the baobhas singing?"

"I heard a racket. Your friends are always kicking up a fuss about something. I don't pay any attention anymore."

"When the baobhas sing it means somebody is going to die. And there's been a cold wind off the plain all day and Big Ears and Golden-Eye have been extremely nervous and . . . it's One-Eye, sir. I just went over to talk to him. He looks like he'd had another stroke."

"Shit. Let me get my bag." No surprise, One-Eye suffering a stroke. That old fart has been trying to sneak out on us for years. Most of the vinegar went out of him back when we lost Goblin.

"Hurry!"

The kid loved that old shit-disturber. Sometimes it seemed like One-Eye was what he wanted to be when he grew up. In fact, it seemed Tobo venerated everybody but his own mother, though the friction between them diminished as he aged. He had matured considerably since my latest resurrection.

"I'm hurrying as fast as I can, Your Grace. This old body doesn't have the spring it did in the olden days."

"Physician, heal thyself."

"Believe me, kid, I would if I could. If I had my druthers I'd be twenty-three years old for the rest of my life. Which would last another three thousand years."

"That wind off the plain. It has Uncle worried, too."

"Doj is always worried about something. What does your father say?"

"He and Mom are still at Khang Phi visiting Master Santaraksita."

At a tender twenty Tobo is already the most powerful sorcerer in all this world. Lady says he might possibly become a match for her in her prime. Scary. But he has parents he calls Mom and Dad still. He has friends he treats like people, not objects. He accords his teachers respect and honor instead of devouring them just to prove that he is stronger. His mother raised him well, despite having done so in the environment of the Black Company. And despite his innate rebellious streak. I hope he will remain a decent human being once he comes into his full powers.

My wife does not believe that is possible. She is a pessimist about character. She insists that power corrupts. Inevitably. She has only her own history by which to judge. And she sees only the dark side of everything. Even so, she remains one of Tobo's teachers. Because, despite her bleak outlook, she retains the silly romantic streak that brought her here with me.

I did not try to keep up with the boy. Time definitely has slowed me. And has left me with an ache for every one of the thousands of miles this battered old corpse has trudged. And it has equipped me with an old man's talent for straying off the subject.

The boy never stopped chattering about the Black Hounds, fees, hobs and hobyahs and other creatures of the night that I have never seen. Which is all right. The few he has brought around have all been ugly, smelly, surly, and all too eager to copulate with humans of any sex or sexuality. The Children of the Dead claim that yielding is not a good idea. So far discipline has held.

The evening *was* chill. Both moons were up. Little Boy was full. The sky was totally clear except for a circling owl being pestered by what appeared to be a brace of night-flying rooks. One of those, in turn, had some smaller black bird skipping along behind it, darting in and out as it prosecuted reprisals for some corvine trangression. Or just for the hell of it, the way my sister-in-law would do.

Likely none of the flyers were actual birds.

A huge something loomed beyond the nearest house. It made snorting noises and shuffled away. What I made out looked vaguely like the head of a giant duck. The earliest of the conquering Shadowmasters had possessed a bizarre turn of humor. This big, slow, goofy thing was a killer. Among the worst of the others were a giant beaver, a crocodile with eight legs and a pair of arms and many variations of the themes of killer cattle, horses and ponies, most of which spend their daytimes hiding underwater.

The most bizarre beings were created by the nameless Shadowmaster now recalled as the First One or the Master of Time. His raw material had consisted of shadows off the glittering plain, which in Hsien are known as the Host of the Unforgiven Dead. It seems appropriate that Hsien be called the Land of Unknown Shadows.

A long feline roar ripped the night. That would be Big Ears or his sister Cat Sith. By the time I reached One-Eye's place the Black Hounds had begun to vocalize, too.

One-Eye's house was scarcely a year old. The little wizard's friends raised it after they completed their own places. Before that One-Eye and his girlfriend, Tobo's grandmother Gota, lived in an ugly, smelly little stick-and-mud hut. The new place was of mortared stone. It had a first rate thatch roof above its four large rooms, one of which concealed a still. One-Eye might be too old and feeble to weasel his way into the local black market but I am sure he will continue distilling strong spirits till the moment his own spirit departs his wizened flesh. The man is dedicated.

Gota kept the house spotless via the ancient device of bullying her daughter Sahra into doing the housework. Gota, still called the Troll by the old hands, was as feeble as One-Eye. They were a matched pair in their passion for potent beverages. When One-Eye gave up the ghost he would be drawing a gill of the hard stuff for his honey.

Tobo poked his head back outside. "Hurry up!"

"Know who you're talking to, boy? The former military dictator of all the Taglias."

The boy grinned, no more impressed than anyone else is these days. "Used to be" is not worth the breeze on which it is scribbled.

I tend to philosophize about that, probably a little too much. Once upon a time I was nothing and had no ambition to be anything more. Circumstance conspired to put immense power into my hands. I could have ripped the guts out of half a world had that been my inclination. But I let other obsessions drive me. So I am here on the far side of the circle, where I started, scraping wounds, setting bones and scribbling histories nobody is likely to read. Only now I am a lot older and crankier. I have buried all the friends of my youth except One-Eye. . . .

I ducked into the old wizard's house.

The heat was ferocious. One-Eye and Gota had trouble keeping warm even in summer. Though summers in southern Hsien seldom become hot.

I stared. "You sure he's in trouble?"

Tobo said, "He tried to tell me something. I didn't understand so I came for you. I was afraid." Him. Afraid.

One-Eye was seated in a rickety chair he had built for himself. He was motionless but things stirred in the corners of the room, usually only visible at the edge of my eye. Snail shells cluttered the floor. Tobo's father, Murgen, calls them brownies after little folk recalled from his youth. There had to be twenty different races of them around, from no bigger than a thumb to half a man high. They really did do work when nobody was looking. That drove Sleepy crazy. It meant she had to work harder to think up chores to keep the Company's villains out of trouble.

An overpowering stench pervaded One-Eye's house. It came from the mash for his still.

The devil himself looked like a shrunken head the shrinker had not bothered to separate from its body. One-

Eye was a little bit of a thing. Even in his prime he had not been big. At two hundred and some years old, with both legs and most of one arm in the grave, he looked more like a shriveled monkey than a human being.

I said, "I hear tell you're trying to get some attention again, old man." I knelt. One-Eye's one eye opened. It focused on me. Time had been kind in that respect. His vision remained good.

He opened his toothless mouth. At first nothing came out. He tried to raise a mahogany spider of a hand. He did not have the strength.

Tobo shuffled his feet and muttered at the things in the corners. There are ten thousand strange things infesting Hsien and he knows every one by name. And they all worship him. For me this intersection with the hidden world has been the most troubling development of our stay in the Land of Unknown Shadows.

I liked them better when they were still unknown.

Outside Skryker or Black Shuck or another Black Hound began raising a racket. Others replied. The uproar moved southward, toward the shadowgate. I willed Tobo to go investigate.

He stayed put, all questions and nags. He was about to become a major pain in the ass. "How's your grandmother?" I asked. Preemptive strike. "Why don't you check?" Gota was not in the room. Usually she was, determinedly trying to do for One-Eye even though she had grown as feeble as he was.

One-Eye made a noise, moved his head, tried to raise that hand again. He saw the boy leave the room. His mouth opened. He managed to force out words in little bursts. "Croaker. This is the . . . last. . . . She's done. I feel it. Coming. Finally."

I did not argue with him, did not question him. My error. We had been through similar scenes a half dozen times. His strokes were never quite fatal. It seemed fate had some last role for him in the grand design.

Whatever, he had to work his way through his standard soliloquy. He had to warn me against hubris because he could not get it into his head that not only am I no longer the Liberator, the military dictator of all the Taglias; I have abdicated claim to captaincy of the Black Company. The Captivity did not leave me rational enough for that task. Nor had my understudy, Murgen, come through sufficiently unscathed. The burden now rests upon Sleepy's sturdy little shoulders.

And One-Eye had to ask me to look out for Gota and Tobo. Over and over he would remind me to watch out for Goblin's wicked tricks even though we had lost Goblin years ago.

I suspect that, should there be any afterlife at all, those two will meet up about six seconds after One-Eye croaks and they will pick up their feud right where they left it in life. In fact, I am a little surprised Goblin has not been around haunting One-Eye. He threatened to often enough.

Maybe Goblin just cannot find him. Some of the Nyueng Bao say they feel lost because the shades of their ancestors cannot find them to watch over them and give advice inside their dreams.

Kina cannot find us, either, apparently. Lady has not had a bad dream in years.

Or maybe Goblin killed her.

One-Eye beckoned with one desiccated finger. "Closer."

Kneeling in front of him, opening my kit, I was about as close as I could get. I took his wrist. His pulse was weak and rapid and irregular. I did not get the impression that he had suffered a stroke.

He murmured, "I am not. A fool. Who doesn't know. When he is. And what. Has happened. You *listen!* You watch out. For Goblin. Little Girl. And Tobo. Didn't see him dead. Left him with. Mother of Deceit."

"Shit!" That never occurred to me. I was not there. I was

still one of the Captured when Goblin stuck the sleeping Goddess with the standard. Only Tobo and Sleepy had witnessed that. And anything they knew had to be suspect. Kina was the Queen of Deceivers. "A good idea, old man. Now, what do I have to do to get you to get up and fetch me a drink?"

Then I started as something that looked like a small black rabbit peeked at me from under One-Eye's chair. This was a new one. I could call Tobo. He would know what it was. There are uncounted varieties of the things, huge and small, some gentle and many definitely not. They just gravitate toward Tobo. In only a few cases, generally involving the most disagreeable sorts, has he taken Lady's advice and bound them to his personal service.

The Children of the Dead worry about Tobo. Having suffered a few hundred years under the heels of the Shadowmasters they are paranoid about outsider sorcerers.

So far the warlords have remained reasonable. None of them want to spark the ire of the Soldiers of Darkness. That might cause the Company to align itself with a rival. Status quo and balance of force are cherished and jealously nurtured by the File of Nine. Terrible chaos followed the expulsion of the last Shadowmaster. None of the warlords want the chaos to return, though what Hsien has now resembles nothing so much as lightly organized anarchy. But not a one is willing to yield a minimum of power to another authority, either.

One-Eye grinned, revealing dark gums. "Not going to. Trick me. Captain."

"I'm not the Captain anymore. I'm retired. I'm just an old man who pushes paper as an excuse to keep hanging around with the living. Sleepy is the boss."

"Still. Management."

"I'm about to manage your scruffy old ass. . . ." I trailed off. His eye had closed. He made a statement by beginning to snore.

Another hoot and holler arose outside, some close by, more far away toward the shadowgate. The snail shells creaked and rustled and, though I never saw a one touched by anything, rocked and spun around. Then I heard the distant bray of a horn.

I rose and retreated, not turning my back. One-Eye's lone remaining pleasure—other than staying drunk—was tripping the unwary with his cane.

Tobo reappeared. He looked ghastly. "Captain . . . Croaker. Sir. I misunderstood what he tried to tell me."

"What?"

"It wasn't him. It was Nana Gota."

3

An Abode of Ravens:
A Labor of Love

Tobo's grandmother, Ky Gota, had died happy. As happy as the Troll could die, which was drunker than three owls drowned in a wine cask. She had enjoyed a vast quantity of extremely high-potency product before she went. I told the boy, "If it's any consolation she probably didn't know a thing." Although the evidence suggested she knew exactly what was happening.

I did not fool him. "She knew it was coming. The Greylings were here." Something behind the still chittered softly in reponse to the sound of his voice. Like the baobhas, the greylings are a harbinger of death. One of a great many in Hsien. Some of the things that had been howling in the wilderness earlier would have been, too.

I said the things you say to the young. "It was probably a blessing. She was in constant pain and there was nothing I could do for her anymore." The old woman's body had been a torment to her for as long as I had known her. Her last few years had been hell.

For a moment Tobo looked like a sad little boy who wanted to bury his face in his mother's skirt and shed some tears. Then he was a young man whose control was complete again. "She did live a long life and a fulfilled one, no matter how much she complained. The family owes One-Eye for that."

Complain she had, often and loudly, to everyone about everything and everyone else. I had been fortunate enough to miss much of the Gota era by having gotten myself buried alive for a decade and a half. Such a clever man am I. "Speaking of family, you'll have to find Doj. And you'd better send word to your mother. And as soon as you can you'll need to let us know about funeral arrangements." Nyueng Bao funerary customs seem almost whimsical. Sometimes they bury their dead, sometimes they burn them, sometimes they wrap them and hang them in trees. The rules are unclear.

"Doj will make the arrangements. I'm sure the Community will demand something traditional. In which case my place is somewhere out of the way."

The Community consists of those Nyueng Bao associated with the Black Company who have not enlisted formally and who have not yet disappeared into the mysterious reaches of the Land of Unknown Shadows.

"No doubt." The Community are proud of Tobo but custom demands that they look down on him for his mixed blood and lack of respect for tradition. "Others will need to know, too. This'll be a time of great ceremony. Your grandmother is the first female from our world to pass away over here. Unless you count the white crow." Old Gota seemed much less formidable in death.

Tobo's thoughts were moving obliquely to mine. "There'll be another crow, Captain. There'll always be another crow. They feel at home around the Black Company." Which is

why the Children of the Dead call our town the Abode of
Ravens. There *are* always crows, real or unknown.

"They used to stay fat."

The unknown shadows were all around us now. I could
see them easily myself, though seldom clearly and seldom
for more than an instant. Moments of intense emotion draw
them out of the shells where Tobo taught them to hide.

A renewed racket arose outside. The little darknesses
stirred excitedly, then scattered, somehow disappearing
without ever revealing what they were. Tobo said, "The
dreamwalkers must be hanging around on the other side of
the shadowgate again."

I did not think so. This evening's racket was different.

An articulate cry came from the room where we had left
One-Eye. So the old man had been faking his snooze after
all. "I'd better see what he wants. You get Doj."

"You don't believe it." The old man was agitated now. He
was angry enough to speak clearly, without much huffing
and puffing. He threw up a hand. One wrinkled, twisted
ebony digit pointed at something only he could see. "The
doom is coming, Croaker. Soon. Maybe even tonight."
Something outside howled as if to strengthen his argument
but he did not hear it.

The hand fell. It rested for several seconds. Then it rose
again, one digit indicating an ornate black spear resting on
pegs above the doorway. "It's done." He had been crafting
that death tool for a generation. Its magical power was
strong enough for me to sense whenever I considered it
directly. Normally I am deaf, dumb and blind in that area. I
married my own personal consultant. "You run into. Goblin.
Give him. The spear."

"I should just hand it over?"

"My hat, too." One-Eye showed me a toothless grin. For
the entirety of my time with the Company he had worn the
biggest, ugliest, dirtiest, most disreputable black felt hat

imaginable. "But you got. To do it. Right." So. He still had one practical joke to pull even though it would be on a dead man and he would be dead himself long before it could happen.

There was a scratch at the door. Someone entered without awaiting invitation. I looked up. Doj, the old swordmaster and priest of the Nyueng Bao Community. Associated with the Company but not of it for twenty-five years now. I do not entirely trust him even after so long. I seem to be the only doubter left, though.

Doj said, "The boy said Gota . . ."

I gestured. "Back there."

He nodded understanding. I would focus on One-Eye because I could do nothing for the dead. Nor all that much for One-Eye, I feared. Doj asked, "Where is Thai Dei?"

"At Khang Phi, I assume. With Murgen and Sahra."

He grunted. "I'll send someone."

"Let Tobo send some of his pets." That would get some of them out from under foot—and have the additional consequence of reminding the File of Nine, the master council of warlords, that the Stone Soldiers enjoy unusual resources. If they could detect those entities at all.

Doj paused at the doorway to the back. "There's something wrong with those things tonight. They're like monkeys when there's a leopard on the prowl."

Monkeys we know well. The rock apes haunting the ruins lying where Kiaulune stands in our own world are as pesky and numerous as a plague of locusts. They are smart enough and deft enough to get into anything not locked up magically. And they are fearless. And Tobo is too soft of heart to employ his supernatural friends in a swift educational strike.

Doj vanished through the doorway. He remained spry although he was older than Gota. He still ran through his fencing rituals every morning. I knew by direct observation that he could defeat all but a handful of his disciples using practice swords. I suspect the handful would be surprised unpleasantly if the duel ever involved real steel.

Tobo is the only one as talented as Doj. But Tobo can do anything, always with grace and usually with ridiculous ease. Tobo is the child we all think we deserve.

I chuckled.

One-Eye murmured, "What?"

"Just thinking how my baby grew up."

"That's funny?"

"Like a broken broom handle pounded up the shit chute."

"You should. Learn to appreciate. Cosmic. Practical jokes."

"I . . ."

The cosmos was spared my rancor. The street door opened to someone even less formal than Uncle Doj. Willow Swan invited himself inside. "Shut it quick!" I snapped. "That moonlight shining off the top of your head is blinding me." I could not resist. I recalled him when he was a young man with beautiful long blond hair, a pretty face and a poorly disguised lust for my woman.

Swan said, "Sleepy sent me. There're rumors."

"Stay with One-Eye. I'll deliver the news myself."

Swan bent forward. "He breathing?"

With his eye shut One-Eye looked dead. Which meant he was laying back in the weeds hoping to get somebody with his cane. He would remain a vicious little shit till the moment he did stop breathing.

"He's fine. For now. Just stay with him. And holler if anything changes." I put my things back in my bag. My knees creaked as I rose. I could not manage that without putting some of my weight on One-Eye's chair. The gods are cruel. They should let the flesh age at the rate the spirit does. Sure, some people would die of old age in a week. But the keepers would hang around forever. And I would not have all these aches and pains. Either way.

I limped as I left One-Eye's house. My feet hurt.

Things scurried everywhere but where I was looking. Moonlight did not help a bit.

4

The Grove of Doom:
Night Songs

The drums had begun at sunset, softly, a dark whispering promise of a shadow of all night falling. Now they roared boldly. True night had come. There was not even a sliver of moon. The flickering light of a hundred fires set shadows dancing. It appeared that the trees had pulled up their roots to participate. A hundred frenzied disciples of the Mother of Night capered with them, their passion building.

A hundred bound prisoners shivered and wept and fouled themselves, fear unmanning some who had believed themselves heroic. Their pleas fell upon unhearing ears.

A looming darkness emerged from the night, dragged by prisoners straining at cables in the hopeless hope that by pleasing their captors they might yet survive. Twenty feet tall, the shape proved to be a statue of a woman as black and glistening as polished ebony. It had four arms. It had rubies for eyes and crystal fangs for teeth. It wore a necklace of skulls. It wore another necklace of severed penises. Each taloned hand clutched a symbol of her power over humanity. The prisoners saw only the noose.

The beat of the drums grew more swift. Their volume rose. The Children of Kina began to sing a dark hymn. Those prisoners who were devout began to pray to their own favored gods.

A skinny old man watched from the steps of the temple at the heart of the Grove of Doom. He was seated. He no longer stood unless he had to. His right leg had been broken and the bone improperly set. Walking was difficult and painful. Even standing was a chore.

A tangle of scaffolding rose behind him. The temple was undergoing restoration. Again.

Standing over him, unable to remain still, was a beautiful young woman. The old man feared her excitement was sensual, almost sexual. That should not be. She was the Daughter of Night. She did not exist to serve her own senses.

"I feel it, Narayan!" she enthused. "The imminence is there. This is going to reconnect me with my mother."

"Perhaps." The old man was not convinced. There had been no connection with the Goddess for four years. He was troubled. His faith was being tested. Again. And this child had grown up far too headstrong and independent. "Or it may just bring the wrath of the Protector down on our heads." He went no farther. The argument had been running from the moment that she had used some of her raw, completely untrained magical talent to blind their keepers for the moments they had needed to escape the Protector's custody three years ago.

The girl's face hardened. For a moment it took on the dread implacability apparent on the face of the idol. As she always did when the matter of the Protector came up, she said, "She'll regret mistreating us, Narayan. Her punishment won't be forgotten for a thousand years."

Narayan had grown old being persecuted. It was the natural order of his existence. He sought always to make sure that his cult survived the wrath of its enemies. The Daughter of Night was young and powerful and possessed all of youth's impetuosity and disbelief in its own mortality. She was the child of a Goddess! That Goddess's ruling age was about to break upon the world, changing everything. In the new order the Daughter of Night would herself become a Goddess. What reason had she to fear? That madwoman in Taglios was nothing!

Invincibility and caution, they were forever at loggerheads, yet were forever inseparable.

The Daughter of Night did believe with all her heart and soul that she was the spiritual child of a Goddess. She had to. But she had been born of man and woman. A flake of humanity remained as a stain upon her heart. She had to have *somebody*.

Her movements became more pronounced and more sensual, less controlled. Narayan grimaced. She must not forge an interior connection between pleasure and death. The Goddess was a destroyer in one avatar but lives taken in her name were not taken for reasons so slight. Kina would not countenance her Daughter yielding to hedonism. If she did there would be punishments, no doubt falling heaviest upon Narayan Singh.

The priests were ready. They dragged weeping prisoners forward to fulfill the crowning purpose of their lives, their parts in the rites that would reconsecrate Kina's temple. The second rite would strive to contact the Goddess, who lay bound in enchanted sleep, so that once again the Daughter of Night would be blessed with the Dark Mother's wisdom and far-seeing vision.

All things that needed doing. But Narayan Singh, the living saint of the Deceivers, the great hero of the Strangler cult, was not a happy man. Control had drifted too far away. The girl had begun altering the cult to reflect her own inner landscape. He feared the chance that one of their arguments would not heal afterward. That had happened with his real children. He had sworn an oath to Kina that he would bring the girl up right, that they both would see her bring on the Year of the Skulls. But if she continued growing ever more headstrong and self-serving . . .

She could restrain herself no longer. She hurried down the steps. She plucked a strangling scarf from the hands of one of the priests.

What Narayan saw in the girl's face then he had seen only one place before, in his wife's face, in her passion, so long ago that it seemed to have happened during an earlier turn around the Wheel of Life.

Saddened, he realized that when the next rite started she would throw herself into the torture of the victims. In her state she might become too involved and spill their blood, which would be an offense the Goddess would never excuse.

He was becoming extremely troubled, was Narayan Singh.

And then he became more troubled still as his wandering eye caught sight of a crow in the crotch of a tree almost directly behind the deadly rite. Worse, that crow noticed him noticing it. It flung itself into the air with a mocking cry. A hundred crow voices immediately answered from all over the grove.

The Protector *knew!*

Narayan yelled at the girl. Attention much too focused, she did not hear him.

Agony ripped through his leg as he climbed to his feet. How soon would the soldiers arrive? How would he ever run again? How would he keep the Goddess's hope alive when his flesh had grown so frail and his faith had worn so threadbare?

5

An Abode of Ravens:
Headquarters

Outpost was a quiet city of broad lanes and white walls. We had adopted the native custom of whitewashing everything but the thatch and decorative vegetation.

On holidays some locals even painted each other white. White had been a great symbol of resistance to the Shadowmasters in times gone by.

Our city was artificial and military, all straight lines, cleanliness and quiet. Except at night, if Tobo's friends got to brawling amongst themselves. By day, noise was confined to the training fields where the latest bunch of native would-be adventurers were learning the Black Company way of doing business. I was remote from all that except for patching up training mishaps. No one from my era was involved anymore. Like One-Eye I am a relic of a distant age, a living icon of the history that makes up so much of the unique social adhesive we used to hold the Company together. They rolled me out on special occasions and had me give sermons that began, "In those days the Company was in service to . . ."

It was a spooky night, the two moons illuminating everything while casting conflicting shadows. And Tobo's pets were increasingly disturbed about something. I began to catch straightforward glimpses of some when they became too distracted to work at staying out of sight. In most cases I was sorry.

The uproar up toward the shadowgate rose and fell. There were lights up there now, too. A couple of fireballs flew just before I reached my destination. I began to feel uneasy myself.

Headquarters was a two-story sprawl at the center of town. Sleepy had filled it with assistants and associates and functionaries who kept track of every horseshoe nail and every grain of rice. She had turned command into a bureaucratic exercise. And I did not like it. Of course. Because I was a cranky old man who remembered how things used to be in the good old days when we did things the right way. My way.

I do not think I have lost my sense of humor, though. I see the irony in having turned into my own grandfather.

I have stepped aside. I have passed the torch to someone younger, more energetic and tactically brighter than I ever was. But I have not abandoned my right to be involved, to contribute, to criticize and, particularly, to complain. It is a job somebody has to do. So I exasperate the younger people sometimes. Which is good for them. It builds character.

I strode through the ground-floor busywork Sleepy uses to

shield herself from the world. Day or night there was a crew on duty, counting those arrowheads and grains of rice. I should remind her to get out into the world once in a while. Putting up barriers will not protect her from her demons because they are all inside her already.

I was almost old enough to get away with talk like that.

Irritation crossed her dry, dusky, almost sexless face when I walked in. She was at her prayers. I do not understand that. Despite everything she has been through, much of which puts the lie to Vehdna doctrine, she persists in her faith.

"I'll wait till you're done."

The fact that I had caught her was what irritated her. The fact that she needed to believe even in the face of the evidence was what embarrassed her.

She rose, folded her prayer rug. "How bad is he this time?"

"Rumor got it wrong. It wasn't One-Eye. It was Gota. And she's gone. But One-Eye is in a pickle about something else he thinks is going to happen. About which he was less than vague. Tobo's friends are being more than normally weird so it's entirely possible it isn't One-Eye's imagination."

"I'd better send someone after Sahra."

"Tobo is taking care of it."

Sleepy considered me steadily. She may be short but she has presence and self-confidence. "What's on your mind?"

"I'm feeling some of what One-Eye is. Or maybe I just naturally can't stand a prolonged peace."

"Lady nagging you about going home again?"

"No. Murgen's last communion with Shivetya has her worried." To say the least. Modern history had turned cruel back in our home world. The Deceiver cult has rebounded in our absence, making converts by the hundred. At the same time Soulcatcher tormented the Taglian Territories in a mad and mainly fruitless effort to root out her enemies, most of whom were imaginary until she and Mogaba created them through their zeal. "She hasn't said so but I'm pretty sure she's afraid Booboo is manipulating Soulcatcher somehow."

Sleepy could not stifle a smile. "Booboo?"

"Your fault. I picked it up from something you wrote."

"She's your daughter."

"We have to call her something."

"I can't believe you two never picked a name."

"She was born before . . ." I like "Chana." It was good enough for my grandmother. Lady would have demurred. It sounded too much like Kina.

And although Booboo might be a nightmare stalking, Booboo was *Lady's* daughter and in the land where she had grown up mothers always named the daughters. Always. When the time was right.

This time will never be right. This child denies us both. She stipulates that our flesh quickened her flesh but she is animated by an absolute conviction that she is the spiritual daughter of the Goddess Kina. She is the Daughter of Night. Her sole purpose for existing is to precipitate the Year of the Skulls, that great human disaster that will free her slumbering soulmother so she can resume working her wickedness upon the world. Or upon the worlds, actually, as we had discovered once my quest for the Company's ancient origins had led us to the time-wracked fortress on the plain of glittering stone lying between our world and the Land of Unknown Shadows.

Silence stretched between us. Sleepy had been Annalist a long time. She had come to the Company young. Its traditions meant a great deal to her. Consequently she remained unfailingly courteous to her predecessors. But internally, I am sure, she was impatient with us old farts. Particularly with me. She never knew me well. And I was always taking up time wanting to know what was going on. I have begun putting too much emphasis on detail now that I do not have much to do but write.

I told her, "I don't offer advice unless you ask."

That startled her.

"Trick I learned from Soulcatcher. Makes people think you're reading their minds. She's much better at it."

"I'm sure she is. She's had all that time to practice." She puffed air out of expanded cheeks. "It's been a week since we've talked. Let's see. Nothing to report from Shivetya. Murgen's been at Khang Phi with Sahra so he hasn't been in touch with the golem. Reports from the men working on the plain say they're suffering from recurring premonitions of disaster."

"Really? They said it that way?" She had her pontifical moments.

"Roughly."

"What's the traffic situation?"

"There is none." She looked puzzled. The plain had seen no one cross for generations before the Company managed the passage. The last, before us, had been the Shadow-masters who had fled the Land of Unknown Shadows for our world back before I was born.

"Wrong question. I guess. How're you coming with preparations for our return?"

"That a personal or professional question?" Everything was business with Sleepy. I do not recall ever having seen her relax. Sometimes that worried me. Something in her past, hinted at in her own Annals, had left her convinced that that was the only way she could be safe.

"Both." I wished I could tell Lady that we would be going home soon. She had no love for the Land of Unknown Shadows.

I am sure she will not enjoy the future wherever we go. It is an absolute certainty that the times to come will not be good. I do not believe she understands that yet. Not in her heart.

Even she can be naive about some things.

"The short answer is that we can probably put a rein-forced company across as early as next month. If we can acquire the shadowgate knowledge."

Crossing the plain is a major undertaking because you have to carry with you everything you will need for a week. Up there there is nothing to eat but glittering stone. Stone remembers but stone has little nutritional value.

"Are you going too?"

"I'm going to send scouts and spies, no matter what. We can use the home shadowgate as long as we only put through a few men at a time."

"You won't take Shivetya's word?"

"The demon has his own agenda."

She would know. She had been in direct communion with that Steadfast Guardian.

What I knew of the golem's designs made me concerned for Lady. Shivetya, that ancient entity, created to manage and watch over the plain—which was an artifact itself—wanted to die. He could not do so while Kina survived. One of his tasks was to ensure that the sleeping Goddess did not awaken and escape her imprisonment.

When Kina ceased to exist, my wife's tenuous grasp on those magical powers critical to her sense of self-worth and identity would perish with her. What powers Lady boasted, she possessed only because she had found a way to steal from the Goddess. She was a complete parasite.

I said, "And you, believing the Company dictum that we have no friends outside, don't value his friendship."

"Oh, he's perfectly marvelous, Croaker. He saved my life. But he didn't do it because I'm cute and I jiggle in the right places when I run."

She was not cute. I could not imagine her jiggling, either. This was a woman who had gotten away with pretending to be a boy for years. There was nothing feminine about her. Nor anything masculine, either. She was not a sexual being at all, though for a while there had been rumors that she and Swan had become a midnight item.

It turned out purely platonic.

"I'll reserve comment. You've surprised me before."

"Captain!"

Took her a while, sometimes, to understand when someone was joking. Or even being sarcastic, though she had a tongue like a razor herself.

She realized I was ribbing her. "I see. Then let me surprise you one more time by asking your advice."

"Oh-oh. You'll have them sharpening their skates in hell."

"Howler and Longshadow. I've got to make decisions."

"File of Nine nagging you again?" The File of Nine—"File" from military usage—was a council of warlords, their identities kept secret, who formed the nearest thing to a real ruling body in Hsien. The monarchy and aristocracy of record were little more than decorative and, in the main, too intimate with poverty to accomplish much if the inclination existed.

The File of Nine had only limited power. Their existence barely assured that near-anarchy did not devolve into complete chaos. The Nine would have been more effective had they not prized their anonymity more than their implied power.

"Them and the Court of All Seasons. The Noble Judges really want Longshadow." The imperial court of Hsien—consisting of aristocrats with less real world power than the File of Nine but enjoying more a demonstrative moral authority—were obsessively interested in gaining possession of Longshadow. Being an old cynic I tended to suspect them of less than moral ambitions. But we had few dealings with them. Their seat, Quang Ninh City, was much too far away.

The one thing the peoples of Hsien held in common, every noble and every peasant, every priest and every warlord, was an implacable and ugly thirst for revenge upon the Shadowmaster invaders of yesteryear. Longshadow, still trapped in stasis underneath the glittering plain, represented the last possible opportunity to extract that cathartic vengeance. Longshadow's value in our dealings with the

Children of the Dead was phenomenally disproportionate.

Hatreds seldom are constrained to rational scales.

Sleepy continued, "And hardly a day goes by that I don't hear from some lesser warlord begging me to bring Longshadow in. The way they all volunteer to take charge of him leaves me nurturing the sneaking suspicion that most of them aren't quite as idealistically motivated as the File of Nine and the Court of All Seasons."

"No doubt. He'd be a handy tool for anybody who wanted to adjust the power balance. If anyone was fool enough to believe he could manage a puppet Shadowmaster." No world lacks its villains so self-confident that they don't believe they can get the best end of a bargain with the darkness. I married one of those. I am not sure she has learned her lesson yet. "Has anyone offered to fix our shadowgate?"

"The Court is actually willing to give us someone. The trouble with that is that they don't actually have anyone equipped with the skills to make the needed fixes. Chances are, no one has those skills. But the knowledge exists in records stored at Khang Phi."

"So why don't we? . . ."

"We're working on it. Meantime, the Court do seem to believe in us. And they absolutely do want some kind of revenge before all of Longshadow's surviving victims have been claimed by age."

"And what about the Howler?"

"Tobo wants him. Says he can handle him now."

"Does anybody else think so?" I meant Lady. "Or is he overconfident?"

Sleepy shrugged. "There's nobody telling me they've got anything more they can teach him." She meant Lady, too, and did not mean that Tobo suffered from a teen attitude. Tobo had no trouble taking advice or instruction when either of those did not originate with his mother.

I asked anyway. "Not even Lady?"

"She, I think, might be holding out on him."

"You can bet on it." I married the woman but I don't have many illusions about her. She would be thrilled to go back to her old wicked ways. Life with me and the Company has not been anything like happily ever after. Reality has a way of slow-roasting romance. Though we get along well enough. "She can't be any other way. Get her to tell you about her first husband. You'll marvel that she came out as sane as she did." I marveled every day. Right before I gave in to my astonishment that the woman really had given up everything to ride off with me. Well, something. She had not had much at the time and her prospects had been grim. "What the hell is that?"

"Alarm horns." Sleepy bolted out of her seat. She was spry for a woman treading hard on the heels of middle age. On the other hand, of course, she was so short she did not have a lot of real getting up to do. "I didn't order any drills."

She had an ugly habit of doing that. Only the traitor Mogaba, when he had been with us, had had as determined an attitude about preparedness.

Sleepy was too serious about everything.

Tobo's unknown shadows began raising their biggest uproar yet.

"Come on!" Sleepy snapped. "Why aren't you armed?" She was. She always was, although I never have seen her use a weapon more substantial than guile.

"I'm retired. I'm a paper pusher these days."

"I don't see you wearing a tombstone for a hat."

"I had an attitude problem once upon a time, myself, but . . ."

"Speaking of which. I want a reading in the officers' mess before lights out. Something that tells us all about the wages of indolence and the neglect of readiness. Or about the fate of ordinary mercenaries." She was in brisk motion, headed for the main exit, overtaking staffers who were not dawdling themselves. "Make a hole, people. Make a hole. Coming through."

Outside, people were pointing and babbling. The moonlight and a lot of fire betrayed a pillar of black, oily smoke boiling up from just below the gate to the glittering plain. I stated the obvious. "Something's happened." Clever me.

"Suvrin's up there. He has a level head."

Suvrin was a solid young officer with maybe just a tad of worship for his captain. You could be confident that neither accidents nor stupid mistakes would happen on Suvrin's watch.

Runners gathered, ready to carry Sleepy's instructions. She gave the only order she could till we knew more. Be alert. Even though to a man we believed that there was no way major trouble could come at us from off the plain.

The thing that you know to be true is the lie that will kill you.

6

An Abode of Ravens:
Suvrin's News

Suvrin did not arrive until after midnight. By then even our dullards understood that there was significance to the agitation of the hidden folk and the crows whose presence gave our settlement its local name. Arms had been issued. Men with fireball poles now perched on every rooftop. Tobo had warned his supernatural friends to stay out of town lest taut human nerves snap and cause them harm.

Everyone of stature available gathered to await Suvrin's report. A couple of subalterns took turns running up to the headquarters' roof to check the progress of the torches descending the long scarp from the shadowgate. Local boys, they seemed to feel that their great adventure had begun at last.

They were fools.

An adventure is somebody else slogging through the mud and snow while suffering from trench foot, ringworm, dysentery and starvation, being chased by people with their hearts set on murder or more. I have been there. I have done that, playing both parts. I do not recommend it. Be content with a nice farm or shop. Make lots of babies and bring them up to be good people.

If the new blood remain blind to reality after we move out I guarantee that their naivete will not long survive their first encounter with my sister-in-law, Soulcatcher.

Suvrin finally arrived, accompanied by the runner Sleepy had sent to meet him. He seemed surprised by the size of the assembly awaiting him.

"Get up front and talk," Sleepy told him. Always direct and to the point, my successor.

Silence fell. Suvrin looked around nervously. He was short, dark, slightly pudgy. His family had been minor nobility. Sleepy had taken him prisoner of war four years ago, just before the Company climbed onto the glittering plain, headed this way. Now he commanded an infantry battalion and seemed destined for bigger things because the Company was growing. He told us, "Something came through the shadowgate."

Jabber jabber, question question.

"I don't know what. One of my men came to tell me he thought he'd seen something sneaking around in the rocks on the other side of the gate. I went to look. After four years of nothing happening I assumed it would be just a shadow or one of the Nef. The dreamwalkers visit us all the time. I was wrong. I never got a good look at the thing but it seemed to be a large animal, black and extremely fast. Not as big as Big Ears or Cat Sith but definitely faster. It was able to pass through the shadowgate without help."

I felt a chill. I tried to reject my immediate suspicion. It was not possible. Nevertheless, I said, "Forvalaka."

"Tobo, where are you?" Sleepy demanded.

"Here." He sat with several Children of the Dead, officers in training.

"Find this thing. Catch it. If it's what Croaker said, I want you to kill it."

"That'll be easier said than done. It's already squabbled with the Black Hounds. They backed off. They're just trying to keep track of it now."

"Then kill it, Tobo." There was no "try to" or "do whatever you can" with this Captain.

I told him, "Ask Lady to help you. She knows those things. But before anybody does anything, we need to set up some kind of protection for One-Eye." If it was a shape-shifting, man-eating werepanther from our homeworld, it could be only one monster. And that creature hated One-Eye with the deepest and most abiding passion imaginable because One-Eye had slain the only wizard capable of helping it regain its human form.

"You think it really is Lisa Bowalk?" Sleepy asked.

"I get that feeling. But you told me it escaped from the plain through the Khatovar gate. And it couldn't get back."

Sleepy shrugged. "That's what Shivetya showed me. It's possible that I just assumed it couldn't get back onto the plain."

"Or maybe it made new friends out there."

The little woman spun, barked, "Suvrin?"

Suvrin understood. "I left them on maximum alert."

I said, "Tobo will have to check the seals on the gate. We don't want it leaking shadows because whatever it was broke through." Though the boy would not be able to do much to stem a real flood. That honor would have to go to his hidden folk friends. Lack of technical knowledge about shadowgates was the main reason we continued to reside in the Land of Unknown Shadows.

"I understand that, Croaker. Can I get to work here?"

I was underfoot. Being considered useless is irksome.

That condition was familiar to most of us whom Soulcatcher had beguiled and captured and managed to leave buried for fifteen years. Our Company had changed during our slumber. Even Lady and Murgen, who had maintained tenuous connections with the outside world, found themselves marginalized now. Murgen did not mind.

The culture of the Company has become quite alien. Almost no northern flavor remains. Just a few little quirks, in how things are done, and my own proud legacy, an interest in hygiene that is completely foreign to these climes.

These southerners did not enjoy a proper terror of the forvalaka. They insisted on picturing it as just another spooky nightstalker like Big Ears or Paddlefoot, which they consider essentially harmless. Near as I can tell they appear harmless only because their victims seldom survive to report any contrary facts.

"A reading from the First Book of Croaker," I told the assembly. It was after midnight. There had been no uproar for a while. The shadowgate was not leaking the Unforgiven Dead. Tobo was trying to pinpoint the intruder but was having difficulties. It was moving around a lot, scouting, plainly unsure how it should view the fact that it had fallen right in among us. "In those days the Company was in service to the Syndic of Beryl."

I told them about another forvalaka, long ago and far away and way more cruel than this one ever could be. I wanted them to worry.

7

An Abode of Ravens:
Night Visitor

Lady and I sat up with One-Eye. Gota had been laid out in the same room. Candles surrounded her. "I see no obvious change in the woman."

"Croaker! Hush!"

"I hear a difference, though. She hasn't complained about anything since we got here."

Playing deaf, One-Eye took a long drink of his product, closed his eye, nodded off. Lady whispered, "It's probably best if he naps."

"Not very lively bait."

"Carrion's good enough to draw this thing. What it wants to kill really only exists inside itself. One-Eye is just its symbol." She rubbed her eyes.

I winced. She looked so old, my love. Grey hair. Wrinkles. Jowls developing. Broadening in the beam. The deterioration had been swift since Sleepy rescued us.

Lucky for me there was no mirror handy. I really do not like to look at that fat, old, bald guy who goes around claiming to be Croaker.

The shadows in the room were restless. They made me nervous. From the beginning of our association with Taglios, shadows have been cause for terror. A shadow in motion meant death could have hold of you any moment. Those sad but cruel monsters off the plain had been the lethal instruments by which the Shadowmasters had earned their fame and had enforced their wills. But here, in the Land of Unknown Shadows, the hidden folk who lurked in the dark were shy but not ordinarily unfriendly—if treated with respect. And even those manifestations owning a history of wickedness and malice now worshipped Tobo and harmed no mortal closely associated with the Company. Unless that mortal was dim enough to irk Tobo somehow.

Tobo lived as much in the world of the hidden folk as he did in ours.

In the distance the spectral cat Big Ears again mouthed his unique call. Native legend says only the creature's prospective victims ever hear that chilling cry. A couple of the Black Hounds bayed. Legend suggests you do not want to hear their voices, either. Interviews with locals lead me to believe that before Tobo arrived only ignorant peasants really believed in most such perils of the night and the wild. Educated folk at Khang Phi and Quang Ninh had been stunned by what the boy had summoned from the shadows.

I glanced at the spear above the door. One-Eye had worked on that for decades. It was as much work of art as weapon. "Hon. Didn't One-Eye start crafting that spear because of Bowalk?"

She paused in her knitting, stared up at the spear, mused, "Seems to me Murgen wrote that One-Eye intended to use it on one of the Shadowmasters but ended up sticking Bowalk with it instead. During the siege. Or was that? . . ."

My knees creaked as I rose. "Whatever. Just in case." I took the spear down. "Damn. It's heavy."

"If the monster does get this far, try to keep in mind that we'd rather catch it than kill it."

"I know. It was my bright idea." The wisdom of which I had begun to doubt. I thought it might be interesting to see what would happen if we could force it to change back into the woman it had been before it had become fixed in its cat shape. I wanted to ask her questions about Khatovar.

Always assuming that the invader was the dread forvalaka, Lisa Daele Bowalk.

I sat down again. "Sleepy says she's ready to send spies and scouts across."

"Uhm?"

"We've been avoiding the facts a long time." This was

hard. It had taken me an age to work up to it. "The girl . . .
Our child . . ."

"Booboo?"

"You, too?"

"We have to call her something. The Daughter of Night is
so unwieldy. Booboo works without being an emotional
calthrop."

"We have to make some decisions."

"She'll . . ."

Black Hounds, Cat Sith, Big Ears and numerous other hidden folk began to give voice. I said, "That's inside the wall."

"Headed this way." She set her knitting aside.

One-Eye's head rose.

The door exploded inward before I finished turning to
face it.

A plank floated toward me in slow motion, slapped me
across the belly hard enough to set me down on the floor on
my butt. Something huge and black with blazing angry eyes
followed the board but lost interest in me in midleap. Still
falling backward onto my back I scored its flank with One-
Eye's spear. Flesh parted. Rib bones appeared. I tried to
thrust on into the beast's belly but did not have enough
leverage. It screamed but could not alter its momentum.

Burning pain seared deep into my left shoulder, not three
inches from the side of my neck. The forvalaka was not
responsible, though. Friendly fire was. My sweet wife had
discharged a fireball projector while I was between her and
her target. There was plenty of fire left, though, when that
ball, its flight path altered, clipped the panther's tail two
inches from its root.

The monster's scream continued. It flung its head back
while still airborne. Its whole frame was in the position her-
alds call rampant.

It hit One-Eye.

The old man made no obvious effort to defend himself.
His chair went over. It shattered into kindling wood. One-

Eye skidded along the dirt floor. The forvalaka ploughed into Gota, tipping the table on which she had been laid out. Lady loosed another fireball. It missed. I fought to get around onto my hands and knees, then to get the head of the spear up, between me and the monster. It fought for its footing while trying to turn at the same time. It slammed into the far wall. I got my feet under me, started to stumble around.

Lady missed again.

"No!" I shrieked. My feet tangled. I came close to landing on my face again. I tried to do three things at once and, naturally, did none of them well. I wanted to get hold of One-Eye, I wanted to get my spearhead back up, I wanted to get the hell out of that house.

Lady did not miss again. But this fireball was a puny one, a near dud. It hit the monster right between the eyes. And just ricocheted off, taking a few square inches of skin along with it, leaving a patch of skull bone exposed.

The forvalaka screamed again.

Then One-Eye's still blew up. Which is what I had expected from the moment Lady's fireball had gone through the wall.

8

Taglios:
Trouble Follows

Mogaba knew there was trouble seconds after he left his rooms, so austerely furnished in shabby regrets. Palace staffers pushed to the sides of the corridors as he passed. Without exception they were scuttling away from the Privy Council Chamber. They must have heard rumors that had not yet reached his ears. Rumors they were sure would displease the Protector, which meant that, soon, someone would be making life unpleasant for someone else and these people hoped to be well out of the way before he started.

"Pride," he said, in a normal, conversational voice to a young Grey runner trying to ease past without attracting notice. "Pride is what did me in."

"Yes sir." Color drained from the young Shadar's face. He did not yet have a beard to hide behind. "I mean, no sir. I'm sorry. . . ."

Mogaba was gone, indifferent to the apprentice soldier. Similar incidents occurred each time he passed through the Palace. He spoke to almost everyone. Those who had watched the habit develop understood that he was talking to himself and did not expect any reply. He was pursuing a running debate with his own guilts and ghosts—unless he was spouting proverbs and aphorisms, most of the meanings fairly obvious but a few convolute and obscure. He was particularly fond of "Fortune smiles. And then betrays." He just could not get into bed comfortably with the truth that he had made that bed himself. He still had difficulty separating "ought to be" from "the way things really are." He was no fool, though. He knew he had problems.

He was certain that he had a much more solid grip on reality than did his employer, though.

Soulcatcher, however, took the view that she was a virtual free agent and refused to be wedded to any particular reality. She believed in creating her own by making her imaginings come true.

Some were quite mad. Few, however, lasted beyond the heated moment of conception.

Mogaba heard crows arguing ahead. Crows infested the Palace these days. Soulcatcher was fond of crows. She allowed no one to harass or harm them. Of late bats had made a claim on her affections as well.

When the crows became vocal the few servants still around started moving much faster. Unhappy crows meant unhappy news. Unhappy news was guaranteed to produce an extremely unhappy Protector. When Soulcatcher was unhappy she did not care who suffered the consequences. But someone surely would.

Mogaba stepped into the council chamber and waited. She would talk to him when she was ready. Ghopal Singh of the Greys and Aridatha Singh of the City Battalions—no relation: Singh was the most common surname in Taglios—were there already. Which meant that Soulcatcher must have been haranguing them about their failure to root out enough enemies, again, before the bad news arrived.

Mogaba exchanged glances with both men. As he believed himself to be, they were good men trapped by impossible circumstances. Ghopal had a flair for enforcing the law. Aridatha was equally talented at keeping the peace without enraging the populace. Both men managed despite Soulcatcher, who loved both chaos and despotism and inflicted each with verve and ferocity, driven by the dictates of whimsy.

The woman seemed to materialize suddenly. It was a talent she used to disconcert lesser beings. A lesser man than Mogaba might have been numbed by the sight of her. The woman had a body the wonders of which seemed highlighted rather than concealed by the tight black leather she wore. Nature had blessed her with superb raw materials. Her vanity had driven her, over the centuries, to keep making improvements through cosmetic sorceries.

"I'm not happy," Soulcatcher announced. Her voice was petulant, that of a spoiled child. Today her look was younger than usual, as though she wanted to spark every young man's fantasy. Although the preening crow on the tall chair back behind her was a distraction once she settled.

"May I ask why?" Mogaba asked. His voice was calm, untroubled. Life in the Palace at Taglios consisted of a disorganized stumble from crisis to crisis. He no longer became emotionally involved. Soulcatcher would turn on him someday. He had made his peace with that already. He would face it calmly when it came. He deserved no better.

"There is a huge Deceiver festival being celebrated in the Grove of Doom. Right now. Tonight." This voice was cool, calm, rational. Masculine. You got used to the changes after a while. Mogaba seldom noticed anymore. Aridatha Singh, only recently promoted, still found the unpredictable chorus disconcerting. Singh was a sound officer and good soldier. Mogaba hoped he lasted long enough to become accustomed to the Protector's quirks. Aridatha deserved better than he was likely to get.

"That's definitely not good news," Mogaba agreed. "Seems I recall you wanting to harvest the timber there while obliterating every last trace of the holy place. Selvas Gupta talked you out of it. Said it would set a bad precedent." Gupta had had secret encouragement from the Great General, who had not cared to waste manpower and time clearing a forest. But Mogaba loathed Selvas Gupta and his smugly holy attitude of superiority.

Gupta was the current Purohita, or official court chaplain and religious adviser. Purohita was a post that had been forced upon the Radisha Drah twenty years earlier by the priesthoods at a time when the princess had been too weak to defy them. Soulcatcher had not yet abolished it. But she had little patience with the men who occupied it.

Selvas Gupta had been Purohita for a year, which incumbency exceeded that of all his predecessors since the establishment of the Protectorate.

Mogaba was confident that slimy little snake Gupta would not last out the week.

Soulcatcher gave him a look which offered the impression that she was peering deep inside him, sorting his secrets and motives. Having paused just long enough to suggest that she was not being fooled, she said, "Get me a new Purohita. Kill the old one if he argues about it." She had an ancient custom of being unpleasant toward priests who disappointed her. Which ran in the family. Her sister had slain hundreds in a single massacre a generation earlier. The exemplary demonstrations of both sisters, however, never seemed sufficient to convince the survivors that they ought to abandon their scheming. They were stubborn. It seemed likely that Taglios would come up short of priests before it ran short of conspiracies.

The crow hopped down onto Soulcatcher's shoulder. She lifted gloved fingers to offer it some tidbit.

"Did you have a response in mind? Something involving my colleagues?" Mogaba nodded toward the Singhs in turn. He suffered little jealousy of either man and did respect each for his abilities. Time and persistent adversity had ground the rough edges off of his once potent sense of self-appreciation.

"These gentlemen were here already, regarding another matter, when the news from the Grove arrived." She offered the crow another morsel.

Mogaba's eyes narrowed the tiniest fraction. He was not to be made privy to that matter?

But he was. Soulcatcher used a cackling crone's voice. "The Greys found several slogans painted on walls today." The crow cawed. Elsewhere, other crows began squabbling.

"Not uncommon," Mogaba replied. "Every idiot with a brush, a pot of paint and enough education to string five characters together seems to be compelled to say something if he discovers a blank piece of wall."

"These were slogans from the past." This was the voice the Protector used when she was focused entirely on business. It was a male voice. A voice like Mogaba imagined his own to be. "Three said '*Rajadharma.*' "

"I've heard the Bhodi cult is making a comeback, too."

Ghopal Singh added, "Two said '*Water Sleeps.*' That's not Bhodi. And they weren't stray graffiti left over from four years ago."

A thrill, half fear, half excitement, coursed through Mogaba. He stared at the Protector. She said, "I want to know who's doing it. I want to know why they've decided to do it right now."

Mogaba thought both Singhs looked cautiously pleased, as though glad to have potential real enemies to chase instead of just irritating people who would otherwise remain indifferent to the Palace.

The Grove of Doom was outside the city. Everything outside was Mogaba's province. He asked, "Was there some particular action you wished me to take in regard to the Deceivers?"

Soulcatcher smiled. When she did that, just that way, every minute of her many centuries shone through. "Nothing. Not a thing. They're scattering already. I'll let you know when. It'll be when they're not ready." This voice was cold but was filled with her evil smile. Mogaba wondered if the Singhs knew how seldom anyone saw the Protector without her mask. It meant that she meant to involve them in her schemes too deeply for them to escape the association.

Mogaba nodded like a dutiful servant. It was all a game to the Protector. Or possibly several games. Maybe making a game of it was how you survived spiritually in a world where everyone else was ephemeral.

Soulcatcher said, "I want you to help catch rats. There's a shortage of carrion. My babies are going hungry." She offered her black-winged spy another treat. This one suspiciously resembled a human eyeball.

9

An Abode of Ravens:
The Invalid

"Am I still alive?" I did not need to ask. I was. Pain was a dead giveaway. Every square inch of me hurt.

"Don't move." That was Tobo. "Or you'll wish you hadn't."

I already wished I did not have to breathe. "Burns?"

"Lots of burns. Lots of banging around, too."

Murgen's voice said, "You look like they whipped your ass with a forty-pound ugly stick, then slow-roasted what was left over an open pit."

"I thought you were at Khang Phi."

"We came home."

Tobo said, "We kept you unconscious for four days."

"How is Lady?"

Murgen told me, "She's in the other bed. In a lot better shape than you."

"She ought to be. I didn't shoot her. The cat get her tongue?"

"She's asleep."

"What about One-Eye?"

Tobo's response was barely audible. "One-Eye didn't make it, Croaker."

After a while, Murgen asked, "You all right?"

"He was the last."

"Last? Last what?"

"The last one who was here when I joined. The Company." I was the real Old Man now. "What happened to his spear? I've got to have his spear in order to finish this."

"What spear?" Murgen asked.

Tobo knew what spear. "I have it at my place."

"Was it damaged by the fire?"

"Not much. Why?"

"I'm going to kill that thing. Like we should have a long time ago. You don't let that spear out of your sight. I've got to have it. But right now I'm going to sleep for a while some more." I had to go where the pain was not, just for a time. I had known One-Eye would leave us someday. I thought I was ready for that. I was wrong.

His passing meant more than just the end of an old friend. It marked the end of an age.

Tobo said something about the spear. I did not catch it. And the darkness came back before I remembered to ask what had become of the forvalaka. If Lady had caught or killed it I had gotten myself worked up for nothing. . . . But I guess I knew it could not be that easy.

There were dreams. I remembered everyone who had gone before me. I remembered the places and times. Cold places, hot places, weird places, always stressful times, swollen with unhappiness, pain and fear. Some died. Some did not. It makes no sense when you try to figure it out. Soldiers live. And wonder why.

Oh, it's a soldier's life for me. Oh, the adventure and glory!

It took me longer to recuperate than it had that time I almost got killed outside Dejagore. Even with Tobo applying his own best healing spells, learned from One-Eye, and urging his edge-of-the-eye friends to help as well. Some of those were supposed to be able to bring a fossil back to life. I felt like a fossil, like I had not enjoyed the advantage of the stasis that had frozen the others while we were prisoners under the plain. There was a lot of confusion inside me. I could no longer figure out how old I am. My best guess is fifty-six, give or take a few years, plus all that time underneath the earth. And fifty-six years, brother, was a pretty damned good run—particularly for a guy in my racket. I ought to appreciate every second, including all the misery.

Soldiers live. And wonder why.

10

An Abode of Ravens:
Recovery

Two months had passed. I felt ten years older but I was up and around—and moving like a zombie. I had indeed been roasted well-done by a jet of almost pure alcohol blowing through the hole that had been drilled by Lady's errant fireball. Everybody kept telling me how much the gods must love me, that I had no business being alive. That had I not been turned the way I was, with the forvalaka positioned perfectly to absorb a lot of the blast, there would not have been much left of me but bones.

I was not entirely convinced that that might not have been the better outcome.

Persistent pain does little to buoy one's optimism or elevate one's mood. I began to develop a certain sympathy for Mother Gota's perspective.

I did manage a smile when Lady began to rub me down with healing unguents. "Silver linings," she told me.

"Oh, yes indeed. Yes indeed."

"Would you look at that? Maybe you're not as old as you think."

"It's all your fault, wench."

"Sleepy's worried about you wanting to avenge One-Eye."

"I know." I did not have to be told. I had had to put up with people like me when I was Captain.

"Maybe you should tone it down."

"It's got to be done. It's going to be done. Sleepy's got to understand that." Sleepy is all business. Her world does not include much leeway for emotional indulgence.

She thinks I just want to use One-Eye's death as an excuse to visit the Khatovar shadowgate, basing her judgment on the fact that I had tramped through Hell for a decade trying to get to that place.

The woman is hard to fool. But she can also get fixed on one idea to the exclusion of other possibilities.

"She doesn't want to make any more enemies."

"More? We don't have any. Not out here. They may not like us much but they all kiss our asses. They're scared to death of us. And they get more scared every time another White Lady or Blue Man or *wichtlin* or whatnot lumbers out of folklore and joins Tobo's entourage."

"Uhn. Is that the spot? I saw something Tobo called a *wowsey* with the Black Hounds yesterday." That is my honey. She can see those things clearly, even over here. "It's as big as a hippo but looks like a beetle with a lizard's head. A lizard with big teeth. To quote Swan, 'It looks like it fell out of the ugly tree and hit every single branch on the way down.'"

Willow Swan seemed to be cultivating a new image as a churlish but colorful old man.

Somebody has to step in and take One-Eye's place. Though I was sort of thinking about picking up the stick myself.

"What do we know about the forvalaka?" I asked. I had avoided asking for specifics before. I knew the damned thing got away. That was all I needed to know until I was prepared mentally to start planning the conclusion of its tale.

"It left its tail behind. It suffered severe burns and several deep wounds and I blinded it partially with my last fireball. It lost several teeth. Tobo has created a number of fetishes using those and bits of flesh torn off by the Black Hounds while it was fleeing toward the shadowgate."

"But it did have what it takes to get back to Khatovar."

"It did."

"Then it's going to be as hard to kill as the Limper was."

"Not anymore. Not with what Tobo has."

"He had your help?"

"I'm ancient in the ways of wickedness. Am I not? Didn't you write something like that a time or two?"

"Especially after I got to know you. . . . Ouch! Well . . . as long as you're a bad girl like you're being a bad girl right now. . . ." I do not recall if I did write the exact words she claimed but I know I recorded those approximate sentiments many years ago. Without exaggerating. "I'm going to go after it."

"I know." She did not argue. They were humoring me. They wanted to keep me quiet. Sleepy was involved in touchy negotiations with the File of Nine. The Court of All Seasons and the monks of Khang Phi were behind us already. The warlords of the File remain unconvinced that it would be wise to give us what we want even though the Company has grown to the point where it has become a serious burden on Hsien's economy. And poses a threat, if the notion of conquest happens to take root. I, myself, do not see one warlord, or even a cabal of warlords, out there, who would stand much more chance than smoke in a high wind if the notion did take us. Most of the warlords are clear on that, too.

They still want Maricha Manthara Dhumraksha—our Shadowmaster Longshadow—desperately. Their hunger for revenge borders on racial obsession. They are not forthcoming about the evils Longshadow visited upon their forbears but we have our sources inside Khang Phi. Longshadow's cruelties had been as capricious as any wickedness of Soulcatcher's but far more terrible for their victims. The need to haul the Shadowmaster up before a tribunal colored every consideration of the warlords, the legal and noble courts, even the several spiritual traditions of Hsien. Maricha Manthara Dhumraksha was the one thing they all agreed upon. Nor did I ever sense a hint of a chance some rogue would try to acquire control of Longshadow in an effort to amplify his own power.

Sleepy did not want a short-tempered, foulmouthed but still influential former Captain stumbling around being sarcastic and opinionated while she was trying to wring the one last concession she wanted out of the File of Nine. She was confident that our years of good behavior would tilt the scale. And if it did not, well, she was the kind of planner who always had a secondary scheme in motion. In fact, she was that wonderful kind of villain for whom the public and obvious scheme might well be only a tertiary effort meant primarily as a smoke screen. Our Sleepy was one wicked little girl.

There are no great sorcerers in the Land of Unknown Shadows. "All Evil Dies There an Endless Death" means that they have persecuted the talented since the flight of the Shadowmasters. But Hsien does not lack or disdain knowledge. There are several huge monasteries—of which Khang Phi is the greatest—dedicated to the preservation of knowledge. The monks do not sort it into good and evil knowledge, nor do they make moral judgments. They take the position that no knowledge is evil until someone chooses to do evil with it.

Even though it has been engineered to wreak havoc upon the human body, a sword is strictly inert metal until someone chooses to pick it up and strike. Or chooses not to do so.

There are, of course, a thousand sophistries spewed by those who wish to deny individuals the opportunity to choose. Which is an arrogant presumption of a divine scale.

This is what happens when you get old. You start thinking. Worse, you start telling everybody what you think.

Sleepy was nervous lest I express an unfortunate opinion to one of the Nine, whereupon, in high dudgeon, the offended party would abandon all sensibility and self-interest and deny to us forever the knowledge we need to repair the shadowgate opening on our native world. She misapprehends my ability to evoke the unfriendly response.

Before the werepanther came I might have stumbled. I might have expressed an actual opinion to a member of the File, some of whom are amongst the most reprehensible generals I have ever encountered. I doubt that, given the opportunity to rule unchallenged, many of them would be more enlightened than the hated Shadowmasters.

People are strange. The Children of the Dead are among the strangest.

I will not upset anyone. I will be diligently supportive of any policy Sleepy sets. I want to leave this Land of Unknown Shadows. I have things to accomplish before I hand these Annals over for the last time. Settling up with Lisa Daele Bowalk is just one. There is the Great General, Mogaba, the darkest traitor ever to stain the Company's history. There is Narayan Singh. For Lady, there is Narayan and Soulcatcher. For both of us there is our child. Our wicked, wicked child.

I asked, "Is there anything besides Longshadow we could offer the File of Nine? Sweeten it just enough to make them move over beside Khang Phi and the Court of All Seasons?"

My sweetie shrugged. "I can't imagine what." She smiled enigmatically. "But it may not matter."

I did not pay sufficient attention. Sometimes I overlook the new truths. These days my Company is managed by sly children and devious old women, not straightforward stalwarts like myself and the men of my time.

11

An Abode of Ravens: Exercise Session

As soon as I healed enough I asked Uncle Doj to let me resume the martial arts exercises I had given up many years ago. "Why are you interested now?" he asked. Sometimes I think he is more suspicious of me than I am of him.

"Because I have time. And the need. I'm as weak as a puppy. I want to get my strength back."

"You chased me away when I offered."

"I didn't have time then. And you were so much more abrasive."

"Ha." He smiled. "You're too kind."

"You're right. But I'm a prince."

"A Prince of Darkness, Stone Soldier." He knew that would get my goat. "But a lucky prince." The old fart indulged in a smirk. "Several of your contemporaries have approached me recently, also motivated by anticipation of those hardships that can no longer be that far ahead."

"Good." Did he know something I did not? Probably a lot. "When and where?"

His grin became evil, revealing bad teeth. Which made me wonder if Sleepy had found anybody to fill the dentistry vacancy left by One-Eye's passing. The old fool had not bothered taking on apprentices.

"When" was the crack of dawn and "where" was the unpaved street outside Doj's small house, which he shared with Tobo's uncle Thai Dei and several bachelor officers of local origin. My fellow victims were Willow Swan, the brothers Loftus and Cletus, who remain the Company's principal architects and engineers, and the exiled ruling prince and princess of Taglios, the Prahbrindrah Drah and his sister the Radisha Drah. Those are not names, they are titles. Even after decades I do not know their personal designations. And they show no inclination to share.

"Where's your pal Blade?" I asked Swan. For a while Blade had been Sleepy's military envoy to the File of Nine, but I had heard that he had been recalled after One-Eye's death. I had not seen him around, though.

"Old Blade's got too much on his plate for anything like this."

Loftus and Cletus both grumbled under their breaths but did not clarify. I had not seen much of them lately, either. I supposed they were working themselves to death building a city from scratch. Suvrin, who arrived just in time to hear what they mumbled, nodded vigorously. "She's going to work us all till there's nothing but grease spots left." I am not sure about Suvrin. I have no trouble imagining him going around endlessly repeating the silent mantra, "Every day in every way I am going to become a better soldier."

"Well, old Blade never was real ambitious," Swan replied. "Except when it came to carving up priests." He seemed to know what he was talking about even if it was not obvious to me.

Clete said, "If we're getting the straight shit from Shivetya there'll be a whole new crop in need of culling when we get home."

The Prahbrindrah Drah and his sister edged closer, eager for hard news from home. Sleepy took no trouble to keep them posted. She did not have much of a diplomatic streak. I had best remind her that she will need their amity once we are back across the plain.

They were not handsome, those two. And the Radisha looked more like the Prince's mother than his sister. But he had been under the ground with me while she rode the Taglian tiger and tried not to lose its reins to Soulcatcher. They strove to remain unobtrusive here, the Prince because he had been our active enemy in the field, the Princess because she had turned on us at the very last moment of our victory over the last Shadowmasters.

Sleepy fixed her for that.

Technically, the Radisha was our prisoner. Sleepy had abducted her. She and her brother will become tools of the Company once Sleepy stages our return. Everyone agrees. But I suspect that the royals have reservations.

"Rajadharma." I said, bowing slightly. I could not resist the taunt, reminding them both that by attempting to betray us they had ended up failing to fulfill their duty to their subjects.

"Liberator." The Radisha returned a tiny bow. I swear, the woman gets homelier by the month. "You appear to be healing well."

"I've got a knack for coming back. But my bounce sure ain't as fast or as high as it used to be. Guess it's old age creeping up." I lied and told her, "You're looking well yourself. You both are. What have you been doing? I haven't seen you for a while."

The Prahbrindrah Drah said nothing. He remained inscrutable. He had been quiet and unexpressive since our resurrection. We had gotten along well, once. But times change. Neither of us were the men we had been during the Shadowmaster wars.

"You're lying like a snake's belly," the Radisha told me. "I'm old and I'm ugly and I'm still ashamed of myself. . . . But you're telling the lie my soul wants to hear. Forget *rajadharma*, though. That accusation has no power to hurt me anymore. From outside. I still crucify myself. I know what I did. At the time I thought it was the right thing. The Protector manipulated me using my sense of *rajadharma*. Once we get back there you'll see us in a different light."

Rajadharma means the ruler's obligation to serve the ruled. When the word is thrown into a ruler's face, or is used as an epithet, it is a savage accusation of failure.

The Radisha is a hard, stubborn little woman. Unfortunately, she will have to get the better of a hard, stubborn, crazy, almost supremely powerful sorceress if she wants to fulfill her expectations for herself.

I glanced at her brother. The Prince's expression had not changed but I sensed that he thought he appreciated the difficulties more fully than his sister did.

Uncle Doj whacked something with a practice sword. The loud crack ended our chatter. "Your canes, please. On the count, commence the Crane Kada." He did not bother to explain what that was to the new guy.

Maybe two decades ago I had observed and briefly joined the Nyueng Bao exercises. Murgen was Annalist then. He had had Gota, Doj and his wife Sahra's brother, Thai Dei, living with him. Doj expected me to remember.

About all I recalled of the Crane Kada was that it constituted the first and simplest of a dozen slow-motion dances incorporating all the formal steps and strokes of Doj's school of fencing. The old priest led from up front, his back to his pupils. Although he was the eldest of us all, he moved with a precision and grace that verged on beauty. But when Thai Dei and Tobo joined us briefly, later, both outshone the old man. It was hard not to stop just to appreciate Tobo's mastery.

The boy made me feel clumsy and inept just standing still. Everything came so easily for him.

He had all the talents and skills he could possibly need. If any question remained, it concerned his character. A lot of good people had worked hard to make sure that he became a virtuous and upright man. Which he did appear to be. But he was a blade not yet tested. True temptation had not yet whispered in his ear.

I missed a step badly, stumbled. Uncle Doj laid his cane across the seat of my trousers as vigorously as if I had been an adolescent. His face remained bland but I suspected that he had wanted to do that for a long time.

I tried to concentrate.

12

Glittering Stone: Steadfast Guardian

The being on the huge wooden throne in the heart of the fortress at the center of the stone plain is a construct. Possibly he was created by the gods, who fought their wars upon that plain. Or perhaps his creators were the builders who constructed the plain—if they were not gods themselves. Opinions vary. Stories abound. The demon Shivetya himself is not disposed to be unstinting with the facts, or is, at best, inconsistent in their distribution. He has shown his latest chronicler several conflicting versions of ancient events. Old Baladitya has abandoned all hope of establishing an exact truth and, instead, seeks the deeper range of meaning underpinning what the golem does reveal. Baladitya understands that in addition to being foreign territory the past is, as history, a hall of mirrors that reflect the needs of souls observing from the present. Absolute fact serves the hungers of only a few disconnected people. Symbol and faith serve the rest.

Baladitya's Company career duplicates his prior life. He writes things down. When he was a copyist at the Taglian Royal Library he wrote things down. Now, nominally, he is a prisoner of war. Chances are he has forgotten that. In reality he is freer today to pursue his own interests than ever he was at the library.

The old scholar lives and works around the demon's feet. Which has to be as close to personal heaven as a Gunni historian can imagine. If the historian does not remain too determinedly wedded to Gunni religious doctrine.

Shivetya's motives for refusing categorical declarations may stem from bitterness about his lot. By his own admission he has met most of the gods face-to-face. His recollections concerning them are even less flattering than those spicing most of Gunni mythology, where few of the gods are extolled as role models. Almost without exception the Gunni deities are cruel and selfish and untouched by any celestial sense of rajadharma.

A tall black man stepped into the light cast by Baladitya's lamps. "Learned anything exciting today, old-timer?" The copyist's fuel expenses are prodigal. He is indulged.

The old man did not respond. He is almost deaf. He exploits his infirmity to its limits. Not even Blade insists that he share routine camp chores any longer.

Blade asked again but the copyist's nose remained close to the page on which he was writing. His penmanship is swift and precise. Blade cannot decipher the complicated ecclesiastical alphabet, except for some of those characters it shares with the only slightly simpler common script. Blade looked up into the golem's eye. That appeared to be about the size of a roc's egg. The adjective "baleful" fit it well. Not even naive old Baladitya has ever proposed that the demon be delivered from the restraint guaranteed by the daggers nailing its limbs to the throne. Neither has the demon ever encouraged anyone to release it. It has endured for thousands of years. It has the patience of stone.

Blade tried another approach. "I've had a runner come from the Abode of Ravens." He prefers the native name for the Company's base. It is so much more dramatic than Outpost or Bridgehead and Blade is a dramatic man fond of dramatic gestures. "The Captain says she expects to acquire the needed shadowgate knowledge shortly. Something is about to break loose in Khang Phi. She wants me to get cracking getting more treasure brought up. She wants you to finish finding everything out. She'll be moving soon."

The copyist grunted. "He's easily bored, you know."

"What?" Blade was startled, then angry. The old man had not heard a word.

"Our host." The old man did not lift his eyes from the page. It would take them too long to readjust. "He's easily bored." Baladitya cared nothing about the Company's plans. Baladitya was in paradise.

"You'd think we'd be a change that would distract him."

"He's been distracted by mortals a thousand times before. He's still here. None of those people are, except those remembered in stone." The plain itself, though older and vastly slower than Shivetya, might have a mind of its own. Stone remembers. And stone weeps. "Their very empires have been forgotten. How much chance is there that this time will be different?"

Baladitya sounded a little empty. Not unreasonable, Blade thought, considering the fact that he looked into the time abyss represented by the demon all the time. Talk about vanity and chasing after wind!

"Yet he's helping us. More or less."

"Only because he believes we're the last mayflies he'll see. Excepting the Children of Night when they raise up their Dark Mother. He's convinced that we're his last chance to escape."

"And all we got to do to get his help is skrag the nasty Goddess, then put his ass away for the long night." The demon's gaze seemed to drill right through him. "Nothing to it. Piece of cake, as Goblin used to say. Though the saying doesn't make any literal sense." Blade lifted his fingers to his eyebrow in a salute to the demon. Whose eyes seemed to be smouldering now.

"God killing. That should be perfect work for you."

Blade was unsure if Baladitya had spoken or Shivetya had entered his mind. He did not like what the observation implied. It echoed too closely Sleepy's thinking, which is why his posh job in Khang Phi is gone and he has charge of operations on the plain, having abandoned banquets and down mattresses for iron rations and a bed of cold and silent stone shared only with unhappy, withered dreams, a crazy scholar, miscellaneous thieves and a house-sized lunatic demon half as old as time.

All his adult life Blade has been driven by a hatred for religion. He has an especial abhorrence for its retailers. Considering his current whereabouts and present occupation it seems likely that he should have restrained his impulse to share his opinions.

Blade could have sworn that, for an instant, a smile played across the demon's features.

Blade chose not to comment.

He is a man of few words. He believes there is little point to speech. He believes the golem eavesdrops on his thoughts. Unless it has become so bored with ephemerals that it no longer pays attention.

That hint of amusement again. Blade's speculation is not valid. He should know better. Shivetya is interested in every breath every brother of the Black Company takes. Shivetya has anointed these men as the death-givers.

"You need anything?" Blade asked the old man, resting a hand on his shoulder briefly. "Before I head down below?" The contact is entirely contrived. But Baladitya cares nothing about the touch, genuine or not.

Baladitya lifted his pen from his right hand with his left, flexed his fingers. "I suppose I should eat something. I can't recall when last I put fuel on the fire."

"I'll see that you get something." The something was sure to be rice and spice and golem manna. If there was anything Blade regretted about his life, it was having lived most of it in a part of the world where a majority of the population include a vegetarian diet within their religion and those who do not mainly eat fish or chicken. Blade is ready to start at whichever end of a spit-roast pig and not stop until he reaches the other.

Blade's command, the thieves, the Company pathfinders, includes twenty-six of the outfit's brightest and most trusted youngsters, all Children of the Dead. They need to be both smart and trustworthy because Sleepy wants to exploit the treasures in the caverns beneath the plain and because they really have to understand that the plain itself will not forgive them if they do the wrong thing. Shivetya has extended his favor. Shivetya sees everything and knows everything inside the gates of his universe. Shivetya is the soul of the plain. No one comes or goes without Shivetya's countenance, or at least his indifference. And in the unlikely event that Shivetya remained indifferent to an unauthorized theft, there was nowhere for a thief to run but back to the shadowgate opening on the Land of Unknown Shadows. That was the only shadowgate under control and functioning properly. That was the only shadowgate not certain to kill the thief.

It was a long stroll across the great circle surrounding the crude throne. That floor is anything but crude. It is an exact one-eightieth scale representation of the plain outside, less the memorial pillars that were added in a later age by men who failed to possess even mythologized recollections of the builders. Hundreds of manhours have gone into clearing the accumulated dirt and dust off its surface so Shivetya can more clearly discern every detail of his kingdom. Shivetya's throne rests upon a raised wheel one-eightieth the size of this.

Decades ago, Soulcatcher's tampering triggered an earthquake that battered the fortress and split its floor into a vast crevasse. Outside the plain the disaster destroyed cities and killed thousands. Today the only memorial of what had been a gap in the floor a dozen yards wide and thousands of feet deep is a red stripe meandering past the throne. It dwindles every day. As does Shivetya, the mechanism ruling the plain heals itself.

The great circular model of the plain rises half a yard above the rest of the floor, which exists at the level of the plain outside.

Blade dropped off the edge of the wheel. He strode to a hole in the floor, the head of stairs leading down. They descend for miles, through caverns natural and created. The sleeping Goddess Kina lies at the deepest level, patiently awaiting the Year of the Skulls and the beginning of the Khadi Cycle, the destruction of the world. The *wounded* Goddess Kina.

Shadows stirred along the nearby wall. Blade froze. Who? No way that could be his people. Or, *what?*

Fear speared through Blade. Shadows in motion often presaged cruel, screaming death. Had those things found a way into the fortress? Their merciless feasting was not a horror he cared to witness ever again. And in particular he did not want to be the main course.

"The Nef," Blade told himself as three humanoid shapes emerged from the darkness. He recognized them despite never having seen them before. Hardly anyone did, outside of dreams. Or maybe nightmares. The Nef were incredibly ugly. Though they might have been wearing masks. The several descriptions available did not agree except as to ugliness. He counted them off. "The Washane. The Washene. The Washone." Names Shivetya had given Sleepy years ago. What did they mean? Did they mean anything at all? "How did they get in here?" The answer might be critical. Killer shadows might exploit the same opening.

As the Nef always did, they tried to communicate something. In the past their efforts inevitably failed. But this time their appeal seemed obvious. They did not want Blade to go down those stairs.

Sleepy, Master Santaraksita, and others who have been in contact with Shivetya believe that the Nef are artificial reproductions of the beings who created the plain. Shivetya brought them into existence because he longed for a connection with something approximating those whose artifice had wrought the great engine and its pathways between the worlds, because he was lonely.

Shivetya has lost his will to live. If he should perish, whatever he has created himself will go with him. The Nef are not yet prepared to embrace oblivion, despite the endless horror and tedium existence upon the plain imposes.

Blade spread his hands at his sides in a gesture of helplessness. "You guys need to polish your communication skills." Not a sound came from the Nef but their growing frustration became palpable. Which had been a constant from the first time anyone had dreamt of them.

Blade stared. He did try to understand. He considered the ironies of the Black Company's adventure across the glittering plain. He was an atheist himself. His journey had brought him face-to-face with a complete ecology of supernatural entities. And Tobo and Sleepy, whom he considered reliable witnesses otherwise, claimed actually to have seen the grim Goddess Kina who, myth suggested, lay imprisoned a mile beneath his feet.

Sleepy, of course, faced her crises of faith. A devout

Vehdna monotheist, she never, ever encountered any worldly sustenance for her beliefs. Though supportive evidence is thin, the Gunni religion only creaks badly under the burden of the knowledge we have unearthed. The Gunni are polytheists accustomed to having their gods assume countless aspects and avatars, shapes and disguises. So much so that, in some myths, those gods seem to be murdering or cuckolding themselves. The Gunni have the flexibility to look at every discovery, as Master Santaraksita has, and declare new information to be just another way of proclaiming the same old divine truths.

God is god, whatever his name. Blade has seen those sentiments inlaid in the wall tiles in several places in Khang Phi.

Whenever anyone strays far from Shivetya, a ball of earthy brown glow tags along. It hovers above and behind one shoulder or another. The ball does not shed much light but in what otherwise would be utter darkness they are sufficient. They are the golem's doing. Shivetya has powers he has forgotten how to use. He might be a small god himself if he was not nailed to his ancient throne.

Blade descended nearly a thousand steps before he encountered anyone headed upward. This soldier carried a heavy pack. "Sergeant Vanh."

The soldier grunted. Already he was winded. No one made more than one trip a day. Blade gave Vanh the bad news because he might not run into him again for days. "Had a message from the Captain. We have to step it up. She's almost ready to move."

Vanh mumbled the sorts of things soldiers always do. He continued his climb. Blade wondered how Sleepy planned to haul off the mountain of treasure already accumulated up top. It was, for sure, enough to finance a pretty good war.

Another thousand steps downward, repeating his message several times. He left the stair at the level everyone called the Cave of the Ancients because of the old men interred there. Blade always stopped to visit his friend Cordy Mather. It was a ritual of respect. Cordy was dead. Most of the others confined in the cave remained alive, enmeshed in stasis spells. Somehow, during the long Captivity, Mather had shed the spells confining him. And success had cost him his life. He had not been able to find his way out.

Most of the old men in the cave meant nothing to Blade or the Company. Only Shivetya knew who they were or why they had been interred. Certainly they had irked someone armed with the power to confine them. Several corpses, though, had been Company brothers when still alive. Several others had been captives before Soulcatcher buried the Company. Death had found them because, evidently, Cordy Mather had tried to wake them up. Touching the Captured without sorcerous precautions inevitably caused the death of the touched.

Blade resisted the urge to kick the sorcerer Longshadow. That madman was a commodity of incalculable worth in the Land of Unknown Shadows. The Company had grown strong and wealthy because of him. It continued to prosper. "How you doing, Shadowmaster? Looks like you'll be here a while yet." Blade assumed the sorcerer could not hear him. He could not recall having heard anything when he was under the enchantment himself. He could not recall having been aware in any way, though Murgen said there were times when it looked like the Captured were aware of their surroundings. "They haven't pushed the bidding high enough yet. I hate to admit it but you really are a popular guy. In your own special way." Not a generous or forgiving or even empathetic man, Blade stood with hands on hips staring down at Longshadow. The sorcerer looked like a skeleton barely covered by diseased skin. His face was locked into a scream. Blade told him, "They still say, 'All Evil Dies There an Endless Death.' Especially when they're talking about you."

Not far from Longshadow is the Company's other insane sorcerer prisoner, the Howler. This one presents a greater temptation. Blade saw no value whatsoever to keeping Howler alive. The little shit has a history of treachery that goes way, way back and a character unlikely to change because of this confinement. He survived a similar Captivity before. That one endured for centuries.

Tobo did not need to learn any of the Howler's evil crap. And Tobo's education was the only excuse Blade had heard for letting the little ragbag live.

Blade paid his deepest respects to Mather. Cordy was a good friend for a long time. Blade owes Cordy his life. He wished the evil fortune had befallen him. Cordy wanted to live. Blade believes he is proceeding on inertia.

Blade continued his descent into the earth, past the treasure caverns that were being looted to finance the Company's homegoing, it was hoped on a spectacularly memorable scale.

Blade is not much given to emotional vapors or seizures of fear. He has a cool enough head to have survived for years as a Company agent inside Longshadow's camp. But as he moved deeper into the earth he began to twitch and sweat. His pace slackened. He passed the last known cavern. Nothing lay below that but the ultimate enemy, the Mother of Night herself. She was the enemy who would still be waiting once all the other, lesser adversaries had been brushed aside or extinguished.

To Kina, the Black Company is an annoying buzz in the ear, a mosquito that has gotten away with taking a sip or two of blood and has not had the good sense to get the hell away.

Blade slowed again. The light following him kept weakening. Where once he could see clearly twenty steps ahead now he could see only ten, the farther four seeming to be behind the face of a thickening black fog. Here the darkness seemed almost alive. Here the darkness felt as though it was under much greater pressure, the way water seemed to exert more as you swam deeper beneath its surface.

Blade found it harder to breathe. He forced himself to do

so, deeply and rapidly, then went on, against the insistence of instinct. A silver chalice took form in the fog, just five steps below. It stood about a foot tall, a simple tall cup made of noble metal. Blade had placed it there. It marked the lowest step he had yet been able to reach.

Now each step downward seemed to take place against the resistance of liquid tar. Each step brought the darkness crushing in harder. The light from behind was too weak to reach even one step beyond the chalice.

Blade makes this effort frequently. He accounts it exercise for his will and courage. Each descent he manages to make it as far as the chalice mostly by being angry that he cannot push past it.

This time he tried something different. He threw a handful of coins collected from one of the treasure caves. His arm had no strength but gravity had not lost its power nor had sound been devoured by the darkness. The coins tinkled away down the stairwell. But not for long. After a moment it sounded like they were rolling around on a floor. Then they were silent. Then a tiny little voice from far, far away cried, "Help."

13

The Land of Unknown Shadows:
Traveling Hsien

The physical geography of the Land of Unknown Shadows closely recollects that of our own world. The essential differences stem from the impact of man.

The moral and cultural topographies of the worlds are completely different, though. Even the Nyueng Bao still have trouble making any real connection here—despite the fact that they and the Children of the Dead share common ancestors. But the Nyueng Bao escaped Maricha Manthara

Dhumraksha and his kin centuries ago, then developed as a cultural island constantly washed by alien waves.

Hsien proper spans roughly the same territories as what were known as the Shadowlands at home when things were going well for the Shadowmasters. The farther reaches of Hsien, that none of us have visited, are more heavily populated than our own. In olden times every town here boasted its kernel of resistance to the Shadowmasters. Few of those groups communicated because of travel restrictions imposed by the master race. Still, when the uprising did come there were local champions enough to ensure success.

The flight of the last Shadowmasters left a power vacuum. The resistance chieftains anointed themselves to fill it. Hsien remains in the custody of their descendants, scores of warlords in constant conflict, few of whom ever get any stronger. Any who appear to be gaining strength are torn apart by their neighbors.

The File of Nine is an anonymous, loose assembly of senior warlords, supposedly drawn one each from the nine provinces of Hsien. This is not true and never has been—though few outside the Nine know it. That is just one more fiction helping keep the current state of chaos alive.

Popularly, the File of Nine is seen as a cabal of secret masters who control everything. The File of Nine would love that to be true but, in reality, they have very little power. Their situation leaves them with few tools they can use to enforce their will. Any real effort to impose anything would betray their identities. So they mostly issue bulls and pretend to speak for Hsien. Sometimes people listen. And sometimes they listen to the monks of Khang Phi. Or to the Court of All Seasons. So each must be wooed.

The Black Company is feared mainly because it is a joker in the warlord deck. It has no local allegiance. It could jump any direction for any alien reason. Worse, it is reputed to include powerful wizards assisting skilled soldiers led by competent commanders and sergeants, none of whom are at all handicapped by excesses of empathy or compassion.

What popularity the Company enjoys essentially arises from its capacity to deliver the last Shadowmaster to the justice of Hsien. And among peasants, from the fact that nervous warlords have reined in their squabbles amongst themselves considerably while they have this unpredictable monster crouched, growing rapidly, to their south.

All the lords and leaders of Hsien, in the last, would prefer that the Company went away. Our presence places too much strain on the state of things as they are and always have been.

I attached myself to the deputation headed for Khang Phi even though I was not yet completely recovered. I would never be one-hundred percent again. I had some blurring in my right eye. I had acquired some truly intimidating burn scars. I would never regain the full range of motion in the fingers of my right hand. But I was convinced that I could be an asset in our negotiations for the shadowgate secrets.

Only Sahra agreed with me. But Sahra is our foreign minister. Only she has the patience and tact to deal with such fractious folk as the File of Nine—part of whose problem with us is that our women do more than cook and lie on their backs.

Of course, of Lady, Sleepy, Sahra and the Radisha I suspect only Sahra can heat water without burning it. And she may have forgotten how by now.

The Company on the move, bound for the intellectual heart of Hsien, was a terror to behold, judging by the response of peasants along the way. And that despite the fact that our party, guards included, numbered just twenty-one. Human souls.

Tobo's shadowy friends surrounded and paced us, in such numbers that it was impossible for them to remain unseen all the time. Old fears and superstitions exploded in our wake, then terror ran ahead far faster than we could travel. People scattered when we approached. It made no difference that Tobo's night pals were well-behaved. Superstition completely outweighed any practical evidence.

Had we been more numerous we would not have gotten past Khang Phi's gate. Even there, among supposed intellectuals, the fear of the Unknown Shadows was thick enough to slice.

Sahra had had to agree, long ago, that neither Lady nor One-Eye nor Tobo would enter the Repose of Knowledge. The monks were particularly paranoid about sorcerers. Hitherto it had suited Sleepy to comply with their wishes. And none of those three were part of our party when we arrived at the Lower Gate of Khang Phi.

There was a strange young woman in our midst. She used the name Shikhandini, Shiki for short. She could easily arouse almost any man who did not know she was Tobo in disguise. Nobody bothered to tell me what or why but Sahra was up to something. Tobo was, obviously, an extra card she wanted tucked up her sleeve. Moreover, she suspected several of the Nine of harboring evil ambitions which would soon flower.

What? Men of power possessed of secret agendas? No! That does not seem possible.

Khang Phi is a center of learning and spirituality. It is a repository for knowledge and wisdom. It is extremely ancient. It survived the Shadowmasters. It commands the respect of all the Children of the Dead, throughout the Land of Unknown Shadows. It is neutral ground, a part of no warlord's demesne. Travelers bound toward Khang Phi, or returning home therefrom, are in theory immune.

Theory and practice are sometimes at variance. Therefore we never let Sahra travel without obvious protection.

Khang Phi is built against the face of a mountain. It rises a thousand whitewashed feet into the bellies of permanent clouds. The topmost structures cannot be seen from below.

At the same site in our world a barren cliff broods over the southern entrance to the only good pass through the mountains known as the Dandha Presh.

A life misspent making war left me wondering if the place had not begun its existence as a fortress. It certainly commanded that end of the pass. I looked for the fields necessary to sustain its population. And they were there, clinging to the sides of the mountains in terraces like stairsteps for splay-legged giants. Ancient peoples carried the soil in from leagues away, a basket at a time, generation after generation. No doubt the work goes on today.

Master Santaraksita, Murgen and Thai Dei met us outside the ornate Lower Gate. I had not seen them for a long time, though Murgen and Thai Dei attended the funeral ceremonies for Gota and One-Eye. I missed then because I was unconscious at the time. Fat old Master Santaraksita never went anywhere anymore. That elderly scholar was content to end his days in Khang Phi, pretending to be the Company's agent. Here he was among his own kind. Here he had found a thousand intellectual challenges. Here he had found people as eager to learn from him as he was eager to learn from them. He was a man who had come home.

He welcomed Sleepy with open arms. "Dorabee! At last." He insisted on calling her Dorabee because it was the first name he had known her by. "You *must* let me show you the master library while you're here! It absolutely beggars that pimple we managed in Taglios." He surveyed the rest of us. Merriment deserted him. Sleepy had brought the ugly boys along. The kind of guys he believed would use books for firewood on a chilly night. Guys like me, who bore scars and were missing fingers and teeth and had skin colors the likes of which were never seen in the Land of Unknown Shadows.

Sleepy told him, "I didn't come for a holiday back in the stacks, Sri. One way or another I've got to get that shadow-gate information. The news I'm getting from the other side isn't encouraging. I need to get the Company back into action before it's too late."

Santaraksita nodded, looked around for eavesdroppers, winked and nodded again.

Willow Swan leaned back, looked up, asked me, "Think you can make it to the top?"

"Give me a few days." Actually, I am in better shape now than I was that evil night. I have lost a lot of weight and have put on muscle.

I still get winded easily, though.

Swan said, "Lie all you want, old man." He dismounted, handed his reins to one of the youngsters beginning to swarm around. They were all boys between eight and twelve, all as silent as if they had had their vocal cords cut. They all wore identical pale brown robes. Parents unable to provide for them had donated them to Khang Phi as infants. These had surpassed a particular milestone on their path to becoming monks. We were unlikely to see anyone younger.

Swan picked up a stone two inches in diameter. "I'm going to throw this when we get up top. I want to watch it fall."

Parts of Swan never grew up. He still skips stones across ponds and rivers. He tried to teach me the art coming to Khang Phi. My hand and fingers will no longer conform to the shape of a proper skipping stone. There is a lot they cannot accomplish anymore. Managing a pen while writing is chore enough.

I miss One-Eye.

"Just don't bomp some asshole warlord on the noggin. Most of them don't like us much already." They were afraid of us. And they could find no way to manipulate us. They kept giving us provisions and letting us recruit in hopes we will go away eventually. Leaving Longshadow behind. We did not inform them that local financing would not be needed to underwrite our campaign beyond the plain.

After four hundred years it has become a given: You keep everybody outside just a little bit nervous. And you do not tell them anything they do not need to know.

Longshadow. Maricha Manthara Dhumraksha. He has several other names here as well. None indicate popularity.

As long as we have the ability to deliver him in chains the warlords will tolerate almost anything. Twenty generations of ancestors cry out for justice.

I suspect Longshadow's wickedness has grown with the retelling, thereby making giants of the heroes who drove him out.

Though they are soldiers themselves the warlords do not understand us. They fail to recognize the fact that they are soldiers of a different breed, drawn on by a smaller destiny.

14

The Land of Unknown Shadows:
Khang Phi

Swan and I stood looking out a window outside the conference hall where we would engage the File of Nine in negotiations. Eventually. It took them a while to sneak into Khang Phi, then change their disguises so their identities would remain unknown. We saw nothing below but mist. Swan did not waste his stone. I said, "I thought I was back in shape. I was wrong. I ache all over."

Swan said, "They say some people here go their whole lives without ever moving more than a floor or two after they finish their apprenticeship and get their assignments."

"Kind of people that balance out you and me," I said. Swan had not traveled as far as I had but at a world's remove an extra few thousand miles does not seem important. I tried to make out the rocky ground we had traversed approaching Khang Phi. The mist just seemed darker when I looked down.

"Thinking about taking the easy way back down?" Swan asked.

"No. I'm thinking being isolated like this might leave you

with a very limited worldview." Not to mention the impact of the scarcity of females in Khang Phi. The few there are belong to an order of celibate nuns who care for the donated infants, the very old and the very sick. The rest of the population consists of monks, all of whom were donated and all of whom are sworn to chastity, too. The more fanatic brothers render themselves physically incapable of yielding to temptation. Which makes most of my brothers shudder and consider them more bizarre than Tobo's shadowy friends. No soldier likes the thought of losing his best friend and favorite toy.

"A narrow view can be as much a strength as a weakness, Liberator," a voice observed from behind us. We turned. Sleepy's friend, Surendranath Santaraksita, was joining us. The scholar has gone native, adopting local garb and assuming the Khang Phi haircut—which is no hair at all—but only a deaf and blind man would take him for a local monk. His skin is more brown and less translucent than that of any native and his features are shaped more like mine and Swan's. "That mist and their narrowness of vision allows the monks to avoid forming worldly attachments. Thus their neutrality remains beyond reproach."

I did not mention Khang Phi's one-time role as an apologist for and collaborator with the reign of the Shadowmasters. That embarrassing dab of history was being expunged by the acids of time and relentless lie.

Santaraksita was happy. He was convinced that in this place learned men did not have to prostitute themselves to temporal powers in order to remain scholars. He believed even the File of Nine deferred to the wisdom of the eldest monks. He was unable to see that if the Nine acquired more power Khang Phi's relationship to the File would soon lapse into subservience. Master Santaraksita is brilliant but naive.

"How's that?" I asked him.

"These monks are so innocent of the world that they don't try to impose anything on it."

"Yet the File of Nine presume to speak from here." The File enjoy issuing bulls which are, more often than not, ignored by the population and warlords.

"They will, yes. The Elders want them to. In hopes that a little wisdom will rub off before their power becomes more than symbolic."

I said nothing about leading horses to water. I made no observations concerning the wisdom of backing a cabal of secret masters in preference to one strongman or the remnant aristocracy of the Court of All Seasons. I did admit, "It does look like they're trying to do what's best for Hsien. But I don't trust anybody who'll bet their pot on guys who hide behind masks." No need to tell him the File have no secrets from us. Little that they do or discuss goes unremarked by Tobo's familiars. None of their identities are secrets to us.

We operate on the assumption that both the File and the other warlords have placed spies among our recruits. Which explains why there is little resistance to our recruiting amongst the Children of the Dead.

It is not difficult to identify most of the spies. Sleepy shows them what she wants them to see. Being a spiteful, vengeful little witch, I am sure she plans to use those spies cruelly at some later time.

She worries me. She has her own old hatreds to redress but their objects escaped life unpunished a long time ago. But there is always the chance she might choose somebody else to take the heat, which would not be to the Company's advantage.

I asked Santaraksita, "What did you want?"

"Nothing special." His face went coolly neutral. He is Sleepy's friend. I make him uncomfortable. He has read my Annals. Despite what Sleepy has dragged him through he cannot yet come to grips with the cruel realities of our sort of life. I am sure that he will not go home with us. "I did hope to see Dorabee again before you went into conference. It could be important."

"I don't know what happened to her. Shiki's missing, too. They were supposed to meet us here." Local mores made it impossible for women to share quarters with men. Even Sahra has to room separately from Murgen, though they are legally married. And Shikhandini's presence saddled Sahra with special obligations. She wanted the holy men distracted but not to the point where they went berserk. Just enough, maybe, so they would give way on a subtle point or two. Though distraction would not be Shiki's principal mission.

Master Santaraksita wrung his hands briefly, then folded his arms. His hands disappeared into the sleeves of his robe. He was worried. I looked closer. He knew something. I glanced at Swan. Swan shrugged.

Murgen and Thai Dei puffed into the room. Murgen demanded, "Where are they?" Thai Dei looked worried but said nothing. He would not. The man seldom says anything. It was a pity his sister could not learn from his example.

Thai Dei knew something, too.

"Haven't shown yet," Swan said.

"The File of Nine will be angry," I added. "Are Sleepy and Sahra dealing some kind of game?"

Santaraksita backed away nervously. "The Unknowns aren't here yet, either."

My companions were a diverse bunch. Once Sleepy arrived we would include five races. Six counting Santaraksita as one of us. Sleepy believes our sheer diversity intimidates the File of Nine.

Sleepy entertains other notions even more strange.

I do not know why she thought cowing them would mean anything. All we needed from them was their permission to research the knowledge needed to mend and manipulate shadowgates. The monks of Khang Phi were willing to share that knowledge. The stronger we grow the more eagerly the monks want us gone. They are more frightened of the heresies we propagate than they are of any armies we might bring back later.

The latter dread keeps the warlords awake at night. But they do want us gone, too, because the stronger we grow here the more real and immediate a threat do they perceive. And I do not blame them for thinking that way. I would do so myself, in their boots. The entirety of human experiences argues on behalf of suspicion of strangers laden with weapons.

The womenfolk made their advent. Willow Swan spread his arms wide and declaimed dramatically, "Where have you been?" He struck a second pose and tried the line another way. Then he went with a third. Making fun.

Sahra told Thai Dei, "Your daughter kept flirting with the acolytes we encountered along the way."

I glanced at Shiki, frowned. The girl seemed almost ethereal, not at all vampish. I blinked but the fuzzy quality did not go away. I blamed my damaged eye. The girl seemed more a distracted ghost than a boy in disguise having fun with a role.

In Hsien's eyes Thai Dei passed as Shiki's father because it was well known that Sahra had just the one son. Her brother, Thai Dei, has managed to remain so obscure that even at the Abode of Ravens the locals never raise a question about the fact that the seldom-seen Shikhandini would have had to have been born while her father was buried beneath the plain. Nor did anyone seem much inclined to ask what had become of the girl's mother. She could be dismissed with a few vague, angry mutters.

Shiki was always empty-headed, always in minor trouble, always considered a threat only to the equilibrium of young men's minds.

Shiki solidified. She pouted. She said, "I wasn't flirting, Father. I was just talking." Her words should have been argumentative but just sounded flat, rote.

"You were told not to speak to the monks. That's the law here."

"But Father . . ."

The act never stopped once it started. There might be watchers. But it *was* an act. And a pretty good one, at least to those of us unaccustomed to dealing with very young women.

Master Santaraksita kept whispering to Sleepy. He must have said something she wanted to hear because her face lit up like a beacon. She did not bother to report to the Annalist, though. These Captains are all alike. Always playing their hands close to their chest. Except for me, of course. I was a paragon of openness in my time.

Thai Dei and his daughter continued to squabble till he issued some loud *diktat* in heated Nyueng Bao that left her sulking and silent.

15

The Land of Unknown Shadows:
The Secret Masters

An old, old monk opened the door to the meeting chamber. The task was a great chore for him. He beckoned with one frail hand.

This was my first visit to Khang Phi but I knew him by his robes, which were dark orange edged with black. They distinguished him as one of the four or five eldest of Khang Phi. His presence made it clear that Khang Phi's monks were deeply interested in this meeting's outcome. Otherwise some midlevel sixty-year-old would have handled the door and then would have hung on to manage the acolytes who were supposed to attend to the comfort of both us and the Nine. Master Santaraksita smiled. Maybe he had had something to do with this meeting having been invested with importance.

Sahra approached the old man. She bowed, murmured a few words. He responded. They knew one another and he did not disdain her for her sex. The monks might be wiser than I had thought.

We soon learned that she had asked if everyone could reduce the ceremony that attends all functions of the Children of the Dead. Formalities imbue every occasion with elaborate ritual. People must not have had much that was practical to do during the reign of the Shadowmasters.

We barbarians do not know the proper forms. The Children of the Dead hoist their noses around us—then sigh in relief because uncomfortable business gets handled quickly when the Black Company is on the far side of the carpet.

Our host scowled at Shikhandini. He was old and bitter and narrow. But! Behold! Not so old and bitter and narrow that a shimmering smile from a beautiful girl would not put a momentary twinkle in his eye. Never that old.

From earliest times our enemies have accused us of fighting dirty, of dealing in trickery and treachery. And they are right. Absolutely right. We are shameless. And this was about as dirty as we could get, having Tobo vamp these old men. They knew women only in the most academic fashion. It was easier than plinking blind men with arrows.

It was all so effortless. Shiki just seemed to float around, not quite all there, not paying much attention, showing none of the enjoyment I expected of Tobo. I mean, what man his age does not enjoy making fools of wise old men? Everything I knew about Tobo suggested he would enjoy that more than most.

I was getting curious. What was going on?

Sleepy claimed the kid was along because she wanted a wizard handy. Just in case. Being paranoid. Having been made that way by lifetimes of treachery from outside. And Khang Phi law would keep Tobo out if he came as himself.

She wanted me to believe.

There would be more. Much, much more. I understand the sneaky little witch better than she suspects. And I approve, thoroughly.

"Move," Sleepy said. She was uncomfortable in Khang Phi. The place is infested with the trappings of strange religions.

The chamber we entered undoubtedly served some high ceremonial purpose when not on loan to the File of Nine. That end where the warlords waited could pass for an altar and its associated clutter. The warlords had seated themselves above us, in front of the possible altar, where five large stone seats were in place permanently. Seven of the Nine were on hand. Chairs had been dragged in for the surplus pair, presumably the junior members of the quorum. All seven wore masks and disguises, which seems to be customary with secret masters—and here possibly a legacy of the Shadowmasters who had found masks and disguises very fashionable. In this case that was a waste of effort. But they did not need to know that. Not right away.

Lady has a talent for rooting out true names and identities. She learned in a deadly school. She has taught Tobo some of her tricks. He unearthed the identities of the members of the File, using his supernatural friends. Knowing who we might find, in the event we developed a corporate inclination to surprise somebody, should prove to be a valuable bargaining tool.

Sahra had dealt with the File before. They were accustomed to her impatience with ceremony. They paid attention when she stepped forward.

Master Santaraksita trailed her by three paces. He would serve as a specialist translator. Though the Children of the Dead and the Nyueng Bao spoke the same language in times past, separation and circumstance have conspired to make misunderstandings common. Santaraksita would have to point out those instances when the parties were using the same word with different meanings.

Sleepy moved a few steps forward but stayed closer to the rest of us than to the warlords.

Sleepy started humming. She was determined to appear

cheerful despite being surrounded by unrepentant heathens.

Sahra stepped forward again. She asked, "Are the File ready to stop objecting to the Company gaining the knowledge we need to repair shadowgates? You have to understand that we won't leave Hsien without it. We're still prepared to turn over the criminal Dhumraksha." The same offer had been before the File all along. They wanted something more but never articulated it—though supernatural espionage revealed that they hoped to gain our support in establishing a much stronger File position. Only they did not dare suggest that themselves before the witnesses that always exist when negotiations take place in Khang Phi.

The masks faced Sahra's way. None of the Unknowns responded. You could sense their exasperation. Lately they had begun to believe, on no creditable evidence, that they had some power over us. Probably because we had not gotten into the sort of pissing contest with any of our neighbors that would have demonstrated the lethal inequalities between their forces and ours. We would devour most of the local armies.

Sleepy stepped past Santaraksita, took position beside Sahra. In passible local dialect she said, "I am Captain of the Black Company. I will speak." Facing a warlord wearing a mask surmounted by a crane's head, she continued, "Tran Thi Kim-Thoa, you are Last Entered of the File." The warlords stirred. "You are young. Possibly you know no one whose life and pain would regain meaning if Maricha Manthara Dhumraksha came back here to atone for his sins. I understand that. Youth is always impatient with the pasts of its elders—even when that past crushes down upon youth's shoulders."

She paused.

Seven silk-clad butts shifted nervously, filling an extended silence with soft rustles. All us Company people grinned, baring our fangs. Exactly like those rock apes around Outpost, trying to intimidate one another.

Sleepy had named the newest of the Nine. His identity would be no secret to the other eight. They had chosen him when last there was an opening in their circle. He would be ignorant of their identities—unless some of the older warlords had chosen to reveal themselves. Each warlord normally knew only those elected to the File after themselves. By naming the Last Entered, Sleepy offered another threat while endangering just the one Unknown.

Sleepy beckoned. "Croaker." I stepped forward. "This is Croaker. He was Captain before me and Dictator to All the Taglias. Croaker, before us we have Tran Huu Dung and six others of the File of Nine." She did not specify this Tran's position in the File. His name caused another stir, though.

She beckoned Swan. "This is Willow Swan, a longtime associate of the Black Company. Willow, I present Tran Huu Nhan and six others of the File of Nine. Tran is a common patronym in Hsien. There are a lot of Trans among the Nine, none of them related by blood."

The next name she offered, after introducing Willow Swan, was Tran Huu Nhang. I began to wonder how they kept themselves sorted out. Maybe by weight. Several of the File carried some surplus poundage.

When Sleepy named the last of the Trans of the File, Tran Lan-Anh, their spokesman, the First, interrupted her with a request for time to confer. Sleepy bowed, offered him no further provocation. We knew that he was Pham Thi Ly of Ghu Phi, an excellent general with a good reputation among his troops, a believer in a unified Hsien, but old enough to have lost his zest for struggle. By the slightest of nods Sleepy let him know that his identity was no secret, either.

Sleepy announced, "We have no interest in coming back to Hsien once we return to the plain." As though that was some dear secret we had held clutched close to our hearts forever. Any spy among us would have reported that we just wanted to go home. "Like the Nyueng Bao who fled to our world, we came here only because we had no choice." Doj would not have accepted her assessment of Nyueng Bao history, brief as it might be. In his eye his immigrant ancestors had been a band of adventurers similar to the forebrethren of the Black Company, who had gone forth from Khatovar. "We're strong now. We're ready to go home. Our enemies there will cringe, unmanned by the news of our coming."

I did not believe that for an instant. Soulcatcher would be pleased to see us. A good squabble would relieve the tedium of her daily grind. Being an all-powerful ruler actually takes most of the fun out of life. In the heyday of her dark empire, my wife had made that discovery, too. Management trivia consumes you.

Lady hated it enough to walk away. But misses it now.

Sleepy said, "We lack only the knowledge to repair our shadowgate, so that our world isn't overrun by the Host of the Unforgiven Dead."

Our spokespeople never fail to harp on that point. It remains central to every statement of our purpose. We would wear the Nine down. They would give in so they would not have to hear about it anymore. They were, however, extremely paranoid about the risk of another otherworld invasion.

If they were hard asses they could try to outstubborn us, hoping we would give up, go home, and have our shadowgate fall apart behind us. That would end our threat permanently.

The power of the File lies in the anonymity of its members. When warlords get together to plot they are restrained by the possibility that among them is one of the Nine. The File publishes any schemes it uncovers, thereby focusing the wrath of warlords not included in the plan. It is a clumsy system but it has kept conflict limited for generations by making it difficult to forge alliances.

Sleepy could expose the File. If they were betrayed, chaos would come baying right behind. Few warlords like having their ambitions held in check—though restraints had to be imposed on all those other villains.

The Unknowns did not like being bullied, either. Those

whose names had been betrayed soon grew so angry the elder monk placed himself between parties as a reminder of where we were.

Being an old soldier, I began a swift inventory of resources available for a fight if some warlord was dim enough to force one. I was not reassured. Our greatest asset was missing.

Where did Shiki go? When did she go? Why?

I needed to keep a closer eye on my surroundings. An oversight this big could turn fatal.

One masked warlord bounded out of his chair. He yipped and slapped his buttocks. We gaped. Silence fell. The man began to gather his dignity. A trill of faint high-pitched laughter sparkled in the silence. Something with humming diamond wings darted about too fast to be made out clearly. It left the room before anybody could react.

Sahra observed, "Most of the Hidden Realm will follow us when we leave. Possibly so much of it that Hsien will no longer be the Land of Unknown Shadows."

Master Santaraksita murmured in her ear. That irked the warlords and the old referee elder, too. The monk was particularly unhappy because the ladies kept spinning those implied threats. But he was cautious. The Company was up to something new. This was frightening. Had the outsiders run out of patience? All Hsien nurtures some fears of the sleeping tiger of the Abode of Ravens. And we make a point of encouraging them.

When I looked around again there was Shikhandini. How? . . .

I studied her, expecting to see some deviltry suggested by her stance or expression. There was nothing there. The kid was stone cold indifferent.

Sahra waved Santaraksita away. He scurried over to Sleepy, murmured some more. Sleepy nodded but did not do anything else. That left the old scholar looking like he was about to panic.

Shiki's disappearance and reappearance made it more obvious than ever that there was something going on. Obvious to the former Captain, anyway. And the former Captain had been told nothing beforehand.

The ladies were into one of their schemes. And that would be the real reason they wanted Shiki along. Shiki brought an awesome array of weapons into the game.

And they had had me convinced that they just wanted the magic handy in case somebody suffered an impulse to be unpleasant, which happens all too frequently when we are around.

The Radisha and the Prahbrindrah Drah still mourn their treacherous impulses.

I told Swan, "This business was a lot more fun when I was the one scheming and being mysterious."

The First of the File said, "Will you do us the courtesy of withdrawing for a moment, Captain? Ambassador? I believe a consensus may be within reach."

While we waited in the antechamber, Swan asked, "Why did he bother asking us to leave? After what happened? Does he really think we won't know what's going on in there?" Things moved in the corners of my vision. Strings of shadow snaked over the walls until I tried to look at them directly. Then, of course, nothing was visible.

"Possibly he didn't catch all the implications." Like the fact that something would be eavesdropping on every word he spoke until the Black Company left the Land of Unknown Shadows. At this late date anything he tried to pull together would be a complete wasted effort.

"Let's go," Sleepy said. "Move out. Croaker. Swan. Quit jacking your jaws and get moving."

"Moving where?" I asked.

"Downstairs. Home. Get going."

"But . . ." This was not what I expected. A good Black Company trick ends up with lots of fire and bloodshed, the vast majority of both not inflicted upon us.

Sleepy growled. It was a pure animal sound. "If I'm going to be Captain I'm going to be Captain. I'm not going to discuss or debate or request preapproval from the old folks. Get moving."

She had a point. I had made it a few times myself, in my day. I had to set an example.

I went.

"Good luck," Sleepy told Sahra. She strode toward the nearest stairwell. I followed. Presumably better trained by Sleepy's predecessor, the others were clattering down those ancient stairs already. Only Sahra and Master Santaraksita remained behind, though Shiki did hover around Sahra briefly, as though interested in a parting hug.

"Interesting," Sleepy observed. "It's such a good mimic that it almost forgets itself."

She was talking to herself, not to the Captain-Emeritus. He no longer needed an explanation. He had seen this stuff before. The ladies were going to take the information that we needed. Santaraksita had located it and had tagged it and now our own people were in the process of collecting it. Tobo was somewhere else, hard at work. One of his spooky friends was masquerading as Shikhandini.

All of which meant that Sleepy was better prepared to travel than I had supposed.

You miss so much when you are laid up.

Things continued to stir in the corners. Movements persisted at the edge of my vision. Always there was nothing to be seen when I looked directly.

Nevertheless . . .

Khang Phi had been conquered. That unvanquishable fortress of enlightenment had been taken and its occupants did not yet know. Most might never find out—assuming the real Shikhandini successfully completed the real mission given to Tobo by Sleepy and Sahra.

Hard to imagine becoming badly winded by running

downhill. I managed. Those stairs went down forever, much farther than when I had gone up at a more leisurely pace. I began to develop cramps. Behind me Sahra and Sleepy kept right on barking and mocking and pushing like they were not almost as old as me.

I spent a lot of time wondering what had compelled me to come along. I was too old for this shit. The Annals did not need to record every little detail. I could have done this One-Eye's way. "They went to Khang Phi and got the knowledge we needed to fix the shadowgates."

Some deep-voiced bell bonged far above. No one had enough breath to explain but no explanation was needed. An alarm was being sounded.

Our fault?

Who else? Though I could imagine scenarios where the File of Nine might be guilty of trying to snuff the Company brain trust.

It did not matter. I reminded myself that Khang Phi is bereft of arms. That the monks abhor violence. That they always yield to strength, then seduce it with reason and wisdom.

Yes, sometimes it does take a while.

I did not feel reassured. I spend too much time hanging around with guys like me.

The air began to whisper and rustle, like a gentle breeze in a time of falling leaves. The sound started in the dimness far below. It rose toward us, met and passed us before I had any real chance to become afraid. I had a brief impression of passing two-dimensional, black, transparent forms accompanied by a touch of cold and a whiff of old mold, then autumn was gone on to adventures far above.

At times the stairway passed behind the outer face of Khang Phi. Windows presented themselves then. Each was filled with an exquisite view of grey mist. Shapes moved within the greyness, never defined. They did not need definition for me to know that I had no interest in making the acquaintance of anything that did not mind having a thousand feet of wet air beneath its toes.

Several times I saw Shikhandini drift downward or rise through the fog. Once she saw me watching, paused, smiled and showed three slim fingers in a delicate wave.

The genuine Tobo was not shy any digits.

What I did not see during our entire descent was even one member of the Khang Phi community. They all had business elsewhere when we passed by.

"How much farther?" I panted, thinking it was a good thing I had lost all that weight while I was recuperating.

I got no answer. No one wanted to waste the breath.

It proved to be much farther than I had hoped. It always is when you are running away.

Ten Finger Shikhandini was waiting with the horses and the rest of our gang when we stumbled out of the unguarded Lower Gate. Animals and escort were ready to travel. All we had to do was mount up and go.

Tobo would sustain the Shiki role till we were home again. The Children of the Dead did not need to know that he was she.

Tobo told his mother, "Sri Santaraksita refused to come."

"I didn't think he would. That's all right. He did his part. He'll be happier here after we're gone."

Sleepy agreed. "He's found his paradise."

"Excuse me," I gasped. It had taken me three tries and a boost from a helpful escort to get myself into the saddle. "What did we just do?"

"We committed robbery," Sleepy told me. "We went in there pretending we were going to appeal to the File of Nine yet one more time. We got them all twisted out of shape by naming some of their names, so they had nothing else on their minds while we stole the books containing the information we need to get home safely."

"They still don't know," Tobo said. "They're still looking the other way. But that won't last. The doppelgangers I left

behind will fall apart before long. Those things can't keep
their minds on business."

"Quit jawing and ride, then," Sleepy grumbled. I swear.
The woman was Annalist for fifteen years. She ought to have
a better appreciation of the Annalist's needs.

The mist surrounded us and seemed to move with us,
unnaturally dense. Tobo's work, probably. Shapes moved
out there but did not come too close. Until I looked back.

Khang Phi had vanished already. It might be a thousand
miles away or might never have existed at all. Instead I saw
things I would rather not, including several of the Black
Hounds, big as ponies, with high, massive shoulders like those
of hyenas. For an instant, as they began to lose color and focus,
an even larger beast with a head like a leopard's, but green,
loomed out of the mist between them. Cat Sith. It, too, wobbled away from reality, like an exaggerated case of heat shim-
mer fading. The gleam of its exposed teeth was the last to go.

With Tobo's help we evaporated into the landscape ourselves.

16

Wastelands:
Night's Children

Narayan Singh released his grip on his *rumel*, the conse-
crated killing scarf of a Strangler. His hands had
become two aching, arthritic claws. Tears filled his eyes. He
was glad the darkness hid them from the girl. "I never took
an animal before," he whispered, drawing away from the
cooling carcass of the dog.

The Daughter of Night did not respond. She had to concentrate hard to use her crude talents to misdirect the bats
and owls searching for them. The hunt had been on for

weeks. Scores of converts had been taken. The rest had scattered in time-honored fashion. They would come together again after the hunters lost interest. And the hunters did lose interest in them before long. But this time the Witch of Taglios seemed determined to collar the Daughter of Night and the living saint of the Deceivers.

The girl relaxed, sighed. "I think they've moved off to the south." Her whisper contained no note of triumph.

"This should be the last dog." Narayan felt no sense of accomplishment, either. He reached out, touched the girl lightly. She didn't shake him off. "They've never used dogs before." He was tired. Tired of running, tired of pain.

"What's happened, Narayan? What's changed? Why won't my mother answer me? I did everything right. But I still can't feel her out there."

Maybe she was not there anymore, the heretical side of Narayan thought. "Maybe she can't. She has enemies among the gods as well as among men. One of those may be . . ."

The girl's hand covered his mouth. He held his breath. Some owls had hearing acute enough to catch his wheezing—should they catch the girl off guard.

The hand withdrew. "It's turned away. How do we reach her, Narayan?"

"I wish I knew, child. I wish I knew. I'm worn out. I need someone to tell me what to do. When you were little I thought you'd be queen of the world by now. That we would've passed through the Year of the Skulls and Kina's triumph and I would be enjoying the rewards of my persistent faith."

"Don't you start, too."

"Start?"

"Wavering. Doubting. I need you to be my rock, Narayan. Always, when everything else turns to filth in my hands, there's been the granite of Papa Narayan."

For once she seemed not to be manipulating him.

They huddled, prisoners of despair. The night, once Kina's own, now belonged to the Protector and her minions. Yet they were compelled to travel under cloak of darkness. By day they were too easily recognized, she with her pale, pale skin and he with his physical impairments. The reward for their capture was great and the country folk were always poor.

Their flight had led them southward, toward the uninhabited wastelands clinging to the northern foothills of the Dandha Presh. Peopled lands were far too dangerous right now. Every hand was against them there. Yet there was no promise the wastelands would be any friendlier. Out there it might be easier for the hunters to track them.

Narayan mused, "Perhaps we should go into exile until the Protector forgets us." She would. Her passions were furiously intense but never lasted.

The girl did not reply. She stared at the stars, possibly looking for a sign. Narayan's proposition was impossible and they both knew it. They had been touched by the Goddess. They must do her work. They must fulfill their destinies, however unhappy the road. They must bring on the Year of the Skulls, however much suffering they must endure themselves. Paradise lay beyond the pale of affliction.

"Narayan. Look. The sky in the south."

The old Deceiver raised his eyes. He saw what she meant immediately. One small patch of sky, due south, very low, rippled and shimmered. When that stopped for half a minute an alien constellation shone through.

"The Noose," Singh whispered. "It isn't possible."

"What?"

"The constellation is called the Noose. We shouldn't be able to see it." Not from this world. Narayan knew of it only because he had been a prisoner of the Black Company at a time when the constellation had been the subject of intense discussion. It had some connection with the glittering plain. Beneath which Kina lay imprisoned. "Maybe that's our sign." He was ready to grasp any straw. He dragged his weary frame upright, tucked his crutch under his arm. "South it is, then. Where we can travel by day because there'll be no one to spot us."

The girl said, "I don't want to travel anymore, Narayan." But she got up, too. Travel was what they did, day after month after year, because only by remaining in motion could they evade the evils that would prevent them from fulfilling their holy destinies.

An owl called from somewhere far away. Narayan ignored it. He was, for the thousandth time, reflecting on the change of fortune that had befallen them so swiftly, after life had gone so well for several years. His whole life had been that way, one wild swing after another. If he could cling to the tatters of his faith, if he could persevere, soon enough fortune would smile on him again. He was the living saint. His tests and trials had to be measured accordingly.

But he was so tired. And he hurt so much.

He tried not to wonder why there was no sense whatsoever of Kina's presence in the world anymore. He tried to concentrate his whole will upon covering the next painful hundred yards. With that victory in hand he could concentrate on conquering the hundred yards that followed.

17

The Land of Unknown Shadows: The Abode of Ravens

It took Tobo ten days to teach himself everything he needed to become a master shadowgate tinkerer. Those ten days seemed much longer for some of us because the File of Nine, defying the express wishes of the Elders of Khang Phi and the lords of the Court of All Seasons, issued a bull declaring the Black Company to be the enemy of the Children of the Dead. It encouraged all warlords to gather their forces and march against us.

That trouble was slow developing. The warlords who were our neighbors knew too much about us to try anything. Those who were farther away were willing to wait until someone else moved first. Most never bothered to call in their troops. And, characteristic of Hsien's politics, the stream of volunteers, of money and materials helping us become an ever greater threat to the Children of the Dead, never slackened.

Tobo finished work on the Hsien-end shadowgate fourteen days after our return from Khang Phi. Despite the war clouds, Sleepy was in no hurry. Sahra assured her that it would be months before anyone got started our way—if they ever did at all. She claimed the warlords could not possibly agree that quickly and move that fast. No need to hurry. Haste causes mistakes. Mistakes come back to haunt you every time.

"You do a good job, you're guaranteed gonna have to pay for it," I told Suvrin. The young Shadowlander had just been informed of his latest honor: He was going to cross the glittering plain to scout and to repair our home shadowgate. Right after Tobo trained him. Tobo would not go himself because he did not want to be separated from his pets. Filled with low cunning, I asked, "How are your writing skills?"

He stared at me for several seconds, eyes big and brown and round in a big round, brown face. "No. I don't think so. I like it in the Company. But I don't plan to spend my life here. This is a learning experience. This is training. But I won't become a lord of mercenaries."

He surprised me, in several ways: I never heard anyone describe their Company time quite that way, though many do join up fully intending to desert just as soon as they are safely away from the trouble that had them on the run. Nor had I noticed, ever, anyone grasp so quickly what it could mean, in the long run, to be approached about becoming the apprentice Annalist.

A stint as Annalist could be a step toward becoming Captain someday.

I was teasing, mostly, but Sleepy did think a lot of Suvrin. The suggestion might not be a joke to her.

"Have fun on the other side. And be careful. You can't be careful enough where Soulcatcher is involved." I went on and on. His patient blank expression and glazed eyes told me he had heard it all before. I stopped. "And you'll hear it all a hundred times more before you go. The Old Woman'll probably write it all down in a scroll you'll have to take along and read before breakfast every morning."

Suvrin put on a febble, insincere smile. "The Old Woman?"

"Thought I'd try it out. I have a feeling it isn't going to work."

"I think you can count on that."

I didn't expect to cross paths with Suvrin again this side of the plain. I was wrong. Only minutes after we parted it occurred to me that it might be useful if I sat in on the shadowgate training.

It occurred to me that I ought to ask the Captain's permission. I was able to resist the temptation.

Lady decided it might be good if she extended her own education, too.

18

The Land of Unknown Shadows:
Due South

Campfires burned on the far slopes, opposite Outpost. Those pesky rock apes had emigrated. The flocks of crows were expanding. Choosers of the slain, I heard them called somewhere. The File of Nine had pulled a half-ass army together far faster than our bemused foreign minister had believed possible.

"At last," I said to Murgen, as he and I shared a newly discovered jar of skullbuster. "To One-Eye." The stuff just

kept turning up. We were doing our best to make sure it did
not fall into the hands of the soldiers. In their hands strong
drink was likely to cause indiscipline. "Your old lady talked
like it'd be next year before they tried anything. If they ever
got anything going at all."

The advent of unfriendly forces had been no surprise, of
course. Not with Tobo handling intelligence.

"To One-Eye. She has been known to err, Captain." He
was starting to slur already. The boy could not hold his
liquor. "Upon rare occasions."

"Rare occasions."

Murgen hoisted his cup in a salute. "To One-Eye." Then
he shook his head. "I do love that woman, Captain."

"Uhm." Oh-oh. I hoped we did not get maudlin here. But
I understood his problem. She got old. We spent fifteen
years in stasis, not aging a minute. A little payoff from the
gods for doing us so dirty the rest of the time, maybe. But
Sahra, who meant more to Murgen than life itself, who was
the mother of his son, had not been one of the Captured.

Which had been lucky for us. Because she had dedicated
herself to freeing Murgen. And eventually she succeeded.
And freed me and my wife and most of the Captured as well.
But Sahra had grown and had changed and had aged more
than those fifteen years. And their son had grown up. And
even now, four years after our resurrection, Murgen still had
not adjusted completely.

"You can get by," I told him. "Bless One-Eye. Put it all
out of your mind. Exist in the now. Don't worry about the
then. That's what I do." In terms of experience my wife had
been ancient centuries before I was born. "You did get to be
the ghost that rode around with her and shared her life, even
if you couldn't touch her." I live with ten thousand ghosts
from my wife's past, few of whom ever got discussed. She
just did not want to talk about her olden days.

Murgen grunted, mumbled something about One-Eye. He
was having trouble understanding me even though I was

articulating with especial precision. He asked, "You never were much of a drinker, were you, Captain?"

"No. But I've always been a good soldier. I've always done what's got to be done."

"I gotcha."

We were outside, of course, watching shooting stars and the constellations of fires that marked the enemy encampment. There seemed to be an awful lot of those fires. More than the reported numbers deserved. Some genius of a warlord was playing games.

"They're not going to come," Murgen said. "They're just going to sit there. It's all for the benefit of the Nine. It's showmanship."

I blessed One-Eye and took another drink, wondered if Murgen was repeating his wife's assumption or his son's. I cocked my head in favor of my left eye. My night vision is questionable even when I am sober.

Murgen said, "I don't think you can imagine the level of fear over there right now. The boy does something to terrorize them every night. He hasn't hurt a louse on one of their heads yet but they're not stupid. They get the message."

You got the Black Hounds strolling through your camp, eating out of your cookpots, or maybe pissing in them, and you have dozens of lesser night things pulling up tent pegs and starting fires and stealing your boots and treasures, you have troubles that will effect morale for sure. The soldiers will not believe the stories you tell to soothe them, however clever you think you are.

"The thing is, if the leadership decides there'll be war, they'll come." I knew. I have been with the Company forever. I have seen men fight under incredibly bad conditions. And, admittedly, I have seen men lose heart when conditions seemed ideal. "To One-Eye. He was a big part of the glue that held us together."

"One-Eye. You know the Fourth Battalion's going up tonight?"

"Up?"

"To the plain. They're probably moving out right now."

"Suvrin can't possibly have the shadowgate ready to go yet."

Murgen shrugged. "I'm just saying what I heard. Sahra telling Tobo. She got it from Sleepy."

Once again the Annalist had not been included in the planning and decision-making. The Annalist was irked. In a former life he had gained a lot of experience planning campaigns and managing large groups of fractious people. The Annalist can contribute still.

In a moment of clarity I understood why I was being left out. Because of the thing that killed One-Eye. Its punishment was unimportant to Sleepy. She did not want to waste time and resources on it. Particularly the time needed to argue with me and those who felt the way I do.

I mused. "Maybe I shouldn't try to avenge One-Eye."

Murgen didn't mind an unexplained shift in topic. He was listening more closely to his own soul, anyway. He did say, "What're you talking about? It's got to be done."

So he agreed with me. It occurred to me that he had known One-Eye longer than anyone else but me. I still thought of him as the new kid sometimes because he was almost the last man to join us while we were still in service to the Lady, in that other world so far away and so long ago that there were moments when I almost waxed nostalgic for those bad old days.

"Here's one more to One-Eye. And I want to know when we're going to start racking up some good old days."

"They're in there, Captain. Here and there. They just don't stick out."

I remembered one or two. But that only got me started thinking about what might have been. About Booboo. And when I mix strong spirits with thoughts of my daughter the weather turns maudlin every time. And we see more and more of that weather as I get older.

"You got any idea what Sleepy's strategy is?" I asked. She

would have one. Scheming and planning is supposedly her long suit. Long enough for her to have outwitted the Radisha and my sister-in-law.

"Not a clue. I knew more about what was going on when I was a ghost."

"You don't go out of body anymore?"

"I'm cured. At least in this world."

Not good, I feared. His loose attachment to his flesh had been the Company's most potent weapon for years. What would we do if we could no longer see what was happening in places we were not at?

You do get spoiled fast.

Something chittered in the darkness. For a moment I thought it was mocking me. But then a huge fireball rolled up into the night across the valley. The unseen thing's amusement was at the expense of the soldiers over there.

"This jar's gone empty," I grumbled, leaning back and shaking a last drop into the back of my mouth. "I'm going to go see if I can't make another one turn up where we found this one."

19

Glittering Stone:
Sneak Away

Doj nodded slightly as Lady and I rode past his place. When I glanced back a minute later he was in the street with several Nyueng Bao henchmen. He was wearing his sword, Ash Wand. Up ahead, Thai Dei, Murgen's brother-in-law and bodyguard, strolled along the street. He was armed, too. If he was moving, Murgen would be, too.

I kept a wary watch behind. This had to be done before Sleepy caught on. Before she could issue orders forbidding it. I would not defy direct orders.

She and Sahra were down in the valley. Tran Huu Nhang had come out under a flag of truce. I had a feeling he would announce that the File of Nine had decided to accept reality. They would never admit it but their army had been defeated without stepping onto the field of battle. It was evaporating. The private soldiers were unwilling to endure the persistent attentions of the Unknown Shadows.

It was all pretty amusing—unless you were one of the Nine determined to make a reputation for the File, or you were a crow with hopes of getting fat. Amusing but handy. I was tired of waiting for a chance to slip away. My need to settle with the Bowalk monster had grown pretty powerful, though I hid it well. I have a number of obsessions that I do not let show.

Officially, the Eleventh Battalion was rotating up to guard the shadowgate. In reality, the Eleventh would be started through to the fortress at the heart of the plain, after nightfall. My gang would be up there much earlier, swiftly moving beyond any hope of Sleepy turning us around. Tobo would cover our backtrail.

I made a sign I hoped would be seen and passed along. We needed to move faster. Sleepy is a resourceful little witch. If there was any way to beat me out of this she might have it figured out already.

It did seem like she was out there by herself on the Bowalk question. One-Eye had a lot more friends dead than he had had while he was alive.

Tobo was at the shadowgate. But he was supposed to be keeping an eye on his mother and the Captain. Before I could say anything, though, he told me, "They're safe. The meet is a face-saving scheme by the Nine. They've realized what they did was stupid. There'll be a lot of ceremony but no admission of anything, like even that they've got an army over there that wanted to do us evil, and before they're done they'll give Mom a bull that grants the Company permission to find and use the shadowgate secrets." He grinned, a kid excited. "I don't think they've been getting enough sleep."

"And why are you here?"

"I have family going through. Don't I?"

Of course he did. I was on edge. "Let's keep moving, people." With Nyueng Bao, old Company hands, my wife and whatnot, I would have just over forty people joining my hunt. For a while. If it dragged on I might not be able to hold them together.

Tobo told me, "Make camp at the first circle. Even if it seems like you can cover a lot more ground before it gets dark." He told Lady, "It's important. Keep him in check. The first circle. So I can catch up when I get away."

Willow Swan called, "Hey, Croaker. If you stand right here and look just right out of the side of your eye, you can see the Nef. In broad daylight."

Swan was on the other side of the Hsien shadowgate. His voice had a dampened, distant quality.

I gave him my best scowl. "Don't forget plain discipline." Shivetya might be our ally and the soul of the plain but there were perils up there even he could not master. The Unforgiven Dead were as hungry for life as ever. Only the roads and circles were safe. Extreme care had to be taken to avoid piercing the protective boundaries. Their master spells would repair them if you did. But you would not be alive to enjoy the result. All that would be left of you was a desiccated husk that had taken a while dying, screaming all the way.

Lately there seemed to be less shadow activity than in the past. Possibly Shivetya had found a way to control them. Maybe even to destroy them. They were a later accretion. He had no use for them. He would love to be rid of them.

Which would be as wonderful for those sad but deadly monsters as it would be for us. They would achieve the release of death at least. A release Shivetya understood. It was a release he yearned for himself.

I started barking at people. "Let's get that equipment out

and moving! Where are those mules? I thought I sent them up here last week." When a lot of people agree with you, you can move a lot of material without drawing much attention. I started work on this as soon as I was sure Sleepy did not intend to pursue it herself.

"Calm down," Tobo told me. And I did. Stunned. Because a kid was saying it to a veteran. And was right. "Come here. Lady, you too." He stepped away from the road, to a rudely made wooden box balanced precariously atop a jagged boulder.

"This same rock is over on the home side," I said. "Your father had a bunker right over there where that bush is. What have you got?"

The box contained what looked like four black glass cylinders a foot long, two inches in diameter, equipped with a metal handle on one end.

"These are keys. Like the Lance of Passion was. The kind you need to get on and off the plain. I made new ones. It's not hard if you have the specifications. Blade has one key. Suvrin has two. One is in place in this gate here. We'll take it away when we leave. Two more are with a couple of the battalion commanders who went up already. You're going to take two with you. Just in case."

He handed me one cylinder and gave the other to Lady. Mine seemed heavier than an object its size ought to be. The handle was silver. I asked, "You just drop it into the hole in the plain, right?"

"Exactly. Remember your repair lessons?" He faced Lady when he asked that. I did sit in on the classes but my wife had gotten a lot better understanding of the process. It would have to be a major emergency before we counted on me doing anything even vaguely related to sorcery.

A stream of mules and men passed through the shadowgate. Each got checked by a sergeant who must have spent his formative years at Sleepy's headquarters. He wanted to make note of every man, every animal, every fireball thrower and other major item of equipment or weaponry. The Nyueng Bao, not really belonging to the Company, were rude to him. I went over and was rude myself. "You're gumming up the works, Sergeant. Go away. Or I'll ask Tobo to sic one of the Black Hounds on you."

The pack was not far off. Nobody could see them, of course, but they made plenty of racket when they quarreled among themselves. And that never stopped.

My threat had the desired effect. The keeper of inventories departed so fast there was almost a whoosh. He would file an official complaint. But that would end up far down the list of my delinquencies.

Tobo overtook me. Most of my gang were through now. The kid bowed to his father, formally polite. He and Murgen had a mutual problem. Neither knew quite how to bridge the gap left by Murgen having been buried during most of the years Tobo was growing up.

The boy told me, in a voice his father was intended to hear, "You'd better push it now. Mom just got word of what you're doing. She'll keep her mouth shut for Gota's sake. For now. But when she hears that Dad is in on it she's going to boil over and head straight for the Captain."

I gave Murgen an ugly look. Didn't tell the old lady you were going out with the guys, eh?

How did Tobo know what his mother had just found out?

The kid snapped his fingers, made a series of hand gestures, said something obscure, apparently to empty air.

A pair of shadows raced across the slope, slanting down from the southwest. They headed straight toward us. I saw nothing to cast them. Then, suddenly, I had a face full of flapping wings, weights on my shoulders and what felt like dragon's talons trying to rip the meat off my collarbones.

Ravens.

"They only look like crows," Tobo said. "Don't ever forget that they're not."

I shuddered. I have lived with this stuff all around me,

decade after decade, but being exposed to it has not made it any less creepy.

Tobo told me. "At my request they've agreed to assume this shape. They'll be your eyes and ears wherever you have to operate without me. They won't have the strategic range you were used to with Dad but they can cover a few hundred miles, fast, and they'll give you a strong tactical advantage. Besides scouting they can carry messages. Be sure to frame those carefully, clearly, without ambiguity, and try to keep them short. Give them an absolutely crystal clear address. Name names and make sure they know who the names belong to."

I turned my head right and left, caught glimpses from the sides of my eyes. It was disconcerting, having those cruel beaks so close. The eyes are the first things the Choosers of the Slain go for on the battlefield.

One bird was black, the other white. They were bigger than the local breed of raven. And the white one had not gotten the shape quite right. It looked like one of its parents had been a startled pigeon instead of a crow.

"If it turns out that I can't catch up and you need to get in touch, they can find me easily."

I am sure I looked grim.

Grinning, Tobo told me, "And I thought they'd go great with your costume. Mom told me you always had ravens on your shoulders when you did Widowmaker, years ago."

I sighed. "Those were real crows. And they belonged to Soulcatcher. The two of us had a sort of understanding in those days. Enemy of my enemy kind of thing."

"You did bring the Widowmaker armor with you, didn't you? And One-Eye's spear? You know you won't be able to come back for anything you leave behind."

"Yes, yes. I have it." This Widowmaker costume armor was not the same outfit that I had worn decades ago. That had gotten lost during Sleepy and Sahra's Kiaulune wars. Soulcatcher probably had it in her trophy chamber. This armor, though mainly for show, came from Hsien's finest armories and had a distinct native flavor. Its black, chitinous lacquer surface boasted inlays of gold and silver symbols that Hsien associated with sorcery and evil and darkness. Some reproduced arcane characters of power once associated with the Shadowmasters. Others went back to an age when Hsien's now-extinct Kina cult was sending out Deceiver companies on crusade. All those symbols were scary, at least in the world where first they had been imagined.

Lady's reconstituted Lifetaker armor was uglier than mine. The stuff on its exterior was less clearly defined and much more creepy because she had insisted on being involved in its design and creation. The inside of her head is filled with spiders.

She did not get any pretend-to-be Choosers of the Slain. She got several ornate little teak boxes and a thin stack of sheets of the strange rice paper preferred by the monks of Khang Phi.

"You have to go. I'll see that they don't send a messenger to order you back."

I grunted. Except for Uncle Doj, who paused to murmur with Tobo, I was the last of my gang through the Hsien shadowgate. Lady squeezed my hand when I joined her on the risky side. She said, "We're off, darling. Again." She seemed excited.

"Again." I could not recall ever being excited by moving out.

Murgen asked, "You want to show the standard now?"

"Not until we're on the plain itself. We're renegades here. Let's don't make Sleepy look small." I had an idea, then. If I could come up with some material . . . we could run up the old Company standard. From before we adopted Soulcatcher's firebreathing skull.

"Good," Doj told me, stepping through the gate. "A bit of wisdom. That's really good."

I began the climb to the plain somewhat numbed by the realization that I was the only living member of the company who recalled our original banner. It had been no more cheerful than today's was but it had been a lot busier. A field of scarlet with nine hanged men in black and six yellow daggers in the upper left and lower right quadrants, respectively, while the upper right quandrant featured a shattered skull and the lower left boasted a bird astride a severed head. It might have been a raven. Or an eagle.

There was nothing in the Annals to suggest when or why that banner had been adopted.

20

Glittering Stone:
Mystic Roads

"Different stars tonight," Willow Swan said, lying back, staring at the sky.

"Different everything," Murgen replied. "Find me Little Boy or the Dragon's Eye."

There was no moon. There is always a moon up in the Land of Unknown Shadows.

The sky on the plain . . . is changeable. It may not boast the same constellation two nights running.

The weather is usually benign. Cold, of course. But seldom rainy, or worse. In my experience. But I was not concerned about rain or snow. Shadow weather worried me.

The sixteen shadowgates are equally spaced around the perimeter of the plain. From each a road of stone of a different color from the plain runs inward to the nameless fortress like a spoke in a wagon wheel. I had seen only two of the roads. One was darker than the surrounding plain, the other slightly lighter. At six-mile intervals along the spokes there were large circles of appropriately shaded material. Those got used as campgrounds though that might not have been their original function. The plain has changed with the ages. Man cannot leave anything alone. The roads were once just mystical routes between worlds. Now they are the only safety out there when the sun sets. When darkness falls the killer shadows leave their hiding places. As we gagged down our rough supper the little light glowing from charcoal fires revealed dozens of black stains oozing over the invisible dome protecting the circle.

"The Slugs of Doom," Murgen said through a mouthful of bread, waving at a nearby shadow. "Much better than the Host of the Unforgiven Dead."

"The man's suddenly developing a sense of humor," Cletus said. "This worries me."

His brother Loftus said, "Be afraid, people. Very afraid. The End Days are upon us."

"You saying it's bad jokes going to bring on the Year of the Skulls?"

I observed, "If that was the case we'd've been dead twenty years ago and the only thing you'd see up there is Kina's ugly face."

"Speaking of ugly." Lady pointed.

We had staked our few square feet of turf at the edge of the circle, where the road to the heart of the plain departed it. I had placed the key given to me by Tobo in the socket in the stone where circle and road came together. Every circle had the sockets. The key sealed the road off. It would keep shadows who got past the protective barriers anywhere else from being able to get us.

"The Nef," Murgen said.

The three creatures at the barrier were plain for everyone to see. They were bipedal but their heads were dissimilar masses of ugliness other Annalists have said they hoped were masks. I could see why—though, seeing them, I got a powerful sense of déjà vu. Maybe I ran into them in a dream. I must have had a few while I was buried. I said, "You know these guys, Murgen. See if you can talk to them."

"Yeah. And after I do that I'll fly off to the sun." No one had yet managed to communicate with the Nef, though it was obvious the creatures desperately wanted to talk. We were so alien to each other that communication was impossible.

"We must be getting a better grasp. We're seeing them when we're awake. We are awake, aren't we?" Historically, the Nef appeared only in dreams. Only in the past year did guards at the shadowgate report catching glimpses the way troops elsewhere made sightings of Tobo's pets.

Murgen ambled over warily. I observed. But I also started keeping an eye on my ravens. Until nightfall they had been almost somnolent, entirely indifferent to the world. The appearance of shadows on the barrier turned them restless, even bellicose. They hissed and coughed and produced a whole range of uncorvine noises. Some form of communication was going on because the shadows responded—though, clearly, not the way the ravens wanted.

The Unknown Shadows of Hsien did share a common ancestry with the Host of the Unforgiven Dead.

Murgen marveled, "I think I'm actually getting what they're trying to tell me."

"What's that?" My wife, I noticed, was watching the Nef intently. Could they be making sense to her, too? But she had no previous experience with the dreamwalkers. Unless while she was a sort of dreamwalker herself, while we were buried.

No, it had to be those three. They had studied us long enough to figure out how to get through. Maybe.

Murgen said, "They want us not to keep heading toward the center of the plain. They're saying we should take the other road."

"Based on what's in the Annals, I'd say they've been trying to get us to do something besides what we want from the first time anybody dreamed them. They're just never able to make themselves clear."

"That would've been me," Murgen said. "And you're right. What I've never figured out, though, is whether they're trying to save us trouble or are pushing their own agenda. It seems to work out both ways."

The tiniest hiss escaped my black raven. A warning. I turned. Uncle Doj had appeared behind Murgen, two steps back, fully armed, staring at the Nef. After watching them for a minute he drifted around the circle to the right, not quite a quarter of the way. Then he shuffled back and forth, squatted, rose up on his toes.

Then Lady went over there. She checked the view from multiple angles herself. "There is a ghost of a road, Croaker." She came back, dug out the key Tobo had given her. I walked back with her. A socket for the key had appeared in the stone surface when no one was watching. It was not there earlier. I had done a one-hundred percent walkaround of the perimeter before we settled down.

Doj said, "The boy told me not to let you waste time trying to make time. Perhaps this is why."

"Murgen. You know about shortcuts and side roads on the plain?"

"They're supposed to exist. Sleepy saw them."

Vaguely, now, I recalled something from my own first passage across the plain.

Lady wanted to plug in her key. I held her back. I said, "All right. If you feel comfortable. Doj? What do you think? Is it safe?" He was as near a real wizard as we had here.

"It doesn't feel wrong."

Not exactly a ringing endorsement. But good enough.

Lady lowered the key into place. In moments the ghost road became more substantial, began to give the impression of a golden glow that was not quite there when you tried to see it. My shoulder ornaments were not pleased. They hissed and spat and retreated to the far side of the circle, where they got into a squabble with something large and dark oozing across the surface of our protection.

Murgen said, "I think they want to enter the circle, Captain. I think they want to cut across."

"Yeah?" The auxiliary road was now more plainly seen than the main way. I mused, "We could hike straight across to the first circle right behind the Khatovar shadowgate." I went and started getting my gear together.

Doj told me, "Not before morning. Tobo told you that we have to stay here overnight."

I glanced around. Obviously, the only way I would get anybody moving again tonight would be by making myself extremely unpopular.

Khatovar had been there for ages. It would be there after the sun came up. My interest in Lisa Daele Bowalk went back farther than my interest in that place, to a city called Juniper, before she made the acquaintance of a Taken known as Shapeshifter. Justice delayed a few hours more would not set the universe wobbling.

I sighed, dropped my stuff. I shrugged. "After breakfast, then."

"Let them go through," Lady said.

"The Nef? You kidding?"

"Doj and I can handle them."

Interesting, her confidence. But it was misplaced. She knew nothing about the Nef. Unless she had met them in her dreams.

I moved people away from potential trouble, creating a clear path. "Everyone ready? Pull the key, then, Murgen." It would be intriguing to see if the plain would let him.

Doj swung Ash Wand around in front of him, exposed eight inches of blade.

The key came out of its seat. Murgen jumped back. The Nef leapt into the circle. And streaked straight across, to the side road. They hit it and never looked back.

"That's definitely weird," Willow Swan said. The dreamwalkers were in a hurry but nobody dwindles that fast. Nor, normally, do they grow transparent as they go. "Slid right back into dreamland."

I wondered, "You suppose I would've slid into dreamland if I'd tried that road?" The road itself began to fade.

Nobody disagreed. Doj mused, "Tobo did say to stay put."

Middle of the night. Something wakened me. Felt like a tiny earthquake. The stars above were dancing. After another jiggle they settled down. And were no longer the stars that had been up there when I laid down. This was a different sky altogether.

"That way!" Doj insisted. It was morning, we were up and Doj insisted on heading back the way we had come.

"The fortress is that way."

"We don't want to go to the fortress," Lady reminded me. "We want to go to Khatovar."

"Which isn't back that way . . . is it?" Tobo had not caught up. I was not thrilled about that.

Willow Swan suggested, "You can go look, Croaker. It wouldn't take that long."

I was tired of arguing, particularly in front of a crowd. I did not want my right to lead to become more questionable than it was already. We all possessed guilty hearts. Me more than any because I bought the Company mystique more than any. "I'll take Swan's advice." I pointed here, there, choosing companions. "You guys get to go with me. Mount up. Let's go."

So we were off to the mule races.

"I don't believe it." I did not. Could not. My eyes had to be liars.

Lying at the rim of the glittering plain I stared down at another landscape with topography resembling that at Kiaulune and at the Abode of Ravens. But here there was no bustling, recovering Kiaulune. There was no fallen castle Overlook, formerly equipped with towers from which Longshadow could look down onto the glittering plain and see what was coming to get him. Nor was there a whitewashed army town with neat ranks of fields on the slopes below it. This country was feral. This country was much more damp than the other two. Wild brush and scraggly trees advanced to within yards of the crippled shadowgate. The works around that were the only recognizable human handiwork visible, and they were in ruins.

"Stay low," Doj advised when I started to rise, which would silhouette me above the skyline. I knew better than that. People who do know better generally get skragged that one time they forget or let something slide. Which is why we pound it in and pound it in and pound it in. "That jungle doesn't mean that there aren't eyes watching."

"You're right. I almost did a stupid. Anybody want to guess how old that scrub down there is? I'd say between fifteen and twenty with a bet that it's a lot closer to twenty."

Murgen wondered, "What difference does it make?"

"The forvalaka broke through this shadowgate about nineteen years ago. She got away. Soulcatcher was too busy burying our asses to chase her, shadows did get after her. . . ."

"Oh. Yeah. She didn't go out alone when she went."

"That's my guess. Shadows got out behind her and wiped out everything we can see from here."

Murgen grunted. Lady nodded, as did Doj. They saw it the same.

Khatovar. My destination for an age. My obsession. Destroyed because we had not had the good sense to cut a young woman's throat in a place now long ago and far away.

The quality of mercy has left me a great, sour role in the theater of my own despair.

Though it is true that it had not seemed important at the time, and we were real busy trying to get out of there with our asses still attached.

21

Taglios:
The Great General

Mogaba leaned back, smiling. "I can't help wishing Narayan Singh continued luck." Relaxed, content, for the first time in years, he found life good. The Protector was in the provinces indulging her passion for religious persecution. Therefore, she was not around the Palace making life miserable for those who actually hauled on the reins, riding the tiger whilst trying to keep the mundane work of government simmering.

His mention of the living saint made Aridatha Singh flinch. It was subtle but the reaction was there. And it was unique. Other Singhs did not react to the name, other than with an obligatory curse, perhaps. This demanded further examination.

Mogaba asked, "Any trouble out there?"

Aridatha said, "It's quiet. You have the Protector out of town, making no ridiculous demands, things settle down. People get too busy making a living to act up."

Ghopal was less upbeat. The Greys were out in the streets and alleys every day. "Graffiti keeps turning up more and more. 'Water Sleeps' most often."

"And?" Murgen asked. His voice was soft but intense, his eyes narrow.

"The other traditional taunts are all there. 'All Their Days Are Numbered.' 'Rajadharma.' "

"And?" Mogaba seemed to have shifted characters the way Soulcatcher did. Perhaps he was aping her style.

"That one, too. 'My Brother Unforgiven.' "

That harsh indictment again. That accusation which always disturbed the incomplete slumber of the part of him guilty about betraying the Black Company to advance his own ambitions. No good had come of it. His life had become enslaved by it. His punishment was to move from one villain to another, always serving wickedness, like a loose woman passing from man to man down a long decline.

Aridatha Singh, eager to move away from talk about Narayan Singh and the Deceivers, interjected, "One of my officers reported a new one yesterday. 'Thi Kim is coming.' "

"Thi Kim? What is that? Or who?"

Ghopal observed, "It sounds Nyueng Bao."

"We don't see much of those people these days."

"Since somebody snatched the Radisha right out of the Palace . . ." Ghopal stopped. Mogaba had begun to darken again, though that failure belonged to the Greys, not to the army. He had been in the territories at the time.

"So. All the old slogans. But the Company all fled through the shadowgate. And perished on the other side because they never came back."

Ghopal knew little about the world outside his own narrow, filthy streets. "Maybe some of them did survive and we just don't know about it."

"No. They didn't. We would've heard. The Protector's had people down there harvesting shadows since they left." People who had been lured into her service by cruelly false promises to teach them her ways and make them captains in her great, unrevealed enterprise.

None of those collaborators survived long. Shadows were clever and persistent. Quite a few found ways to escape from novices long enough to destroy their tormenters and be destroyed themselves.

Soulcatcher made sure conditions for disaster remained ripe.

Mogaba closed his eyes, leaned back again, steepled his dark fingers. "I've enjoyed not having the Protector around." Getting those words out casually was difficult. His throat was tight. His chest felt like a huge weight was pressing in on it. He was afraid. Soulcatcher terrified him. And for that he hated her. And for that he loathed himself. He was Mogaba, the Great General, the purest, smartest, strongest of the Nar warriors produced by Gea-Xle. For him fear was supposed to be a tool by which he managed the weak. He was not supposed to know it personally.

Silently, within, Mogaba repeated his warrior's mantras, knowing habits ingrained since birth would hold the fear at bay.

Ghopal Singh was a functionary. Very good at managing the Greys but not a natural conspirator. That was one attribute that had recommended him to the Protector. He did not apprehend the message lurking on the edges of the Great General's statement. Aridatha Singh, in some ways, was as naive as he was handsome. But he did understand that Mogaba was sneaking up on something that could be a great watershed in all their lives.

Mogaba had championed Aridatha's elevation because of his naivete concerning the complex motives of others and because of his enthusiastic idealism. Rajadharma was a lever that Mogaba was sure would move Aridatha Singh.

Aridatha peered around nervously. He had heard the old saying that in the Palace the very walls have ears.

Mogaba leaned forward, lit a cheap tallow candle from a lamp and took the fire to a stoneware bowl filled with a dark liquid. Ghopal held his tongue even though the animal product offended him religiously.

The bowl's contents proved to be flammable, though they produced more unpleasant black smoke than they did flame or light. The smoke spread out across the ceiling, then crept down the walls and flowed out the doors. Its progress was marked by squeaks and chitterings and an occasional complaint from an unseen crow.

Mogaba said, "We may have to get down on the floor for a few minutes, till the smoke thins out."

Aridatha whispered, "Are you really proposing what I think you're proposing?"

Mogaba murmured, "You may not have the same reasons I do but I think we'd all be better off if the Protector no longer held her position. Particularly the Taglian people. What do you think?"

Mogaba had expected Aridatha to agree easily. The soldier believed in his obligation to the people he served. And he did nod.

Ghopal Singh was his main worry. Ghopal had no obvious reason to want change. The Greys were all members of the Shadar religion, traditionally with little influence in government. Their alliance with the Protector had given them power out of proportion to their numbers. They would be reluctant to lose that power.

Ghopal glanced around nervously, completely failing to note Mogaba's intense examination. He blurted, though in a whisper, "She has to go. The Greys have believed that for a long time. The Year of the Skulls couldn't be much more terrible than what we've suffered from her. But we don't know how to get rid of her. She's too powerful. And too smart."

Mogaba relaxed. So the Greys were *not* enamored of their benefactor. Interesting. Excellent.

"But we'll never get rid of her. She always knows what everyone around her is thinking. And we'll never be able not to think about it because we'll be so scared. She'll sniff it out in about ten seconds. Really, we're walking dead men now, just for having considered it."

"Then get your family out of town now," Mogaba told him. It was Soulcatcher's habit to exterminate her enemies root and branch. "I've been giving this a lot of thought. I think that the only way it could be managed would be to have everything in place and strike before she has a chance to look around and pick up clues. We might engineer it so that she arrives exhausted. That might give us the edge we need."

Aridatha mused, "Whatever it is, it will have to be sudden and massive and a complete surprise."

"She'll begin to suspect," Ghopal said. "There are too many people loyal to her, because without her they'll be dead themselves. They'll warn her."

"Not if we don't get carried away. If just us three know what's happening. We're in charge. We can give any orders we want. People won't question us. There's trouble on the streets and it's getting worse. People will expect us to do something about it. Plenty of others hate the Protector. They'll feel free to act up while she's away. That gives us an excuse to do almost anything we want. If we mainly use people whose loyalty to the Protector is absolute, letting them do most of the work and carry the messages, there's no reason she should suspect anything until it's too late."

Ghopal looked at him like he was whistling in the dark. Maybe he was. Mogaba said, "I've opened my mouth here. I've committed myself. And I have nowhere to run." They were natives. They could vanish into the territories. There was nowhere he could hide. And a return to Gea-Xle had been out of the question for twenty-five years. The Nar back home knew all about what he had done.

Aridatha mused, "Then every day in every way we should do our jobs to the utmost on the Protector's behalf—until we create a rattrap we can close like this." He clapped his hands.

"We'll only get one chance," Mogaba said. "Five seconds after we fail we'll all be praying for death." He waited a moment during which he checked the smoke. Its usefulness was almost exhausted. "Are you in?"

Both Singhs nodded but neither showed an unbound eagerness. The truth was, it was a poor bet that any of them would survive this adventure.

Mogaba sat in his quarters staring out at a full moon. He wondered if it had been too easy. Were the Singhs genuinely interested in ridding Taglios of the Protector? Or had they just played along, sensing that he was the more deadly threat at the moment?

If they were not committed he would learn the truth only when Soulcatcher sank her teeth into his throat.

He was going to be an intimate acquaintance of fear for a long time to come.

22

Khatovar:
Invasion

Swan volunteered to slither down to the shadowgate with me. I demurred. "I think I'll take my sweetheart. We don't get many chances to get away together." And she would have a steadier hand than I would when it came to working on the shadowgate. Which, even from the head of the slope, could be seen to need restoration.

After examining the shadowgate from a closer vantage, I told my beloved, "Bowalk really tore it up getting through."

"She had shadows gnawing on her. According to what Sleepy says Shivetya showed her. Tell me you'd be gentle and not slam the door if you had those things after you."

"I don't even want to think about it. Are we safe? Is anything out there watching?"

"I don't know."

"What?"

"I have a little power here on the plain. A dim one-hundredth of what used to be. But outside the shadowgates I might as well be deaf, dumb and blind. All I can do is pretend."

"So Kina is alive, then?"

"Possibly. If I'm not just tapping Shivetya or some residual, ambient power. The plain is a place of many strange energies. They leak in from the different worlds."

"But you believe you're bleeding Kina again. Don't you?"

"If I am, she's not just sleeping, she's in a coma."

"There!"

"There what?"

"I thought I saw something move."

"That was just the breeze stirring the branches."

"You think so? I'm not inclined to take chances."

The sarky witch said, "You stand guard. I'll work on the gate."

If she did I could not tell. She was less active than I would have been.

We were through. Into Khatovar. I did not feel like I had found my way into paradise. I did not feel like I had come home. I felt the letdown I had expected almost from the moment I had become aware that my lust to find Khatovar had been imposed upon me from without. Khadi's Gate was a wasteland.

Clete and Loftus started laying out a camp close enough to the gate that we could make a quick getaway if that became necessary. I was still at the gate itself, surveying this world where the Black Company had been born.

Definitely the disappointment I had anticipated. Maybe even worse.

Something stirred the hair on the back of my neck. I turned. I saw nothing but had a distinct feeling that something had just come through the shadowgate.

I caught movement in the edge of my vision. Something dark. A shape both large and ugly.

One of the Black Hounds.

The back of my neck went cool again. Then again.

Maybe Tobo was coming after all.

The darker of my two ravens settled onto a nearby boulder. After a shower of hisses directed nowhere in particular, it cocked a big yellow eye my way and said, "There are no occupied human dwellings within fifty miles. The ruins of a city lie under the trees below the rocky prominence to the northeast. There are signs that humans visit it occasionally."

I gaped. That damned bird was better-spoken than most of my companions. But before I could strike up a conversation, it took to the air again.

So there were people in this world. But the closest were at least three days away.

The promontory the bird mentioned was the place where the fortress Overlook had stood in our own world. The ruins likely occupied the same site as Kiaulune.

Another chill on the neck. The Unknown Shadows continued to come through.

I went down to camp. The engineer brothers were old but efficient. It was livable right now—as long as we got no rain.

The rain would be along before long. It was clear it rained often here.

Fires were burning. Somebody had killed a wild pig. It smelled heavenly, roasting. Shelters were going up. Sentries were out. Uncle Doj had appointed himself sergeant of the guard and was making a circuit of the four guardposts.

I waited till Murgen found something to occupy him, beckoned Swan and Lady. "Let's think about what we do now." I looked my wife in the eye. She understood what I wanted to know. She shook her head.

There was no Khatovaran source of magical power she could parasitize.

I grumped, "I didn't expect towers of pearl and ruby beside streets of gold, but this is ridiculous." I checked Doj and Murgen. They showed no interest in us yet.

"Sour grapes." Swan sneered, heading straight for the critical point. "That's a whole world out there. Damned near empty, it looks like. How do you expect to find one insane killer monster?"

"I got to thinking about that while I was standing up there looking at all this. Amongst other things. And I think I've had an evil epiphany."

Lady contributed to the Annals and tried to keep up with

her successors. She shook her head, said, "There isn't much in what she wrote."

Swan glanced around. Nobody was close. In a soft voice he said, "She hasn't been writing the histories since you came back, has she?"

I asked, "What's that mean?"

"Over the years Tobo and Suvrin and some of their cronies have visited most of the shadowgates. They visited the Khatovar gate several times."

"How do you know?"

"I sneak around. I listen when I'm not supposed to hear. I know Suvrin and Tobo came out here while you were wounded. Just the two of them. And later, while we were in Khang Phi, Suvrin went out again. Alone."

"Then I'm right. We've been jobbed. How come you didn't mention this before?"

"It had to do with Khatovar. I figured you were behind whatever was going on."

Lady made a growling, chuckling sound that told me she had a handle on the truth. "That devious little witch. You really think so?"

Swan asked, "What am I missing?"

I told him, "I think we're out here raiding Khatovar not because I'm so damned clever but because Sleepy wants us old farts out from under foot when she breaks out into the homeworld. I'll bet the whole damned force is moving right now. And Sleepy won't have a single one of us asking questions or giving advice or trying to do things our own way."

Swan took a while to think about it. Then he took a while to look around at the gang who had elected to defy the command authority to pursue revenge on One-Eye's killer. He said, "Either she is *really* an astute little bitch or we've been around so many sneaky people so long that we see machinations everywhere we look."

"Tobo knew," I said. Tobo had to be part of it. He let his

father and Uncle Doj come out here. . . . "You know, I'm so paranoid I'm going to put a guard on the gate from the other side. And I'll fill them up with lies about how a demon in the guise of one of our people might try to sabotage the gate so we can't get back out of Khatovar."

Neither Lady nor Swan argued. Swan did remark. "You *are* paranoid. You think Sahra would let Sleepy get away with leaving Thai Dei, Murgen and Doj trapped out here?"

"I think it's a mad universe. I think almost anything somebody can imagine happening can happen. Even the cruelest, blackest sin."

Lady asked, "And what do you intend to do about it?"

"I'm going to kill the forvalaka."

Swan said, "Murgen's noticed that something's going on. He's headed this way."

"I'm going to play the game. Tobo sent a bunch of his pets through after us. Let's make sure they can't get back out unless we let them go. We'll use them to find Bowalk. Then we'll kill her."

23

Glittering Stone:
Fortress with No Name

Sleepy reached the fortress at the heart of the plain by the expedient of refusing to be steered elsewhere. Shivetya's helpful shortcuts were not going to divert her from examining the root of her scheme for conquest.

There was one temporal power greater than the greatest sorcery. Greed. And she owned the wellspring of a flood of what the greedy held most dear: gold. Not to mention silver and gems and pearls.

For thousands of years fugitives from many worlds had

hidden their treasures in the caverns beneath Shivetya's throne. Who knew why? Possibly Shivetya. But Shivetya would not tell tales—unless they advanced his cause. Shivetya had the mind and soul of an immortal spider. Shivetya had no remorse, no compassion, knew only his task and his will to end it. He was the Company's ally but he was not the Company's friend. He would destroy the Company instantly if that suited an altered purpose and he was in a position to do so.

Sleepy meant to cover her back.

She approached Baladitya. "Where's Blade?"

Baladitya had begun gushing discoveries he had made since being handed his mission. Sleepy felt a twinge of guilt. She remembered Baladitya's kind of excitement, long ago and far away. But being responsible for thousands of people, pursuing a timetable with very little slippage built in, left no opportunity for simple pleasures. That made her cranky and curt, sometimes.

"He's down below. He doesn't come up much anymore."

Irked, Sleepy looked around for someone young enough to gallop a mile down into the earth. She spied Tobo and Sahra arguing. Not exactly unusual. But not so frequently lately. They had been butting heads since Tobo entered puberty.

One of Tobo's djinn could get down there faster than the youngest pair of legs. "Tobo!" Sleepy beckoned.

Exasperation flashed across the boy's face. Everyone wanted something from him.

He did respond. He showed no defiance. He never did. His calm half-caste face settled into perfect nonexpression. Nor did his stance in any way betray what he might be thinking. Sleepy seldom saw anyone so inscrutable. And yet he was so young.

He just stood waiting for her to tell him what she wanted.

"Blade is down below somewhere. Send one of your messengers to tell him I want him up here."

"Can't do it."

"Why not?"

"I don't have any here. I've explained before. The Unknown Shadows hate the plain. It's very difficult to get them to come up here. Most of those who do come refuse to have anything to do with people. I don't want them to have anything to do with people. It puts them in a bad temper every time. You have a whole regiment cluttering up the place. There must be a man somewhere who doesn't have something else to do."

Sarcastic infidel. There were twelve hundred men cooling their heels around the fortress, waiting to lead the treasure train, doing nothing useful in the interim. "I was looking for something a little faster." Once the Company was on the barren plain, even with Shivetya working wonders, there was little time to waste.

There had been no good news from Suvrin, either. Tobo should have gone with him. Or Doj or Lady, at the very least. Someone better equipped to deal with the Unknown Shadows. But at the very least there should have been word that a bridgehead had been established.

Baladitya said, "Then you'd better go down there yourself. Because he isn't going to respond to any lesser authority."

"What? Why?"

"Because he hears voices calling him. He's trying to figure out what to answer them."

"Darn!" Sleepy broke out in what, for her, was a blistering blue streak. "That wrangle-franging mudsucker! I'm going to . . ."

Tobo and Baladitya grinned. Sleepy shut up. She remembered times when her Company brothers would get her going to see just how creative she would be in avoiding use of common profanity. She muttered, "I should've written you people the way you really are. Not you, Baladitya. You're actually a human being." She glared at Tobo. "You I'm beginning to wonder about."

"For a nonbeliever," Baladitya said, of himself.

"Yes. Well. There're more of you lost souls than there are those of us who know the Truth. I must be God's Beacon in the Land of Our Sorrows."

Baladitya frowned, then caught on. Sleepy was actually poking fun at her religion's attitude toward those outside it, all the unbelievers who made up the population of the Land of Our Sorrows. Which, in an earlier age, when the Vehdna were more numerous and more enthusiastic about rescuing the infidel from damnation, had been called the Realm of War.

Only Believers lived inside the Realm of Peace.

Sleepy snapped, "Tobo, stop trying to sneak away. You're going down there with me. Just in case he really is hearing voices."

"That sounds to me like a real good reason for everybody else to stay away."

"Tobo."

"Right behind you, Captain. Ain't nobody gonna sneak up on your back."

Sleepy growled. She never got used to the informality and irreverence, though it had been a firm fixture of Company culture since long before her advent.

The soldiers mocked everything and bitched about the rest. Yet the work got done.

Sleepy conscripted a half dozen more companions while hurrying to the stairway down. All from Hsien. She marveled at the results of her relentless training regimen. Many who had joined the Company had been the dregs of the Land of Unknown Shadows, criminals and fugitives, bandits and deserters from the forces of the warlords, and fools who thought a turn with the Soldiers of Darkness would be a great adventure. Sleek, strong and confident, they put on a show now, after months of intense preparation. The clash of steel, probably closer than they anticipated, would be their final tempering.

Sleepy's descent led her past dozens of men still carrying treasure toward the surface. From behind her Tobo asked, "You sure you aren't overdoing the tomb robbing? We've already got enough to make the whole mob rich." A fact not lost on some recruits of less than unstained provenance. But temptation was easy to resist when you knew only your Captain could get you off the plain alive and that the Unknown Shadows would hound you pitilessly if you tried anything after you were off.

"We can't beat the Protector with eight thousand men, Tobo. We need secret weapons and force multipliers. Gold fills both roles."

Sometimes Tobo was troubled by his Captain. At some point, during her copious free time, she had gotten too close to a library centered around military theory. At times she tended to regurgitate notions like "strategic center of gravity" and "force multipliers" just when that would leave her listeners uncomfortable and concerned.

Tobo was also concerned because the old folks, the veterans, Croaker and Lady and the others, approved. That meant that *he* was not getting it.

"We'll take time out here," Sleepy said when they reached the level of the ice caverns where the Captured had been held. "You men," she said to those she had had follow, "I want four of you to take a couple of sleepers up top. Longshadow and the Howler. Howler is going to travel with us. With Tobo. A work party will take Longshadow to Hsien for trial. You two. Stay with us."

The ice caverns seemed timeless, changeless. Frost soon obscured the smaller signs of any traffic. The dead could not be told from the enchanted except on close examination by someone who was knowledgeable.

Sleepy continued, "You men don't go in there until we call you. You even breathe on those things sometimes, somebody dies." Which, upon close examination, could be seen to have happened before. The corpses included several of the

Captured as well as a handful of the mystery ancients whose presence Shivetya had yet to explain.

There was a great deal the demon would not share.

Sleepy told Tobo, "We want these two to go upstairs without them waking up."

"I have to break stasis. Otherwise they'll die as soon as we touch them."

"I understand that. But I want them kept in a condition where they can't cause trouble. There won't be anybody there to control Longshadow if he wakes up all the way."

"Let me do my job."

Touchy. Sleepy posted herself between the boy wizard and the cavern entrance in case curiosity overcame the good sense of the soldiers. She marveled at how quickly the ice reasserted itself, at how delicately cobweblike were some of the structures around the sleeping old men. Beyond Howler, now, there was little evidence of the trampling the place had taken when the Captured were released. The cavern floor tilted upward back there, turned, and the cave itself got tight enough to force an explorer to crawl. If you went back far enough you reached a place where the most holy relics of the Deceiver cult had been hidden during an ancient persecution. The Company had destroyed them, giving particular attention to the powerful Books of the Dead.

Sleepy was quiet for a long time after she sent the two sleeping sorcerers to the surface. She and Tobo and two young Bone Warriors resumed their descent into the earth. Sleepy had two things on her mind: The first was the identity of the source of the pale blue light leaking through the ice of the cavern of the old men, to illuminate the human hoard, and second, "What is the center of gravity of the Taglian empire?" She was more interested in the latter. The former was just a curiosity. It did not matter. Probably just the light of another world.

"Soulcatcher," Tobo replied. "You don't have to think about that. If you kill the Protector you're left facing a big snake with no head. The Radisha and the Prahbrindrah Drah step up and announce themselves and the whole thing is over with." He made it sound simple.

"Except for hunting down the Great General."

"And Narayan Singh. And the Daughter of Night. But the Protector is the only part we can't manage using the Black Hounds."

Sleepy did not miss the way his voice went hollow when he mentioned the Daughter of Night. He had met the witch when she was the Company's prisoner, before the flight to the Land of Unknown Shadows. Sleepy had not failed to notice the impact the girl had had then.

The Captain missed very little. And forgot nothing. And seldom made an error.

But setting up the old folks to put themselves out of the way, so they would not be peering over her shoulder, proved to be an error of the first order.

The Captain found Blade standing in front of a wall of blackness, rigid, a lantern dangling from his left hand. It was obvious that he had spent a lot of time there. Empty fuel containers littered the steps. The contents of those containers had been meant for Baladitya and the rangers mining the treasure hoards.

The Captain was irked. "Blade! What? . . ."

Blade gestured for silence. He whispered, "Listen."

"For what?"

"Just listen." And when Sleepy had just about exhausted her store of patience, he added, "For that."

She heard it plainly, though remote, weak, echoing. A cry of, "Help."

Tobo heard it, too. He jumped. "Captain . . ."

"Summon your Cat Sith. Or one of the Black Hounds."

"I can't do that." He would not tell her that he had exceeded his instructions by sending most of the Unknown Shadows to help Croaker and Lady.

"Why not?"

"They'd refuse to come down here."

"Compel them."

"I can't. They're partners, not slaves."

Sleepy grumbled to herself about damnation and consorting with demons.

"You can't go any farther than this," Blade said, answering a question that had not been asked. "I've tried a thousand times. There isn't enough willpower in the Company to move another step downward. I can't even throw one of these oil jars."

Sleepy asked, "Are any of them full?"

"Over there."

Sleepy picked up three full pots. She dropped two at Blade's feet, told him, "Step back." The oil from the broken jars could not be intimidated by a supernatural darkness. "Now light it."

"What?"

"Set it on fire."

With considerable reluctance Blade tilted his lantern and let a few drops of burning oil spill.

The stairwell filled with flame.

"Damn!" Tobo squealed. "What did you do that for?"

"Can you see now?" Sleepy had an arm up to shield her face from the heat.

The blackness had not been able to overpower the flames.

Tobo told her, "Just two more steps down there's a floor. With coins scattered around on it."

Sleepy lowered her arm. She stepped past Blade. Tobo followed. Stunned, Blade again tried to push forward. He staggered. There was none of the resistance he expected.

Why not, suddenly?

Blade was sure there would have been no change had he started a fire himself. "Captain, I'd be very careful."

The darkness had been waiting.

"Help!"

The voice was louder and more insistent. And clear enough to be recognized.

Tobo echoed Blade. "Captain, be very careful indeed. This isn't possible. The man has to be dead."

"Help!"

Goblin's plaints sounded increasingly urgent.

24

Khatovar:
The Unholy Land

We had been in the holy land of my imagination for four days. Nothing had been gained. Something had been lost. An old Company hand named Spiff was dead. Likewise, Cho Dai Cho, alias JoJo, the Nyueng Bao who had been One-Eye's indifferent bodyguard for so long.

Shadows had gotten them the first night. Killer shadows that had escaped the glittering plain after the forvalaka's breakout had damaged the Khatovar shadowgate. Shadows that had depopulated this part of Khatovar.

Once we knew they were there we had little trouble luring and destroying them. We had had plenty of experience. But the alarm method was awfully unpleasant.

It could have been worse. The fact of regional devastation had inspired everyone to a higher state of readiness.

During subsequent nights we eliminated a total of nine shadows. I hoped that augured well for the rest of this world. I hoped they were now that uncommon.

The Black Hounds helped destroy the shadows. They hated their undomesticated cousins from the plain. And feared them greatly. Though these shadows seemed much less aggressive than those we had encountered in the past.

They ranged afar, too, and found no living people south of

Khatovar's equivalent of the Dandha Presh. Of the forvalaka they found little sign, either. Its trail, though, they were able to uncover. Apparently it was so plain my ravens suspected that it had been left that way on purpose.

"You really want to cross those mountains again?" Swan asked.

Lady remarked, "He looks exhausted already, doesn't he? And we haven't walked a foot."

I admitted, "This would be a great time to have one of those flying carpets."

"There're a lot of things we could use. Several of the black stallions from Charm would be handy. So would a hundred more fireball throwers. You wouldn't steal Sleepy's horse."

"Well, I couldn't, could I? It's the last one left. She'd notice it was missing."

"But she isn't missing you and me and the rest of these droppings beneath the roost of the rooks of dim wittedness."

"That's a cute image," Swan said. "Here come the lead birds of the flock." Murgen. Thai Dei and Uncle Doj were approaching. Like the rest of the band they wanted to know, "What now?" and I had promised to tell them this afternoon.

Murgen asked, "So what're we going to do, boss?"

"Go get it. We can't stay here. The shadows wiped out almost all the game."

They just kill. They will kill bugs if the passion takes them. Large animals they overlook only when they have the opportunity to suck the life out of something human.

Murgen asked, "You think that's why she didn't hang around here?"

Only part of it. "She does have to eat." A glance around told me the fire in their bellies for revenge no longer burned so hot.

Doj said, "But there is food here. And it's not that hard to find. I've seen wild pigs and a species of miniature deer that I didn't recognize. I've seen rabbits and several kinds of smaller rodents. I'd say there was food enough if she wanted it. I'd also say the shadows haven't been active here for a long time. Otherwise I wouldn't have seen the animals I have. The monster had to be rejoining her allies. And the shadows had to be sent. To spy on us."

I said, "Do go on."

"I've considered several alternate frames for the evidence. Maybe it does add up to nothing more than the surface picture. A raid by an insane monstrosity. But I think that is just too simple. I feel there has to be more. Insanity and revenge as motives don't seem adequate. But if she's working with someone local . . ."

I had been supposing almost from the moment I broke out of my coma. I did not have enough information to support my guesswork, though.

I grunted.

"The monster had to know she would be pursued. The Soldiers of Darkness have that reputation. And they've tried to kill her before, with much weaker provocation."

"And Goblin also tried to help her, as I recall. Which she repaid by turning on him before he could do her any good."

Doj continued, "She had to get through two shadowgates to reach Hsien. Which she knew, somehow, was where One-Eye could be found. Both shadowgates, as far as she knew, were damaged. So even if she was safe on the roads she could expect to be vulnerable at the gates. But she didn't get hurt. And then the distance between the gates would be a long one if she got no help from Shivetya. We have no reason to believe he helped her. On its face it looks like it would've been too long and too dangerous and too hungry a journey if One-Eye's murder was all she hoped to accomplish and could expect no help managing it."

I turned to Lady, then looked back to Doj. He was as smart as I was. "I see. Of course she couldn't have managed without help. With the shadows and, especially, with food. She had no chance to feed while she was in Hsien. The Hounds were after her all the time."

Lady chipped in, "Then she had help from helpers who expected a sizable payback. What might that be?"

"How about the same thing we worked for four years to dig out of the Land of Unknown Shadows?" Murgen said. "The secrets of the shadowgates."

Heads nodded. I asked, "How would they know? And why would they want it? To stop this gate from leaking? Didn't Shivetya say they always repair themselves to that level? Tobo and Suvrin never found any that were open, did they?" I assumed Doj would be familiar with Tobo's adventures.

All eyes were on me. Murgen suggested, "This is Khatovar. Source of the Free Companies."

"More than four hundred years ago. Closer to five, now. They might not even remember."

"Probably not."

"And they must have some knowledge of shadowgates. They got Bowalk through this one, in and out of Hsien, then back through here again. Without destroying anything."

Lady said, "Another thing we can infer is that someone here knows something about controlling shadows."

"We can?"

"Implicit in the fact that Bowalk made it to Hsien and back again. As well as in the fact that we should've had more shadows to deal with here if a horde did break out and devastate the world when Bowalk came through the gate the first time. There's game, Doj says. If those were feral shadows we destroyed they would've killed all the game. Those things were here to watch us."

I growled. "Damn! Murgen. All that time at Khang Phi. You ever hear tell of any Shadowmasters that never were accounted for? We're not going to have to butt heads with Longshadow's long-lost mom, are we?"

"They're accounted for. Any that turn up here would have to be home grown." Which was possible. Two of the three we had destroyed in our world were exactly that. One had been one of the Lady's henchwomen believed dead but gone fugitive instead.

Continued talk led to the notion that we might have been lured to Khatovar specifically so we could be stripped of whatever knowledge we might possess.

Even now Lady remained a tremendous repository of arcane information.

I went off alone with my raven companions. One I told to take the Unknown Shadows out scouting, ranging as far as necessary to find the nearest natives. The other I sent to find Tobo. It carried a detailed and honest report, just as if Sleepy had sent us to Khatovar and expected regular communiqués.

I hoped Tobo might have some useful suggestions. I hoped he knew more about Khatovar than he had pretended.

Neither Lady nor I could sleep. The white raven had not taken long to find people. An army was headed our way, though it was still on the far side of the mountains. The for-valaka was there, accompanying a family of wizards who, according to reports from Tobo, were the uncontested over-lords of modern Khatovar.

Tobo's source was indirect. He had consulted the scholar Baladitya, who took our questions to the demon Shivetya. Shivetya then tacitly acknowledged his ability to monitor events in the worlds connected to the glittering plain.

The rulers of Khatovar were a sprawling, brawling, turbulent clan of wizards known as the Voroshk, which was simply their family name. The founding father's talented blood had bred true. And often. He had been a man of immense appetites. There were several hundred Voroshk today. Their regime was cruel. Its sole purpose was to further enrich and empower the Family. Following the disaster caused by the forvalaka's breakthrough into Khatovar, the Voroshk had learned to manage the shadows. It would be the Voroshk who had sent the shadows we had destroyed.

Kina, or Khadi, was no longer worshipped in the world

bearing the name that meant Khadi's Gate. The Voroshk had exterminated the Children of Kina.

Nevertheless, once each year, sometime during the time when the Deceivers would have celebrated their Festival of Lights, somebody managed to strangle a member of the Family and get away.

Chances were good that the Voroshk knew their history well enough to recall that the Free Companies of Khatovar had gone out as missionaries on behalf of the Mother of Night. They might well dread the Queen of Darkness's return.

My own supernatural allies were under instruction to avoid notice except in instances where Khatovar's shadows could be picked off without risk of our secret strength being revealed.

Her face against my chest, Lady murmured, "These Voroshk sound like bad people, hon. As bad as any you've run into before."

"Including you?"

"Nobody's as bad as me. But you need to worry about this. There's a whole family of them. And they don't squabble amongst themselves. Much. Even when I had the Ten on their shortest rein they were always trying to stab each other in the back."

There was a message there, under her teasing. I held her and told her, "I'll retreat to the plain rather than risk the confrontation. We can always sneak back here some other time." But I would not be happy if I had to let Bowalk get away yet again.

I drifted off wondering about the minds of the Voroshk. Wondering about this mysterious world that had sent our forbrethren out so long ago, on a crusade that had gotten lost. Were the Voroshk unwitting pawns of Kina? Could they be yet another device by which the Dark Mother might try to bring on the Year of the Skulls?

"No," Lady said when I suggested it aloud. "We know
whose role that is."

"Don't want to think about Booboo, hon. Just want to go
to sleep."

25

Glittering Stone:
The Revenant

G oblin denied nothing. "She kept me alive somehow.
She intended to use me. But she never did anything to
me. I spent most of the time sleeping. Dreaming ugly
dreams. Probably her dreams."

The little wizard's voice was barely a whisper. It husked.
He seemed permanently on the verge of tears. The irrepress-
ible spirit that had made him the Goblin of old seemed to
have fled.

His audience did nothing to make him welcome or feel
wanted. He was not welcome or wanted. He had spent four
years sleeping with the Queen of Night, the Mother of
Deceivers.

"She lives in the bleakest place you can imagine. It's all
death and corruption."

"And madness," Sahra added without looking up from the
trousers she was mending.

Tobo asked, "Where's the Lance?"

Goblin had been asked before. The Lance of Passion was
the soul of the Company. As much as the Annals did, it tied
past and present together. It went all the way back to the
Company's departure from Khatovar. It had symbolic power
and real power. It was a shadowgate key. And it was capable
of causing a Goddess terrible pain.

Goblin sighed. "There's nothing but the head left. Inside

her, from when I stabbed her. She made it migrate through her flesh. She's taken it into her womb."

The Captain, obviously uncomfortable with this heathen talk, snapped, "Would any of you infidels care to explain that? Tobo?"

"I don't know anything about religion, Captain. Not the practical stuff, anyway."

"Anybody?"

None of the infidels had a thought.

Sleepy had a few. One was that Kina was not a real Goddess. Kina was just an incredibly powerful monster. All the Gunni Gods and Goddesses were nothing but powerful monsters. There was only one God. . . . She continued staring at Goblin, wondering if he was worth believing, wondering if the best course was just to kill him. The silence stretched. Goblin remained immensely uncomfortable. As he should be, considering the circumstances and his limited ability to explain what had happened to him.

There was no way anyone would ever trust him.

The Captain said, "I have a thought, Tobo."

Silence stretched again as the boy waited on her and she waited for him to ask what her thought was. Grown-up silliness.

Sahra said, "Why don't we have Goblin go help Croaker with Khatovar? He'll be more comfortable with his old friends, anyway."

Sleepy gave her a dirty look. Then Tobo did the same. Sahra smiled, bit the thread she was using, put her needle away. "That's done, then."

Goblin's froglike face had lost the little color that had survived his time underground. It lost all expression. The man within was trying hard to remain unreadable. In trying he gave away the fact that he did not want to join the expedition to Khatovar.

Maybe he just dreaded facing the forvalaka again.

"I think that's a wonderful idea," the Captain said. Coldly.

"Croaker sent a raven whining for help. He has all those unpredictable soldiers and sorcerers headed his way. Goblin. You can still cut it, can't you? Sorcery-wise? You haven't lost the knack?"

The sad little wizard shook his head slowly. "I don't know. I'd have to try. Not that I would be any good against a real talent even on my best day. I never was."

"It's decided. You'll take the Khatovar road. Everyone else. We're done here. We're moving out. Tobo, find the Chu Ming brothers. They're going to go with Goblin."

The news that movement was imminent spread quickly. The remaining troops were glad to hear it. They had stayed here in this uncomfortable, frightening place far too long while the higher-ups fussed about nothing. Rations were growing short, despite all the years of preparation.

26

Khatovar:
Hunkered Down

I returned from consultations with the white raven. "They've reached the downhill side of the pass."

Lady observed, "They're moving fast, then."

"They've begun to wonder if we suspect something. They've begun to wonder why so few of their shadow scouts come back and why the few that do never came close to us. So they left their infantry and heavy cavalry and artillery behind in an effort to get here before we can do a lot to get ready if we do expect trouble. The bird tells me they're also preparing some sort of surprise but it couldn't get close enough to find out what."

Swan grumbled, "I don't understand why they weren't just sitting here waiting for us."

"Probably because there's not much here to eat, it's a long way from where things are happening and they couldn't know when we'd arrive. Or even if we would. They have an empire up north to keep in line. And if they were camped out here, chances are we'd just not bother to come off the plain. Also, I would imagine that they really expected us to follow the forvalaka once we understood what had happened here. So they could trap us north of the Dandha Presh. In familiar territory, closer to home. Which I would've run into if I didn't have the Blacks Hounds and whatnot to go scouting.

"On top of the distance for them, there're a raft of superstitions about this country. Plus there's just been a change in the head of the Voroshk family. Somebody called the Old One died unexpectedly about the time we climbed onto the plain. His replacement seems to be more action-oriented."

"And you got all that by talking to crows?"

"They're smart birds, Swan. Smarter than a lot of people. They make wonderful scouts."

Doj asked, "What is our strategy now?"

"We sit tight. We wait. We let the Black Hounds play. They like to tease horses."

Everybody looked at me with that exasperated expression I recalled from those days when I was the Captain and played my cards close to my chest. I shuddered, forced myself to open up further.

"They've separated a small light cavalry force in order to make more speed. The Unknown Shadows will start tormenting the horses after nightfall. Subtly, of course. We don't want to lose them. The bigger ones are going to work on the forvalaka by letting her see them as One-Eye's ghost. I'm hoping she'll rush on down here ahead of her friends. So we can kill her and get out before they get here." There. I had shared.

I felt lousy. I felt like something was sure to go wrong now that I had talked about it.

Silence. Which stretched. Until Murgen finally asked, "Will it work?"

"How the fuck should I know? Ask me again this time tomorrow."

Lady asked, "What're we going to do about Goblin?"

"Keep an eye on him. Don't let him get near One-Eye's spear." That all seemed self-evident to me.

Silence stretched again. Then Swan said, "Here's a thought. Why don't we leave Goblin here when we pull out?"

I grumped, "I thought he was your friend."

"Goblin was. But we've already decided that this can't be the Goblin we knew. Right?"

"But there's a chance the Goblin we knew might still be inside him waiting to be let back out. Like the rest of us when we were buried under the plain."

"And us guys who weren't aren't so sure about you."

"Just say I've developed a soft streak. We'll treat the guy like Goblin till he does something that makes us want to hang him. Then we'll string him up." I had to posture some. It was expected of me.

Murgen observed, "The Captain is still solving her personnel problems by exiling the questionables to Khatovar."

"And that's funny?" Because he was smiling.

"Of course it is. In the sense that neither you nor I nor Lady would've considered doing anything like that while we were in charge."

"Everybody's a sarcastic social critic," I told Lady. "Don't you let on that you can't kick Goblin's ass all the way to Hsien when he gets here. I'll try to keep him so busy he doesn't have time to get into trouble. But it'll help if he believes he has to walk a narrow line, too."

"He won't have to be convinced of that. He isn't stupid."

"How much longer you going to need us?" Swan asked. He had begun shuffling a deck of cards. Murgen and Thai Dei seemed eager to join him in a pastime that had made a comeback during our sojourn in the Land of Unknown Shadows.

"Go ahead. There's not much to do now but wait. And watch Uncle Doj sneak around with all those snail shells like he can't even conceive of the idea that anybody would be alert enough to notice." That was how the Unknown Shadows had crossed the plain and gotten here. So who on my team was in cahoots with Tobo and the Captain?

I could not wait forever, though. Nor did I have any intention of facing any Voroshk soldiers. My only quarrel with the Voroshk sprang from their presumption that the Company existed only as an as yet untapped resource.

I deplore that attitude wherever I encounter it.

There was a full moon in Khatovar that night. I went strolling in the moonlight. My ravens came and went: They traveled like lightning as long as I did not try to watch them do it.

The Unknown Shadows are every bit as wicked and dangerous as Hsien folklore indicates. It was almost too easy for them to taunt and lure the forvalaka away from the umbrella of protection offered by the Voroshk sorcerers.

27

Shadowlands:
Breakout

The Captain slithered up beside Suvrin, lifted her head just enough to be able to see the shadowgate separating the plain from home. "We're only thirty miles from where you were born, Suvrin." She had tried for years now to think of a better nickname than Suvrin, which meant Junior in Sangel, his native tongue. She had not found anything more exotic that fit.

"Less. I wonder if anybody'll remember me."

Behind them thousands waited anxiously. Hungrily. Way too much time had gotten wasted crossing the plain. Sleepy brushed aside a twinge of guilt.

"How many of them are there?" she asked. A camp lay just below the shadowgate. Built on the remains of old Company camps, it looked to have been there a long time. Its shelters had a makeshift but permanent appearance. They were part of a squalor which characterized all things military under the Protector's rule.

"There are fifty-six people. Including nine women and twenty-four children."

"That isn't exactly enough to stop a breakout attempt."

"We aren't why they're there. They're armed but they aren't real soldiers. They don't pay any attention to the road or the gate. During the day most of them just work their fields." Several feeble examples of primitive agriculture lay scattered along the banks of the creek at the bottom of the hill. "I thought about jumping them but decided I'd better wait till Tobo could look them over. I think they're really here because of the shadows."

"We'll send commandos down after sunset. Roll them up before they know what hit them." The Captain was not pleased with her protégé's indecision.

Suvrin said, "Better have Tobo check them out first. Really. They're always more active after dark."

"Excuse me?"

"It's almost twilight now. Hang on. You'll see what I mean."

"Don't make me wait all night, Suvrin." Sleepy eased back. Once she could rise without being seen from below she did so, strode to her waiting staff. "There's a garrison in our way. Not a large one. Shouldn't be any trouble because they don't appear to be expecting anything. I want to make sure none of them get away once we move. Runmust. Iqbal. Head back up the road. Have everybody fall out. Maintaining plain discipline. Tell them to eat. To get their weapons ready. No fires permitted, though. We don't want to show any smoke or light. We might not go in till after midnight but I want everyone ready to go when I say it's time to go."

Relays of messengers carried word back along the column.

"There. Watch. That's what I mean," Suvrin said, pointing. Tobo and the Captain lay to either side of him. The garrison below had begun an exhaustive examination of the area around the shadowgate, illuminating the area from several directions using a variety of sources of light. "They're obviously looking for leaks right now. It'll get more interesting in a minute."

Soon afterward a three-man team brought up a thin-necked earthenware jar of about a gallon's capacity mounted in a wooden rack which they crowded right up against the sorcerous boundary that prevented the shadows, the Unforgiven Dead, from leaving the plain.

The lighting was bright but still not good enough for even Tobo's sharp young eyes to discern clearly what was going on but, whatever they were up to, those people were being extremely cautious.

"I've got it!" Tobo said after watching intently for about ten minutes. "They're trying to catch shadows. They've got a tiny little hole bored through the barrier there and they're hoping an overeager shadow will pop through it into their jar."

"They work for Soulcatcher," Sleepy said, maybe just to dampen the boy's enthusiasm. She now understood why Suvrin had been so cautious.

"Of course they do. Who else? We need to think this over. If she has a whole bunch of shadows under her control. . . ."

"It's too late to turn back." As though he had suggested anything of the sort. Sleepy rolled onto her back, rubbed her forehead with her left hand. The stars above were the stars of her childhood. She had not seen them for far too long. "I missed our stars."

Suvrin replied, "I did, too. I've spent a lot of time here just enjoying them."

"You haven't sent even one scout through yet?"

"I really haven't had the chance. I didn't want to commit you to anything by taking everything into my own hands. Anyway, I had to fix the gate before I could do anything else and I've gotten maybe an hour a night when I could get down there to work on that."

"It's ready, now, though. Isn't it? I've got twelve thousand men up here. Don't tell me we have to wait some more."

"You can go through any time."

Tobo grunted. "The Nef."

Sleepy rolled back onto her stomach. Sure enough, the dreamwalkers had appeared down by the locals. They remained transparent. They jumped and gestured. The workers beyond the barrier ignored them.

"They can't see them," Tobo said.

The Nef abandoned their effort to communicate with the shadowcatchers and swept upslope to harangue the watchers on the lip of the plain.

"What're they trying to tell us?" Sleepy asked.

Tobo replied, "I don't know. I can actually hear a whisper sometimes but I still can't understand them. If Dad was here. . . . He was almost a dreamwalker. I think he might understand them a little bit."

"It's probably safe to assume that there's something they don't want us to do. That's what it always has been once somebody does figure it out. But doing what we want hasn't ever led to trouble for us. Has it?"

The wait stretched. Suvrin said, "It's always like this." He rolled over. "Why don't we watch for shooting stars?"

Tobo said, "I'm going down there. I want to hear what they're saying."

"Ignoring the fact that they'll see you, when did you learn to speak Sangel?" Sleepy asked.

"I've picked up a few words from Suvrin. We had to do

something during those tedious journeys to the shadow-gates. Although I don't think these guys will be speaking anything but Taglian. They have to be people the Protector trusts. Meaning people whose families are where she can eat them up if she's disappointed with anybody's behavior. They aren't going to see me."

Doj had taught him well. He was all but invisible descending that slope, using no magic at all. The shadow-catchers noticed nothing. But the dreamwalkers did. They became agitated. Then the few shadows in the vicinity, not swarming beside the road with all their kin, hoping some soldier would stupidly break the protective barrier, also began to scoot from hiding place to hiding place erratically. One darted up and through the pinhole into the earthenware jar.

The shadowcatchers congratulated one another. In a moment they had both jar and barrier sealed, the latter with an almost invisible bit of bamboo. Tobo sensed powerful spells in its wood. Soulcatcher did not want the more potent shadows pushing through that valve.

The capture of a single shadow satisfied the shadow-catchers. They packed up for the night.

"That's it?" Sleepy asked.

"That's the first time I've actually seen them catch one," Suvrin replied. "I guess it doesn't happen very often."

Moments after the shadowcatchers left, Tobo stepped through the shadowgate into the world of his birth. Suvrin had made his repairs correctly.

The boy took a deep breath. He listened to the soft noises made by the commandos already coming down from the plain. There had been no alarm as he had passed through the shadowgate and there was none when the commandos began to ease through. Plainly, the Protector did not fear the south. Though she had leapt up from the grave a few times herself, she did not anticipate that kind of refractory behavior on the part of her enemies.

"Water sleeps," Tobo told the night, and began to cast a spell that would send the shadowcatcher crew into a deep sleep. He had learned the spell from One-Eye, who had stolen it from Goblin over a hundred years ago.

Always his thoughts found their way back to Goblin.

Kina was the Mother of Deceivers. Suppose she had done nothing whatsoever to the little wizard? Nobody would believe that. And nobody would ever trust him again. Tons of time and resources would be wasted keeping an eye on him.

Was that it? Was Goblin just a diversion? Was there any way to find out?

He was supposed to be on fire with the creative brilliance of youth. He ought to be able to devise something workable.

The prisoners looked on in wide-eyed amazement as battalion after battalion marched down off the plain. An army this size had not been seen since the Kiaulune wars. Soulcatcher had won the laurels in that round because the Company had been hopelessly outclassed in matters of sorcery.

The Radisha Drah and the Prahbrindrah Drah had prominent places in that parade. Clad in imperial finery, accompanied by dozens of Taglian royal banners, their presence was a declaration Sleepy wanted made early and often.

It was a declaration that was wasted here, of course, because none of these witnesses would be allowed to carry the news out ahead of the advance of the invasion force. But Sleepy thought it would be a good idea for the Prince and Princess to begin practicing to reassume their historic roles.

Suvrin was gone already. As were scores more pickets and scouts and recon soldiers. The Soldiers of Darkness were loose. Poor Suvrin was having to run ahead again, now tasked to close the southern end of the pass through the Dandha Presh. A job for which he needed no special training. It was the one he had held at the time when Sleepy had taken him prisoner, while on her way to release us poor old Captured from our durance beneath the plain.

Once Suvrin was sure the pass could not be used by rumor-mongers from the south side he was supposed to go on through and seize the military works at Charandaprash. Which were likely to have no garrison at all, considering Soulcatcher's attitude toward her armed forces.

Suvrin would know that layout well before he got there. Tobo had brought sack after sack of old snail shells off the plain once the way was open. An unseen flood had begun to spread across the region once known as the Shadowlands. Tobo would know everything his creatures knew. Tobo would have those creatures carry the news to anyone else who needed to know it.

Tension ran high and continued to rise. Those who knew Soulcatcher knew she would hear of the invasion eventually. Her response was sure to be violent and showy, swift and unpredictable and nothing anyone wanted to endure.

28

The Taglian Territories:
The Blind Measures of Despair

Narayan groaned when the girl wakened him. He regained control quickly, however. The Protector was out there somewhere, never closer than she had been these past two days. The Daughter of Night's valiant efforts, using talents she did not understand, had been just enough to prevent their capture. But it was a close thing every day. And the game might not last much longer. He and the girl had nothing left. If the Protector brought in some of the shadows she controlled . . .

"What is it?" he breathed. He fought the pain that was with him always nowadays.

"Something's happened. Something big. I can feel it. It's . . . I don't know. It's like my mother woke up, took a look around, then went back to sleep."

Narayan did not understand. He said so.

"It was her. I know. She touched me." From confusion the girl moved swiftly toward assurance and confidence. "She wanted me to know that she's still there. She wanted me to hang on. She wanted me to know things will be getting better soon."

Narayan, who had known the girl's birth mother well, suspected the child took after her aunt, the Protector, far more. The Protector was changeable. The Daughter of Night's moods could shift with a change in the breeze. He wished she were more stable, like her mother. Although Lady could become obsessively focused. For example, she was determined to even scores with him and the Deceiver cult. She had been Kina's tool but had no love or respect whatsoever for the Goddess.

"Did you hear me, Narayan? She's there! She's not going to lay low much longer."

"I heard. And I really am as excited as you are. But there are wonders and wonders. We still have to get away from the Protector." He indicated the sky to their west. Crows swarmed not half a mile down the long, scrubby slope.

Soulcatcher had her obsessions, too. This chase had gone on forever, successfully for neither party thereto. Did the Protector have no other work to do? Who was managing Taglios and its territories? Deviltry was sure to flourish in her absence.

From the beginning of the chase Narayan had been confident that Soulcatcher would get bored and would turn to something else. She always did.

But not this time. This time she was dogged.

Why?

No telling with the Protector. She might have had a vision of the future. She might be unable to think of a more amusing hobby. She was twisted inside. Her motives might not always make sense even to her.

The crows began to fan out to the north of what must be Soulcatcher's position. They seemed to be interested in a slice of pie arc. They drifted on the breeze, not working hard, slowly moving away. Narayan and the Daughter of Night watched without moving. Crows were sharp of eye. If the two most holy Deceivers could see them, the crows could see the Deceivers in turn—if the girl's erratic talent failed for even a moment.

A single bird glided to the southeast, rather drunkenly, Narayan thought. Soon no black bird could be seen in any direction.

Narayan said, "Let's move on now. While we can. You know, I think that haze down south might be the Dandha Presh. We'll be in the mountains in another week. She won't have a hope of catching us there."

He was whistling in the dark. And they both knew it.

The Daughter of Night led the way. She was far more mobile than Narayan. Frequently she grew impatient with Narayan's inability to keep up. Sometimes she cursed him and hit him. He suspected that she would desert him if she had any other resource. But her horizons never did extend far beyond the boundaries of their cult and she understood that the living saint had far more influence with the Deceivers than did any ill-schooled female messiah whose status as such was accepted only because it bore the living saint's chop of authenticity.

Narayan's lagging actually saved them. The girl was squatting in brush, looking back with ill-concealed irritation. "There's a clearing. It's big. Not much cover. Shall we wait until dark? Or should we work our way around?" It was much too difficult for her to keep them invisible when they were in the open.

Narayan sometimes wondered what she might have

become had she grown up with her birth mother. Lady would have turned her into a dark terror by now, he was certain. Not for the first or even the hundredth time he wished Kina had allowed him to sacrifice Lady the day he had claimed the newly born Daughter of Night. His life since would have been much easier had the woman died then. "Let me look."

Narayan crouched. Pain clawed his bad leg as though someone was slashing him with a dull knife. He peered out at a stony waste almost devoid of life—except for a stunted, twisted stump of a tree smack in the middle. It stood just over five feet tall. There was a familiar feeling to it. He had not seen it before but knew he should recognize it. "Don't move," he told the Daughter of Night. "Don't even breathe fast. There's something not quite right out there."

He froze. The girl froze. She never questioned him in these things. He was right every time.

It came to him eventually. He whispered. "That's the Protector, that stump. Wrapped inside an illusion. She's used the trick before. I heard about it when I was a prisoner of the Black Company. It was one of the devices she used when she was stalking them and they kept telling each other to look out for it. Look carefully at the root of that branch that twists around twice and ends in a cluster of little twigs. See the crow hiding there?"

"Yes."

"Back away carefully. Slowly. What? . . . Freeze!"

The girl froze. She remained unmoving for many minutes, until Narayan began to relax. She murmured, "What was it?" Neither the stump nor the crow had done anything alarming.

"There was something. . . ." But he was no longer sure. It had been there in the corner of his eye for an instant but not there when he looked directly. "Over by that big red boulder."

"Hush!" The girl stared in another direction. "I think . . . There. Something . . . I can't see anything but I can feel it. I think it's watching the tree. . . ."

Grrr!

Both felt rather than heard the growl from behind them.

Such was their self-discipline, after years on the run, that neither so much as flinched. Something large and dark and not quite there trotted past. The living saint's mouth opened wide but no scream came forth. The girl drifted closer to him without making any sudden movement.

What seemed like a series of large black cutouts of an unfamiliar animal flickered across the open ground. It looked nothing like a dog. It had too many limbs. But in its brief moment beside the stump it lifted a hind leg and loosed a river.

And then, of course, it was not there anymore. But Soulcatcher was, in her own form. And she was in a towering rage.

"Something has changed," Narayan gasped through his pain.

"Something more than Mother."

Something more than the Mother of Night.

Something that, from that moment onward, left them feeling as though they were being watched every moment—even when they could see nothing around them anywhere.

29

Khatovar:
The Lords of the Upper Air

My ravens worked hard. Within the same hour I learned that Sleepy had broken out into our homeworld and that the forvalaka had left the Voroshk and was rushing our way. I began issuing orders immediately. Bowalk could not possibly arrive for hours but I wanted to make sure that each of my companions was exactly positioned and that all of my resources could be brought to bear almost instantly.

Willow Swan followed me around reminding me that

most of the fussing I was doing was exactly the sort of half-ass officiousness I resented from Sleepy.

"You want to make your future home in Khatovar, Swan?"

"Hey, don't kill the messenger."

I grunted unhappily, went and collected my sweetheart. "It's time we got dressed up. Get ready for the show."

"Ooh!" she said. "I've always had a weakness for men in black with birds on their shoulders."

Our preparations were complete. Our dozen surviving fire-ball projectors were positioned, I felt, to perfection to bring the forvalaka under saturating fire as she attacked me. If that did not destroy her itself it would drive her to me, directly onto One-Eye's black spear. I looked forward to our confrontation. That was unusual for me. I am not one of those men who enjoys the killing side of this business.

The ravens had the monster just an hour away. People were having a last meal so we could get the fires all put out before it arrived. There was a pig that Doj had killed. It went fast. Not many vegetarians in my crew.

Murgen joined Lady and me where we were playing paper, rock, knife with Willow Swan. "Goblin's here. He just came over the rim of the plain. There's two guys with him. That's a good look for you." He had not yet seen the new Widowmaker armor in action.

"Bless the Captain and her infinite wisdom," I grumbled. "That was quick. Let's keep an eye on the little shit." Like that needed repeating. I asked Lady, "Should I put him to work?"

"Absolutely. Right out front. One-Eye was his best friend, wasn't he?"

"Murgen, when he gets down here, after we talk to him, I want him positioned down there where I put the pair of two-inchers. We don't know if either of those has anything left in them. Then have those guys fall back to cover the approach to the shadowgate. You and Thai Dei stay with Goblin."

Murgen offered me a carefully blank look.

"If you have to, stick him. Or bop him over the head. If he gives you a reason."

"Which might be?"

"I don't know. You're an intelligent adult. Don't you think you can tell if he needs smacking around?"

"Don't you think that that's what those guys with him are there for?"

I had not thought of that. It did seem probable. "Are they men we know well enough to trust completely?"

"I couldn't make out who they were yet when I came over here."

"Then the instruction stands."

I studied Goblin intently. I had not seen him since before I had gone underground. He had aged a lot. "Last I knew of you, you'd deserted."

"I'm sure One-Eye explained all that." The voice was the same but there was an indefinable difference in the man that, probably, had more to do with time and the betrayals of memory than it did with any evil new within him, but I have never gone far wrong by being suspicious.

Goblin's stature approached the extreme low altitude end of normal humanity. And he was wide, despite not having eaten well in recent years. And he had almost no hair at all anymore. Nor did he smile readily. He seemed infinitely tired, as though he labored under a weight of weariness that stretched all the way back into antiquity.

My long nap in the cave of the ancients had not been all that restful, either.

"One-Eye was a notorious liar. The way I heard it—fifteen years after the fact—was that it was all your idea and he just got dragged along."

"The Captain was satisfied." He did not argue and he did not make light. And that was the last clue I needed. There was no humor left in this Goblin. That was the big change.

"Good for her. You've arrived just in time. The forvalaka is only minutes away. We're going to kill it this time. You didn't lose any of your skills while you were trapped, did you?"

Something stirred in the deeps of his eyes. It seemed cold and angry but might have been just his irritation because so many pairs of eyes peered at him so intently, so suddenly.

"Captain?"

That had to be one of the real old hands. Everyone else was out of the habit, though many still called Lady "Lieutenant" because Sleepy never filled that position officially. Sahra did much of the work despite her official status as an outsider.

Why did we set such store by these tiny distinctions?

"What?"

"There's movement out there. Probably the Black Hounds coursing the forvalaka. Which means the monster is getting close."

"Full alert. Murgen, show Goblin his post." I clattered and clanked. The armor was mainly costume but it was real and it was heavy.

"Captain!" From farther away. "Down there!" A man stood out of his concealment, pointing.

I gawked.

"Shit!" Lady exploded. "Why the hell didn't your crows tell us about that?" She dove for cover.

Three flying things were headed toward us from the west, in a V formation. My man had spotted them so far away that, despite their speed, we had time to observe their approach. Eagle-eye there was a guy who deserved a bonus.

The flyers had made the mistake of approaching at an altitude calculated to avoid the notice of the Unknown Shadows. That left them completely vulnerable to detection by the naked eye because it silhouetted them against the clear blue sky on the one day the weather chose to be neither overcast nor rainy.

Lady snapped. "You concentrate on the shape changer, darling. This is a diversion. I'll deal with it." She shouted orders. I boomed a few of my own.

She was wrong, of course. The forvalaka was the diversion for those flying Voroshk—though Bowalk would be convinced that the reverse was true. Once they moved closer the airborne sorcerers appeared to be rippling lumps clinging to long fenceposts. They were wrapped in and trailed acres of something resembling black silk cloth.

They must have had some reason to believe that we would not be able to see them. They made no effort not to be noticed.

When they slowed their approach I suspected immediately they wanted to coordinate timing with the forvalaka—and I was right.

A burst of screams and dark fury erupted a scant hundred yards from our most forward post. Unknown Shadows were all over the forvalaka. Exactly as they were supposed to be, suddenly and briefly, at that point.

The moment Bowalk stopped charging to rip at the spooks they faded away.

For that moment she made a wonderful target.

The fireball projectors opened up.

Unfortunately, most that worked sped their blazing, unpredictable missiles toward the Khatovaran sorcerers. Only two light bamboo pieces remained trained on the monster. And one of those gave up the ghost after projecting just one bilous green ball that flew in erractic skips and jerks but did graze the beast along the flank scars she had gained during our previous encounter. She took a solid hit in the shoulder from the other projector.

She could scream.

I did not look away. Lady kept talking, keeping me informed. She told me the flyers had been surprised completely. That made me suspect that there had been little honesty between Lisa Daele Bowalk and the Voroshk sorcerers.

They should have known. All of them.

The Voroshk were not entirely unprepared for trouble. They had surrounded themselves with protective spells which did shunt the lightest fireballs aside—usually from the path of the leader into those of the trailing two. But those spells could not turn everything and they weakened quickly.

I was bracing to receive the charge of the forvalaka when one of the flyers streaked across in front of me, behind Bowalk, tumbling, all that silk aflame. A scream ended abruptly as the sorcerer impacted somewhere to my right.

My strategy was to channel the forvalaka toward me and One-Eye's spear, hurting it as much as possible as it approached. I had mounted the black spear in the end of a twelve foot bamboo pole to give myself a little added reach. Once Bowalk was pinned, the people with the fireballs could finish her off. Assuming One-Eye's spear had not lost its potency with his death.

And assuming the people with the fireballs were not busy with the distraction overhead. I risked a glance. The lead flyer was circling back. Whatever he had intended to do he had not, because he had been forced to concentrate on his defenses instead. The remaining Voroshk had come to a halt several hundred yards east of us, smoldering, drifting on the breeze, evidently still alive but just barely. Before I shifted my attention back to the forvalaka I noted that that flyer was gaining altitude very slowly.

A swarm of javelins and arrows buzzed around the werepanther. The darts were all poisoned. Just in case a few did penetrate her skin.

Wonder of wonders! A lot of arrows were sticking. A sort of black haze seemed to cover the monster, making the boundary between her and the rest of the universe appear poorly defined.

Lady was yelling. A lot. Fire discipline was critical. We would be able to create no new fireball-spitting bamboo poles until we were safely back in our own world. Half of those we started this fight with were out of action already. The guys had not been in a real fight for years but they did remember what was what. The fireballs stopped going up even before my wife started yelling again. Several men did take the opportunity to put fireballs into the forvalaka, though. Poor Lisa had no friends.

She was not as invulnerable as I had expected. She began to stagger drunkenly well before I had hoped she would respond to the poisons. The endurance and stamina of her kind were legendary and in our experience were exceeded only by the ferocious vitality of the sorcerers who had belonged to the circle that had been known as the Ten Who Were Taken. Of whom Soulcatcher and the Howler were the last. Of whom there would be no survivors much longer.

I was determined. I had a whole list of people who were going to blaze the way to hell for me.

Now the monster was up again, evidently shaking off the effects of missiles and fireballs and chemicals. She was gathering herself for the charge that would get her in amongst us and render her safe from our most dangerous weapons just when she could start using her jaws and claws.

I do not know what the Voroshk tried to do. I know the fireballs flew again, there was a shudder in the ground like somebody had hit it a few yards away with a ten-thousand-pound hammer, then the forvalaka launched herself my way in a sort of weak, half-hearted leap, one hind paw dragging in the dust. Smoke came off her at a dozen points. The stench of burnt flesh preceded her.

I glimpsed the last Voroshk streaking across the sky behind the monster. He was tumbling.

Bowalk batted at my makeshift pike as she flew toward me. Her effort was weak and slow. The head of One-Eye's spear entered and passed through the flesh of her right shoulder, which had been injured badly already. I felt it bounce off bone. She screamed. Her weight ripped my weapon out of my hand even though I had the butt of the bamboo pole set firmly against the ground.

Her momentum spun her around. She managed to slap me with a paw and send me ass over appetite before she landed and became preoccupied with the black spear. My armor withstood her claws. I barely knew up from down for a moment but I did keep my head attached to the end of my neck.

I regained possession of my bamboo pole but not of the spear. The forvalaka was writhing around, screaming and snarling and snapping at the spear while my comrades were careful to stay out of her way. The occasional arrow or javelin continued to dart in, when there was no risk of a miss.

The Voroshk remained out of the struggle. One burned on the slope east of us. One rose higher and higher, now yielding streamers of smoke. The last circled cautiously, either looking for an opening or just observing. Each time he started to dart in, a score of bamboo poles pointed his way, offering to welcome him. I suspect most were dead. But he could find out the truth of that only the hard way.

A huge black sword of a design similar to Doj's Ash Wand came with the Widowmaker costume. I drew it as the forvalaka tried to come at me. I felt almost foolish behind the excitement and fear. It had been decades since I had used a sword anywhere but in practice sessions with Doj. I did not know this one at all. It might be little more than a showpiece. It might snap the first time I struck a blow.

The shapeshifter staggered forward a few steps. Someone hit it a glancing shot with a fireball. Javelins and arrows continued to arrive. It snapped at the wound where One-Eye's spear stood forth, again. The arrows and javelins all fell out eventually but not that black spear. It was working its way slowly deeper.

I stepped in, struck. The tip of my blade bit several inches into the big cat's left shoulder. She barely stumbled. The wound bled for seconds only, then closed, healing before my eyes.

I struck again, near the same site. Then again. Not despairing. Her vitality was no surprise. But her wounds were not healing as fast as once they had. And that spear was worming its way deeper. And she seemed to be losing the will to fight.

Shouts!

The healthy Voroshk was boring in on me, coming fast, his protection turning first the fireballs rising to meet him, then the arrows and bolts. I pranced around and braced myself to flail away when he got close enough. He raised one hand as if to throw something. But before he could, my white crow appeared out of nowhere and hit him from behind. In the head. His chin slammed against his chest.

I doubt he suffered any damage but he did forget me for the moment. He flailed at the raven. The ghost bird had secured a perch on his shoulder and was trying to peck his eyes.

Even up close I could see no face. That was hidden by wraps of the same cloth enshrouding everything else.

I swung away but misjudged the Voroshk's speed. My blade chopped into the post he was riding a foot behind his butt and tore itself from my hands. Then he hit ground. Then, howling, he bounced into the air and streaked away in a lazy curve that tended northward, all the while spinning round and round the axis of his flying post. His robes or cape or whatever billowed all over the sky. Tatters tore loose and fluttered down.

The forvalaka continued to weaken. Cautiously, some men left cover and surrounded the beast. Lady and Doj joined me within striking distance. Each carried one of the debilitating fetishes Tobo had created using the tail and bits of skin Bowalk had left behind when she killed One-Eye. Lady had shown him what to do. The fetishes were particularly effective because Lady and Tobo had had Lisa Daele Bowalk's true name to work with.

I said, "Swan, take a squad to check out the one that's

burning over there. Be careful. Murgen, keep an eye on the other two." The Voroshk who had streaked off rolling was under control again and headed our way at a crawl, gaining altitude, moving toward the Voroshk who remained airborne and still rising slowly. That one had begun drifting with the breeze and showing some evidence of actual flames.

I asked my darling, "Darling, is there any chance you're keeping an eye on Goblin?" Our mysteriously resurrected brother had remained extremely quiet during the exchange of greetings between the Voroshk family and the Black Company. Unless I had missed something while I was preoccupied.

"There are two guaranteed-good bamboo poles aimed at him right now."

"Excellent. You are going to be able to make more of those things once we get back home, aren't you? They're the best weapons we've ever had."

"I'll make some. If there's time. Once my sister knows we're back we're going to get extremely busy."

Egg-yolk light suddenly drenched the world. It faded before I looked up and saw a thousand-armed starfish of a cloud blossoming where the smoldering Voroshk sorcerer had been drifting.

The other Voroshk was headed north again, this time end over end. And someone was falling directly toward us, vast expanses of black cloth fluttering behind, smoke boiling off that. There was no sign of the log the Voroshk had been riding. Its fall seemed terribly slow.

Meantime, undistracted from his task, Willow Swan was bellowing across the slope. He wanted a stretcher.

Lady observed, "That one is still alive."

"We have a hostage. Somebody poke that thing with a pike. It's probably playing possum." The forvalaka had stopped struggling. It lay on its back, tilted slightly to one side, both hands grasping the shaft of One-Eye's spear.

"Hands," Murgen said as Thai Dei prodded the monster with one of the longer fireball projectors.

"Hands," I said, too. The change was coming over her. The change she had longed for ever since we had murdered her lover-master Shapeshifter, way back during our first assault on Dejagore.

Lady said, "She's dying." She sounded both puzzled and a little disappointed.

30

Khatovar:
Then Start the Fire

A rising shriek rushed us from above. The falling, flailing Voroshk smashed through the leaf roof of a shelter. The shrieking stopped. Bits of roof flew upward. I said, "Murgen, go check that out."

When I looked back to the forvalaka, I discovered that Goblin had joined us. He pushed through the crowd and stood over the monster, staring down. She was about halfway changed, her arms and legs having become a badly scarred, naked woman. She was aware enough to recognize Goblin.

The frog-faced little man said, "We tried to help you and you wouldn't let us. We could've saved you but you turned on us. So now you pay. You mess with the Company, you pay." He started to reach for One-Eye's spear.

Men jumped every which way. Half a dozen bamboo poles swung toward Goblin. Crossbows came off shoulders.

The little wizard's mouth opened and closed several times. Then his hand slowly withdrew.

I guess news of One-Eye's dying words had gotten around.

Goblin squeaked, "Maybe you shouldn't have rescued me."

Lady told him, "We didn't," but did not expand upon her remark. She drew me away. "He has something to do with Bowalk dying so easily."

I glanced over there. "She isn't dead yet."

"She should have been much tougher."

"Even considering the fetishes and One-Eye's spear?"

She thought about that. "Maybe. When she's done dying you'd better make sure that thing is hard to reach. I don't like the look in Goblin's eye when he stares at it."

That look was there now, though the little wizard showed no inclination to do anything certain to inspire a swift and violent response.

Swan and his gang were approaching, four of the men at the corners of a makeshift litter. Trotting ahead, Swan puffed, "Wait'll you get a look at this, Croaker. You ain't going to believe it."

At the same moment Murgen called for another stretcher. So the other Voroshk had survived, too.

Swan was on the mark. The girl on the stretcher was impossible to believe. Maybe sixteen, blonde, as gorgeous as every boy's fantasy. I asked my wife, "Darling, is this for real?" And to Swan, "Good job, Willow." He had bound and gagged the girl so as to disarm most of a sorcerer's simpler tricks.

Lady said, "You men get back." There was not much left of what the girl had been wearing. And more than a few of the guys were the sort who would count her fair game for having tried to attack us. Some were the sort who would dish out the same treatment to a male captive. They might be my brethren but that did not make them less cruel men.

Lady told Swan, "Take Doj back over there and collect anything you can find that belonged to her. Her clothing and that thing she was riding in particular." And to me she said, "Yes, dear, she's the real thing. Except for just a touch of makeup. I hate her already. Goblin! You come over here and stand where I can see you."

I stared down at the Voroshk girl, not focusing on the lushness and freshness of her but on the blondness and whiteness. I have read all the Annals, all the way back to the first volume—albeit, admittedly, a several-generations-removed-from-original copy—that had been begun before our forebrethren ever left Khatovar. Those men had not been tall and white and blond. Could the Voroshk be another out-world scourge like the Shadowmasters of my own world and Hsien?

At that moment Lady removed her helmet, the better to menace me for staring. And I realized she was quite white herself, even if not blonde.

Why expect the peoples of Khatovar to be any more homogeneous than the peoples of my own world?

Murgen and his crew came jogging up, carrying another body on another crude litter. The first had escaped most of the effects of impact and fire. This one had been less fortunate.

"Another girl," I observed. That fact was hard to ignore. She was more obvious than the first.

"Younger than the other one."

"But just as well put together."

"Better, from where I'm standing."

"They're sisters," Lady growled. "You have an idea what this means?"

"Probably that the Voroshk had so little respect for us that they sent out some kids so they could get in some practice. But after what's happened, Daddy and Grandpa will take a closer interest." I beckoned. "Gather round, gentlemen." Once everyone not doing something closed in, I said, "In a short time we're probably going to have a sky full of unfriendly company. I want you to start pulling up stakes and getting the animals and equipment back through the gate. Right now."

Lady asked, "You think that third one will make it back to the Voroshk army?"

"No way will I bet against it. My mother's optimistic children have all been dead for fifty years." I glanced at the forvalaka. It was almost entirely Lisa Bowalk now. Except for the head. "Looks like some mythological beast, don't she?"

She was not dead yet. Her eyes were open. They were no longer cat's eyes. They begged. She did not want to die.

I told Lady, "She doesn't look any older than the last time I saw her." She was still a young and attractive woman—for one whose formative years had been spent surviving the worst slum of a truly ugly city. "Hey, Cratch. Grab Slobo. I want you guys to bring all the firewood over here and pile it on this thing."

Goblin said, "I'll help."

"I'll tell you what, runt. You want a job, you can build me a couple of good litters so we can take our new girlfriends with us."

Lady asked, "Are they fit to travel?"

"The older one could probably get up and limp along on her own if she was conscious. I'll need a closer look here before I can tell how bad this one's hurt, though."

"You watch what you're poking and squeezing, old man."

"You'd think that, at your age, you'd have developed a little better sense of humor, old woman. Don't you understand that every profession has its perks? A surgeon gets to poke and squeeze."

"So does a wife."

"I knew I forgot something when we did that ceremony thing. Shoulda brung a lawyer. Cratch! Nobody touches that spear till we start the fire. And I'll do any touching that gets done. Where are my birds? I've got to get the Black Hounds called in." We could not leave them here. They were going to be critical weapons in the war with Soulcatcher. Sleepy was, probably, missing them desperately already.

Swan and three others approached, straining to carry the post the older girl had ridden. Swan puffed. "This goddamned thing weighs a ton!" The four of them started to drop it.

"No!" Lady barked. "Gently! You recall what happened to the other one? Up there?" She pointed. Smoke or dust or whatever still smeared the sky. There was still an occasional crackle of toy lightning inside the cloud, too. "That's better. Goblin! Doj! Come and take a look at this thing."

"Check this cloth," Swan said, offering me a bit of black rag.

It felt like silk and seemed almost weightless. It stretched when I pulled it without tearing or getting any thinner. Or so it seemed.

"Now watch this." Swan stabbed the cloth with his knife. The knife did not penetrate. It did not cut when he slashed, either.

I said, "Now isn't that a handy little trick? We're lucky we had the bamboo. Honey, check this out. Show her, Swan. You, men. Get the post thing on the other side of the gate. Let's get moving, people! These folks can fly. And the next bunch that shows up aren't likely to be as friendly." No one really needed my encouragement, though. A solid line of men, animals and equipment was moving upslope already. The older Voroshk girl was headed uphill already, too, bound to Goblin's first litter.

When Swan finished showing that cloth to Lady, I told him, "See if you can't find a log or post in one of the huts that might look like that flying thing from a distance."

Lady, Goblin and Swan all stared at me. This time I stood on my command right and did not explain. I had a hunch the Voroshk would not want to lose the post. Which my comrades might understand but if I said so they would just ask for further explanations.

I said, "This one has broken bones, bad burns, punctures, cuts and abrasions and probably internal injuries."

"And?" Lady asked.

"And so I think she won't be much use to us. Probably die on us. So I'm going to do the best I can for her, then leave her for her own people."

"Going soft in your old age?"

"Like I said, she'd be more trouble than she's worth. Plus, the sister ought to be up and around in no time. So if I do right by the one I leave here, the Voroshk might be less inclined to run around behind us trying to get vicious."

"What're they going to do?"

"I don't know. I don't want to find out. I just take into account the fact that they were able to get Bowalk onto the plain and off again, once each way, without wrecking any shadowgates. I'm hoping they don't have what it takes to move an army the same way."

"They wouldn't need to grab us if they did. Odds are, Bowalk's trip was possible because of what she was and the fact that she'd bulled through it all once before."

I looked at the forvalaka. Even its head was Lisa Daele Bowalk now. The same Lisa Bowalk who ruined Marron Shed a thousand subjective years ago. Her eyes were shut but she was still breathing.

We would have to fix that.

Lady told me, "Cut off her head first. Then start the fire."

31

Khatovar:
The Opened Gate

The Voroshk were not sneaks. They came out of the northwest in an angry swarm, eager to get at us. There were at least twenty-five in the first wave.

My people were all on the uphill side of the shadowgate but many of the Unknown Shadows had not made it back. I had left snail shells scattered around the woods so they would have somewhere to hide. I would get them out later, once the excitement was over.

The swarm streaked in, vast flutters of black cloth billowing. Even though they could see that we were beyond the shadowgate and our main body was already on the plain they dropped down and streaked over our empty camp, shedding a rain of small objects which turned little patches of ground into puddles of lava and caused vegetation to combust almost explosively. None of our shelters or corrals survived. But nothing touched the injured girl or the forvalaka's funeral pyre.

"Glad I don't have to run between those raindrops," I said. A couple of the Voroshk had tried to award me that experience but the barrier between Khatovar and the plain repelled their missiles easily. And ate their magic right up. They did not activate, even when they dribbled to the ground.

Lady said, "They're all kids, too."

The members of the swarm all seemed to do whatever they wanted, going their own ways, yet none of them collided. Once their assault failed to produce results most of them settled to earth around the injured girl.

On my side of the shadowgate we leaned on bamboo poles and watched.

A trio of latecomers formed the second wave. They appeared several minutes after the first flood. "These will be the leaders," Lady said. "Being a little more cautious than the youngsters." Even more black fabric billowed around these three.

"The highest ranking members of the Family making the journey," I conceded. "There sure are a lot of these people. Considering the size of the army they brought." Not counting the Voroshk themselves, my spies numbered the approaching force at about eight hundred. The light cavalry hurrying ahead numbered fewer than fifty men. There was a good chance we could have beat them up if they had not had all those post riders in the sky looking out for them.

When they grounded, the Voroshk flyers did stand their conveyances on end, like fenceposts that would not tip over without a push from a human hand.

The elders circled a few times before they set down. Then they took time to examine the unconscious child before paying any more attention to us.

I gave a small hand signal as soon as we were on. Men on the slope who had been hanging around gawking resumed moving. The Voroshk chieftains were allowed to see the other girl being led away and what looked like four men lugging a captured flying fencepost. While the heart of my heart and I posed just behind the gate in our best killer costumes. I know there was a huge smirk hanging around inside my helmet.

Out there among the Voroshk, so far ignored but not unnoticed, the headless corpse of our ancient enemy crackled and popped inside a roaring fire. I wished we still had the Lance of Passion to show those guys, too. My ravens had not been able to tell if the Voroshk were aware of who we really were.

I said, "The past always comes back." I waved. Then I told Lady, "I think it might be a real good idea if we got going now. Their good feelings about us having taken care of that kid just aren't going to last."

"You've probably stretched it too long already, showing off." She started up the slope. She did not look at all bad in that armor. She set a brisk pace for such an old gal, too.

Soon all the flying sorcerers were staring uphill, pointing and jabbering at one another. They seemed to be much more excited about us carrying off their flying log than they were about us taking the girl. Maybe she was not anyone important. Or maybe they figured she was old enough to look out for herself.

One of the elders stepped away from that fluttering black crowd. He had a small book in his hand. He turned a couple of pages, found the one he wanted, ran a finger along a few lines as he read. A second elder nodded and apparently repeated what he had to say, with gestured accompaniment. After a moment the third elder took it up, his gestures similar but not in step with those of the other two.

"It's a round," I told Lady. We had overtaken the slowest of our people. "Row row row." I made some gestures myself. "You do anything you're going to be sorry."

The Voroshk all spun, presenting their backs to us.

The flash was so bright it blinded me for a moment. When my sight returned another of those hundred-legged starfish of brownish-grey smoke had materialized. This one was not upstairs. This one was right where the shadowgate had been. Centered right where I had hidden the captured flying post under some "abandoned" tenting.

"Warned you," I murmured.

"How did you know?" Lady asked.

"I'm not sure. A hunch, I guess. Uninhibited intuition."

"They've just killed themselves." There was almost a hint of compassion in her voice. "They'll never stop the shadows from flooding through that."

Some of the Voroshk already recognized the magnitude of the disaster still unfolding. Black fluttering shapes scattered like roaches suddenly exposed to the light. Flying posts took to the air, streaked northward so violently that bits of black cloth ripped off and fluttered down like dark autumn leaves.

The three elders held their positions. They stared our way. I wondered what was happening inside their heads. Almost certainly not any recognition of the fact that the disaster was a direct result of the magnitude of Voroshk arrogance. I have never met one of their kind who would admit any fallibility whatsoever.

I was sure there would be some grand squabbles over where to fix the blame during the time they had left. Human nature at work.

"What are you thinking?" Lady asked.

I realized that I was no longer moving, that I was just watching the Voroshk watch me. "Just looking around inside me, trying to figure out why this doesn't bother me the way it would have years ago. Why I recognize the pain more easily now but am not touched by it nearly so much."

"You know what One-Eye used to say about you? You think too much. He was right. You don't have any more obligation to him. Let's go back to our own world, see about spanking our little girl and getting my baby sister straightened up." Her voice changed severely as her thoughts turned. "One thing I demand. Still. Narayan Singh. I want him. He's mine."

I winced inside my helmet. Poor Narayan. I said, "I still have one thing to do here."

"What?" she snapped.

"After those three leave. I have to get Tobo's friends back."

She grunted and resumed walking. She had to make sure the road across the plain could be closed behind us, so that we would not become victims of the explosion, too.

32

The Shadowlands:
The Protector of All the Taglias

Soulcatcher's survival instincts had been honed to a razor's edge by centuries of adventures among peoples who considered her continued good health a liability. She sensed a change in the world long before she had any idea what that change might be, good or ill or indifferent, and ages before she dared hazard a guess as to its cause.

At first it was just that sense. Then, gradually, it became the pressure of a thousand eyes. But she could discover nothing. Her crows could find nothing either, other than the occasional, unpredictable, flickering glimpse of their quarry, the two Deceivers. That was ancient news.

Soulcatcher abandoned the hunt immediately. It would

not be difficult to get close to the Deceivers again.

She learned nothing more before nightfall—except that her crows were extremely unsettled, getting more and more nervous, less and less tractable and increasingly inclined to jump at shadows. They could not make clear the nature of their malaise because they did not understand it themselves.

That began to grow clearer as the twilight gathered. Messengers interrupted Soulcatcher's meditations to inform her that several of the murder had fallen prey to a sudden illness. "Show me."

She made no effort to disguise herself as she followed her birds to the nearest feathered corpse. She picked it up, rolled it carefully in her gloved hands.

It was obvious what had killed the crow. Not illness but a killer shadow. No cadaver looked like one did after a shadow finished with it. But that could not be. It was still light out. Her tame shadows were all in hiding and there were no rogue shadows around anymore. Nor would wild shadows have wasted themselves on a crow when there was human game in the vicinity. She should have heard Narayan Singh and that wretched niece of hers screaming long before any crow. . . . There had been no sound from the bird whatsoever. Nor had there been from any of a half dozen others the murder knew to be gone. The survivors had plenty to say. Including stating plainly that they were not about to stray away from her protection.

"How can I fight this if I don't know what it is? If you won't find out for me?"

The crows would not be bullied or cajoled. They were geniuses for birds. Which meant they were just bright enough to have noticed that every one of the dead had been completely alone when evil had befallen them.

Soulcatcher cursed them, then calmed herself and convinced the most valiant birds that they had to, therefore, do their scouting in threes and fours until darkness closed in completely. At that point she would have bats and owls and her own shadows available to take over.

Darkness came. As the Deceivers correctly observe, the darkness always comes.

With nightfall came a silent but horribly vicious warfare with Soulcatcher poised at the eye of the storm.

Initially she had to hold on desperately against unknown assailants until her own shadows could bring in enough swift reinforcements. Then, spending shadows profligately, she took the offensive. And when dawn came, and she was almost without supernatural allies because of the cost of the struggle, she gave way to exhaustion, having gained a knowledge of a portion of the truth.

They were back. The Black Company were, with new formations, new allies, new sorceries, and still without a dram of mercy in their hearts. These were not the Company she had known in younger years but they were the spiritual children of the cold killers of the olden days. No matter what you tried, it seemed, you could kill only men. The ideal lived on.

Ha! An end to the boredom of empire stood at hand.

Bravado and pretense did not lessen the inexplicable fear. They had fled onto the plain. And now they were back. That had to mean much more. She needed to interrogate shadows who had existed on the glittering stone during those silent years. When there was time. Before she did anything else she had to do what she always did so well: survive.

She was out here hundreds of miles from any support. She was besieged by things that would not yield to her will or sorcery and which she could detect, it seemed, only through her own shadows or when one of them attacked her directly. They were as fierce as shadows but strange. They were more otherworldly than her spirit slaves and seemed possessed of a higher order of intelligence.

Each one she extinguished personally infected her with both a vast sorrow and with the certainty that she was battling only the most feeble of their kind. Always there was a powerful presentiment of demons or demigods to come.

What she could not comprehend was why all this frightened her so. There was nothing here more deadly or threatening or bizarre than a thousand perils she had faced before. Nothing here matched the sheer dark menace of the Dominator in his time.

There were infrequent moments when she still longed for those dark and ancient times. The Dominator had taken her and all her sisters, had made one of them his wife and another his lover. . . .

He had been a strong, hard, cruel man, the Dominator. His empire had been one of cruelty and steel. And Soulcatcher had revelled in its pomp and dark glory. And would never forgive her rival, her last surviving sister, for having brought all that to an end. Blame the death of the Dominator on the White Rose if you wanted. Soulcatcher knew the truth. The Dominator never would have gone down if his whining virgin of a wife had not helped his destruction along.

And who had fought and conspired so hard after their resurrection to keep the Dominator in the ground? His loving wife, that was who!

She would be back. She would be out there somewhere, wherever the Black Company had been hiding. She was not here yet but she would be soon. Having been buried alive again would be no impediment to the inevitable, that grim moment when they would settle their differences face-to-face.

Soulcatcher could will herself blind in some quarters, despite centuries of cynical experience. She would not see that fortune could be just as erratic and insane as she was.

Soulcatcher's powers of recuperation were tremendous. After a few hours of rest she rose and started walking northward, her stride long and confident. Tonight she would gather an army of her own shadows around her. Never again would she be as threatened as she had been the night before.

So she told herself.

By late afternoon her confidence was as high as ever it had been and fragments of her mind were already peeping past today's crisis to scout out what might be done to sculpt the future.

Soulcatcher had long been intimate with the knowledge that horrible things could and did happen to her but always she had enjoyed the certainty that she would come through everything alive.

33

Khatovar:
Leave-taking

Looks clean," Swan said. Murgen and Thai Dei grunted agreement. I nodded to the Nyueng Bao. What he had to say meant something here. His eyes were still as sharp as those of a lad of fifteen. I was damned near blind in one and could not see out the other.

"Doj? What do you think? Did they run away? Or did they sneak back just in case *we* sneaked back?" Element of surprise no longer my ally, I did not want to run into the Voroshk again. Especially not those old men. They would be bitter and in a mood to drag me down to hell with them.

"They went away. They went back to prepare for the onslaught. They know horror and despair are headed their way but they also know they're strong enough to weather it if they remain calm and work hard."

I suspect I gaped. "How do you figure all that?"

"It's just a matter of mental exercise. Take what we know about them, about sorcerers as a whole, and about human beings in general, and the rest follows. They've been through this before, in a smaller way. They'll have worked out what to do if it happened again. All this empty country, from here to the other side of their Dandha Presh, will serve the same function as the cleared ground surrounding a fortress expecting to be besieged."

"You've convinced me. Let's just hope they're not so ready that they figure out how to come looking for us after they wrap up their pest problem." As badly as the shadow-gate and nearby barrier had been damaged I doubted the Voroshk would have much energy to spare for generations.

Swan said, "He had me for a minute, too, but here comes the argument that proves what I always knew: Uncle Doj is full of shit."

A half dozen billowing black forms had emerged from the vegetation down the slope. They were walking very slowly, two by two, hands extended away from their sides, their flying posts tagging along behind at waist height.

I said, "I don't know what the fuck is going on but I want Goblin and Doj ready for anything. Murgen, you and Thai Dei spread out so we can hit them from in front and both sides with fireballs." Me and my pals had three live poles, literally all our band had left. Lady said there were just six usable fireballs between the three. She hoped.

One for each of the Voroshk.

Swan said, "You sure we really need to round up those spooks? Life would be a lot easier. . . ."

"Right here. Right now. But what happens back home when we've got Soulcatcher coming at us and we yell for Tobo to let loose the Black Hounds and there ain't no Black Hounds? And the rest of the Unknown Shadows say, 'Fuck that shit! I ain't getting skragged for these guys who wouldn't even try to bring the Hounds out of Khatovar.' "

Swan growled. Goblin sneered, "A little passion, Captain? I thought you'd lost it all."

"When I want shit out of you, runt, I'll kick it out. What did he just say?" The Voroshk had stopped coming toward us. One had spoken. And, O wonder, his words sounded like something I ought to understand. "Say that again, buddy."

The sorcerer got the idea. He repeated himself, loudly and slowly, the way you do with the hard of hearing, the dim of wit and foreigners.

"What is that noise?" I asked. "I know there were words in there that I should recognize."

"Remember Juniper?" Goblin said. "It sounds like he's trying to speak what they spoke there."

"Makes sense. Bowalk came from Juniper. So listen close." Goblin had served in Juniper, too. A *long* time ago. I have a knack for languages. Could I get enough of this one back fast enough to do us any good? We did not have many hours of daylight left.

Something began to get past the fact that the Voroshk had a horrible accent and his grammer was atrocious. He butchered tenses and inverted his verbs and subjects.

Goblin and I compared notes as we proceeded. The little wizard had never spoken the language well but he had had no trouble understanding it.

"What's going on?" Swan demanded. He was holding one of the bamboo poles. It was getting heavy.

"Sounds like they want us to take them with us. That they think the end of the world is coming and they don't want to participate."

Goblin nodded, agreeing. He added a caveat, "But I wouldn't trust them for a second. I'd always assume they were sent to spy on us."

"Yes," I said. "I'd do that with just about anybody."

Goblin ignored the jibe. "Make them strip. Bone naked. Doj and I can go over their clothes like we're looking for nits."

"All right. Only I'm taking Doj with me to help collect my snail shells." I began telling the Voroshk what they had to do if they really wanted to go with us. They were not pleased. They wanted to argue. I did not argue even though I hoped to get my hands on a flying post or two so Lady and Tobo could study them. Damn, having a few of those sure would be handy.

I told the Voroshk, "If I don't see naked bodies I'd better see the backs of people getting away. Anybody who isn't doing one or the other by a count of fifty will die where he's standing on his dignity." The language came back to me quite well, though I did not really make my statement that clearly. The two Voroshk who were probably the brightest began disrobing almost immediately. They proved to be as pale and blond as the girls we had seen already, though red with embarrassment and shaking with fury. I watched carefully, not with much interest in their flesh. How much determination they put into something humiliating would give me a hint or two about their sincerity.

It was too much for one young woman. She got just far enough for her true sex to become evident before she found that she could not finish.

"Better run, girl," I said. And she did. She hopped aboard her flying log and scooted.

Her desertion had a definite impact on one of the young men. He changed his mind even though he was already naked. I did not hurry him as he dressed.

That left four, three boys and a girl, all in their early to middle-teens.

I waved uphill, confident that by now Lady would be watching and could guess what I needed. She is clever that way. And shortly a couple of guys were headed downhill lugging bundles of odds and ends with which to dress our prisoners.

They did not yet quite understand their new status.

I brought them through the shadowgate one at a time, watching carefully. I did not expect them to try anything but I am alive at my age because I make a habit of being ready for trouble when it seems most unlikely. I asked, "Anybody got any reason to think whoever goes out the gate is going to get into trouble?" To their further humiliation the Voroshk kids found themselves with their hands bound behind them as soon as they were dressed.

The fellow with the feeble command of Juniper's lingo protested the indignity. "It's only temporary," I assured him. "Just while us few are on the outside." I shifted to Taglian. "Murgen, Swan, Thai Dei, you keep these guys on a short leash."

Bamboo poles lashed the air. Despite age and its attendant cynicism, those guys could put on a show of enthusiasm. Mainly faked. Swan promised me, "Anything happens to you, there won't be anything left of them but grease stains and toenails."

"You're a good man, Swan. Doj, you go through first." The elderly Nyueng Bao drew the sword Ash Wand and stepped through the damaged shadowgate into Khatovar. He positioned himself. I said, "Your turn, Goblin." By hand sign I told Murgen not to be shy about flinging a fireball at surprise targets outside.

What followed was anticlimactic. I took a sack around to all the places I remembered seeding earlier and collected snail shells. Those in which something had hidden itself had a distinct feel.

My ravens returned while I was involved in the harvest. They reported the Voroshk feverishly preparing for nightfall. They believed our defectors were genuine. Terror and panic were spreading across the world as fast as Voroshk messengers could fly.

The birds made the recovery of our shadow companions much easier. They let me know which shells were a waste of time and where to find the ones I had forgotten. We were all back through the shadowgate an hour before sunset.

Goblin was still examining the clothing removed from the Voroshk kids. The little wizard piped. "This is some truly amazing material, Croaker. I think it might be sensitive to the thoughts of whoever is wearing it."

"Is it safe?"

"I think it's completely inert as long as it isn't in contact with whoever is keyed to wear it."

"A little something more for Tobo to play with during all the spare time he's going to have in the middle of a war. Bundle it up. Put it on a mule at the front of the column. We need to get going." I shifted languages, told the unhappy youngsters, "I'm releasing you now. I'm going to bring you back out here, one at a time, so you can get your posts. You won't be allowed to ride them. You'll travel at the rear of our column." I went on to tell them about the dangers of the plain while they were following instructions. Their fear of the shadows gave me a good chance to retain their attention. I tried to impress them that a screw-up on the plain would kill not just the fuck-up but the whole crew, so they should not expect my people to be gentle if their behavior was unacceptable.

I was the last of the Company to leave Khatovar's soil. Before I departed I indulged in a little personal ceremony of farewell, or perhaps of exorcism.

The youngster capable of some communication wanted to know, "What is the meaning of what you just did?"

I tried to explain. He did not get it. In time I determined that he had never heard of the Free Companies of Khatovar. That he knew almost nothing of the history of his world before his ancestors had taken power. That, furthermore, he did not care.

He seemed a shallow young man, overall. No doubt his companions were much the same.

The Company was going to be a revelation for them.

Lady and I stayed at the end of the road, waiting to make sure we had sealed it successfully against shadow incursions. The sun set. The sense of presence that comes when a large number of killer shadows are gathering grew powerful as darkness came. A rising excitement informed that presence, as though the Host of the Unforgiven Dead knew that some change had taken place even though they could not come out and scout around in the daytime.

The skies remained clear over Khatovar. The moon rose just before sunset, so there was ample silvery light to reveal the opening stage of the shadow invasion. A trickle of small explorers gradually slithered through the shattered boundary. The scream of a dying pig reached us. More shadows descended the slope. Though they did not appear to be communicating with one another, somehow more and more and bigger and bigger shadows became aware of the opportunity.

"Look there," Lady said. A line of Voroshk flyers had begun passing near the moon. Before long little balls of light were bubbling into existence within the dense vegetation down the slope. "Maybe something like our fireballs."

The fireballs had been created, originally, to destroy the floods of darkness the Shadowmasters insisted on throwing against us.

"They're going to put up a fight, anyway. Will you look at that?" That being the Nef.

"The dreamwalkers are going out? I wonder why."

"Too bad we couldn't let the shadows all get out, then slam the gate shut behind them."

Even Shivetya would agree, I supposed. He was not pleased with some of the improvements made on his plain during recent millennia.

Lady said, "We should get moving. And you might want to put some thought into what to do with our new children once we get to the other end and they become tempted to run away."

Yes. I should. We did not need any more psychotic sorcerers getting under foot.

34

The Shadowlands:
Tobo's Chores

Tobo finished interviewing the black raven that was not really a bird, sent it racing back to Croaker. He found his mother and Sleepy with Sleepy's usual fellow travelers studying a map of the territories north of the Dandha Presh. They were trying to determine the most favorable route northward, once the force finished crossing the mountains. Little colored patches represented the last known positions of the Protector and of Narayan Singh.

Sleepy asked, "News from Croaker?"

"He's finished it. He's on his way. But it turned stranger than he expected." He relayed the full report.

Sleepy told him, "You'll have to go back. We can't risk the chance of another gang of sorcerers getting loose over here."

"I suppose." Tobo had no enthusiasm for that.

"I don't like it. Why didn't he just kill them after he had their flying things and that remarkable clothing?"

"Because he doesn't do things like that." Not to mention the fact that dead people are not real cooperative when it comes time for them to share their knowledge.

"No. He lets people get away with stuff, then hunts them down thirty years later." She made a growling noise. "How can I keep moving if I don't have you here?"

"If Croaker is on this side all the Unknown Shadows will be on this side, too. The Black Hounds will be running out front in no time. A day or two later we'll be able to see what's going on anywhere we want to look." Sleepy needed that reassurance. She was worried about everything going on out where she had no ability to see. Reminding her that most people, including most captains, went through whole lives far more blind than she had ever been, did nothing to improve her temper.

Sleepy was spoiled. Throughout her association with the Company, one way or another, we had owned some ability to find out what was happening far away from us. You let anybody have something for a little while, they soon consider it their birthright. Sleepy was very much no exception to that rule.

Goblin crabbed, "I understand that you need Tobo here before you can let the prisoners leave the plain. But why shouldn't the rest of us go ahead? We aren't getting anything useful done just sitting here."

"You're getting done what I want you to get done. Now be quiet. Before I gag you."

I became impatient myself before Tobo finally appeared. He was subject to the constraints of normal travel. We had no flying carpets anymore, though there was hope that the Howler might create some once he was reawakened. (Nobody had yet tried.) And now there was the possibility we might gain the secrets of the Voroshk flying posts.

Tobo came in astride the superhorse that had attached itself to Sleepy. Bred originally to serve the Lady of the Tower up north, a number had come south with the Company. This was the last known survivor.

"How long do those things live, hon?" I asked Lady as Tobo approached.

"Maybe forty years. At the extreme. This one is pushing the limit."

"Looks pretty spry." Despite having run forty miles the animal looked almost fresh.

"I did good work in those days."

"And you miss them now?"

"Yes." She would not lie to me. She did not love me any less for missing being what once she had been, either. Near as I can tell, she never regrets anything she does, good or evil. I wish I could be that way.

Tobo dismounted right outside the shadowgate. I passed him through. He got straight to business, though he smiled and waved to his father and uncle and Doj. "You have five prisoners? All major wizards?"

"I don't know about that. They could be complete notalents, far as I can tell. But they did go flying around on fenceposts wearing a kind of super-fabric that Goblin says can be manipulated by thoughts. This comes across as a 'You'd better be careful, Croaker' kind of sign."

"We can communicate with them?"

"We have two brothers whose father studied and managed Bowalk while she was in Khatovar. The father could force Bowalk to resume human shape for an hour or two sometimes, but he couldn't keep her there. He thought the problem was a dead-man-loop Shapeshifter built into the shape-changing spells. Shifter didn't trust her. The loop activated when One-Eye killed him.

"Anyway, this Voroshk's kids picked up some of Bowalk's native tongue from being around her, which has been for all of their lives. When the Voroshk blew up the shadowgate one of them got the bright idea that he could talk us into taking them to safety somewhere else. He rounded up some friends who were just as scared and came to us. He assumed we all spoke the same language as the forvalaka. He had some strange notion that we would recognize the innate superiority of the Voroshk and take his bunch in as honored guests. He couldn't imagine it being any other way because that's the only way it could be in Khatovar. He's vain, stupid and arrogant. They all seem to be. The other brother more so. He won't even talk."

Tobo smiled a little unpleasantly, perhaps recalling similar attitudes amongst Hsien's warlords. "I expect they've all suffered one disappointment after another."

"Absodamnlutely. Life has become an unimaginable hell

for these kids. I have to remind them over and over that they're still alive."

"Let's go meet them, shall we?" The kid looked like he was excited by the challenge.

As we approached the refugees I warned Tobo, "They're all gorgeous but I really don't think they have a brain between them. At least they show every sign of being slow learners."

We stopped several yards from Khatovar's forlorn children. They huddled together beside the road as Black Company men and mules began to move out through the shadowgate. Only one of the girls had ambition enough to look up. The little one. The one we had taken prisoner.

She stared at Tobo for half a minute. Then she murmured something to her companions. They looked up, too. Only the ringleader and his brother betrayed their native arrogance. And it had not been that long or arduous a journey.

They seemed to sense something in Tobo that was not apparent to me. It awakened hope. Several babbled questions in their own language.

"When they stop yammering tell them who I am. Don't feel like you have to be entirely honest, either."

"A little exaggeration couldn't hurt?"

"Hardly ever."

The interview lasted longer than I anticipated. Tobo was remarkably patient for his age. He worked hard to make the Voroshk understand that they were no longer in the land of their fathers, that here it did not matter who they were or who their parents had been. In our world they were going to have to sing for their supper.

We broke for a snack. The Voroshk and their guards were the only people left on the plain side of the shadowgate. I told Tobo, "I admire your patience."

"Me, too. Already I want to kick some of them. And it's not really all patience, anyway. I'm trying to learn more about them by reading what they don't say and what they do let slip. You're right. They don't seem very bright. Though I'm guessing that's as much because of the way they were educated as it is any natural stupidity. They have no idea whatsoever of their own past. None! Never heard of the Free Companies. Never heard of the Lance of Passion. Didn't know that some really great wizards from Khatovar erected the standing stones that are all over the plain, at great peril to themselves from shadows. Didn't even recognize the name Khatovar, though they do know Khadi as some vague, old-time demon that nobody cares about anymore."

"How do you know that? About the memorial stones."

"Baladitya got it from Shivetya. You did notice that the runes on the flying logs are almost identical to the ones on the standing stones?"

"I didn't notice that, no. Mostly I've kept busy watching Goblin. The little shit speaks a bit of the language. He's been sneaking around talking to them."

Tobo chewed and nodded and looked thoughtful. "You ask him about it?"

"Hardly. I don't trust that guy, Tobo. One-Eye told me not to just before he passed."

"Nobody is going to trust Goblin for a long time, Croaker. And he knows that as well as anybody else does. He'll be the carefulest Goblin you ever saw. You won't even recognize him."

"We're talking about Goblin here. He can't help himself."

"He got into most of what he got into because One-Eye dragged him along. Think about it, Croaker. If he's some-how turned into Kina's tool, his assignment will be a long-term one. 'Bring on the Year of the Skulls' kind of stuff. He won't get himself killed trying something trivial."

I grunted. That made perfect sense on a rational level but I remained unconvinced. Goblin was Goblin. I had known him for a long time. The things he did did not always make sense, even to him. I asked, "What'll we do with the Voroshk?"

"I'm going to educate them."

Damn! I did not like the way he said that.

He replaced my guards with his own cronies, Taglians led by a senior sergeant called Riverwalker. All these guards were fluent in the language of Hsien and possessed a working knowledge of Nyueng Bao, which was a close cousin of the language spoken in the Land of Unknown Shadows.

Tobo instructed the guards, then the prisoners. Through me. Explaining the facts of life. "These men will be your teachers. They will teach you languages and the skills you will need to get along in this world. They will expose you to our religions and laws and the ways we have for getting along with one another."

The boy doing the translating started to protest.

Riverwalker smacked him in the back of the head hard enough to knock him down.

Tobo continued, "You have to understand that you're guests. You bought passage out of Khatovar with your knowledge. Your lives will be as comfortable as we can make them so long as you cooperate. But we are at war with ancient and powerful enemies. We won't be inclined toward patience with anyone who doesn't cooperate. Our patience will be especially short with people we consider dangerous. Do you understand?"

Tobo waited for me to finish translating. I asked an extra time to make sure the kids really grasped the gravity of the situation. Youngsters have a hard time getting it when the cruel and deadly applies to them personally. They also tend to agree to almost anything just to stop hearing about it.

Tobo had me tell them, "The rest of today and tonight you can rest. Tomorrow you'll begin an intensive education in Taglian. While we're hurrying to catch up with the rest of our army. I'll travel with you and will help you as much as I can."

The leader boy wanted to argue again. He had not listened closely enough to what he was translating. Riverwalker knocked him down again. Tobo told me, "That one's going to be trouble."

"There's a good chance they all will be. They couldn't get along at home." They had to be misfits. Shifting languages, I told the kids, "If you make yourselves more trouble than you're worth these people will kill you. Come on. I think I see some chow waiting to make our acquaintance."

One of the girls said something in her own language. The captive, not the one who had come along with the boys.

I responded to the whine. "Tell her she can't go home. It's too late for that."

Meantime, Tobo remarked, "But everybody here is running away from something."

"Some," I stipulated. "How soon do you think we'll get a chance to sit down somewhere? I've got a lot of writing to catch up on."

Tobo laughed. "You'd better stage a coup, you want a chance to sit down. Sleepy won't take time off until the corpses are piled high enough to make fences."

The Voroshk seemed to enjoy their evening meal. They were hungry enough to appreciate anything. We started teaching them Taglian nouns. Tobo studied both them and the wonders they had brought with them. He seemed less impressed by their flying posts than he was by the clothing they were no longer permitted to wear.

He told me, "Those posts look like a variation on the same sorcery Howler uses to operate his flying carpets. I should be able to work it out eventually. If I can get around some spells that're meant to make the posts destroy themselves if they fall into the wrong hands."

I told him about the two I had seen explode.

"Pretty potent self-destruct, then. I'll be careful."

"Be careful of those girls, too. I think the little one's already staked you out."

Come morning the leader kid could not be wakened. He was alive, all right, but no one could rouse him. "What did you do?" I asked Tobo, whispering, having leapt to a conclusion involving Tobo wanting the potential troublemaker out of the way without us losing access to his post and clothing.

"I had nothing to do with it."

Lady examined the boy after I did. She said, "This looks a lot like the coma Smoke went into for so long."

I agreed. But Soulcatcher had been responsible for that, we believed. And there was no way this could be her doing. The Unknown Shadows knew every move she made. And would turn aside any monsters she sent against us. I wondered aloud, "Were any of your invisible friends around here last night? Maybe they saw something."

"I'll check."

By dint of ferocity I got the unconscious kid's brother to admit that he could communicate. I made him understand that they needed to bind his brother onto one of their posts. Otherwise he would get left behind when we moved out.

The kids were terrified.

"Handy disaster," Lady remarked.

"Yeah. But for whom?"

35

Taglios:
The Message

Mogaba swore softly but virulently, foully and steadily. Crows had been arriving for over an hour, each bird carrying a fragment of a long message from the Protector. Being birdbrained, no one crow could carry much of the whole. And because they were vulnerable to a thousand misfortunes, every fragment had to be sent again and again.

The Great General hated putting these puzzles together and this one was the worst ever, by an order of magnitude.

There should not be this many crows in the whole world.

He had twenty scribes working on the message already.

Some points became clear quickly.

He sent for Aridatha Singh and Ghopal Singh. This message would affect all of them.

By the time the others arrived, enough of the puzzle had come clear for Mogaba to reveal what, for him, was the most critical detail. "They're back."

Aridatha jumped, startled by Mogaba's intensity. "Back? Who's back?"

"The Black Company. The Protector destroyed them. Right? Root and branch. Right? But now she says they're back. They're patching her message together in the next room right now."

Ghopal asked, "What are you talking about?"

"There's a huge message coming in from our employer. She's given up her quest. She's on the run, headed home. The Black Company is pouring through the shadowgate. Thousands strong. Well-armed, well-clad, well-trained. With the Radisha Drah and Prahbrindrah Drah in their train and blessing them. And we have nothing much in their way for hundreds of miles. She's headed back here. She expects to lose her ability to watch them shortly. They have some unfamiliar kind of supernatural help coming off the plain with them. Evidently something like the shadows but more dangerous because they're smarter."

Aridatha observed, "Sounds like pretty good intelligence gathering for somebody who's on the run from an enemy who knows her capabilities." Singh's handsome face had lost some of its color. His voice had gone husky.

"A thought which did not escape me. She is Soulcatcher, after all. On the other hand, though, she can't learn anything when there isn't anything to see."

Aridatha and Ghopal nodded. In all ways, except in their hearts, they remained dedicated servants of the Protector.

Mogaba said, "The enemy being familiar with the Protector's

capabilities means they'll try to take them away from her. We don't know who's in charge but doctrine is doctrine. They'll try to blind her first, then they'll try to take away her capacity to communicate. They couldn't have come at a better time for them. She's a hundred miles from nowhere. She can't spread the word much faster than rumors will spread. And you know the news that the Radisha and her brother are coming back will spread like the plague."

Ghopal said, "I'll seal this part of the Palace off, then. We don't want those people in there running to their temples or whatever and telling too much of the truth to someone who'd use it as a tool against us."

"Do that." That would look good to the Protector's invisible spies. But, on the other hand it might be very useful to have some of the news get out. Taglios might fall into a state of chaos. A state in which there would be opportunities. Chaos could be very useful. Chaos could make wonderful camouflage.

Perhaps when the Protector was nearer Taglios.

Right now it was necessary to prepare for the advent of the Company. That would be expected from all quarters.

Where did they find so many men? Or shadows of their own? What other surprise cards did they have in their hand?

Some, surely. That was their nature.

Mogaba said, "We've got to leak some of the news. Like it or not. We have to get ready for war. We're headed for a fight. Unless we give up without a struggle. I don't plan to do that myself. I couldn't live with the consequences."

The Singhs exchanged glances. The Great General showing a sense of humor? Remarkable.

Ghopal said, "People are afraid of the Black Company."

"Of course they are. But when was the last time they won? We beat them over and over during the Kiaulune wars." Mogaba was proud of his work back then. His thinking and planning had contributed to every Taglian triumph.

"But we didn't wipe them all the way out. The trouble

with the Black Company is that if you leave even one of them alive, before long they're coming right back at you again."

"My brother unforgiven." That slogan haunted Mogaba's nightmares. He had his regrets.

"How soon can we expect the Protector?" Ghopal asked. "I'll have preparations to make."

Mogaba said, "She was on foot when she started sending her message. But she'll get to a courier station eventually. Then she'll start making good time. I wouldn't count on having more than another two or three days if she gets in a real hurry."

Ghopal grunted unhappily.

Mogaba nodded. Nothing ever went easily.

Aridatha asked, "Did she catch the Deceivers?"

Once again Mogaba thought the man betrayed a curiously skewed interest. Possibly a personal interest. "No. I told you, she said she was breaking off the chase. Enough. We all pretty much know what we need to do. Aridatha, I want the entire courier battalion here as soon as possible. The garrison commanders will need to be advised. I'll let you know right away if any critical news comes in."

Watching the message continue to approach final form, the Great General reviewed his unit commanders and the readiness and reliability of their commands. He was troubled. At first glance it would seem he could call up the resources of an empire. But the Protector had not concerned herself with the upkeep of her armed forces when she was not directly and immediately threatened. And she was not remotely popular, never had been and never wanted to be. She preferred rule by raw strength.

The Prahbrindrah Drah and his sister returning was particularly troubling. They had been popular in their era and in time's crucible had gone through the first stages of sanctification already. Some would hail them as liberators. Hell, if

Croaker was still alive they might give him his old title back.

There would be desertions, both at high levels and among the soldiers. Mogaba was more concerned about the troops. The nobility and senior priests, who owed their positions to the Protector, would play it carefully. Taglios had received several painful lessons regarding the price to be paid for betraying the Protector.

Where would it be best to bring the Company to battle? And how could he force battle upon them if they were reluctant to hazard a major encounter?

He was sure that his best chance lay in forcing an early confrontation, before what forces he did have began to evaporate.

36

The Nether Taglian Territories: The Barrens

Soulcatcher hastened along the bank of a creek that was almost as still and deep as a canal, looking for a way to cross. She had miscalculated when she had chosen to cut across these moors and downs to reach the shabby stronghold at Nijha. Clinging to the road would have meant a longer walk but there would have been bridges for times like these.

When she encountered obstacles of this sort she had no choice but to guess which way to turn. She did not know the country. She was blind. There were no bats or owls to send scouting. There were no shadows tonight. She had sent all those to safety, along with her crows. She knew she was capable of dealing with the hobgoblins following her around.

Something rose from the water behind her. It had a shape

like a horse. A voice whispered in her ear, telling her to come and ride. She barely glanced at it, and then only in total scorn. These things might be smarter than shadows but they could not be by much. How stupid did they think she was? She did not have to be familiar with the folklore of Hsien to understand that the water horse would drag her under.

She ignored the monster, not knowing it was an afanc, actually of centaur shape rather than equine. A half hour later she ignored one of its cousins, which took the semblance of a giant beaver. Then there was one resembling a crocodile, though this creek was four hundred miles from anywhere warm enough to support those giant reptiles. They all whispered to her. Some of them even knew her true name.

She found a plank footbridge evidently put in place by the seldom-seen, horse-stealing natives of these highlands. As she started across, something whispered to her from underneath. She did not understand its words but their menace was plain enough.

"You don't want me crossing, come up and do something about it." The voice she chose was that of a small child who was severely annoyed, but not frightened.

Something came up. It was huge and dark and ugly. In spots it glowed with a leprous inner light. It had way too many teeth. They stuck out of its mouth at all angles. It would have trouble when it came time to eat.

All those teeth and fangs snapped open as the monster prepared to lunge.

Soulcatcher's gloved right hand drifted forward. A spray of sparkling dust floated onward to meet the evil spirit.

It screamed.

Soulcatcher leapt off the bridge an instant before it shattered to kindling. She backed away, watched the fiend thrash and melt. From behind her mask came a soft wee sound like a little girl's skip-rope song, with a refrain that went, "It was fun to watch you die."

37

The Taglian Territories:
Somewhere North of Charandaprash

The Daughter of Night actually seemed to be thriving now that the Protector was stalking them no longer. Narayan was worried.

"You're always worried," she chided. She was happy. Her voice was musical. The light of the campfire made her eyes sparkle—when it did not make them glow red. "If someone is after us you worry about getting caught. If we're safe you worry about me not being a perfect replica of this image of the Daughter of Night you've invented inside your head. Narayan, Narayan. . . . Papa Narayan, what I want more than anything is somehow to fix it so you don't have to do this anymore. You've been the one for so long. . . . You deserve to put it all down now and relax."

Narayan knew that was not possible. Never would be. He did not argue, though. "Then let's bring on the Year of the Skulls. Once Kina returns we can loaf for the rest of our lives."

The girl shivered, seemed puzzled. Then she shuddered violently. She grew more pale, leaving Narayan wondering how she managed that when she was always as pale as death to begin. She stared out into the night, obviously troubled.

Narayan started to dump dirt—piled there for that purpose—onto the fire.

The girl said, "It's too late."

A huge shape rose behind her—then faded away as though dispersed by the wind.

"Kid's right, old man," said a voice Singh had not heard for years and was hearing again far sooner than he had hoped.

Iqbal and Runmust Singh—no relation to Narayan—

appeared at the edge of the firelight, wavering, as though they were a mist coalescing. Other men appeared behind them, soldiers in a style of armor Narayan had never seen. Amongst the soldiers he saw drooling red-eyed beasts of species he had never seen before, either.

Singh's heart redoubled its wild pounding.

The girl observed, "Now we know why my aunt quit chasing us."

Runmust Singh agreed. "Now you know. The Black Company is back. And we're not happy." Runmust was a great shaggy Shadar whose sheer size was oppressive.

Iqbal Singh smiled, perfect teeth glistening in the middle of his brushy beard. "This time you'll have to deal with your mother and your father." Iqbal was as shaggy and nearly as huge as his brother but somehow less intimidating. The girl remembered him having a wife and several children. But. . . . Did he mean her birth mother? Her natural father? But they were supposed to be dead.

Her knees went watery. She never had seen her natural parents.

The living saint was unable to keep his feet. Kina was going to test him yet again. And he had no energy left to spend in the fight for his faith. He was too old and too feeble and his faith had worn too thin.

Runmust gestured. The soldiers closed in. They were careful men who made certain they did not get between their captives and the crossbows threatening them. They put the girl's hands into wool-stuffed sacks, then bound her wrists behind her. They gagged her gently, then pulled a loose woolen sack over her head. They were aware that she might work some witchery.

Narayan they placed up on an extra horse, then tied him into the saddle. They were doing him no kindness. They were in a hurry. He would be too slow if they made him walk behind them. They were more gentle with the girl but her immediate fate was identical.

Their captors were not gratuitously cruel but the girl was sure that would change when they found themselves with adequate leisure time. The strange young soldiers in the clacking black armor seemed highly intrigued by what they could see of her pale beauty.

This was not the way she had imagined herself becoming a woman. And her imagination had been extremely active for several years.

38

The Taglian Territories:
The Dandha Presh

We were high in the pass through the Dandha Presh when the news arrived. The grinding weariness dragging my ancient bones down slipped my mind. I was at the head of the column. I stopped walking, moved aside, watched all the tired mules and men trudge past. Man and animal, we hoped the main force had not stripped Charandaprash of food and fodder.

The Voroshk had sunk deep into exhaustion and despair. Tobo traveled with them, talking all the time, trying to teach them through their pain and apathy. The kids had not had to walk anywhere ever before.

Their flying logs followed right behind.

Lady finally came up. I joined her. I sensed that rumor had reached her already, even though nobody seemed to have any breath to waste on conversation. Rumor is magical, maybe even supernatural.

I told her anyway. "Runmust and Iqbal have captured Narayan and Booboo. They never stopped heading our way after Soulcatcher left off chasing them."

"I heard."

"You as nervous as I am?"

"Probably more." We trudged along for a while. Then she said, "I never got a chance to be a mother. I never got a chance to learn how. After Narayan kidnapped her I just went back to being me."

"I know. I know. We have to keep reminding ourselves not to get emotionally entangled in this. She isn't going to think of us as Mom and Dad."

"I don't want her to hate us. And I know she will. Being the Daughter of Night is her whole life."

I thought about that. Eventually, I told her, "Being the Lady of Charm was your whole life once upon a time. But here you are."

"Here I am." Her lack of enthusiasm would have disheartened a lesser man than I.

She—and I—were of an age now where we spent too much time wondering how things might have gone had we made a few different choices.

I had plenty of regrets. I am sure she had more. She gave up so much more.

Willow Swan went puffing past with some remark about old folks slowing everybody down. I asked, "You guys keeping an eye on Goblin?"

"He don't fart without we don't know about it."

"That goes without saying. The whole countryside knows."

"He's not getting away with anything, Croaker."

I was not confident about that. Goblin was a slick little bastard. If I had the time I would stay right beside him myself, step for step.

Lady said, "Goblin hasn't done anything suspicious."

"I know. But he will."

"And that attitude is beginning to win him some sympathy. I thought you ought to know."

"I know. But I can't help recalling One-Eye's warning, either."

"You noted yourself that One-Eye would try to get his last lick in from beyond the grave."

"Yeah. Yeah. I'll try to take it easier."

"We need to move a little faster." The rear guard was almost up to us.

"We could lag behind and sneak off into the rocks for a while."

"Maybe you're not as worn out as you thought, then. Get a move on." And after a moment, "We'll talk about that tonight."

Some motivation, then.

39

Taglios:
The Great General

Thus far Mogaba had contained the worst reaction to the seething rumor cauldron that Taglios had become. His most useful tool was the carefully placed half-truth. His representatives did not deny that something big and dangerous was going on down south. They did, however, suggest that it was an uprising by the same sort of Shadowlander troublemakers who had supported the Black Company during the Kiaulune wars. They were milking that connection from the past, trying to intimidate opponents and encourage friends. There was no Black Company anymore.

Rumor had not yet discovered the Prahbrindrah Drah and his sister. Mogaba would offer the suggestion that those people were imposters when stories did begin to circulate.

"This is actually going better than I expected," the Great General told Aridatha Singh. "None of the garrison commanders have refused their marching orders. Only a handful of the senior priests and leading men have tried to pretend neutrality."

"I wonder if that state would persist if we lost the Protector."

Mogaba had been trying to find out for some time. The Prahbrindrah Drah had yet to produce an heir. His only living relative was his sister, who had run Taglios and its dependencies for years in fact, if not in name. At one point she had proclaimed herself her brother's successor. Though the culture militated against a female ruler she might be allowed to take over again if her brother preceded her in death. No one knew what would happen if brother and sister were both gone, as most of the population believed them to be.

The question was entirely an intellectual exercise, these days. Power in Taglios belonged to the Protector almost exclusively.

Mogaba never pressed his questions beyond a purely speculative level. None of his respondents suspected a deeper purpose. Nor did anyone volunteer to participate in an effort to get rid of the Protector, though it was no secret that most Taglians would prefer to do without Soulcatcher's protection.

Communications with Soulcatcher had ceased. The crow population had suffered a dramatic decimation, whether from disease or enemy action remaining unclear. Their numbers had been dwindling for decades, until murders in the wild were almost unknown. Bats could not carry significant messages. Owls would not. And there was no one at the Taglian and trained to manage and communicate with shadows. That was a rare talent indeed and the Black Company had exterminated the brotherhood who had shared it back when they were still running things their way.

Soulcatcher had scoured the Shadowlands, whence those people had sprung, length and breadth. She had turned up just a few old women and very young children who had survived all the wars and purges. They seemed to be a people unrelated to any other in the south, had been unknown there before the advent of the Shadowmasters, and among themselves had a oral tradition of having come from an entirely different world. Those old women and babies had lacked any useful knowledge or talent.

When his duties granted the time, Mogaba walked the main route from the Palace to the city's southern entrance. The walls had been under construction for decades and remained unfinished but the southern gate complex, the most important, had been completed and put into use ages ago. By channeling traffic through its bottleneck the state managed to tax all incoming travelers.

He was looking for the perfect place to put an end to the Protectorate. Four explorations had not revealed it yet. The obvious sites were just that: obvious. Soulcatcher would be alert. She was intimate enough with human nature to realize that rumors fed by the crisis in the south would reawaken opposition to her rule.

There seemed to be no way to manage it in the streets. And the longer it was delayed the more certain she was to become suspicious of her captains. It would be impossible for them to conceal their nervousness.

It would have to be instantly upon her arrival or immediately upon her entering the Palace. Or never.

They could forget the whole thing, go back to being her faithful hounds, and wait with her for the disaster from the south.

When Mogaba thought of the Company he shuddered and was most sorely tempted to abandon the plot against the Protector. Soulcatcher would be a potent weapon in that war.

The gate. The south gate. It had to happen there. The complex had been engineered for exactly that sort of thing, although on a larger scale.

When he returned to the palace he found Aridatha Singh waiting. "There was a messenger, General. The Protector has reached Dejagore. She took time out to review the troops assembling there, though it would seem the enemy isn't that far behind."

Mogaba made a face. "We don't have much time left, then. She won't lag long behind our couriers." Unspoken, but understood, remained the fact that they were running out of time to chose their final commitment.

Then Mogaba grunted. He had realized, suddenly, that the Protector could pluck the whole opportunity right out of their hands. Easy as snapping her fingers.

40

The Taglian Territories: Below Lake Tanji

We overtook Sleepy in the hills beyond the north shore of Lake Tanji. Lady hurried ahead. She knew better but could not help herself.

Runmust Singh's rangers were still somewhere out ahead of the main force. They were close enough for their camp-fires to be seen across the barrier hills but recent hard rains had flooded the ravines and creeks between here and there. Which was the only reason we had caught Sleepy so soon. The flooding had slowed her down.

"It won't be long," she told us. "Unless we get more rain. These washes drain fast."

I knew. I fought the Shadowmasters across these hills, many years ago.

My wife was exasperated. She turned on Tobo, who, with his father, was renewing acquaintances with Sahra. "When are you going to learn enough about those damned posts so we can use them?" A little flooding would slow nobody if we could fly.

Tobo told Lady the truth, which was the last thing she wanted to hear. "It might be months yet. Maybe even years. If we're all so anxious to become more mobile, why don't we wake the Howler up and make a deal for some flying carpets?"

Debate was immediate and brisk with almost everyone feeling a need to offer an opinion. Goblin, Doj, Lady, Tobo, Sahra, Willow Swan, Murgen, Goblin again. Even Thai Dei looked like he had a viewpoint, though he kept it to himself.

I realized that Sleepy had not stated her opinion. In fact, her eyes had glazed over. She was far, far away. Her intensity was disturbing.

One by one, the others fell silent. A foreboding emotional murk began to gather. I looked for Unknown Shadows but saw nothing. What was going on?

Tobo spoke up first. "Captain? What's the matter?" Sleepy had begun to lose color. I got up to go find my medical kit.

Sleepy came out of it. "Tobo." Her voice was so intense silence spread in all directions. "Did you remember to restore the shadowgate so it won't collapse if Longshadow dies?"

The silence deepened. Suddenly we were holding our breaths. And staring at Tobo. And every one of us knowing the answer even if we had not been there and did not want it to be true.

Sleepy said, "They've had him in Hsien for as long as we've been here. He was a frail old man. He won't last."

Without saying a word Tobo started getting ready to travel. Groaning, I clambered to my feet and began getting my stuff together, too. Tobo began telling his father and Uncle Doj how to manage the Voroshk. "You have to keep them engaged. Keep them trying to learn. Keep them away from Goblin. You'll need to force-feed the sick one. I don't think he's going to last much longer."

I was not sure I overheard that last remark. He spoke very softly.

He was right. The kid was slipping away. I could not stop it.

I looked hard at Lady, who had shown no sign of getting ready to do what had to be done. I told her, "You need to come. Following Tobo you're our best gate mechanic." I offered a hand.

Murgen, I noted, was paying his son's instructions no attention. He was getting ready to travel, too.

Lady's expression hardened. She accepted my hand. Upright, she stared northward. The fires in Runmust's camp were not visible now. Rain was falling between here and there.

Several others, including Willow Swan, quietly began getting ready to travel, too. No names were named, no orders were given. Those who needed to go or thought their presence would be useful began packing. Nobody grumbled. Nobody said much of anything at all. We were all too tired to waste energy doing anything but what had to be done.

No fingers got pointed, either. It took no genius to understand that Tobo had been swallowed up by his own workload, with people wanting something more from him every minute. Sleepy bore the heaviest responsibility. It was her job to see that everything got done. She should have had a checklist. But she had been singleminded in her desire to move faster than resistance could coagulate in front of her.

For that she could not be faulted. The Company had seen no fighting yet, though nearly a quarter of the Taglian empire could be accounted disarmed. It was the most remote and lightly populated quarter but the strategy remained sound.

The wealth Sleepy had brought off the plain would let her exploit the territories we held far more effectively than would Soulcatcher's capacity for generating terror allow her to exploit what she held.

Of course, if the shadowgate collapsed all that would be moot. Our world would be in greater danger than Khatovar. Unlike the Voroshk, we could not defend ourselves.

Tobo did not bother collecting the few bamboo fireball

throwers left. If we became desperate enough to need them that handful would not do any good.

There were eight of us. Tobo and his father, me, Lady, Willow Swan, and Thai Dei because Murgen never got out of rock-throwing range of Tobo's uncle. Then there were two older-than-average hardcases from Hsien, solid veterans of the warlord conflicts. One we knew as Panda Man because his real name sounded like that. The other was Spook. He was Spook because he had green eyes. In Hsien demons and haunts are supposed to have green eyes.

The Unknown Shadows refuse to conform. Every one of those haunts that I have actually seen had the more traditional red or yellow eyes.

Many of the Unknown Shadows traveled with us. At night, under the moon when it made its infrequent, shy appearances, the ground surrounding us seemed to be a sea in motion. Tobo's pets did not mind being seen just now.

Before long my two ravens rejoined me. I had seen nothing of them since shortly after we had left the shadowgate.

Tobo told me, "I've sent scouts ahead. Now I'm going to ride ahead, too." He was mounted on Sleepy's superhorse. "The rest of you follow me as fast as you can."

He surged ahead. Most of the churning darkness went with him, though we retained enough shadowy outriders that no danger would take us by surprise.

"I'm sorry," I told Lady.

"Not your fault this time." She was not happy, though.

"You gotten anything out of Kina yet?"

"No. Nothing but a few infrequent touches while we were up there with Sleepy. They were pretty faint and probably just because we were close to Booboo."

Damn. "You think we can get back to the gate in time?"

"You think Longshadow will fight for life if he knows that the only thing he can accomplish is to save the people who pulled him down and turned him over to his oldest enemies?"

That was not the answer I wanted to hear.

41

The Nether Taglian Territories: Leaves of Misfortune

Runmust and Iqbal rode northward slowly, at a pace their whole band found comfortable. Life would not be too hard until the Captain caught up. She would be put out because the rangers did not meet her as soon as possible. She would get over it.

The prisoners were given no opportunity to enjoy life, but they were not tormented directly. The Singhs would not have allowed that even had they known that Sleepy would not mind.

There was no formal arrangement between the Singhs and the dark spirits out of Hsien but Unknown Shadows paced them always. Communications remained crude. Runmust generally just got a really bad feeling when it was time to watch out. The problem was his. A religious failing. He was allowed no congress with demons. His innate human knack for rationalization had not yet exonerated the Unknown Shadows from being spawn of darkness.

Runmust began to have one of those bad feelings. It grew worse fast. Iqbal's uneasiness said that he had been touched, too. Even some of the soldiers were becoming troubled.

Quick hand gestures. The ranger team halted. Everyone dismounted. Scouts crept forward while the men assigned the duty for the day began moving the prisoners and horses into a gulch off the road.

The warriors of Hsien could be remarkly quiet and patient. Runmust admired their skill in using the available cover in terrain, boasting only tangled, scrubby brush, rocks and lots of gullys. He could not do what they did. Of course, he was twice the size of the biggest and a decade older than the oldest.

Minh Bhu, one of the best, intercepted him in his slow advance, after signing for absolute silence.

Minh brushed leaves aside and smoothed a patch of dirt. He used a forefinger to sketch the ground ahead, indicating the approximate positions of a well-chosen ambush site.

Runmust signaled a general withdrawal. He looked for crows or other creatures traditionally associated with the enemy. He saw nothing. "How could they know we were coming?" he asked when he was far back enough to whisper. "How many of them are there?"

Minh shrugged. "We're not going to get a head count. There are a lot more of them than there are of us. And as for how did they know, from that hilltop you can see all the country we crossed the last two days. They were probably just sent out to see if this is the route north the Captain picks." He pointed back south. The dust and sparkle of the main force were obvious.

"Why an ambush?"

"They can see there aren't many of us. It would look like a chance to take some prisoners."

"Uhm." Runmust scanned the slope. Could he turn the tables on those people? He wished he had developed a more intimate relationship with the Unknown Shadows. "Iqbal. Talk to me."

"We're outnumbered, we should back away. There's no reason to get in a fight. Or even make contact. We've got important prisoners to protect. So let's stay away and wait for the Captain."

Iqbal was a married man. He did not favor major risks.

Even so, Iqbal was right. Withdrawal was the only course that was not crazy. Runmust asked, "What would they do if we did stroll into their trap?" He wished he could catch a couple of them. A few questions answered would tell a lot about enemy plans and what the other side thought was happening.

"They see Sleepy coming. They'll pull out pretty soon."

"Why do I keep getting more and more nervous?" Runmust knew the Unknown Shadows wanted him to know something and he just was not hearing it.

In the hills ahead horses began screaming. Men cursed. Several dozen arrows rose into the air, fell where the enemy evidently thought the rangers were hidden. None of the arrows came close.

Muttering curses himself, Runmust waved his men back again. They began slipping away. Wildly sped arrows fell all across the slope. "Idiots," Runmust muttered. "Recon by fire." The Protector's soldiers would charge any outcry. Or any other obvious reaction. They were an opportunity to inflict disaster just waiting to happen.

A Taglian soldier sprang up not ten feet from Runmust, barking in pain as he swatted his ass. Runmust froze, hoping the Taglian was too preoccupied to notice him—though now he heard other Taglians pushing through the dry brush and knew he could not sneak off fast enough to get away untouched.

Iqbal carried a fireball launcher. He was supposed to use it as an emergency signal, not as a weapon. It was believed to contain just one charge. It was ancient. There was no guarantee it would work at all.

Iqbal, unseen by the man who had now spied Runmust, rotated, the handgrip trigger on that piece of bamboo.

An intense yellow ball slammed right through the Protector's man and rattled around in the brush behind him. In seconds a dozen fires were burning.

Runmust and Iqbal ran. No point doing anything else now.

They had almost reached the gully hiding the animals and prisoners when a random arrow found the unprotected meat of Runmust's right thigh. Singh flung forward in an uncontrolled dive. His beard protected his face as he ploughed through the brush but he left large tufts behind. He squealed with the unexpected pain.

Iqbal stopped to help.

"Get out of here!" Runmust growled. "You have Suru-vhija and the children." Which moved Iqbal not at all.

The Taglian troops blundered down the hillside, scattered, in no order, without discipline or thought. Officers, sergeants and men, they had no practical experience and very little training. They had come out of the Nijha fortress because Soulcatcher had told them they might achieve a startling triumph. But once the situation on the ground deviated from their expectations they were lost.

Stumbling, dragging the leg with the arrow still embedded, Runmust clung to and leaned on Iqbal. Both men heard the exultant Taglian soldiers plunging through the brush behind them, swiftly bringing the inevitable.

The rangers were men chosen from those who had seen prior action serving the warlords in Hsien and who both understood Company doctrine and accepted it. They set an ambush of their own. The Taglians came to it as though guided by maleficent demons.

The result was a bloodbath. It was a tactical triumph for the Black Company. It was not unalloyed by bad news. In the end, in the heat of the moment, the rangers did fail to acknowledge doctrine. They did not fade away while the Taglians were confused and panicky. They maintained contact in hopes of making sure Runmust and Iqbal escaped.

The Singh brothers did survive. But when the light cavalry, flung forward by Sleepy right after she recognized the fireball signal, arrived they found most of the rangers wounded or dead after having been overrun. The horsemen pursued the fleeing Taglians. They cut down most of the enemy wounded and stragglers.

Sadly, they failed to recapture the Daughter of Night.

A particularly bright Taglian officer had recognized what he had stumbled across and got the girl moving to the rear immediately. Her grub-colored skin had given her away.

When that day's sun set it was a tossup which side would

consider the encounter the greater disaster. The Company had lost a huge treasure and some of its most valuable men, at least for a while. The Taglians had endured a huge massacre with only one sullen, if exotically beautiful, pale, dirty young woman to show for all the deaths.

42

The Nether Taglian Territories:
After Battle

The Captain herself reached the scene of the fighting just an hour after its end. She stomped around. She nagged the survivors with questions. Most of the rangers had survived but only two had managed without suffering serious wounds. Sleepy interrogated prisoners even more emphatically. The cavalrymen had retained sense enough to capture a few Taglians who offered to surrender, presuming they would continue to cooperate to save their skins.

None of the prisoners knew anything about the Daughter of Night. None even knew that name.

The Captain's prowling took her near Narayan Singh. She kicked the old cripple. "Hellspawn." She turned, bellowed, "Why didn't we know about this ambush ahead of time?"

Some bold soul told her the truth. "The Unknown Shadows probably did know. But nobody asked them. Tobo is the only one who knows how to talk to them the way it takes to get them to do the kind of spying you want."

Sleepy growled. She kicked Narayan Singh again. She paced. "What do we know about this fort?"

Blade came forward. He would save the others. Sleepy's wrath fell less heavily upon him. Usually. Some thought she was a little afraid of Blade. In fact, she was just not sure of him, though he had been around longer than she had. Like

Swan and Sahra, he was not actually a sworn brother of the Company. But he was always there and always involved.

Blade said, "The old Captain established it. It was a remount station for the first courier post. The wall got added because the natives kept trying to steal the horses. Soulcatcher eventually expanded the fort and garrison during the Kiaulune wars because she wanted a stronger presence here in case her enemies tried to sneak north this way. Assuming she did here the way she did everywhere else, she forgot the place as soon as the fighting was over. The garrison might be a hundred fifty or two hundred. Plus hangers-on."

"Pretty big gang for out here."

"It's a big territory. And half of them are out of business now."

"What're the fortifications like?"

"I've never been there. I hear they're barely good enough to stop horse thieves. Which means not real impressive. Some kind of rock wall, since that's the available material around here. I've heard there's a ditch that was never completed. Didn't you come this way when you ran south? Didn't you see it?"

"We took a trail west of here. The old trade road. We avoided the courier routes."

"You might send some cavalry to surround the place before they can move the girl out."

Sleepy mused, "It's probably too late to stop them yelling for help."

Blade said, "I don't think you need to worry about sneaking. By now Soulcatcher's got the whole Taglian empire alerted."

Sleepy grunted. Then she sent for cavalry officers. And after she sent them off she visited Runmust and Iqbal. Those two had been close friends for two decades. She asked Iqbal's wife, Suruvhija, "What did the surgeon say?"

"They'll recover. They're Shadar. They're strong men. They fought well. God will watch over them."

Sleepy glanced at Sahra, who was helping tend the wounded. Sahra nodded, meaning Suruvhija was not just wishful thinking.

"I'll include them in my prayers as well." Sleepy squeezed Suruvhija's shoulder reassuringly, thinking the woman was too perfect to be real. At least as men saw wives. But she was Shadar, too, and she believed, and the roles of all members of the family were clearly defined by her religion.

Sleepy took time to talk to Iqbal's children, too. They were bearing up bravely. As they would, for they were good Shadar, too, despite the strange lands and societies they had seen.

When she was around Iqbal's children, Sleepy sometimes even vaguely regretted having abandoned the woman's role. But that never lasted more than a few seconds.

"Blade. Pass the word. I want the whole gang up to this fort before sunset. If that's possible. Once they see some numbers I'm sure they'll give up."

Blade told her, "You know you have to stop before long. The animals need time to graze and recover. And we have a tail of stragglers that has to stretch all the way back to Charandaprash."

People got hurt or sick or just could not keep up. It irked Sleepy but it was a fact of life. Her strength was down maybe a thousand men already. That would worsen rapidly if she continued to drive hard.

"When they get here the most worn-out ones can take over as our garrison." That was a tactic as old as soldiering.

She would not admit it but she needed a rest herself. She could not imagine when she would get one, though.

43

The Taglian Shadowlands:
The Shadowgate

Seem like there's much point dragging my weary ass over there?" I asked Lady. There was just enough dawn-light to show the vague outline of the slope leading up to the shadowgate. Which was still miles and miles from where we had spent the night. This part of the journey was one of those where you spend the whole day trying not to look ahead because every time you do it seems you have not gotten ten feet closer. Way to our left a smoky haze concealed the New City and the lower half of ruined Overlook. A lot of unpleasant memories connected us with those places.

"What do you mean?" My sweetheart was as tired and morning-cranky as I was. And her bones were a lot older than mine.

"Well, we didn't get killed last night. That means the gate hasn't collapsed yet. Old Longshadow's still holding out."

"Evidently."

"Wouldn't that mean Tobo's got everything under control? So why beat ourselves up getting on over there?"

Lady smirked at me. She did not have to tell me. We would cross the valley because, in the end, I would want to see everything for myself. Because I would want to get it all into the Annals, right. She had chided me fifty times during the ride south because I was trying to work out a way to write on horseback. I could get so much more done if I could do it while we were traveling.

Then she chirped, "You are getting old."

"What?"

"A sign of advancing age. You start obsessing about how much you have to get done in the time that you have left."

I made noises in the back of my throat but did not argue.

That kind of thinking was familiar. So was being unable to fall asleep because I was tracking my heartbeat, trying to tell if something was wrong.

You would think a guy in my line of work would make his peace with death at an early age.

We ran into several locals while crossing the valley, the bottom land of which was decent farmland and pasture. We did not receive one friendly greeting. I did not see one welcoming smile. Nobody raised a hand in defiance but I had no trouble feeling the abiding resentment of a tormented nation. There had been no serious fighting in these parts for years but the adult population were all survivors of the terrible times, whether they were natives or immigrants who had come in to settle the depopulated lands and to escape even worse horrors elsewhere. They did not want the evils of the past to return.

This land had suffered grotesquely under the Shadowmaster Longshadow. It had continued to suffer after his defeat. The Kiaulune wars devoured most everything that Longshadow and the Shadowmaster wars had not. And now the Black Company had returned. Out of the place of glittering stone, an abode of devils. The season of despair appeared to be threatening again.

"Can't say I blame them," I told Lady.

"What?"

I explained.

"Oh." Indifferently. Some attitudes never wither. She had been a powerful lord a lot longer than she had been just another tick on the underbelly of the world. Compassion is not one of the qualities that endeared her to me.

We found Tobo impatient with our dawdling. "I see the old gal's still here," I said of the shadowgate. Lady and I produced our keys and let the crew cross over, Murgen first so he could make sure his boy still had all his arms and legs and fingers and toes.

"It is," the wonder child confessed. "But probably only

because Longshadow still hasn't left the plain."

"What?" Lady was irritated. "We made promises. We owe the Children of the Dead."

"We do," Tobo said. "But we won't be allowed to kill ourselves. Shivetya knew we forgot to disarm Longshadow's booby trap so he kept Longshadow from leaving."

"How do you know that?"

"I sent messengers. That was the news they brought back."

Lady's mood had not improved. "The File of Nine will be smoking. We don't need them as enemies. We may have to flee to the Land of Unknown Shadows again."

"Shivetya will release Longshadow the second we finish refurbishing our gate."

My companions were nervous. Willow Swan was pale, sweating, dancing with anxiety and, most of all, un-Swanlike, silent. He had not, in fact, spoken all day.

Thinking about the shadows can do that to you if you have witnessed one of their attacks.

Tobo asked, "You two ready to go to work?"

I shook my head. "Are you kidding?"

Lady said, "No."

Tobo told us, "I can't finish this alone."

I replied, "And you can't finish it with assistants so tired they're guaranteed to make mistakes. I have a premonition. Longshadow will keep till tomorrow."

Tobo admitted that he would. Shivetya would see to it. But he did so with poor grace.

Lady said, "Let's go set up camp." Murgen, Swan and the others probably should have been doing that instead of standing around being anxious.

Once we crossed the barrier Lady wondered, "Why is Tobo in such a hurry?"

I snickered. "I think it might have to do with Booboo. He hasn't seen her for a long time. Sleepy says he was completely smitten."

While I spoke her expression transformed from curious to completely appalled. "I'd hope not."

Murgen suggested, "There were two rather attractive Voroshk girls. One of them might have something to do with it."

44

The Shadowlands: Gate Repairs

The dreamwalkers came during the night. Their presence was so powerful that even Swan, Panda Man and Spook saw them. I heard them speak clearly although I never understood a word.

Lady and Tobo did get something out of them.

They put their heads together over breakfast. They decided that the Nef wanted to warn us about something.

"You think so?" I sneered. "There's a new interpretation."

"Hey!" Tobo chided me. "It has something to do with Khatovar."

"Like what, for example?"

The youth shrugged. "Your guess is better than mine. I've never been there."

"Last time we saw the dreamwalkers they were headed out into Khatovar in the middle of all the shadows on the plain. You think they saw something they think we ought to know?"

"Absolutely. Any idea what?"

Lady asked, "Have you had your Unknown Shadow friends try to talk to the Nef?"

"I have. It doesn't work. The Nef don't communicate with the plain shadows, either."

"Then what was the Unknown Shadows' problem last night? The Black Hounds kept carrying on so bad they woke me up several times."

"Really?" Tobo was puzzled. "I never noticed."

Nor did I. But I am deaf and blind to most supernatural stuff. Plus, for once, I had not been tossing around listening for my heart to stop.

"Let's get to work."

"Booboo isn't going anywhere, kid."

Tobo frowned. Then got it. He did not become embarrassed or defensive. "Oh? Oh. You don't know? She's already gone. There was a fight with the garrison from Nijha. Runmust's troop got overrun. The Taglians captured the Daughter of Night. Sleepy has cavalry trying to run them down now."

I shook my head and grumped, "It won't do her any good. A million horsemen won't be enough now."

"Aren't you pessimistic."

"He's right," Lady opined. She lapsed into an old northern language I had not heard since I was young and which I never had understood completely. She seemed to be reciting a song as a poem. It had a refrain that went something like, "Thus do the Fates conspire."

We were on the inside of the shadowgate, hard at it. Tobo was making tiny, elegant adjustments to the strands and layers of magic that made up the mystic portal. The training I had received had elevated me to the level of a semiskilled bricklayer. Compared to me Tobo was the sort of master artisan who created panoramic tapestries by weaving them instead of embroidering them. I was nothing but the lead finger man on the bow-tying team.

Even Lady was little more than a hodcarrier on this job. But hodcarriers are needed, too.

"Thanks for the compliment," Tobo said after I tried out my similes. "But I'm mostly doing embroidery and plain old-fashioned knot tying on broken threads. Parts of this tapestry were plain outright crippled. It'll never be completely right, even if it's stronger than when it started."

"But you can weasel Longshadow's booby trap out of there?"

"It's kind of like lancing a boil and cleaning it out, but yes. He actually made a pretty crude job of it. Obviously, he didn't know much about shadowgates. He did know that there was no one in our world who knew more. What he didn't understand was that there were more keys."

"Of course he knew," I said. "That's why he sent Ashutosh Yaksha, his apprentice, to infiltrate the Nyueng Bao priests at the temple of Ghanghesha."

Tobo looked puzzled, like he did not recall that story.

"He knew they had a key there and he wanted it. So he could get back to Hsien. If you don't know that story you'd better corner your uncle. Because that's what he told Sleepy."

Tobo smiled weakly. "Well, maybe. I suppose."

"What do you mean, you suppose?"

Lady paused what she was doing. "Don't play Doj's games, Tobo. You won't be fooling anybody. I was there. Inside the white crow. I know what the man said."

"That's probably it. Doj told Sleepy a bunch of stories. Some were probably true but some he probably made up. Stuff he thought might be true because it sounded plausible based on what he did know. Master Santaraksita spent years searching the records at Khang Phi. The history of our world's Nyueng Bao isn't much like what Doj might've wanted you to believe."

"Which was it?" I mused aloud. "Was he lying or making it up?" I have known plenty of people who would not admit ignorance even in the most obvious circumstance.

Tobo said, "Master Santaraksita says our ancestors left Hsien as fugitives, sneaking out like snakes using a secretly manufactured key. They were trying to get away from the Shadowmasters. There was supposed to be a regular, gradual evacuation across the plain. Because they were persecuted followers of Khadi they did favor the organizational structure we've seen in other bands of believers but those people weren't mercenaries and they weren't missionaries. They weren't a Free Company. They weren't a band of Stranglers. They were just running away because the Shadowmasters insisted they had to give up their religion. Master Santaraksita says their priests probably made up a more dramatic history after they'd been settled in the river delta for a while. After several generations spent wandering. Before they arrived the only people in the swamp were Taglian fugitives and criminals and a few remote descendants of the Deceivers Rhaydreynek tried to wipe out. Maybe the Nyueng Bao wanted to impress them."

Tobo's hands never stopped moving while he talked. But their movements had nothing to do with what he was saying. He was mending things that I could not see.

"How much did Doj lie?" I was determined to pin that on him. I never did trust that old man.

"That's the intriguing part. I don't know. I don't think he really knows. He did tell me that a lot of what he told Sleepy originally he said just because it sounded believable and like something she wanted to hear. When you get right down to it, except for his skill with Ash Wand, Uncle Doj is a bigger fraud than most priests. Most priests actually believe what they preach."

Lady said, "Sounds like he's spent time hanging around with Blade."

Tobo continued, "The key my ancestors used to cross the plain was created secretly in Khang Phi. It went back to Hsien so the next group of fugitives could use it. They never got the chance."

"But they had the golden pick." Which was the key that Sleepy eventually found and used to get onto the plain so she could release us Captured from underneath Shivetya's fortress.

"That must have been the key that belonged to the Deceivers who hid the Books of the Dead back in Rhaydreynek's time. They must've hidden the pickax under the temple of Ghanghesha. The temple has a long history. It started out as a Janaka shrine. The Gunni took over and used it as a retreat. Then the survivors of Rhaydreynek's pogrom chased the Gunni out. But they faded away. Nyueng Bao folklore talks about bitter fighting over doctrine in the early days. A century later Gunni holy men from the cult of Ghanghesha began to come back to the swamp. Eventually most Nyueng Bao forgot Khadi and adopted Ghanghesha. A few generations back the pick turned up when the temple was being repaired. Somebody realized that it had to be an important relic. It wasn't till more recent times, when Longshadow, and later Soulcatcher, found out about it, that anyone realized how important it had to be."

"What about the pilgrimages?"

"Originally people from Hsien were supposed to meet our people at the shadowgate with news from home and more refugees. But the Shadowmasters found out. Plus on this side my ancestors lost touch with the past. Contrary to legend, and unlike the way things are now, there wasn't that much pressure from outside. Hanging on to old ways and old ideas wasn't that important a way to maintain the identity of the Nyueng Bao.

"Whatever Doj says, most Nyueng Bao aren't devoted to tradition and keeping the old ways. Most don't remember anything anymore. You saw that while we were in Hsien. The Nyueng Bao aren't anything like those people over there."

Lady and I exchanged looks. Neither of us assumed Tobo was telling any more of the truth than Doj ever had. Though the boy was not necessarily lying consciously. I glanced at Thai Dei. He gave nothing away.

I said, "I've been wondering why Doj never found any Path of the Sword guys over there."

"That's easy. The Shadowmasters wiped them out. They were the warrior caste. They kept fighting till there weren't any of them left."

I had, for years, wondered why a sword-worshipping cult would be part of a people descended from a band of worshippers of Kina, who, in my world, did not believe in shedding blood. I still did not know. But now I knew that nobody else was likely to know, either.

I told Lady, "I'm surprised Sleepy never picked up on the fact that the supposed priest of this Nyueng Bao band went around carving people into steaks."

"Deceiver people at that," she added. "He slaughtered them by the score at Charandaprash."

Tobo is a clever young man. He understood that we did not find his version of history more convincing than Doj's.

I still was not sure whether he believed what he was saying.

It did not matter.

Lady poked me. She whispered, "Murgen and Willow Swan have drawn my attention to an interesting phenomenon. You'll want to see for yourself. Tobo, drop doing what you're doing and look at this, too."

By then I knew it would be something I did not want to see. Thai Dei, Murgen and the others were debating the best places to take cover already.

I turned. Lady pointed. A trio of Voroshk flyers, appearing only slightly larger than dots, hovered above the rim of the plain. They were way up high and a long way away, motionless.

I asked, "Anybody want to guess how well they can see us?"

Lady said, "They can tell we're here but that's it. Unless they have a farseeing device."

"What're they doing?"

"Scouting around, I imagine. Now that their gate is gone they can get onto the plain whenever they want. During the day they're safe as long as they stay off the ground. And they probably won't have much trouble with shadows even at night if they stay high up. We've never seen shadows go higher than ten or fifteen feet above the surface of the shielding."

"Think they're looking for us? Or are they just looking?"

"Both, probably. They'll want revenge. And maybe even a safe new world."

The Voroshk did not move while we were talking. I pictured similar trios ranging to all points of the plain, perhaps hoping they could open the way without us. "Tobo, can they get off of the plain?"

"I don't know. They won't be able to here. Not without one of my keys. I'll install something that'll kill them if they try."

I admired his confidence. "Suppose they have somebody as slick as you are? What's to keep him from undoing your spells the way you're undoing Longshadow's?"

"Lack of training. Lack of the knowledge we got out of Khang Phi. You have to know a little about these things to redo them."

Lady asked, "Can they break through the gateway into Hsien?" The knowledge was there.

"I don't know. They got the forvalaka through. Maybe they could shove their own people through on a slow, one-at-a-time basis. They never tried before. But they've never been desperate before. And time isn't on their side."

"What about Shivetya? What's his take on this?"

"I'll find out. I'll send a messenger in just a minute."

One of the soldiers from Hsien—Panda Man, I think—asked, "What about the men with Longshadow? If he hasn't left the plain. One is my cousin."

Tobo drew a long, deep breath. "My work is never done."

Lady said, "If you're going to do something you'd better do it fast. They have a key. It's at risk."

"Damn! You're right. Captain, I'm going to borrow your ravens. Lady, lean out the gate and yell for Big Ears and Cat Sith. They'll hear you. Tell them I want them. It's an emergency."

"One damned thing after another," I grumbled. "It never lets up."

"But you're alive," Swan said.

"Don't you be jumping around on the other side of your

own argument." We amused ourselves with some good-natured bickering while Tobo sent supernatural messengers off to Shivetya, the guards at the Hsien shadowgate, Long-shadow's keepers, and our folks up north.

Along the way Murgen asked his son, "What's to keep those jokers up there from just flying off the plain? I remember times when crows came and went." And he used to do so himself, all the time

"They could do that because they come from our world. Crows from any other world we wouldn't have seen at all. Even if they were there. Yes. The Voroshk can fly out any time they want. But when they do they'll end up in Khatovar. Every time. If they want to get off the plain into another world they'll have to come onto it through their shadowgate and leave it through another shadowgate. Shivetya restructured it that way."

It can be confusing. I guess that happens where realities overlap, with a deathless demigod in the middle who feels compelled to make it hard for the human species to realize its darkest potential.

45

Nijha:
The Stronghold Falls

There were fewer than fifty soldiers to hold Nijha's walls, most of them injured already and all of them thoroughly terrified after having endured a night overrun by the Unknown Shadows.

The defenders were accorded the honors of war and allowed to march out without their weapons, taking their families and what possessions they could carry. They were admonished to clear the road whenever the Black Company passed.

* * *

If the Nijha stronghold had surrendered any faster Sleepy would have worried that she was walking into a trap. As it was, she did send Doj in first to make sure Soulcatcher had left her no special little gifts.

She had not.

"Put Narayan somewhere where he can't embarrass me," Sleepy ordered after the stronghold had been declared secure. "I'll decide what to do with him in a day or two." She would have preferred handing him over to Lady and Croaker right away. "Battalion, regiment, and brigade commanders and all senior staff are to assemble in the local headquarters building in one hour."

Sahra asked, "You think there'll be room? I really thought this place would be bigger."

"So did I. Even though we knew it was a glorified remount station. Gosh, I wish Tobo was here instead of down there."

"So do I." Sahra hated having her whole family so far away. She had become accustomed to having a real family again during our years in Hsien. "I've been thinking. Wouldn't it be reasonable to keep Tobo and Murgen from going to the same dangerous places?"

"Like the shadowgate?"

"Like that. Or anywhere else where one bad blow could take them both away."

Sleepy understood Sahra's agony. Sahra had lost two children and one husband to malignant fortune already. The husband did not trouble her much. His removal had improved her life. But rare is the mother who will not ache forever over the loss of her little ones.

All part of the wondrous cruel experience of the siege of Jaicur, or Dejagore, that has twisted so many members of the Company and burdened them with vulnerabilities and obsessions that will shape their minds and souls for as long as they survive.

"That's a good idea," Sleepy said. "Although you can count on getting resistance from the men. Can you imagine Runmust and Iqbal being willing to go anywhere where they're not elbow to elbow with each other?"

Sahra sighed. She shook her head slowly. "If the Gunni are right about the Wheel of Life then I must have been something more wicked than a Shadowmaster in a previous life. This one never stops punishing me."

"Let me tell you, it's harder being Vehdna. You don't have other lives to blame it on. You just go crazy trying to figure out why God is so angry with you in this one."

Sahra nodded. The moment had passed. She was in control again. "You'd think I would've made my peace with this life by now, wouldn't you?"

Sleepy thought that she had, about as well as she could, but did not say so. She did not want to push Sahra back onto the path of self-examination. That could get tiresome fast.

"We have a major staff meeting. I want your help. I want you to think in broader terms. I'm rethinking my strategy. The distances are turning out to be too great for a headlong rush. We're getting weaker fast while our enemies are getting stronger. I want your thoughts on different approaches."

"I'll be all right. I have to have these spells once in a while just to get by."

46

Nijha:
The Darkness Always Comes

Darkness came to Nijha. With it came an almost super-natural silence. Within the crude walls the senior commanders were clustered with Sleepy and Sahra. Outside, the soldiers were cooking, repairing harnesses and equipment, or, mainly, just sleeping the sleep of the exhausted. A night's rest was never enough to recover fully from a hard day's march. Weariness accumulated, and more so when a force covered a lot of miles in a hurry.

For the first time since his liberation Goblin found himself unsupervised, overlooked, forgotten. He did not trust his observations for a while. These were sneaky people. Possibly they were testing him.

Eventually it became evident that he really was running free, unmonitored. This was early in the game and way remote but no better opportunity was ever likely to arise.

Narayan stirred warily, though his despair was such that he could generate little concern about his own continued well-being. Already he had been separated farther, if not longer, from the Daughter of Night than ever before since her birth. If he lost her there would be no reason to go on. It would be time to go home to Kina. There would be nothing more he could do. And there was little chance he would get any opportunity ever again, anyway. He was alive now only because these people were saving him as a plaything for the girl's birth parents. Again.

His days and hours were numbered and once again his faith was being tested sorely.

He heard a faint, breathy sound that seemed vaguely familiar. And it should be, he thought. His heart began to hammer. That was a Deceiver recognition sign meant for use in darkness exactly like this, where the usual hand signals would not work. He murmured countersigns. The effort set off a coughing fit.

The exchange continued until Narayan was satisfied that he had been located by a religious brother. He asked, "Why have you come? It won't be possible to rescue me." He used the secret Deceiver cant, which amounted to the final test. It would, at least, advise him of the status of his visitor. Not many recent converts were yet that advanced in their studies.

"The Goddess herself has sent me to relay her love and her esteem and her appreciation of all your sacrifices. She bid me to assure you that your rewards will be great. She wants you to understand that her resurrection is nearer than any nonbeliever suspects. She wants you to know that your efforts and your trials and your steadfast faith have made the difference. She wants you to know that her enemies soon will be overwhelmed and devoured. She wants you to know that she's watching over you and that you'll stand at her side when we celebrate the Year of the Skulls. She wants you to know that of all those who have ever served her, even of her many saints, you were her most favored."

47

The Shadowgate:
The Repairmen

The encampment below the shadowgate became the hub of a flood of Unknown Shadow traffic as Tobo tried to head off the Voroshk threat. He remained especially worried about Longshadow's keepers till Shivetya somehow assured him that they were invisible to Voroshk eyes.

"Do you trust him?" Lady asked. She being the most naturally paranoid of any of us at the shadowgate. "He might try to make a better deal with the Voroshk."

"What better deal? We're going to give him what he wants. Without trying to control him or even to get much out of him."

"Bet he thinks we're too good to be true, then." She was in a mood.

I asked, "What happened to the golden pickax? The Deceiver key to the shadowgates."

After a pause to make up his mind about what to admit, Tobo said, "I left it with Shivetya. We may need it again. When it's time to kill Kina. I couldn't think of any other place where it would be safer from her followers." He was troubled as he looked the rest of us over. He was thinking he should have kept that to himself. The golden pickax was an extremely holy Strangler relic that could also be used to help set Kina free.

He was afraid that at least one of us was sure to tell somebody what we had just heard.

It was a long night followed by what promised to be a longer day.

For the uninvolved members of the band these were trying times. There was nothing for them to do but play cards and wonder if the people of the New City would be crazy enough to attack us.

Panda Man and Spook mostly watched the game. They did not do well when they played. Tonk is one of the simplest games ever invented, rules-wise, but a huge part of it is the table talk that goes along with the actual picking up, discarding and laying down of cards. A group accustomed to one another is an entirely different animal from one where the players barely speak the same language. Wherever the Company stops for fifteen minutes a tonk game soon develops. The tradition began ages before my time. It will persist long after I am gone.

Gone. I tried to imagine what life might have been like had I left the Company sometime in the past. My imagination was not up to the task. I confess. I do not have the strength of personality to abandon everything I know, even when all that is just a meandering, unhappy path that, too often, wanders through the outlying marches of hell.

I was a zombie most of the day, carrying that hod for my young bricklayer while most of me was elsewhere, boldly adventuring across those fields of might-have-been.

Sometime late in the afternoon I told Lady, "I probably should tell you this more often. I love you and I'm glad Fate conspired to bring our lives together."

I stunned her into silence. I know Swan and Murgen gaped and spent some time trying to figure out if I thought I was dying.

The Voroshk had not overlooked us. They were cautious. They showed themselves briefly several times during the day. Their customary arrogance seemed in abeyance.

Once I left my own preoccupations behind I asked Tobo, "What do you suppose they're up to?" We had talked about it before but I am never entirely comfortable taking a sorcerer's motives at face value.

"Looking for hope. Or anything that will give them an edge. I expect that, right now, their world is more like hell than almost anything any priest ever imagined. Most of the surviving shadows from the plain must be running loose there. One family of sorcerers, however wonderful their weapons, just has no chance to stop what's happening. Not before the devastation reaches the scale of an end of the world catastrophe."

Once upon a time I might have felt bad for the Voroshk and the people of Khatovar. This time when I examined my soul I found not much more than indifference within me.

"How much longer before you've finished making all your modifications?" Lady demanded. She was anxious to head north. From oblique remarks I gathered that she wanted to rejoin the main force before disaster struck it. What she could do to avert a disaster was beyond me. She did not have enough magic currently to start a fire without adding flint and steel to the mix.

"Ten minutes, tops," Tobo replied. "There's this one last braided strand that needs reweaving and we'll have us not just a completely healthy shadowgate, it'll be the toughest there ever was. Tough enough that what happened to the Khatovar gate can't happen here. In fact, it's already all those things. What this spell rope is going to do is create a little pocket of darkness that's invisible from outside so killer shadows can be turned into invisible sentries. They'll be there ready to jump out at anybody who tries to get through who isn't already approved by us or Shivetya."

"Neat," I said. Lady scowled. She was determined to believe that we were placing too much trust in the golem.

She seemed unable to recognize that trust was not a large part of this equation.

She said, "We're going to have company in a minute."

I looked up. Two Voroshk sorcerers were coming down the slope, following the old road, inside what would have been protection if they had not blown up their own shadow-gate. A third post-rider remained a dot above the horizon, a remote witness. I asked, "You think they did more damage getting through the barrier and onto the road?"

After only a glance, Tobo said, "No. I think they came in the far end and flew here, following the roads. The other one paced them from above."

Admirable stupidity, I thought. The two at ground level had no chance of getting back out before dark. Did they think we would protect them from the night? If so they were huge daydreamers.

The Voroshk dismounted a hundred yards away. They walked toward us like walking was a foreign experience. Riding the flying fencepost had to be a huge status symbol back in Khatovar. So huge, walking was never done where your inferiors could see you.

"How long now?" Lady asked Tobo.

"Fifteen seconds. After that I'll fake it for a bit. Then we all step back through the gate. Are Dad and the others alert?"

Alert was not strong enough a word. A variety of missile weapons were ready. So was one fireball projector but it would not see use while the Voroshk remained on the plain side. The barriers could be damaged by fireballs. Arrows and crossbow bolts, however, could pass through and the wounds they made would heal in moments.

Not that arrows were likely to accomplish much against these chunky old men.

They did seem overweight. They projected an aura of fatness behind the constant stirring of their black cloaks.

"There. I think that should do it," Tobo said.

Click. Click. Click. That swiftly we three backed through the shadowgate into our own world. Tobo sealed the way. We waited. The kid said, "One of these will be the father of our two troublemakers."

Probably. The Voroshk did appear interested in communicating. They knew someone on our side spoke the language of the forvalaka.

Their luck was in. Of all the Black Company people who could have been there with Tobo they got me and Lady.

They would get no happiness out of that, though. Their kind rubbed me the wrong way. I would make nothing easy for them.

48

The Shadowgate:
The Warlords of the Air

These Voroshk, who actually introduced themselves—as Nashun the Researcher and the First Father—both spoke the language of Juniper. Nashun the Researcher had by far the best command. Neither had social skills of a sort likely to put a smile on the face of many mothers. It was clear that the demonstration of manners toward persons outside the family was an exercise with which they had little familiarity.

After the introductions I stated the obvious. "You people sure got yourselves into big trouble."

You could feel the Voroshk closing their eyes and sighing inside all that black material.

"We will survive," the boss Voroshk declared. He strained to keep anger and arrogance out of his voice. He had less success with confidence, which made me wonder if he did not really mean it.

"No doubt. What I saw of your family's capabilities impressed me. But honestly, you realize that your family's survival will require more than just fending off the shadows."

Nashun made a dismissive gesture with one gloved hand. "We come to you because we want our children back."

He spoke clearly and slowly enough that Lady caught that. She made a surprised little noise that might have been half a laugh.

"You're out of luck. They may prove useful. Nor have we any incentive to give them back."

Their anger seemed a palpable force.

Tobo felt it. He said, "Warn them that any power they use to try to break through will bounce back at them. Tell them that the harder they try the worse they'll get hurt."

I translated. Our visitors were not impressed by anything a boy said. Neither did they experiment. They did recall events at their own shadowgate. The Researcher said, "We are prepared to make an exchange."

"What do you have to trade?"

"You still have people on this plain."

"Go for it. They're covered. When the dust settles you'll be picking up dead family members." Of that I was confident. Because Tobo trusted Shivetya completely. "You're powerful but ignorant. Like an ox. You don't know the plain. It's alive. It's our ally."

Smoke should have rolled out of their ears. Goblin sometimes did that in the old days. But these men had no sense of humor.

Their desperation overcame their anger.

"Explain," Nashun hissed.

"You know nothing about the plain but you're arrogant enough to believe that your power will be supreme there. In a realm of the gods. Evidently you don't even know your own world's history. The people you're facing, that you believe you can threaten, are spiritual descendants of soldiers sent out from Khatovar five hundred years ago."

"What happened before the Voroshk does not signify. However, you demonstrate ignorance of your own."

"It *is* of consequence. You want something from the last Free Company of Khatovar. And you don't have anything to offer in exchange. Except, possibly, that disdained history and a little contemporary knowledge."

Neither man commented.

Lady told me, "Ask them why they want these kids back so bad. They're safe over here."

I asked.

"They are family," the First Father said.

His voice had a quality which made that seem not only plausible but possibly even true.

I said, "They're a long way away. They've been travelling northward steadily since they arrived. One is deathly ill."

"They have their *rheitgeistiden*. They can get down here in a few hours."

"I think this guy is for real," I told Lady. "He's really got some mad-ass notion that I'd give those kids their toys and turn them loose, just on his say-so. They sure don't have to work to survive in Khatovar."

The Researcher picked up the one word. "I mentioned your ignorance. Listen, Outsider. Khatovar is not our world. Khatovar was one city of darkness, where damned souls worshipped a Goddess of the night. That evil city was expunged from the earth before the Voroshk arose. Its people were hunted down and exterminated. They have been forgotten. And they will remain forgotten. Never will any Soldier of Darkness be permitted to return."

Once upon a time, on a lazy day, ages before he had become the vessel he was now, Goblin had told me that I would never get to Khatovar. Never. It would forever remain just beyond the horizon. I could get closer and closer and closer but I would never arrive. So I had imagined I had set foot in Khatovar. But I had only been to the world where Khatovar had existed once upon a time.

"Time itself has evened the score. That which Khatovar sent out came back. And the world that killed Khatovar will die."

"Did you catch that?" Lady asked.

"Huh? Catch what?"

"He used the world evil. We don't hear that much in this part of the world. People don't believe in it."

"These guys aren't from this part of the world." I returned to the language of Juniper. "Given a complete, working breakdown on the construction and operation of your flying logs, and of the material from which your clothing is made, I'd say we could give you what you want."

Lady did her best to keep the others up-to-date on what

was being said. She did not always get it right.

Nashun the Researcher could not grasp the enormity of my demand. He tried speaking three different times, failed, finally turned to the First Father in mute appeal. I was sure his hidden face was taut with despair.

I told my guys, "It might be wise to back away from the shadowgate. These people are about out of patience."

I felt wonderfully wicked. I always do when I frustrate overly powerful, responsible-to-no-one types who think all existence was created only for their pleasure and exploitation.

I told the Voroshk, "It'll be dark soon. Then the shadows will come out." And, as the Voroshk exchanged glances, I borrowed from Narayan Singh. "When dealing with the Black Company you would do well to remember: Darkness always comes."

Lady's expression was one of less than one hundred percent approval when I turned away. "That could've gone better."

"I let my feelings intrude. I should know better. But talk wasn't going to get us anywhere, anyway. They think too much of themselves and too little of everyone else."

"Then you're giving up the dream of returning to Khatovar."

The Voroshk made their first furious attempt to bust through the shadowgate.

I did warn them.

They did not want to listen.

It was worse than I had imagined it could be.

It was worse than Tobo had predicted.

The countermagical blast hurled both sorcerers all the way up the slope to the edge of the plain, bouncing and tumbling all the way. By some miracle neither broke the barrier protecting the road. Maybe Shivetya was watching over then.

One still had shown no sign of recovering when I gave up

watching. I told Tobo, "I reckon it's time to go, now. Those guys might have gotten the message this time."

I did not look back. The trials the Voroshk faced left me confident that they would never become a problem to my world.

As we descended the hill I asked, "Anybody think there might be a connection between the Shadowmasters and the Voroshk? They seem to have gotten their start about the right time. And the Shadowmasters tried to sever all connections with the past in Hsien. It was just too big a job. I wonder what we'd find out if we talked to some ordinary farming stiff over there?"

"I can ask Shivetya," Tobo said. "And the prisoners." But he did not sound particularly motivated.

49

Nijha:
Place of the Dead

Sahra kept calling for more torches. As though bringing in enough light would nullify the disaster. By the time the Captain arrived there were fifty torches, lamps and lanterns illuminating what had been a stable before the Company arrived.

"Strangled?" Sleepy asked.

"Strangled."

"I'm tempted to use the word 'ironic' but I fear there's no irony in it at all. Doj. That white raven of Croaker's was hanging around outside. Find it. There were little people hanging around here, some of them supposedly watching Singh. I want to know what they saw."

Sleepy had a good idea what she would hear from the Unknown Shadows. It would be a variation on reports she had had before. She said, "I'll want to send the news south, too."

Nothing happened around the Black Company without some hobyah there to witness it. The soldiers from Hsien understood that perfectly. They took it for granted. They tended to be well-behaved. But someone without experience of life in Hsien would not take the Unknown Shadows as seriously.

A minute later, Sleepy asked, "I don't suppose anyone's seen Goblin, have they? I don't reckon anyone knows who was supposed to be watching him?"

Riverwalker said, "He was right over there till a minute ago."

Sleepy looked, considered, muttered, "No doubt right up to the second I decided to consult the Unknown Shadows about what they saw." Which would have been the same moment he would have realized that his recent history was no mystery to anyone. The moment when he realized that Sleepy had been paying out the hangman's rope while seeing what she could learn.

Riverwalker asked. "Want him rounded up? In one piece?"

"No." Not now. Not when the best wizard she had was an old, old man whose skills, outside using a sword, were too weak even to put hexes on people and animals. "But I wouldn't mind knowing where he is." Doj could manage that. The Unknown Shadows communicated with him. Sometimes. When the mood took them. "What you do need to do right now is get extra guards around the Voroshk. Goblin showed a lot of interest in them while we were traveling. I don't want anything happening to them and I don't want them wandering off." It did not occur to her to reinforce the company responsible for the comatose sorcerer Howler. But Fortune stood behind her there.

Goblin, it developed, had grabbed a couple of fast horses and some loose supplies and had gotten himself out of

Nijha, headed north, all without attracting any particular notice. Sleepy very nearly indulged in profanity when she received the report. Someone pointed out that the little wizard always had had that knack. Sleepy growled, "Then somebody should have been watching for him to take advantage of it."

Uncle Doj told her, "I can't stop him or control him but I can make life miserable for him."

"How?"

"His horses. The Black Hounds can have a lot of fun with them. And when he tries to lead them to water . . ." He chuckled wickedly.

"Send them." Sleepy beckoned Sahra. "I kept leaning both ways during the meeting. Looking for a sign. I've just had it. We're not going to rush in anymore. We'll move ahead slowly, into more hospitable country, and stop somewhere where we can support ourselves without much trouble. We'll wait till everyone catches up. And issue a call for volunteers willing to support the Prabrindrah Drah and the Radisha." If anyone even remembered them.

"Wait especially for my son. Yes." Sahra was angry and unhappy but too tired to fight much. "Now that Murgen is no longer the major tool."

"Especially for Tobo, yes. Tonight it was clear that without Tobo we're in trouble bad."

Sahra said nothing more. She was tired of fighting a battle in which even the men she wanted to protect refused to honor her concern.

50

The Taglian Territories:
The Palace

The Taglian field army slowly assembled astride the Rock Road in lightly settled country midway between Dejagore and the fortified crossings over the River Main at Ghoja. Another, less powerful force, consisting of troops from the southern provinces, assembled outside Dejagore. And a third gathered outside Taglios itself. There seemed no reason to suspect that the force at Dejagore should have any trouble denying that city to a force such as that the Black Company was bringing up. Mogaba expected his enemies to swing west once they descended from the highlands, possibly marching as far as the Naghir River, which they could follow north, then swing eastward again and try to get over the Main at one of the lesser downriver crossings. He intended to let them march and march and wear themselves down. He intended to let them do whatever they wanted till he slammed the door shut behind them. Once he had them north of the Main he could build a ring around them and slowly squeeze.

The Great General was feeling quite positive. Taglios was restive but not rebellious. Even the most remote garrison commanders were bringing their soldiers to the assembly points with their units at near strength even though some harvesting would commence in the far south before the end of the month.

Harvest season inevitably precipitated higher desertion rates.

Best of all, the Protector was staying away. Her tinkering and interference always made his task more difficult. And, of course, it was always his fault when a bastardized plan fell apart.

The Great General gathered his senior staff and inner circle, which included a dozen generals as well as Ghopal and Aridatha Singh. He told them, "The plan appears to be coming together perfectly. With a couple of nudges and timed withdrawals I think we can lead them to the ford at Vehdna-Bota. I still wish we had better communications with the Protector. But she can't find enough crows anymore. Some plague is wiping them out. I seldom hear from her more than once a day. And then, often as not, she'll waste time on weather news or a flue epidemic in Prehbehlbed." Nor were there any shadows about, nor any of the Protector's lesser spies. Mogaba did not mention that. Taglians were dedicated conspirators. Let them continue to think that there might be eyes in the corners, watching.

Only his own conspiracy need go forward.

The Great General had more to preoccupy him than how to isolate and destroy his enemy. He suspected there was a definite question about the identity of Taglios' most dangerous foe.

Something about this incarnation of the Black Company had Soulcatcher so concerned that she insisted on focusing all her attention there. Something about this incarnation of the Black Company had touched almost everyone of substance within the Taglian empire, though news of their return had barely had time to spread and there were no eyewitness reports available at all. All customary enmity and internal friction seemed to be dwindling at a time when, normally, factionalism should be exploding as old antagonists tried to use the situation to their advantage.

And Mogaba had found that he was thinking less and less about the practicalities of eliminating the Protector, more and more obsessively about destroying the Black Company. Not just defeating them but obliterating them. To the last man, woman, child, horse, mule, flea and louse.

After decades of unhappy fortune Mogaba was naturally

wary of everything—including his own emotional state.

He had begun keeping a personal journal the day he had made the decision to betray Soulcatcher, to track his thoughts and emotions during the subsequent, stressful days. It was a journal he opened only in brilliant sunlight. It was a journal he would destroy before actually taking action against the Protector because there were names in it he did not want betrayed if he failed—and was lucky enough to die before she captured him.

Lately he had noticed an evolution in his thinking about the Company. An accelerating evolution. A frightening evolution.

He had become suspicious of his own reason.

Following a general meeting to consider policy for the empire the Great General met with the men responsible for the capital city.

"Kina is active again," Mogaba murmured. Ghopal and Aridatha listened politely. He was referencing events from before their time, that they knew only by repute. "She's doing that thing where she gradually shapes everyone's prejudices."

They offered him blank looks.

"Not history buffs, eh?" Mogaba explained. "The strangest part was, nobody ever wondered why they were terrified. They just didn't remember that three years earlier they'd never heard of the Black Company."

Ghopal said, "What you're saying is, the Strangler Goddess has a particular fear of the Black Company. She wants the whole world to climb all over them and destroy them. Even if blood has to be spilled."

"Isn't this an interesting quandary," Aridatha said. "If we can overcome the Black Company, we'll still have to deal with the Protector. If we knock her down, too, then we'll still have to handle the Stranglers and Kina, in order to prevent the Year of the Skulls. Wave after wave. No end to it."

"No end to it," Mogaba agreed. "And I'm getting to be quite an old man." He had begun to nurture an outrageous notion almost as soon as he had determined that he was being manipulated. "There are a couple of old records I want to check. I want you both back here same time tomorrow."

The Great General did not lack courage. The next evening he led Ghopal and Aridatha into the brightly lit room. He presented a more convincing case for his belief that Kina had awakened, drawing heavily upon excerpts from copies of Black Company Annals residing in the national library.

Aridatha Singh said, "I believe you. I just wonder what happened to wake her up again."

"Ghopal?"

"I'm not sure I understand. But I don't think I have to. Aridatha does. I trust his wisdom."

"Then I'll talk to Aridatha. But you listen." Mogaba chuckled.

Aridatha listened to his idea, the reasoning behind it, frowning all the while. Ghopal seemed aghast. But he kept his mouth shut. Aridatha went off alone with his thoughts. After a while he nodded reluctantly and said. "I have a brother in Dejagore. I'll find a reason to go visit. I know some people who might listen to what you have to say if it's me doing the talking."

"What?"

Aridatha said, "You recall a few years ago when the Company underground here started kidnapping people? Willow Swan, the Purohita, and so on? I was one of the people they snatched."

Ghopal wanted to know why, and Mogaba wondered how he had gotten away.

"I got away because they let me go. They only picked me up because they wanted to show me off to somebody they were holding already." Aridatha took a long, deep breath and revealed his great secret. "My father. Narayan Singh. They were showing him their power."

"Narayan Singh? *The* Narayan Singh? The Strangler?" Ghopal asked.

"That Narayan Singh. I didn't know. Not till then. Our mother told us our father was dead. She believed it, I think. The Shadowmasters conscripted him into their labor battalions during their first invasion, before the Black Company ever arrived from the north. I was the youngest of four children. I'm pretty sure the older ones knew the truth. My brother Sugriva moved to Dejagore and changed his name. My sister Khaditya changed hers, too. Her husband would die of mortification if he knew."

"You've never mentioned this before."

"I think you can understand why."

"Oh. I do. That's a cruel burden to bear." Mogaba already found himself responding to the Deceiver connection. With exactly the sort of paranoid fear everyone did to any Deceiver connection. It was inevitable. Aloud, he said, "I wonder how those people ever trust each other?"

Aridatha replied, "I suspect you'd have to be inside and a part of it all to understand. I think the biggest part of it, though, would be their faith in their Goddess."

The Great General looked at Ghopal Singh. "If the Greys have objections I need to hear them now."

Ghopal shook his head. "Only one Grey is going to know about this. For now. The others wouldn't understand."

"Aridatha. You have someone you trust to take charge while you're gone?" The City Battalions did not know they were part of a conspiracy to free Taglios from its protector. It was necessary to keep firm control there.

"Yes. But no one in the know. If you have unusual requests you'll have to justify them based on what's going on in the city." The soldiers understood that their role was to keep the peace if the population became too restive for the Greys alone.

Mogaba asked, "Are there enough provocations to make any excuses sound good?"

Ghopal showed a large array of teeth. Shadar were proud of their well-kept teeth. "That's almost amusing. Since the news reached the street that the Black Company really is back, there's actually been less related graffiti. As though real Company sympathizers don't want to risk identification and the non-Company vandals responsible for most of it suddenly don't want to be identified with any terror that's for real."

"Terror?"

"You were right, what you said last night. There's a growing fear of the Company out there. Like you said, it was in olden times. I don't understand but it's helping keep the peace just when I expected a lot more trouble."

"If you need provocations and the villains don't provide them, feel free to create your own. Aridatha, you know what needs doing. Do it. As quickly as possible. Before events move so fast they rob us of more chances." Though it could happen almost momentarily, Mogaba had abandoned any real hope of catching the Protector unaware as she returned to the city.

At the moment it seemed she did not plan to return until the Black Company invasion was settled.

51

The Taglian Territories: The Middle Ground

Soulcatcher, in full leather and fuller ire, stalked the perimeter of the encampment midway between Ghoja and Dejagore. A dozen frightened officers followed, each silently appealing for mercy to his choice of god or gods. The Protector in a rage was a disaster no one wanted to experience. Her excesses made no more sense than do those of a tornado.

"They haven't moved. For six days now they've hardly taken a step. After hurtling northward like the storm itself, so fast we were killing ourselves trying to pull something together fast enough to stop them. What're they doing? What

changed suddenly?" As always when she was under stress
Soulcatcher was a babble of conflicting voices. That added to
the uneasiness of the men tagging after her. None had had any
experience with her before her arrival in camp. The actuality
was more unnerving than the stories predicted. She seemed
every bit as cruel and capricious as any god. Several graves
beyond the perimeter attested to the violence of her temper.

These sycophants would never find out but those who
died had been chosen only after extended supernatural espionage. Not one had been a devoted servant of the Protectorate. Each had said so aloud. Additionally, none had been
particularly competent leaders and that had been clear to
their soldiers and compatriots. They had attained their positions through nepotism or cronyism, not ability.

Soulcatcher was culling her officer corps. She was disappointed that necessity prevented her from doing more. That
corps was terrible. But she would take no responsibility for
that. Of course.

How poor would it have been without the efforts of the
Great General? Probably an awful, corrupt joke without a
punchline. Without Mogaba's dedicated nurturing there
would have been little to assemble here.

How to keep it here? The desertion rate was supportable
now but showing signs of rising. Was that the enemy strategy? Wait until the Taglian armies melted because of the
demands of the approaching harvest? Would they charge
north again then? It sounded like a Black Company sort of
thing to do. Indications were, they had the wealth to maintain a force in the field a long time.

Mogaba's messages indicated his own suspicions concerning a similar strategy. He was tailoring his own
approach toward getting his enemy to take the long way
around, into a trap.

Soulcatcher did not believe there would be any chance to
trap the Black Company. Their intelligence resources were
much too wonderful. While her own continued to fade. All

species of crows were becoming endangered. Mice, bats, rats, owls, those sorts of creatures had no range. There seemed to be no modern sources of quality crystal or worthy mercury with which to create a scrying glass or bowl. The shadows she still controlled were few and feeble and frightened and she refused to risk them in enemy territory, often because each time she did a few more would not come back. And for now she was cut off from her only source of replacements.

She glanced skyward, saw vultures circling to the north, over woods which ran from right to left for as far as she could see. The growth followed a shallow stream. Her sister had won a small victory over the Shadowmasters there, ages ago, soon after the Black Company had suffered the disaster that led to the siege of Dejagore.

"I'm going to walk up there and see what those vultures find so interesting."

No one gave in to the urge to protest.

Maybe the vultures would dine on her.

"None of you need to come with me."

Relief was obvious.

52

The Nether Taglian Territories:
Lady Made Grumpy Noises

Lady was in a towering rage. I could not recall ever having seen her so close to losing control. "How the *hell* could they let that happen? Somebody was supposed to stay in that little shit's pocket every second!"

No one bothered to respond. She did not want answers. Not really. She wanted somebody to hurt.

Tobo was quietly busy talking to things that were there only when you looked away. Big things, little things, human-looking things and things that had escaped from madmen's nightmares. Goblin was going to be found. Goblin was going to be tracked and harassed and hurt if at all possible, all the live-long day. Insofar as this fragment of the Company was concerned Goblin was going to be the main mission from this day forward. He was to be hunted down and exorcised—or exterminated—before he could engineer any more disasters on Kina's behalf.

Though long out of practice and definitely out of the habit, Lady hurled a deadly spell at an inoffensive scrub pine. The tree began to wilt almost immediately.

"What the hell was that?" I demanded. "I thought you couldn't . . ."

"Be quiet. Let me think." So astonished was Lady that she forgot to be angry about Goblin.

I was quiet. I gave her all the thinking room a girl could want.

Was there a silver lining inside our latest black cloud?

My at-the-moment not very lucky wife called, "Tobo. Next message you send north, ask if the little shit got away with one of the gate keys. Or anything else unusual."

Tobo made little gestures to the air, then replied, "I checked on that already. He got away with nothing more than two horses and one saddle. Not even a sausage. He's probably eating bugs. The only unusual thing mentioned is that nobody noticed him. An eventuation almost certainly artificial in origin."

"Because?"

"Because he's being damned hard to notice right now. The Black Hounds shouldn't be having trouble finding and following him. But they are. He's as elusive as a ghost. Each time they do make contact it's because he's been following the road, without deviating, and they can just wait for him to show up."

"Following the road where?"

"North. Toward the junction with the Rock Road.

Though because he isn't talking his plans are unclear."

Tobo still had a sense of humor about what was going on.

I asked Lady, "How did you manage to murder that tree?"

She mused, "A good question. Without a good answer. I never felt any sharpened Kina presence."

"You think it might have to do with Goblin? We know Kina must've put a piece of herself into him or he wouldn't even be alive."

"I would've sensed something before. I think. Tobo. Did you feel anything weird about Goblin?"

"Of course." The boy was curt. He was trying to work. Old folks kept interrupting. "He wasn't Uncle Goblin anymore. But he wasn't any more powerful than he was before, either."

I said, "Maybe it was something that didn't come out until he got the chance to kill Narayan."

Debate on the why increasingly focused on the fact that crippled old Narayan had been in no shape to run or do anything on behalf of his Goddess and, if left in our hands, would have been compelled to reveal whatever he knew eventually. And while most of us would view his murder as a betrayal by his Goddess, what we knew of Deceiver doctrine suggested that he might actually see it as a reward. Having been strangled for the Goddess, Narayan would go directly to Deceiver paradise where, no doubt, his rewards would be commensurate with his service.

I tend toward the cynical view where religion is concerned.

After a silence so extended I decided she was not listening, my beloved responded, "You might just be smarter than you look. She'd expect us to be suspicious enough to watch every breath Goblin took. So she'd want him to seem as normal as possible until he got a solid chance to get away." She began to pace. "Poor Goblin. That would've been mostly him, maybe even really trying to help his old friends as much as he could. And he'll still be partly Goblin, but a prisoner inside his own body." The hollowness of her voice indicated that she might have been through that herself, once upon a time.

"Which tells us nothing of his purpose. Or of Kina's."

"She's in prison. She wants out. That doesn't take any special figuring."

"But there'll be a grand plan. Old Goblin didn't get his soul eaten up just so he could be flung across the pond of the world like a skipping stone. He's going to go somewhere and he's going to do something and if he gets away with it all the rest of us are going to end up really sorry."

Lady grunted. She was still mostly angry.

I said, "He headed north. What's up there that would interest Kina?"

Tobo interrupted his sweet talk with his pets. "Booboo." He sounded as unhappy as I felt. "He's going to take Narayan's place watching over the Daughter of Night."

"Yeah. Only there'll be a big chunk of Goddess in him so he'll be a lot more dangerous than Narayan ever was."

Lady glared around her with an expression that made me think she did not have much trouble seeing Tobo's friends. "Do you think my sister can be made to hear one of those?"

You could have heard a stack of pans drop. Even the animals quieted down.

I asked, "You have something in mind?"

"Yes. We send her a message. Tell her what's going on with Goblin. It's as much in her interest to stop him as it is in ours."

"And she has a personal interest," Tobo reminded us.

I understood immediately but Lady needed it explained. "Goblin is the reason Soulcatcher has a bad leg."

"Oh. Of course. I remember now."

She ought. She was there, spying on everything through the eyes of a white crow, during the kidnapping of the Radisha. That same night Goblin managed to trick Soulcatcher into springing a booby trap. The result had been serious and irreversible damage to her right heel.

Tobo said, "She gets around pretty well now. She wears a special boot and brace and is supported by several specialized spells. She only limps when she's really tired."

"Ah. She'll definitely want to chat with Goblin, then. She's always been a sore loser."

"Just a thought," I offered. "What happens if Soulcatcher turns Goblin into her own version of the Taken? And maybe Booboo, too? Word is, there were times when she showed a few powers of her own."

"Make a slave out of a Goddess?" Lady was incredulous. I raised an eyebrow. She protested, "What I did wasn't the same thing at all. What I did was pure parasitism. I wormed in so she couldn't get me out without hurting herself."

"And now you're getting a little of that back?"

"But it doesn't feel the same. Tobo. Can you send a message to my sister or not?"

"I can try. In fact, I *can* do it. Easily. The real question would be whether or not she'd listen."

"She'll listen or I'll kick her butt."

It took all of us a moment to realize she was joking. She did so so rarely.

Tobo began concentrating on the task of getting an extended message to Soulcatcher.

Again I cautioned, "There's a risk in this."

Lady just made one of her grumpy noises. She was turning into a cranky old witch.

53

The Taglian Territories:
· A Haunted Wood

Soulcatcher glanced back before entering the wood. "So where are they all?" And in a firm male voice she demanded, "What happened to all the suck-ups?"

Another voice, "Somebody should've wanted to kiss up."

A puzzled voice asked, "They always do, don't they?"

"Are we losing it here?"

"I don't like it."

"This isn't fun anymore." Petulant, spoiled child voice.

"Most of the time we're just going through the motions. There aren't any challenges here."

"Even when there are it's almost impossible to get impassioned enough to care."

Most of those voices were businesslike but jaded.

"It's hard to keep going on fuel like hunger for revenge alone."

"It's hard to be alone, period."

That remark brought on an extended silence. Soulcatcher did not have a voice for expressing the emotional costs of being who she was. Not out loud. Ferocious mad-killer sorcerers do not whine because nobody likes them.

The growth along the creek had a sharp boundary. In another time the land must have been groomed by human occupation. Soulcatcher listened. The wood, which was a little more than a mile wide, seemed remarkably silent. There should have been a racket from work parties harvesting firewood and timber for use around the camp. But there was nothing. And she did not recall authorizing a holiday. Something had frightened the soldiers away.

Yet she sensed no danger.

After a moment, though, she did detect a supernatural presence.

She glanced upward. Those vultures continued to circle. They were lower now. They seemed to be wheeling above the presence she sensed.

Warily, she probed farther and deeper. She had remarkably well-honed senses when she cared to concentrate.

This presence was like nothing in her experience. Something like a powerful shadow, yet with a strong implication of working intelligence. Not a demon or some such otherworldly entity, though. Something that felt like it was a part of nature but still having about it a hint of not belonging to this world. But how? Not of this world but not otherworldly? . . . Something very powerful but not driven by malice. At the moment. Something timeless, accustomed to patience, mildly impatient right now, again a smart-shadow thing like those stalkers down south had been.

Soulcatcher extended her senses to their maximum. This thing was waiting for her. For her alone. It had repulsed everything but those vultures. She had to be careful. Despite her ennui she did not want to trigger a fatal ambush.

There was nothing.

She stepped forward.

She did so while assembling a quiver of sudden and deadly spells. She squinted behind her mask, looking for this thing that wanted to see her.

It grew stronger but less focused as she moved toward it. For a moment it seemed that it was all around her—even while being in one place somewhere ahead of her. When she did arrive where her senses told her it ought to be, she saw nothing.

That place was a small clearing just off the Rock Road, across the shallow stream. She saw several Vehdna grave markers and a few Gunni memorial posts with time-gnawed prayer wheels on top. This must be where her sister fought the Shadowlander cavalry during her flight from Dejagore. In a time so long ago that she still had believed Narayan Singh to be her friend and champion.

Sunlight tumbled through the leaves overhead. It dappled the clearing. Soulcatcher settled on a rotten log that protruded from what might once must have been an earthwork. "I'm here. I'm waiting."

Something large moved at the edge of her vision. She got the impression of a black feline. But when she turned she saw nothing.

"So that's the way it's going to be, eh?"

"Thus it must be. Ever." The response seemed to come from nowhere in particular and it was not clear whether she heard it with her ears or inside her head.

"What do you want from me?" Soulcatcher used a deep masculine voice heavy with menace.

The presence was amused, not intimidated. "I bring a message from your old friend Croaker."

Croaker was no friend. In fact, she was distinctly piqued with that man. He had not been entirely cooperative when she had tried to seduce him and now he had refused to stay buried after she had tried to kill him. Still, he was the reason she had a head on her shoulders these days. And that tiny edge would be why this communication was arriving in his name.

"Go ahead."

The whatever-it-was did as she bid. As she listened she poked around in an effort to fathom its true nature. While searching for some handle she could grasp to make it over into an agent of her own.

It sensed what she was doing. It was amused. Not troubled. Not frightened. Not inclined to react. Just amused.

Soulcatcher reviewed the story carefully once the spook had finished relating it. It sounded plausible. If incomplete. But why expect those people to be entirely forthcoming in such a situation?

Try as she might she could discover no obvious trap. They

sounded worried down there. This news could explain their sudden shift of strategy.

Goblin possessed by Kina. Narayan Singh dead. The Daughter of Night running loose. . . . Not running loose at all! In the hands of her troops, on the Rock Road somewhere south of Dejagore, very probably looking for an opportunity to get loose.

Goblin might arrange that.

She bounced up off the rotten log, ennui gone. "Tell Croaker he can consider communications opened. I'll take steps to deal with the situation. Go! Go!"

A flicker. Like a shadow passing through and deserting at the same time. It left a deeply felt chill and one more uncertain glimpse of an impossibly large, catlike form moving away at an impossible pace.

From the nearby Rock Road came the rattle and clop of a large party headed south. Camels seemed to be involved. That meant civilians. There were no camels in her armies. She hated camels. They were filthy animals with nasty tempers even on their best days.

She leapt across the creek and hurried to the edge of the woods, emerging not a hundred feet from where a caravan was doing the same. Civilian it was, but most of the wagons and camels and mules would discharge their cargo in her camp.

The caravaners spied her. They were startled. And frightened.

Her blood was moving again. She always enjoyed the impact she made when she appeared unexpectedly.

As she turned and raised her gaze to the circling vultures she thought she glimpsed a familiar face among the merchants and teamsters. Aridatha Singh? Here? How? Why? But when she looked more closely she saw no Aridatha. Maybe it was just someone who looked like Singh. Maybe it was her reawakened zest reminding her that it had been a long time since she had enjoyed a man. Aridatha Singh had a definite masculine allure. Few women failed to notice that, though he seemed entirely unaware of the effect he had.

Time enough to think about that after she alerted Dejagore and got troops of cavalry out to round up her niece, that willful, difficult child.

There must be some way to gain control of her and add her talents to the arsenal of the Protectorate. Possibly she might even take Goblin—despite the fact of his possession.

Goblin never had been much of a wizard.

How sweet revenge was when it arrived after a long delay.

Then let that bitch Ardath and all her dogs come on! A lot of ancient debts would get paid off.

As she approached the encampment ditch she glanced back to consider the vultures again.

The carrion birds had broken their circle. Only a few remained in sight, cruising the sky in search of something rank and tasty again.

Soulcatcher found a voice she had not used since she was young. With it she began to sing a song of springtime and young love, in a language recalled from the springtime of life, when love still lived in the world.

The sentries were extremely frightened.

54

The Taglian Territories: The Thing in the Cesspit

I have a question," Murgen said. The stronghold at Nijha was in sight. "Who's going to tell Sleepy we're in bed with the Protector?"

I replied, "I don't reckon anybody has to. Not putting it that way, anyhow."

"She's a reasonable woman," Lady opined. "She'll understand what we did and why."

Tobo laughed. Murgen just grinned weakly. The boy wizard said, "You must not have been paying attention. Or you must've mistaken the Sleepy I know for somebody else."

I told him, "She'll get over it. How's Soulcatcher doing on cutting Booboo off?"

"She has pickets out in a line south of Dejagore. The line keeps spreading out wider, to either side of the Rock Road. She doesn't entirely trust me to send her solid information. And I'm not giving her everything I know because I don't want her guessing how well I can keep an eye on her. She's not talking about this to her captains, by the way. My guess is she's afraid she'll start losing them if they begin worrying about Kina."

What a bold lot we were. When first the Company arrived in the Taglian Territories a fixed part of Taglian culture was that the Goddess was never named lest her attention be attracted. If a name just *had* to be used people would reference the watered-down avatar from Gunni myth, Khadi.

The fact that the name Kina is now widely used in daily speech is one more indication of the magnitude of the impact the Company has had these past few decades.

Maybe those old-timers had been right to be terrified of us. We have shaken a civilization to its foundations. And its future does not look bright.

They asked for it. All we ever wanted was to pass on through.

"We won't have to deal with Sleepy for a few days yet," Tobo told us. "She's moving out of the highlands onto the plain, following the south bank of the Viliwash right now. She's only moving a few miles a day. The countryside there has enough of a surplus to support her easily. She's started trying to recruit. In the name of the Prahbrindrah Drah. The Prince and his sister are showing themselves off."

I had a feeling they would not sell well in those parts. That was territory that had been conquered by the Black Company in Taglios' name. "What about Booboo?"

"Almost up to the Protector's picket line now. Sticking to

the Rock Road. The Black Hounds have instructions to make sure she gets caught."

Lady grumped, "I thought she was caught already. That she was a prisoner."

"That's true. But right now she seems content to have it that way. I understand that her guards aren't nearly as attentive to her security as they ought to be."

Having read Sleepy's Annals I was not surprised. Booboo seemed capable of having a mind-numbing impact on nearby male-type people.

"Then that's something you need to let my sister know. Otherwise she could get a surprise that would leave all of us unhappy."

We were approaching the Nijha wall. I said, "You experts ought to give this place the once-over. See if our bitty old buddy left any evidence behind." That earned me frowns and scowls. Here came a chance to rest and I was talking about more work. Not for me but for them. I changed the subject and asked Lady, "You said Sleepy burned the Books of the Dead? The real ones? You were a direct witness?"

"I was a witness through the white crow. She burned all three of them. Shivetya himself has their ashes. He's been having Baladitya dispose of them a pinch at a time by having them carried away by anyone who's traveling the plain."

Tobo said, "I moved a lot of them back when Suvrin and I were exploring the plain. What's up?"

"An old man natural's curiosity, I guess. Everyone, and the Deceivers seemed to agree, thinks the Daughter of Night—or whoever inherits her job if she fails—will have to have the Books of the Dead to complete the rituals of the Year of the Skulls. No books, no resurrection. Right?"

I did not get an answer. There was no answer anyone could give. In actual fact nobody really knew. Possibly not even my befuddled daughter or poor old Deceiver and now very dead Narayan Singh.

Lady stipulated, "The old witch is still in there trying, isn't she?"

"Isn't she?"

Lady and Tobo found nothing of interest at the Nijha post. Goblin had not shed his skin or left any secret Deceiver hex signs. He had just started running while the getting was good, as soon as somebody realized that he might be responsible for Narayan's murder.

Uncle Doj rejoined us at Nijha. So did some stragglers who had accumulated there. Sleepy would not have much trouble with desertions. These men knew no one outside the Company and spoke not a word of Taglian or any other local language.

With the stragglers added we would number more than a hundred when we resumed traveling. Of the original group we lacked only Spook and Panda Man, who had been awarded the dubious honor of staying behind to watch the shadowgate.

Once she finished looking for other evidence, Lady cornered Doj. "Where's the body?"

"Huh?" The old swordmaster was baffled.

"Narayan Singh. What did you do with his corpse?"

Tobo and I exchanged looks. That question had not occurred to either of us. It might be a good idea to make doubly certain just who had died. Narayan Singh had been a veritable Prince of Deceivers, beloved of Kina.

One of the injured men left to garrison Nijha volunteered, "They threw him in the old cesspit, then filled it with dirt and rock from the new latrine, ma'am. Which was built according to your specifications, sir."

I have had a reputation as a martinet along those lines ever since I joined the Company. And when health, hygiene and waste disposal are handled my way the Company tends to experience significantly fewer disease problems than do people who do not do things my way. It remains impossible to reason with some men, though, so I just give orders and make sure they are carried out.

"Dig him up," Lady directed. And when nobody rushed to grab up picks and shovels she began to glow darkly and swell up and even to develop fangs.

Then people started looking for tools.

"That was interesting," I told her.

"Been working on it since I ambushed myself and that tree. It doesn't take much effort or power but it ought to be visually impressive."

"It definitely was that."

The exhumation satisfied Lady. There was a body. It resembled Narayan Singh, even including his bad leg. And it was unnaturally well preserved considering where it had been buried.

"Well?" I asked after she had gone so far as to open the body up. I do not know what she expected to find.

"It does seem to be him. Considering who he served, who seemed to love him, I was almost certain there wouldn't be a body. Or it wouldn't be Narayan's if there was."

The truth was, she had not wanted it to be Narayan. She did not want Singh evading her vengeance this easily.

"There's no dramatic unity in real life," I told her. "Save it up and take it out on Goblin."

She offered me a wicked look.

"I mean on the thing that's taken possession of Goblin." The real Goblin would be my oldest surviving friend.

She carved Narayan's corpse into little pieces. She left a trail of those for the bugs and buzzards over the next several days. But the man's head, heart and hands she kept in a jar of pickling brine.

I did not ask why or if she had a plan. Narayan's escape had left her in much too black a mood for small talk.

A couple of times I did overhear her cursing the fact that there were no great necromancers left in the world.

She would call Narayan back from paradise or hell to make him pay for taking our daughter.

The smaller Voroshk girl, the captive, came out to see us. In not bad Taglian she told us, "Sedvod just died." She stared at Tobo the whole time.

I went to check. The sick boy had, indeed, passed on. And I still had no idea why.

I figured the Goblin thing probably deserved the blame.

55

The Nether Taglian Territories: Along the Viliwash

Sleepy surprised us all. She was irked about us dealing with Soulcatcher but she made no great fuss. "This situation isn't the one I prepared for. Tobo. I trust you're taking steps to prevent the Protector from observing what we're doing."

"She sees what we want her to see. Which means she doesn't see what we're doing, only what our mutual enemies are doing."

Which was not much on Booboo's part. Despite her best effort to vanish during the night after her captors first encountered Soulcatcher's pickets, she remained a captive. She would be turned over to Soulcatcher herself within a few days.

Goblin, moving faster than the girl's captors were, had been gaining ground fast and Tobo now placed him only about thirty miles behind. I suggested that he would be more trouble to Soulcatcher than Booboo ever could.

Thinking out loud, I said, "I wonder if this is how myths get started."

People looked at me like they were not sure they wanted to know what that was all about.

I explained. "Here we've got a bunch of people visiting strange places most people couldn't get to even if they wanted. We've got close relatives squabbling and even trying to murder each other."

"That's reaching," Murgen said.

"I like it," Tobo said. "A thousand years from now they'll remember me as the god of storms. Or something."

"Or something?" his father asked. "How about the small god who makes littler rocks out of runty stones?"

Earlier Tobo had gotten caught making stones explode. He had been doing it for the sheer joy of watching them shatter and hearing the fragments ricochet. He was embarrassed. But you have got to have fun once in a while. Today's Company is not nearly as much fun as it was when I was young.

I snickered. "We marched forty miles every day. Uphill all the way. In the snow. When we weren't in the swamp."

"What?"

"Thought I'd start practicing for when I get really old. How do you make rocks explode?"

"Oh. That's easy. You just kind of feel what they're like inside. You find the water. You make it hot enough and the rock goes boom."

Find the water. Inside a rock. And the rock goes boom. Right. I had to ask. I changed the subject. "How are those Voroshk kids doing?" Despite everything he had to do, Tobo found time to spend with our captives.

It was amazing how much the kid could handle in a day.

I could recall when life worked that way for me. Back when we were marching up all those hills. With cold, wet feet.

"Uncle Doj has them speaking Taglian like they were born in the delta, in the shadow of the temple of Ghanghesha."

"Excellent." He was poking fun, of course.

"They're picking up the language. Shukrat and Magadan could get by now. Arkana is having trouble but she's catching on. None of them are mourning Sedvod. Gromovol, the brother, is being stubborn. He doesn't like not being the only conduit. He likes to be in control. Of something. But even he is making progress."

"Gromovol is the pain in the ass, then? Which're which with the other names? I haven't heard any names before."

"That's because they hadn't given up hope that their family would rescue them from their own dumb mistake. Even more than the Gunni do, they believe their names can be used against them. There's a connection with their souls."

"Which means that Shukrat and Magadan and whatnot won't actually be real names."

"They're real public names. Work names. Just not true names."

"I've never understood the concept but it's one I've learned to live with. Which one is which?"

"Shukrat is the shorter girl. The one who crashed."

"The one who's working up a crush on you."

Tobo ignored me. The ability to ignore seems to be coupled with a talent for sorcery. "Arkana is the ice queen. Which I definitely would not mind melting. Magadan is the quiet guy."

Magadan, in my estimation, would be the dangerous one. If he so chose. He observed and studied and prepared. He did not bluster or invoke the threat of powers from a world away. "Did you tell them what happened at the shadowgate?"

"They didn't want to believe me but they did enough to decide to introduce themselves. Enough to conclude that they're likely to be a part of our world for a long time to come."

"You did remind them that that's what they asked for?"

"Sure. Shukrat even managed to joke about it. She has a

great sense of humor. For a girl. Who *didn't* ask to be here."

Considering the females in his experience I could see how he might think a feeble sense of humor was a sex-linked characteristic. Only Iqbal Singh's wife ever smiled and joked. And Suruvhija's lot was the poorest of all the women associated with the Company.

"But all you can see is long legs, long blonde hair, big blue eyes and a monumental set of gazoombies." Once we got up into settled country we needed to find the kid a whore. Twenty years old and never been laid.

On the other hand, harnessing all that energy the way we were right now had a lot to recommend it. We were not headed into an era where we could let our most talented wizard be distracted by nature.

Maybe we should find him a traveling companion.

I could just imagine what his mother would say about that.

"The future," I said, raising my hand as though holding a drink. "We have to get Swan and Blade set up in the brewing business."

Murgen said, "That's what I miss most about One-Eye, too."

"Here's a thought. Maybe Goblin will get so thirsty he'll shake Kina off and set up a still."

I had to mention Goblin. That took the pleasure out of the moment.

Everybody who remembered the old Goblin had to deal with those memories each time the man's name came up. Those memories were going to be treacherous if ever we confronted the revenant himself. Even if they caused just a moment's hesitation.

If we had to go after Goblin hard we would be better served to send people from Hsien. They would not be sentimental about him. Their exposure was entirely hearsay.

I did not want to hasten the day.

I asked, "Tobo, now that we've slowed down, what are we

going to do about the Howler?" An entire infantry company had been saddled with that sleeping sorcerer from the day he and Longshadow had been brought up out of the earth. That company had no other duties but transporting and protecting the Howler. "Something's got to be. If she don't wake him up and make a deal we'd better kill him. Before Soulcatcher figures out that we've got him and steals him so she can use him herself."

I was worried that Sleepy was not taking the Howler seriously enough. She had no experience of him. Not enough to understand just how dangerous he could be, which was just as dangerous as Soulcatcher. And he was crazier than she was.

The Howler was no dedicated enemy of ours though he had worked against us far more often than otherwise. His nature seemed to make him a follower. He gravitated toward where the strength seemed to be. He was so powerful I would prefer he was with us rather than not. Or, if not with us, dead.

"There's a certain amount of debate. Sleepy would rather just leave him for the jackals. Mom would, too, only she keeps having these premonitions. You know how big premonitions are with the women of the Ky family."

"One got your mom and dad together."

"No use crying over spilled milk," Willow Swan said. "How about somebody tells Sleepy if she's not going anywhere in a hurry why don't we set down in one place? It's a pain to set up and tear down every day if we're not going anywhere."

Our northward drift did allow for a lot of camp time. I used it to work on these Annals. Lady used it to get several wagon loads of large bamboo poles collected so she could begin manufacturing a new generation of fireball projectors. Tobo used it to teach the Voroshk youngsters. I joined him occasionally. The boy Magadan seemed to have a healing touch. We needed to nurture that.

Arkana remained the ice queen. Shukrat grew more

relaxed with us. And Gromovol decided he wanted to become my buddy—in support of whatever scheme was shaping up inside of him.

Although he did not spread it around, Tobo figured out the basics of riding the Voroshk flying post. At least, a particular flying post. I suspect Shukrat helped him. It was her post he sneaked out in the middle of the night, indulging all of a young man's joy in adventure.

56

The Nether Taglian Territories: The Manor at Gharhawnes

Ten days into the Amble on the Viliwash we had traveled barely forty-five miles. A third of those we covered in a single day when it became apparent, to the amazement of all, that there really were people in the Taglian Territories disinclined to celebrate liberation from the Protector's reign. A coalition of regional nobles and priests tried to resist, then tried to hole up in a stout manor called Gharhawnes. In the field Tobo used his talents to weaken their will to resist, before the soldiers got a real chance to beat up on them.

We surrounded the manor at dusk. Fires sprouted. The outer wall of the manor house seemed to boil with a dark mist as the Unknown Shadows stormed the place.

Results did not become obvious for hours. Tobo's friends preferred to be indirect. And preferred the cover of darkness.

We had the place surrounded. Our bonfires sent harmless shadows scampering over the manor walls. I told Sleepy, "This place looks nice and comfy, Captain. We're in no hurry. We could hang around here for a while. Long enough to learn its name."

She was underwhelmed by the suggestion. "Gharhawnes."

"Bless you."

"Gharhawnes is the name of the place, you idiot."

"And it's the best place we've seen. Maybe we should set up the prince and his sister here. Sort of get them back into the swing of being royalty." The gods knew they got no practice with us savages. We just dragged them hither and yon like so much duffel, in case they became useful someday.

"Don't you have some writing to do? Or a boil to lance?"

"Not at the moment. I'm all yours and full of advice."

Before she could put together a suitable reply without using profanity, a party of several men slipped out of the manor, bringing women and children with them.

I had a feeling our camp looked pretty impressive.

It was supposed to look like a horde was on the move.

Tobo and his parents materialized. The boy said, "The haunts are working faster than I thought they would." He extended an arm, hand palm downward, then whispered in what sounded like the language of Hsien. A moment later a cry of rage came from a high manor window where a pair of archers had been about to snipe at the defectors. One somehow managed to fall through the opening.

The Captain said, "Have those things start whispering that anyone who surrenders before dawn will be allowed to take their possessions with them. They'll even be allowed to go home unharmed if they take an oath to the Prahbrindrah Drah. Captives taken after sunrise tomorrow will be conscripted into our forced labor battalions."

We did not have forced labor battalions. But those were a part of siege warfare and were often the fate of prisoners of war and peasants who were insufficiently fleet of foot. The threat was plausible. And the Black Company had a long reputation for being unimpressed by caste, noble birth, or priestly status, too.

Once it was clear we would provide covering fire to defectors a flow developed. Usually the soldiers set to keep deserters from using the posterns were the first to come over.

The people engineering the resistance were not popular with their conscripted followers.

So some folks wanted to see the Protectorate continue but the people who had to do the work were not interested. The few I got to talk to had no real convictions in the matter. Who ruled made little difference in their lives. But it was getting on toward harvest time.

One of the great truths was getting some exposure to the light here.

Our men entered the manor early next morning. I was still asleep. Tobo's pets spread confusion. Our men cleaned up behind them. None of our people died. There were few wounds of any consequence. Sleepy felt magnanimous. She turned most of the men of standing over to the Radisha and her brother for judgment. Only those Tobo identified as irredeemable creatures of the Protector faced the Company justice.

"Spread that around," Sleepy told Tobo. "Make it sound a lot bigger than it was."

"Tonight little people will be whispering in the ears of sleepers everywhere within two hundred miles."

57

The Nether Taglian Territories: The Resurrection

That far Taglian province shared religions with the rest of the Taglian Territories, with the majority being Gunni. It's language was closely akin to that spoken around Dejagore. Sleepy could manage the dialect with only a little practice.

What I called a manor house was really more like a village completely enclosed within a single blockish structure. The principal building material was an unbaked brick kept carefully plastered so it would not wash away in the rain.

Inside there was an open central square with both cisterns and a good well. Stables and workshops opened on it all around. The rest of the structure was a warren of halls and rooms where people obviously lived and worked and ran shops and lived life as though the place was indeed some sort of city.

"It's a termite mound," Murgen told me.

"The Prince and his sis ought to feel right at home. It's as bad as the Taglian Palace. On a miniature scale."

"I want to know what they ate. The smell is overpowering." The odors of spices clogged every hallway. But that was true in every Taglian city and town. These odors were just an alien mix.

Thai Dei caught up. He had actually allowed Murgen out of his sight for several minutes. Maybe he was slowing down, too. He brought a message. "Tobo says to tell you that Sleepy has decided to take a chance on wakening the Howler."

You could tell Thai Dei was worried because that was one of the longest speeches I ever heard the man make.

Sleepy chose to undertake the awakening with full pomp, ceremony and drama. Following an evening meal we gathered in what had been a temple hall, when everyone was rested, well fed and supposedly relaxed. The place of worship was poorly lit and boasted far too many multiheaded and multiarmed idols in its corners to lead me to consider it strictly benign.

None of the idols represented Khadi but all Gunni deities make me uncomfortable.

I was present in a demigod role myself. I appeared as the creepy armored monster Widowmaker. I do not enjoy the role.

My dearly beloved, on the other hand, just loves any excuse to assume the guise of Lifetaker. For a few hours she can wear the ugly armor and pretend that these are still the good old days when she was something much more wicked than this Lifetaker thing is supposed to be now.

Our role in the proceeding was to sit there in the gloom with colorful worms of sorcery slithering over us. We were supposed to look intimidating while others got the real work done.

Tobo just came as Tobo. Hell, he did not bother putting on a clean shirt and trousers. But he did bring his Voroshk students.

The rest of the audience consisted of senior officers and regional notables who had come in, mainly, to assess the Prahbrindrah Drah and to discover what they would need to do to weather our presence.

Conquerers do come and go.

The hall was crowded. All those bodies produced a lot of heat. And I was inside that armor, sitting motionless on a stool behind the action, One-Eye's black spear held upright in my right hand. That was supposed to be my entire part.

It mostly involved not fainting in front of witnesses.

Sleepy had set the stage pretty well, with the low lighting and enough advance rumormongering to make the audience understand that the Howler was both foaming-mouth mad and yet a sorcerer who was as powerful as the Protector.

Poor Howler. Despite his part in the Shadowmaster wars he was almost forgotten now.

The Voroshk, I noted, eventually settled right up front. Tobo was treating them as good friends, particularly the well-rounded, freckled little blonde. He chattered with her until Sleepy growled and told him to get on with it.

Even I felt a little let down by the awakening. Tobo indulged in no mumbo jumbo and no showmanship. He felt that his part was no more exciting than working in a stable.

But his effort was more impressive to thoughtful minds. A few people, maybe the right people, understood that Tobo was so good he could make something big look routine.

I thought the boy's efforts said a lot about his character, too. His ego did not need a lot of feeding.

I noted that three out of four Voroshk got it right away. Gromovol actually got it, too, but he did have an ego disease.

Tobo freed Howler from his long trance in a matter of minutes.

I do not know the whole story. You never do with their kind of people. But I do know that Howler is ages older even than Lady. He was one of the men who helped her first husband, the Dominator, build the Domination, an empire that collapsed into the northern dust about the time the original Black Company crossed over from Khatovar. Howler's pain and deformity are a legacy of that time. So is the kind of thinking that led Soulcatcher to proclaim herself Protector.

The woman does not have the obsessive focus and drive necessary to create a true replica of that old empire of darkness.

I never have seen Howler outside the layered rags he wears, rags so long unchanged that a whole ecology has developed between the Howler's skin and the surrounding world. It includes numerous invertebrates, molds, mildews and a variety of small green plants.

The Howler is smaller than Goblin or One-Eye ever were but Lady insists that that was not always the case.

When Tobo finished, the almost shapeless little ragbag sucked in a deep breath, then let out one of the shrieks that had given him his name. It seemed an egalitarian mix of agony and despair. I shivered despite the heat. It had been a long time since I had heard one of those cries. I could have waited a lot longer to hear this one.

The little wizard sat up.

Swords made metallic sounds. Spearheads dropped. Several of the half dozen existing, new-production fireball projectors swung to point Howler's way.

But he did nothing more. He was at least as disoriented as the worst of the rest of us when he awakened.

Tobo signalled. A man stepped forward with a pitcher of water. Howler would be fiercely thirsty. He would drink as much as he was allowed for the next couple of days. The first few of us to be awakened four years ago had made ourselves sick drinking too much water.

We learned to ration.

Howler wanted water by the gallon, too.

He did not get it.

He opened his mouth. A terrible howl came out. He could not control that frightful habit.

As rationality returned the little wizard looked around and was not pleased with his situation. He did not recognize anyone immediately. He asked, "How long has it been?" He used a tongue of the north so ancient no one but Lady spoke it. She translated into the language of Hsien, adding, "Right now he thinks he's been resurrected into a whole new age."

I suggested, "Break his heart fast. We don't have time to waste."

Howler asked questions again, in a series of languages, trying to elicit an understandable response.

I watched him wilt as he began to acknowledge the possibility that he had been asleep so long that the nations of his own age had been forgotten. But he was not entirely numb mentally. Though they differed in detail from the originals he soon recognized the armor Lady and I wore. And recalled who was who. He addressed himself to Lifetaker. The language he chose was an old one that they had shared in another age. There had been a time when I could read it, written, but could only guess at the meaning of the spoken words.

Just when everyone started to relax he let rip another bone-chilling shriek.

Lady announced, "Howler sees the general situation. Once he's had a little more explained I think he'll be amenable to an alliance."

I used the language of Hsien to respond. "Howler has

been part of my life most of my life. And all that time he's been one of the people trying to kill me. I don't think I can be real comfortable having him on my side."

"Well, that would be stupid, wouldn't it? We don't have to trust him, darling. The Unknown Shadows will keep him trustworthy."

Of course. "And you do remember his true name. Which you could pass along to Tobo."

"If I have to."

I nodded, thinking it might be a damned good idea for her to tell Tobo right away. Because the Howler was not the sort to be shy, reluctant or slow about eliminating a threat.

Howler let rip another terrible cry.

Sleepy had begun to simmer because she did not know what was going on.

Lady talked to the Howler about our situation while I told the Captain what was going on.

The Howler howled. There was some passion in this cry. He did not like the situation at all. But he had been there before and my sweetie was amply blunt in making it clear that there would be only one other choice available.

One reason the Howler had become the Howler was his powerful aversion to death. Nor did he have any reason to love Soulcatcher, who had buried him in a hope that that would last forever. And who had played him cruelly a time or two farther in the past.

The little sorcerer howled again.

In the language of Hsien I wondered aloud, "Tobo, do you think Shivetya has the power to cure this little shit's screaming?" It really got distracting after a while.

Tobo shrugged. "Possibly." He was not paying much attention. "I can find out." He was trying to hear what Riverwalker was whispering to Sleepy. Riverwalker had been called away a few minutes earlier. He was back now with Suvrin and a cavalry officer named Tea Nung. Nung's troop was supposed to have picket duty so I supposed something important had happened out there.

Sleepy nodded, said something affirmative. Riverwalker, Suvrin and Tea Nung withdrew. Sleepy started to snap something at them but whatever the thought was, it had come too late. Sleepy shifted her attention back to the matter at hand. She seemed less than totally focused now. She had developed a case of the fidgets. And she seemed to have brightened up.

She leaned over to confide something to Sahra.

Sahra was startled. Then she became smiley and conspiratorial, possibly even teasing.

The Captain did appear to be embarrassed.

Lady coughed indiscretely to cue me that it was Widowmaker's turn to speak to our leader. So I said, "Captain, the Howler would be honored to throw in his lot with the Black Company. He'll create flying carpets for us and he'll help with our weapons program. I wouldn't trust him a whole hell of a lot, though. And I'd keep him away from the Voroshk." All this stated in the language of Hsien, so the little sorcerer would not follow.

The youngsters remained in their unhappy clump, trying to understand. Almost perky little Shukrat understood enough Taglian already to keep her companions accurately posted as to what got said in that language.

Riverwalker and Suvrin returned. A tall, handsome man accompanied them. He was dusty and obviously exhausted but he was alert. He ran an inquisitive eye over everyone. He seemed to recognize several people. He even bowed slightly to the Radisha.

Sleepy rose to greet him. There was a deference in her manner I had not seen before, though it was so subtle as to lurk on the border of imagination. Obviously this was someone she knew. But not someone she cared to announce. After a tentative clasping of hands she, Sahra, Riverwalker and a few others, including the Radisha, slipped away.

I wondered immediately if they had not done something stupid by bringing the man into a crowded hall when a meeting with him needed to be private. Yet a glance around showed me nobody buzzing. Excepting Sleepy's cronies from her years underground in Taglios.

Might the visitor be some Company brother who had been left behind? Or some past ally?

The glance around also showed me all the Gunni idols apparently stirring. That had begun to divert the attention of the audience. Tobo was grim with concentration. He had his spectral allies hard at work.

That pretty boy had to be somebody special.

A moment later Widowmaker moved for the first time during the festivities. He stood up suddenly. The tip of his spear snapped down, pricked the rags surrounding the Howler, who had managed to stifle his screams and was in the process of beginning to ooze away.

Lifetaker's great black sword fell an instant later, blocking his line of sight.

58

Gharhawnes:
The Traitor General

It was deep in the night when a limping Runmust Singh dragged me out of bed. Out of a real bed. It had been ages. And this one came with a real woman in it. Runmust insisted that she had to get up, too. The Captain wanted us both.

Lady was grumbling something about restructuring the chain of command when we left our cubicle. We ran into Murgen right away. He was waiting for Thai Dei, who had not gotten a personalized wake up call. Sahra was nowhere in sight.

I asked, "When are you two going to work it out so you can go your own ways?" Thai Dei was one of very few

Nyueng Bao still dedicating himself to bodyguarding.

"I don't think that'll happen," Murgen said. "He doesn't have anything else since Narayan died."

"Ah." Thai Dei's son had been slain by Stranglers. Thai Dei was another who had been waiting in line to get some paybacks.

The obligation to protect Murgen had become a convenient fiction for both men. I should have recognized that a long time ago. I who have made such a big deal out of brotherhood for so many years.

Thai Dei bustled up. We set off after Runmust. I said, "Singh, you should let me take a look at that leg. It should've healed faster than it has."

"It'll mend fine once I get some real rest, sir. And I believe we expect to stay here for some time."

What good would that do if the man refused to take the opportunity to rest?

I could have Tobo knock him into a coma.

Runmust led us to a room barely big enough to fit a dozen people. Sleepy and Suvrin, the Prahbrindrah Drah and his sister, Tobo and Sahra were there already. So was the handsome stranger.

"Sit," Sleepy said. Then she got straight to the point. "This is Aridatha Singh." Beside me, Lady winced, recognizing the name and thinking of her trophies. "Aridatha commands the City Battalions in Taglios. He, the Great General and Ghopal Singh, who commands the Greys, form the triumvirate who're running Taglios while the Protector is out of town. Aridatha tells me that he and they—the Protector's top henchmen—have decided they need to get rid of her."

From one side, in back, Willow Swan grumbled, "Ghopal Singh is a general now? He was a damned sergeant when he worked for me."

Aridatha responded, "The Protector prides herself on her ability to recognize outstanding talent."

A joke of sorts had passed between the two. I guess you had to have been part of the situation to follow it.

While we sat around with our mouths hanging open, looking intelligent, Sleepy told the outsider, "These people are here to offer their advice. That's Croaker. He was the Liberator, once upon a time. That's Lady. That's Murgen. They've all led the Company at some time. The others you'll recall from the last time we met." She passed over Thai Dei, which lent him an air of mystery, nor did she introduce the Prahbrindrah Drah.

I asked, "Did Mogaba send you?"

"I volunteered. Because your Captain knew me. And because your Company has no personal grievance with me."

Lady stirred. She was willing to invent one.

Sleepy said, "It would seem that there are limits even Mogaba refuses to exceed. And Soulcatcher has managed to discover them."

Aridatha said, "You have ancient grievances with the Great General.

"I want you to know that he isn't an evil man. He *is* an obsessed man, though his obsession has weathered away with age. He's realized that history won't record his name on the roll of great conquerers. There's no longer time. He hasn't entirely made his peace with that but he does see that it's his own fault. Because of his untimely defection during the siege of Dejagore he has been forced to serve a procession of deranged and incompetent masters. But that's of no moment now.

"Between us, he, Ghopal, and I have concluded that Taglios should be spared any more torment by the Protector. She's like a deadly rot. She's destroying everything slowly. Even our religions and culture. And the only force able to put an end to that is the Black Company."

Murgen suggested, "You guys could whack her yourselves. She's not immortal. And she trusts you. As much as she trusts anybody. That gets you close enough. . . ."

"That plan was in place even before you people resurfaced. But she's stayed away from the city since the beginning of that crisis. Her messages to the Great General all affirm her determination to keep after you until she's accounted for every member of the Black Company personally. She was extremely put out because so many people who were supposed to be dead started turning up alive."

"Believe me, I know how exasperating that is," Lady said. "For twenty years I chased the Deceiver Narayan Singh. The man had more lives than a cat."

Aridatha caught the past tense. "Has the living saint of the Deceivers passed to his reward, then?"

"He got away from me through the only exit he had left." Lady sounded extremely bitter. Like she thought Singh had beaten her by cheating blatantly. Her hatred of Narayan was stronger than I had suspected.

"Then that's one distraction that no longer needs concern us."

"Incorrect," Sleepy said, reclaiming control. "The Daughter of Night is still out there. And Kina still hopes to bring on the Year of the Skulls. Whatever else happens, Kina and her followers still have to be managed. Tell my associates why we should trust anything you tell us, Aridatha."

"I am, of course, damned to walk in the shadow of a man I met only once in my life, after I was a grown man, and then for only a few minutes, several years ago, in your presence. That's the legacy of the Deceivers. The cult destroys trust. My answer is, all men should be judged by one standard: their behavior. By the deeds they do. The gesture of good faith I have to make in this instance is, I think, generous."

Sleepy interrupted. "Aridatha has a brother who lives in Jaicur. Under an assumed name. This brother, real name Sugriva, is going to help us take the city. He'll scout out the best gate for us to get at in the middle of the night. We'll use it to prance in and take over before anyone can put up a fight."

I opened my mouth to argue but stopped before anything stupid came out. Sleepy's mind was made up. All I could do was my best to make sure everything worked out right. "Soulcatcher has an army between here and there. One that outnumbers us, I hear."

"And one that's little better than a rabble, according to Aridatha. Some of the poorer soldiers are armed only with hammers, pitchforks, sickles and such."

"A guy goes away for a few decades, everything turns to shit," I said. "I had everybody tall enough to reach his mother's hand armed up, once upon a time. What happened to all those weapons?"

Riverwalker explained, "When the Protector took over, times got so bad that almost anybody with anything to sell sold it. Weapons were a glut on the market. The steel got forged into other things."

"And the Protector didn't care," Aridatha said. "The Great General finally gave up trying to make her see the point of maintaining arsenals in peacetime. I think it won't be long now until she understands what he was talking about."

Sleepy told us, "It isn't necessary to trust Aridatha or Mogaba to test Jaicur's defenses. We're expected to swing west toward the Naghir River. We'll make a show of doing just that. But Blade, with the light cavalry, will split off the rear of the column and loop back around eastward. The hidden folk will find a route along which the horsemen can approach Jaicur unobserved. In the meantime, the main force will turn again and head for the Rock Road north of Jaicur. That ought to stir up an ant's nest. And make Soulcatcher forget Jaicur completely for a few days."

Why had Sleepy bothered calling the rest of us in? She had it all worked out already. And pretty soundly, I thought.

Tobo said, "We do have a more immediate problem than that, Sleepy. You brought General Singh in during the reanimation ceremony. And he's been seen around camp. It's inevitable that some of our outside visitors will be Soul-catcher's creatures. And it's possible one of them recognized him."

Sleepy admitted, "I didn't think fast enough. I'm open to corrective suggestions."

"I'm already working on it. But I do want to warn you. I don't think I can be a hundred percent successful in identifying them and cutting them off."

"Then you'd better consider what would be the best way to warn the other conspirators in Taglios, hadn't you?"

Aridatha said, "Ghopal and the Great General won't be taken unawares. The Protector possesses no means of traveling faster than the rumor of her coming. When she heads for Taglios they'll know before she gets there. And what she brings with her will betray her intentions."

I nodded. The reasoning seemed sound. And you did have to be really sneaky to outfox Mogaba. Soulcatcher was not sneaky these days. She had developed the habit of just bulling straight ahead because she was the biggest power around.

Sleepy elected to assume a stance which made it look like we were just going to sit and rest. But Tobo scouted the country north of Gharhawnes in ever greater detail, sometimes even going out in person, when he went flying with Shukrat.

The two of them were getting very chummy.

In private I observed, "This is getting distinctly weird. We're allies with Soulcatcher against our daughter and Kina. We're allies with the traitor Mogaba against your sister. We're allies with a demigod whose price for supporting us is that we murder him."

Lady chuckled weakly. "You did say it has a mythic ring."

"You know something? It's got me scared."

She stared at nothing, waiting for me to explain.

"Scared in a generalized way, not scared like when we're in a fight. Scared of the shape the future might take." I had a bad, bad feeling. Because on the surface everything looked just too marvelous for the Black Company.

59

With the Middle Army:
When Guests Arrived

The Goblin creature proved difficult to catch. What should have taken just a few days took two weeks and, in the end, necessitated Soulcatcher's personal intervention—with, to her chagrin, considerable coaching from the shadowy cat thing she could never quite see and never quite ambush and bind to her own service.

In the meantime she amused herself with the girl.

The Daughter of Night was imprisoned in a cage inside Soulcatcher's tent. That was the largest and most ostentatious tent in the midway camp. The girl had been stripped naked, then had been decorated with a variety of chains and charms. She would not be guarded by or even approached by anyone male. Soulcatcher knew only too well how men could be manipulated by the women of her blood.

Though the girl did not seem interested in listening, Soulcatcher said, "To this day I'm not quite sure how you and that old man managed to get away from me. But I have some suspicions. And it won't happen again. You're far too important to your mother to be running around loose." The voice Soulcatcher selected was annoyingly pedantic.

The girl did not respond. She was alone in her own reality. This was not her first time as a prisoner of someone who planned to use her. She could be patient. Her moment would come. Someone would slip up. An impressionable guard would be assigned. Something. Somewhere, sometime, she would have an opportunity to deceive someone into loving her long enough to want to set her free.

The girl's continued indifference pricked Soulcatcher into trying to hurt her with news she had wanted to reserve. "He's dead, you know. Your old man. Narayan Singh. He was strangled. They threw his body in a cesspit."

That blow did strike home. But after an initial flinch and a brief, black look the Daughter of Night lowered her eyes and settled back into her pose of patient indifference.

Soulcatcher laughed. "Your freak Goddess has abandoned you."

To which the girl offered her only spoken response since her capture. "All their days are numbered." Which was like a slap in Soulcatcher's face. It was one of those slogans Black Company–inspired graffitists had used to taunt her for years.

Soulcatcher snatched a whip, flailed away without doing the girl much harm. The cage itself prevented that.

Someone shouted for Soulcatcher's attention from outside the entrance to her tent. In that respect her soldiers were well-trained. They did not bother her with trivia.

Responding, Soulcatcher found a gaggle of soldiers with a dead man on a crude litter. The corpse was twisted. Its features were severely distorted. Raindrops slid off the ruined face like tears. "You," she said, picking a man. "Tell it." A cavalryman covered with mud, he must have been on picket duty.

"This man came up from the south. He gave the proper recognition signs. He told us that he was bringing you important news about traitors but wouldn't say anything else."

"He arrived healthy? How did he get this way?"

"Just before we got to camp he stood up in his stirrups and screamed. His horse reared and threw him. After he hit the ground he shuddered and twitched and made gurgling noises trying to scream. And then he died."

"Traitors?" No doubt there would be many of those to pay off before this played out. These situations brought them out from under every rock and bush.

"That's all he said, ma'am."

"Bring him inside. It's possible I can still get a little something out of him. Be careful where you track your mud." She stepped aside, even held the flap for the soldiers. Reluctantly, a few found courage enough to bring the body forward. Soulcatcher's soldiers shared a common opinion that it was not good to catch the Protector's eye. These stepped carefully, leaving as little mud and moisture as possible.

In a merry young voice Soulcatcher observed, "You must all have mothers."

Soulcatcher had the corpse partially stripped, disassembling its apparel thread by thread, when there was another disturbance outside the tent entrance. Irked, she responded, hoping this would be the news she had been awaiting so long: that Goblin had been captured at last.

As she was about to open up she caught motion from the corner of her eye. She spun. For an instant she thought she glimpsed a tiny man, maybe eight inches tall, ducking down behind the corpse.

The racket outside remained insistent.

It was not the news she wanted. The soldiers there—they always came in groups—pushed one of their number forward. "A courier just came in, ma'am. The enemy is on the move again. Westward."

Mogaba had called it right, then. "When did this start?"

"The courier will be with you in a minute, ma'am. With dispatches. He had some physical needs he couldn't put off before he could see you. But the command staff insisted you get the main news immediately."

In a casual tone, Soulcatcher observed, "The drizzle seems to be letting up."

"Yes, ma'am."

"Get that courier here as fast as possible."

"Yes, ma'am."

The reports from the south did indeed have the rested Black Company forces moving westward but not on the track previously anticipated. Part of their journey would have to be made without the benefits of roads, over rough terrain.

Soulcatcher said, "They must be striking for Balichore by the shortest route. Why? Can anyone tell me what's special about Balichore?" Soulcatcher controlled a sprawling empire she knew only a little about.

After an extended silence someone tentatively suggested, "That's the farthest upriver heavy barge traffic travels. Cargos have to be portaged and loaded on smaller boats or onto wagons."

Someone else recalled, "There's some kind of problem with rocks in the river. A whatchamacallit. Cataract. The Liberator once ordered a canal built around it but the project was abandoned. . . ."

A couple of pokes in the ribs were necessary before the speaker recalled who was responsible for the neglect of public works in recent times.

Soulcatcher did not respond, however. She concentrated on the transport idea.

A large portion of the Company had barged up the Naghir River after fleeing Taglios five years ago. Could this new Captain be in a rut? Or was she thinking she could catch Taglios by surprise, from the river side, where there were no walls and no defensive works and the peoples of those poorer quarters tended toward nostalgic recollections of the Prahbrindrah Drah, the Radisha and even the Liberator.

Soulcatcher asked, "Does anyone happen to know how long it takes to get a barge down the Naghir, through the delta channels, and upriver to Taglios?" She knew barges manned by veteran crews traveled day and night, unlike soldiers afoot or on horseback.

Another disturbance at the entrance arose before anyone produced a reliable answer.

The drizzle had ended, she discovered. Yet the men demanding attention were covered with mud. And they had brought her a present.

"For me? And it's not even my birthday."

Goblin was a present who looked way the worse for use. He was bound and gagged. His head and hands were wrapped in rags as well. His captors had been determined to take no chances.

Soulcatcher gloated. "He stumbled into one of my traps, didn't he?"

"Yes he did, ma'am."

There were hundreds of those out there, taking many forms. Soulcatcher had begun to put them out as soon as it had become evident that the new, improved Goblin could evade the best efforts of her soldiers. "He's still alive, isn't he?" If he was dead her concern that he might have allowed himself to be caught would slide down her list of worries.

"Your instructions were perfectly clear, ma'am."

Soulcatcher memorized that man's face. He was mocking her behind a mask of rectitude. She preferred open defiance. That she could crush without mystifying anyone. "Take the mask and gag off. Set him up over here." The Daughter of Night, Soulcatcher noted, was interested enough to forget to hide her interest.

She could not know the little wizard's significance, could she?

No. Impossible. The girl was just doing what she did whenever anything happened inside the tent. She paid attention because she might learn something useful.

Soulcatcher waited until she judged that Goblin was sufficiently recovered. She told him, "Your former brothers really don't like turncoats, do they?"

Goblin stared at her with eyes colder, deeper and more remote than those of the Daughter of Night. He did not reply.

She stepped closer. Her mask was just a foot from his face. She purred, "They came to me for help settling your account."

Goblin twitched but remained silent. He did try to look around.

He smiled when he glimpsed the Daughter of Night.

Soulcatcher said, "They told me all about it, little man. They told me what you are now. They expect me to just kill you because of what you did to my foot. They really just want you dead." She rubbed her gloved hands together. "But I think I'm going to be a lot cruder." She giggled.

"All their days are numbered," Goblin said in a whisper. The voice borrowing the taunt only vaguely resembled that of the man who had gone down into the earth to challenge the Dark Mother.

"Some more closely than others." Soulcatcher's voice was old and emotionless. Her right hand lashed out, sliced across Goblin's face. Blades a half inch long on the ends of her fingers destroyed his eyes and the bridge of his nose. He shrieked, at first as much in surprise as in pain.

The Protector turned on the men who had brought the prisoner in. "Bring me another cage like the one the brat is in." The cage did in fact exist already. Such had been her certainty that she would capture Goblin.

The blacksmith had orders to create three more, suitable for housing her sister, her sister's husband, and that treacherous Willow Swan.

Later, in Taglios, she meant to work with a glassblower to bottle them all so they could be displayed outside the entrance to her palace. They would be kept alive and fed until they drowned in their own ordure.

Such was the fate that the Dominator often bestowed upon his most important enemies, in his time.

60

Gharhawnes:
Tobo and the Voroshk

The Howler certainly kept busy. He completed his first functional four-passenger flying carpet two days after the soldiers marched westward. Gharhawnes seemed deserted, though there were enough of us around to bloody a bunch of noses the morning the former tenant took a notion to steal his home back.

Sleepy had a dozen carpets on order, from single-rider scouts to a monster she hoped would carry twenty soldiers. I do not know who she expected to fly them. Only Howler and Tobo—and, possibly, the Voroshk—had the power to manage the things.

I insisted that we have a couple of modest-sized carpets first. Those should not take too long to make and would be the size most useful to us right away. And since I was in charge of the left-behinds and the Dejagore strike I got what I wanted. Well, I got the one carpet.

Tobo had the flying post thing figured out, too. Both Shukrat and Arkana seemed eager to get along now. One or the other would allow Tobo to borrow her post when he wanted to run out to visit Sleepy, which he did by night so he would not be seen from the ground. I never felt comfortable when he did that. We had too many potentially unpleasant and unfriendly people back here in the manor. Including a lot of hostages from the leading families of the region.

Both Magadan and Gromovol were increasingly determined not to be won over, each for his own reasons. I told Magadan, "I'd be tempted to send you two home just so I don't have to worry about what's going on behind my back." I was not worried, really. Tobo's supernatural friends saw everything.

Magadan told me, "I don't want to go home. Home no longer exists. I want to be free."

"Sure. You Voroshk showed what you can do when you're free. I've spent my life killing people like you. That's people who believe it's their destiny to make slaves out of people like me. I'm in a war with another one of them right now. I'm not about to cut you loose and let you start making peoples' lives miserable, too."

None of which was absolutely true but it did sound good. And Magadan bought it. Some. The part that really was true. That I would kill him before I turned him loose on the world.

That was the moment when he decided he might want to go home after all. From then on he brought that possibility up each time we crossed paths. The hidden folk said he was sincere. He was trying to get the other kids to go along with swapping what knowledge they had for an escort back across the place of glittering stone.

Lady did not believe it. She thought we should put him and Gromovol down because of the trouble they could cause.

My sweetie has a very direct approach to problem-solving.

Sometimes I do find what little conscience I retain a damnable handicap.

Howler, though, did successfully work his way out of the top ten on my shit list. Tobo's appeal to Shivetya had resulted in word from the golem saying he did have the ability to intervene in Howler's screaming and shrinking problems. Shivetya did not have much of a reputation as a liar so even Howler took him at his word. After which the smelly little wizard became extremely cooperative.

Though we still had no cause to trust his long run intentions. Nor he any call to trust ours, either.

Lady cornered Tobo. "We have a dangerous situation, here. And like a pet cobra it's going to bite us someday. We have to do something."

The boy sounded puzzled. "What're you talking about? Something about what?"

"Those Voroshk. They aren't as strong or as bright as we first thought but there are four of them and only one of you."

"But they're not going to. . . ."

"Pardon me for being an old cynic," I said. "Magadan keeps telling me, in so many words, that he wants to be anywhere that isn't here with us. And there's at least the implication that he'll do whatever it takes if we don't help him go home. And Gromovol is going to be trouble eventually because his personality requires it. If you go out to visit Sleepy or just on a flying date the rest of us are stuck here with no better hope than the Howler."

"And speaking of flying," Lady said, "don't you *ever* go out with both of those girls again. Hush! You're only familiar with the women you've grown up around. I'm telling you right now that Arkana is exactly like Magadan. But she has one more weapon than he does and she means to use it to cloud your mind."

"But . . ."

"Shukrat I'm not sure about. There's a chance Shukrat is exactly what she seems."

I agreed. The kid was likable. And according to Tobo the hidden folk agreed. They offered no reason not to trust her.

Tobo was not used to arguing with anybody but his mother, even when he thought he was right. He did not want to think ill of Arkana but would not fight us.

Lady demanded, "So how do we make sure of them? You have to think of something before we move against Dejagore. We'll be scattered, distracted and extremely vulnerable then. And because you spend time with the girls, out amongst the rest of us, all four will know what's going on. They can plan accordingly."

Again Tobo did not get a word in before I said, "I would be."

Lady reminded him, "You've never been a prisoner."

"Now there's a joke. I was born a prisoner. A prisoner of a prophecy by an old woman who died years before I was born. A prisoner of the expectations of all you people. Gods, I wish Hong Tray was wrong and I could've been a normal kid."

"There aren't any normal kids, Tobo," I told him. "Just kids who fake it better than the rest of us do."

"And that name. Tobo. That was my baby name. Why does everybody still call me that? Why didn't we ever have a ceremony to give me a grown-up name?"

Nyueng Bao do that. And Tobo was years past the appropriate birthday.

Lady told him, "You'll have to take that up with Uncle Doj. Meantime, the other thing needs addressing right now. Blade is moving already. In three more days Sleepy will curl back to the northeast and it'll be too late to stop anything. I want to be sure that we won't get stabbed in the back just when things get exciting."

An hour after we nagged him Tobo asked Shukrat to go flying. He borrowed Arkana's log. Arkana was not pleased. When an hour later she told me Magadan had said he did not mind if she used his post to join Shukrat and Tobo I told her, "But I mind. If you need to talk to Tobo do it when he gets back."

Arkana was the brightest of the Voroshk. She recognized that things were tightening up.

When Tobo did return he stayed just long enough to round up Magadan. He took Magadan flying. It was the first time Magadan had been aloft since he had entered our keeping. He did not appear excited, which I would have expected.

They returned within a half hour. Magadan's hand-me-downs, appropriated from Gharhawnes' former occupants, were ragged. He looked like he had been in a fight and the other guy had kicked his butt. A good long way.

Tobo gave instructions for Magadan to be isolated, then found Arkana and took her for a fly.

The ice queen, I noted, had replaced her confiscated robes with native garb that served her to considerable visual advantage.

"Down, boy!" Lady said.

"It's a good thing I didn't run into her before I met you, isn't it?"

That earned me a not entirely playful swat.

Arkana came back looking rougher than Magadan had. And she was not smiling.

Tobo had Arkana put in with Magadan. He collected Gromovol.

Gromovol was not interested in going anywhere with Tobo. Tobo insisted. They were not gone long. Once they returned Tobo had the Voroshk returned to their quarters. He gathered their flying posts in the main hall. Lady and I joined him.

I asked, "What was that all about?"

"I took them out and dueled with them. Except for Shukrat."

I stopped Lady before she explained—probably at great length—how unsmart doing that could have proven. Sometimes she could fuss as much as Sahra. I said, "I'm sure there was a reason."

"I wanted to find out just how much we really do have to fear from them."

"And?"

"They're frauds. The only power they really have is what they draw from their post and their clothing. Without those even Shukrat isn't as powerful as One-Eye was at the end. Gromovol is about Uncle Doj's equal. Lady, even as weak as you are right now, you could manage any of them but Shukrat."

I snorted. "I guess that would explain why Gromovol's pop was anxious to get the kids back. Were most of the Voroshk limited talents? Were most of them carried by a few strong members of the clan?"

"I'd guess that's likely. The point, though, is that for right now there's a better chance our Voroshk will attack us with knives than with sorcery." He looked at us, saw no obvious eagerness to embrace his theory. "Don't you think that if they had any real power they would've used it to try to escape?"

I realized that he was upset. He had believed he was making friends with the Voroshk. Our worries had led him to test that and he had learned that his friends were not as close as he had hoped.

"You're telling us we don't have to kill them to be safe," Lady said.

"That, too."

"You have the Unknown Shadows at your command and you didn't figure this out until today?" Lady can find something to suspect in everything. I would suggest we retire and settle down somewhere where we do not have to worry all the time but she would suspect me of ulterior motives.

"I've thought it for a long time," he admitted sullenly. "But the hidden folk can't report things that they don't hear. The Voroshk don't discuss their weaknesses. Or much of anything else, actually. Because of their present situation nobody likes anybody very much anymore."

I said, "I didn't want to kill them, anyway. Maybe I'd like to thump Gromovol a little, now and then, but . . ."

"So that's settled. Heck, turn them loose if you want. Once they've had a dose of the real world they'll come back. Meantime, let me get to work on these things."

Lady asked, "You've finally found their secret? You can make more?"

"I've learned how to change who they recognize as their master. None of the Voroshk know how the posts are made. They're not even sure of the theory behind them. I know more than they do just because I've studied the things. I don't yet know how they pull their magical power. But I don't know how I do that, either. Someday I will know. But it'll be a long, slow, dangerous process, finding out. They're booby-trapped."

I told him, "Life is booby-trapped, kid."

As we left the hallway Lady was speculating on whether the original Voroshk had invented their magics or if they had just stolen them from an ingenious but unwary predecessor. I did not care, so long as no Voroshk made my life more difficult than it already was.

61

The Taglian Territories: Nightfliers in Dejagore

Three flying posts formed the goose flock formation. Tobo had the point with Willow Swan riding pillion. Swan was in the throes of an apparently severe religious relapse, muttering a continuous polysyllabic one-word prayer. With his attitude toward heights he would be bruising Tobo by hanging on so tight. His eyes would be closed so intently that he would have muscle cramps all the way back to his ankles.

Lady and Shukrat flew the other posts. Lady had Aridatha Singh aboard behind her. Shukrat carried Uncle Doj.

Murgen, Thai Dei and I shared the flying carpet with the Howler, whose shrieks were being contained inside a big glass bowl sort of thing Lady had put over his head. It worked well enough to save trouble with people who did not know we were coming.

Murgen and Thai Dei were along only because Sahra had to be placated. She did not want her baby going into harm's way alone. People everywhere were irked because the boy's father and uncle had had to be flown back to Gharhawnes before the raid could be launched. But Sahra had been stubborn and loud and Sleepy had given in rather than lose a friend.

Sahra's recollections of and fears of Dejagore remained abiding and debilitating.

I hoped Murgen and Thai Dei handled it better, though at takeoff time Murgen had been sweaty, pallid, shaking and appeared to be having trouble breathing. And Thai Dei had seemed more self-engrossed than ever.

I had spoken to each alone and had tried telling each that I was counting on him to keep an eye on the other and carry him if the emotional strain became too much. I have found that assigning major external responsibilities like that can get many of my brothers through times of deep emotional stress.

Howler kept the carpet in the pocket of the formation. We moved northward at a pace that created a cold wind strong enough to pull the tears out of my eyes. Murgen and I occupied the carpet's rear corners. I told him, "I'd forgotten just how much I don't like this. Why didn't I send some of those eager young bucks from Hsien?"

"Because you're just like every other recent Captain of the Company. You've got to have your pointy nose right in the middle of things so you can make sure things get done your way."

Up ahead Tobo lifted the shutter on a red lantern. He winked the light several times. There was an answering signal from the ground, miles off our track and much farther forward than I expected.

Blade and the cavalry had made good time and were already in the ring of hills surrounding Dejagore. The moon would rise in an hour. It would provide the light they needed to filter through the hills and descend the inner slope.

We passed over the rim and discovered the scattered lights of Dejagore. We slowed to a crawl. The flying posts gathered together. Aridatha tried to explain to Tobo where we needed to go.

I told Murgen, "You should've gone with Tobo. You know Dejagore better than anyone else."

"Dejagore twenty-five years ago, maybe. It's a whole new city since my day. Aridatha belongs with him. It's only been weeks since he was there."

Few details could be distinguished by starlight but as we moved closer the walls and main buildings matched my recollections almost exactly.

The logs formed up in line astern with Lady and Aridatha leading. Howler fell in behind. We resumed moving.

Ten minutes later we were on the ground. Five minutes after that Aridatha hustled us into his brother's shop.

Sugriva Singh seemed to be a shorter and older version of Aridatha. He had done well for himself. He had the whole downstairs of a building for his business and everything above for his family—none of whom were ever in evidence.

Sugriva's past good fortune assured his deep displeasure at our invasion. All of a sudden he had ten villains in amongst the vegetables and only his brother and the bountiful little blonde did not look willing to roast him for a prank. He had a great deal to lose here. And maybe more to lose if he did not cooperate. The Strangler cult was hated in the extreme in Dejagore. Just a whisper about his relationship to the living saint of the Deceivers would destroy him and just about anyone who had ever spoken to him.

Aridatha dispensed with introductions. Sugriva did not need to know his visitors. Chances were, he recognized a few of us anyway.

Aridatha told his brother, "Our father is dead. He was murdered a few weeks ago. Strangled."

Sugriva was the elder by a decade. He remembered the Narayan Singh who had sold vegetables and doted on his children before the invasion of the Shadowmasters. He was stricken as Aridatha had not been stricken. "And that should be no surprise, should it? Is that what you mean?" Sugriva said through tears that might have been due as much to rage as to pain.

He needed a few minutes to collect himself.

To his credit Sugriva Singh did not rail against the inevitable. He understood exactly how his arm was being twisted and, though events were not going to proceed quite like Aridatha had led him to expect during his previous visit, he chose to cooperate. He wanted to get it over as fast as he could, then he would pray that the new administration would be as indifferent to him as he was to the one presently in place.

Things were not exactly working out the way Aridatha had hoped they would, either.

Sugriva said, "You haven't chosen the best night to do this. The moon is going to expose anyone moving toward the city from outside."

Tobo chuckled. "You might be surprised. The night is our friend, brother Sugriva."

"I rather expect you'll find that my father believed the same thing, young man."

And his father's son? Sugriva had been unhappy, even angry, when we turned up, but not really surprised. What kind of vegetable dealer was not surprised to be wakened in the night? Inside a city that closed its gates with fanatical devotion when the sun's lower limb touched the western hilltops?

Could Aridatha's big brother be some sort of crook?

Aridatha told his brother, "The reason we're troubling you is that we don't know how the gatekeeping is managed."

"You told me before. I looked into it. There's a company of soldiers assigned to each gate. The west gate is the most closely controlled because it sees more traffic than the other three put together." One of Dejagore's quirks was that most of today's roads to the city joined outside it, to the west, so there was not much traffic elsewhere. The north and south gates were used only by people involved in agriculture and its produce.

"The east gate looks like it should be the easiest to seize and control," Sugriva said. A true road did connect with the east gate but there was little out that way but a few distant villages. "The guards are slackers, at all levels. None of them are natives. None of them are old enough to remember the last time Jaicur was attacked." Sugriva had adopted the local accent and the local name for the city when he had assumed a Dejagoran name.

The trouble with the east gate was that Blade was west of Dejagore. But he was well ahead of schedule. There was time, before sunrise, if he hustled.

Tobo suggested, "Lady, why don't you go tell Blade that it has to be the east gate?"

"Because I'm going to be getting dressed."

Widowmaker and Lifetaker were coming to the party. They had been away for far too long.

Half a minute later Shukrat said, "I guess it's time to find out if you can really trust me, Tobo."

I jumped in before the boy could speak. "I suppose so. Tell Blade not to waste time. We need as much of the night as we can get. And we won't stay unnoticed long once we start. Tell him we'll be waiting when he gets to the gate."

A smile tickled Shukrat's freckled, almost pudgy face. She bounced up onto her toes and gave Tobo a peck on the cheek. Bold, bold behavior by any standard in this part of the world. They must do things differently among the Voroshk.

She bounced away. Tobo was completely flustered. I grinned till Lady poked me in the ribs. Evidently I was enjoying the bouncing part a little too much.

Murgen said, "I suggest we get to work here, folks. I don't want to be inside these walls a minute longer than I have to." He was holding it together but the strain was obvious.

Thai Dei was frazzled, too, and with even better reason. A lot of people very close to him had died here during the siege. No matter how tough a man pretends to be, such losses gnaw at his soul. Unless he is not human at all.

"The man has a point," I said. "Start getting ready."

Lady and I had the most to do. We had a big show to put on. We retreated into a small separate room, colder than the main shop. As we strove to turn ourselves into walking nightmares I asked, "Hon, have you really got that post-riding stuff figured out?"

"It isn't that hard. Except for staying on. Any idiot could do it. There are some little black rods and slidy things you move around. You go up or down, or faster or slower, or whatever, when you do. Why?"

"It occurs to me that it might be better for us and him both if we got Aridatha back to Taglios. He's been gone a long time. Mogaba needs to have him back where he can show him off before news of tonight's business gets around."

She did not stop donning the Lifetaker armor but did look at me in a way that I do not see often. It was like she was looking right through me, at all the secret places inside. It was frightening sometimes.

"All right. We'll have to move fast if I'm going to be aloft before daylight."

"Will the log make it that far?" Not knowing how those things worked I did not know what you might have to feed it, like a horse. The posts did seem to work on a different principle than Howler's flying carpets, which required a strong-willed, powerful sorcerer to drive them. They demanded his undivided attention every moment they were aloft.

"I'm sure it will. What do you want me to tell Mogaba?"

The long-time taunt, "My brother unforgiven," came to mind, along with, "All their days are numbered." But this was not the time.

62

Dejagore:
The Occupation

My original intention had been to make a huge show of our invasion. I do like a big ration of drama. Lightning. Thunder. Fireworks. But I waited until we had the gate open to let it start.

Early on there were alarms from the south wall as a tide of darkness and whispers passed by. But no sentry saw a single horsemen. They spied only vague shapes that stirred secret fears of things far darker and crueler than any conquering soldier.

The city was restless and troubled but remained unaware of our presence. It did sense approaching change.

The thunder and lightning came after Blade's men started coming through the gate, six hundred men in Hsien's strange armor, under strict orders not to betray their humanity until the city was captured. Most Dejagorans were Gunni. The Gunni believed in demons who could take human shape to make war on men. And most of the people of the outlying Taglian Territories had by now heard that the Company was allied with ghosts and devils.

Each soldier had a bamboo wand carrying a banner affixed to his back. The color of the banner declared the man's unit affiliation while characters painted on the banner stated that unit's martial slogan. Widowmaker and Lifetaker rode at the head of the invading column. She carried a burning sword. Widowmaker carried One-Eye's spear, which was crawling with maggots of light. His shoulders bore a salt-and-pepper set of oversized ravens.

And, even so, much of the city slept on.

Ugly worms of fire crawled over our hideous armor.

Bannermen marched ahead flailing big flags supposed to be our personal ensigns.

Witnesses brought out by the flash and boom and the rattle of horseshoes remembered old stories and ran away weeping.

Yet most of the city slept on.

Doj, Murgen, Thai Dei and Swan remained at the gate, holding the hostages we had taken there. Aridatha stayed out of sight at his brother's place. Howler, Tobo and Shukrat circled high above. Howler's glass bowl continued to contain his shrieks. We hoped he would remain a secret for a while.

The real fireworks began when we reached the citadel, where the Protector's still-sleepy governor deluded himself into thinking he could refuse to surrender and make it stick.

Fireballs flew. The citadel gate exploded. Holes appeared in its walls. People inside began to scream.

Every dark place in the streets had something moving inside it. Hundreds of somethings, many of them vaguely familiar in those instants when anything could be clearly discerned.

Those flooded in through the broken gate of the citadel. They weaseled through the holes in its walls.

Lifetaker and Widowmaker followed moments later.

The terrified inhabitants of the tower put up no fight at all. Our sole injury was a broken arm suffered by a dimwit who tripped over his own big feet and rolled down a stair.

Lady and I stood atop the citadel. The city below still was not fully aware that it had been conquered. I said, "It hurt a lot less getting here tonight than it did last time."

"That was the night we made Booboo."

"Which was a real booboo."

"Not funny."

"That was the night One-Eye made the enemy that stalked us for twenty years, too."

"We'll make new enemies this time. I have to go if I want to have any hope of getting Aridatha into Taglios unnoticed."

"I don't think you can, tonight. Not without flying so

damned fast the wind rips the skin off your face."

"I'll see if Tobo can't help."

It was difficult to kiss her good-bye. We still wore all the costume armor.

63

The Taglian Territories: The Middle Army

The Protector's reconnaissance troops had warned her that something unusual was taking shape. The warning confirmed her suspicions. Her nonhuman spies had been having almost no success keeping track of the enemy. Which meant the enemy was taking pains to be less visible.

Soulcatcher raised the state of alert and stepped up training. She redoubled her own, personal preparations.

When word of the disaster at Dejagore reached her—one lone rider managing to get through with the news—she had known for fourteen hours already that the Company main force had left its westward track and had begun hustling up a line that would slice between her Middle Army and the newly orphaned force outside Dejagore.

That would evaporate within days, she presumed. Many of those soldiers came out of the city itself—a disproportionate percentage of them officers—while the rest would now hear the call of the harvest much more loudly.

What the hell had happened down there? The messenger had brought very few details, just word that the city had awakened to find itself occupied. The invaders had been swift and thorough. They seemed to have had outstanding intelligence. Heavy sorcery might have been involved.

"The next fight won't be so one-sided," she promised her officers. "Next fight they'll have to deal with me. Me like they haven't seen me in a long, long time." She was angry and awake and no longer handicapped by any shred of boredom. She was feeling more alive and filled with hatred and bitterness than she had for a generation.

Within hours her new mood had electrified those around her.

Officers who failed to become equally electrified quickly suffered permanent replacement.

64

Dejagore:
The Orphaned Army

After losing their base at Dejagore the generals of the fading, confused army nearby ineptly tried to invest the city in a way that would not result in economic disaster. Then, six days after the fall, news came that the enemy main force was rushing straight toward them.

There had been skirmishes with the cavalry occupying Dejagore. Those had not gone well for the locals. And now ten times as many well-disciplined, perfectly-armed, trained killers were about to fall on them.

A third of the army went home under cover of darkness the night after the news arrived. Those who stayed endured almost continuous psychological torments by things they could never see.

The murderous army from the south never materialized. That was never necessary. The Dejagoran soldiers in the Taglian force all deserted. The cavalrymen occupying Dejagore scattered the army's steadfast core without outside help.

65

Taglios:
The Palace

Mogaba's level of discomfort—he would not think the word "fear"—had risen substantially since Aridatha's return. The stakes kept rising. The risks kept expanding. Lady had been seen by Palace servants. So far those believed they had seen the Protector, whose comings and goings were secretive and unpredictable. But someday Soulcatcher might overhear some mention and know she could not have been two places at once. Nor would she believe the manifestation to have been one of the haunts now regularly seen in the maze of passageways for which the Palace was famed.

Mogaba told Ghopal and Aridatha, "I'm tempted to drop everything and run."

Ghopal asked, "Yeah? Where would you go?" It might not be as personal but his doom was every bit as certain as Mogaba's was if the Black Company reconquered Taglios and restored the ruling family. Life would turn cruel for any Shadar who had belonged to the Greys.

"Exactly." Mogaba ran his palm over the top of his head. Keeping it shaved required less and less work. "So I remind myself what honor demands."

Aridatha said little. He had not talked much since his return. Mogaba understood. Singh had seen things he did not want to believe were true. He had learned things about the stakes that left him paralyzed with indecision. There appeared to be no road leading toward the light. Wherever he turned he beheld another face of the darkness.

It was important to Aridatha that he do what he perceived to be the right thing.

Singh's visit with his brother had fueled him with a determination to offset some of the evil his father had done.

Aridatha was Gunni by faith but his character was much
more suited to the Vehdna religion. He thought *this* was the
life where wrongs had to be made right.

Mogaba said, "The news from the south is uniformly dis-
asterous. The Black Company is meeting very little resistance. They have superior sorcery, superior weaponry, superior
troops, equipment and leadership. Not to mention intelligence
so good we're wasting our time trying to keep anything secret.
So it seems our fates actually depend on how fast those people
can get here. The Protector won't stop them. They'll pluck the
strings of her ego, tickle her pride, and just when she thinks
she's ready to make her kill they'll hit her in the back of the
head with a sledgehammer she'll never see coming. You have
to be more than just powerful to deal with those people. You
have to be more than clever and treacherous. You need to be
psychic."

Ghopal asked, "Then why don't we ride down there and
take charge?" He smirked.

"Not funny. Two reasons. First, she doesn't want me to.
She still thinks we can get them into a pocket between us. I
don't know how. And, more importantly, if I got anywhere
near her there'd be no way I could hide my thoughts and no
opportunity to put them into effect before she could protect
herself. You two, you might be a little luckier."

Ghopal observed, "The city is remarkably calm in spite of
the news."

Tidings of the fall of Dejagore were making the rounds
but hardly anyone seemed to feel that the Protector was in
any peril herself. There had been no disorders. Graffiti was
becoming more common, though. Mostly the same old
taunts, though rajadharma was becoming more common.
Then there was a new one: You shall lie in the ashes ten
thousand years eating only wind. And one not seen for years
had reappeared: Thi Kim is coming.

No one knew quite what that meant. Maybe not even its
framers. Some people thought "Thi Kim" might be a

Nyueng Bao phrase. In which case the name could mean something like Walking Murder.

If it was not Nyueng Bao it made even less sense. Or no sense at all.

Aridatha asked, "If we do nothing to support her and she gets beaten, how do we defend ourselves?"

Mogaba said, "I'm going to tell you right now, *you* don't have a problem unless the Protector wins. The Company and the royals have no quarrel with you. You've done a good job running the City Battalions. If you just sit on your hands you'll probably end up inheriting my job."

Aridatha shrugged. "You must have talked about these things when *she* was here."

"Oh, yes. She said nobody would chase me very hard if I had sense enough to take off before they occupied the city."

Ghopal asked, "They're that confident? That they can discount your help? What about me?"

"She's that confident. Which is probably too confident. She didn't say anything about you. She didn't know who you were. She suggested that if you think you have reasons to fear the return of the royals you should join me in looting as much treasure as you can before you run away."

"Shadar don't abandon their oaths of service."

Aridatha, with little to fear from defeat, suggested, "Let's just do our jobs. Like we've always done. And see what opportunities Fortune places in our hands."

Sarcastically, Ghopal responded, "Of course. The Black Company and the Protector could end up destroying each other. Like a couple of rams getting their horns locked."

A consideration which left all three men thoughtful, with Mogaba in particular reflecting on how fate might write the joke that would end with that unexpected punchline.

66

The Taglian Territories:
Midway Between

Oh, we looked good, ten thousand strong, all lined up as if for a parade. Every man wore his armor. Every man had his personal banner whipping in the breeze. Every battalion wore its own color of armor. Every weapon was perfectly honed and polished. Every horse was groomed and caparisoned as though for review. Every standard was in place and gloriously new. We were a general's wet dream, pretty and dangerous, too.

The gang opposite us, though they outnumbered us three to one, looked like they would be no challenge. Men over there were still trying to find their assigned places in ranks.

Good as it all looked I had my doubts about the wisdom of offering battle, however confident our guys were and however much confidence the men opposite us lacked. But Sleepy wanted to crush them fast and harry Soulcatcher back to Taglios where, because she would be hard-pressed, she might not be wary enough to elude ambush by Mogaba and his henchmen.

She was assuming too much would go our way. When things are going good is when you really have to watch your back.

But I was not the Captain. I could only advise, then do my part in the show once a decision had been made.

Tobo was more confident than Sleepy was. He believed the enemy only needed a nudge to crack. One vicious shock and they would collapse. He guaranteed it.

Trumpets sounded the ready. Drums began to talk, counting the cadence for the advance. A thousand men would remain in reserve. Well behind them were the recruits we had acquired. Those surrounded the Radisha and her brother, nominally forming the royal lifeguard. They would be used only in desperation.

The trumpets sounded the advance. The ranks stepped out, lines dressed, cadence perfect, weapons exactly on line. Positioned in front of the wings, Lifetaker and Widowmaker lit off in blinding flashes and began to advance themselves. But they halted before they entered missile range.

From that closer vantage I could see that Soulcatcher had formed her troops up in three successive forces with a hundred yards of separation each between them. The frontline unit was the most numerous but looked like the lowest quality. The second formation appeared much more solid.

That was a device I understood, having used a variant myself. But you have to be confident that your real fighters will not catch the panic of the scrubs when they run away.

There were things going on behind Soulcatcher's third line but they were too far away to be made out clearly.

Then the advancing soldiers made seeing much more difficult. Then the next stage of enchantments surrounded me, concealing me from enemy eyes, making it impossible for me to see anything either.

67

The Taglian Territories: Inside the Middle Army

"This is going to be tricky," Soulcatcher reminded staff officers compelled to take her genius on trust. Her previous demonstration, during the Kiaulune wars, had come before their time.

The enemy trumpets sounded the ready. His drums began to rumble.

Soulcatcher said, "Once they sound the advance they'll be too busy to spy on us."

The advance sounded.

"I want the word spread on the second line that the collapse of the first line is part of my plan. Tell them it's a deliberate ruse. I don't want anybody running because the first line does. Tell them that anybody who does run is guaranteed worm food. Then tell the third line the same thing about the first and second lines. I want them to believe I'm luring the enemy in where I can use sorcery to destroy them. And I want the reserves backed off to the edge of the wood. Right away."

"But that means . . ."

"Forget the camp. If we don't win this fight the camp won't matter. I want the reserves spread out along the edge of the woods so they can collect up men who run away and get them organized. But before they do that I want them in here to move my guests back to the north bank of the creek."

Blank looks stared her way.

Anger began to creep into her voice. Anger they knew to be the sort that soon saw corpses arriving on the cemetery ground outside camp. When Soulcatcher was angry enough she would not let the Gunni burn, and thus purify, the bodies of those she had slain. "Form them at the edge of the woods! Ready to kill any cowards!" Then in a calm, almost beatific voice she added, "If the soldiers fail to rally and throw back the enemy their generals won't long survive defeat." Soulcatcher had very strong feelings about how this engagement should proceed. "In fact, the wise general will make plans not to outlive his standard bearer. His passing will be much less painful that way."

She had been preparing for days. But she was compelled to fight with flawed weapons. The most rigid control had to be exercised.

"Get busy!" She stepped past the officers, left the tent, climbed up a reviewing stand that would let her see the action. As she took her place there the enemy, with the precision of a drill team, collided with her forward deployment.

The slaughter was slighter than she had anticipated. The enemy seemed content to shatter opposing formations. They did not pursue. They halted, removed wounded, dressed their ranks and repaired their equipment. And took their time doing it. Which pleased the Protector. That meant more time for the beaten companies to collect themselves at the edge of the wood.

Soulcatcher glanced back as men carried her prisoners' cages out of her tent. Goblin, his eyes regenerated already, offered her a little mocking salute. The girl looked straight at her and smiled.

One more time and she would throw the brat to the soldiers for a few hours. That would take the sass out of her.

The soldiers managing the removal seemed calm enough, despite the terrified fugitives beginning to enter the camp.

Soulcatcher was irritated at herself for having overlooked the chance that the fugitives might not flee all the way to the woods. She should have had the palisade demolished.

No matter. Only a few would take refuge here.

She gave orders to seal the gates.

The enemy resumed his advance.

The second line gave a better account of itself but the outcome was identical. The troops broke without doing much real damage to the foe.

This time none of the fleeing soldiers got into the camp.

Once again the enemy stopped to handle his wounded and dress his lines and repair his armor. The cavalry screening the enemy flanks were having trouble holding back. Soulcatcher guessed that discipline would crack once the third Taglian line fell apart.

Those idiots had better be ready back at the wood.

Soulcatcher left her vantage as the enemy sounded the advance again. "Very businesslike, this new Captain. But how well does she think on her feet?"

Very businesslike, Soulcatcher's personal removal to the wood, where she growled new orders at her officers before she retired to the big tent she had had prepared, as a pretended forest getaway and as a place where she could meet messengers from the allies who were trying to butcher her now. Goblin and the Daughter of Night had been deposited there.

Both prisoners seemed amused by her arrival. As though they had shared some particularly hysterical joke, entirely at her expense, just a moment before she appeared.

Soulcatcher paid them no attention. She was much more concerned about how troubled her sister would have grown because of the absence of sorcery on the battlefield. If no one became too suspicious for another fifteen minutes . . .

68

The Taglian Territories:
Fire on the Middle Ground

Behind the brilliant fog of light masking Widowmaker I climbed down off my horse, then clambered onto the Voroshk flying post I would share with my former understudy, Murgen. The post had Magadan's name painted on it in his native script. Over on the left, Lifetaker, too, was preparing to soar with that noted devotee of high flying, Willow Swan. All of the flying logs were ready to go up, each surrounded by an absurd wicker and bamboo framework carrying numerous makeshift attachments.

Somewhere back where I could not see them, Tobo and Howler were getting ready to take up a flying carpet creaking under the weight of warlike unpleasantries. The screaming wizard was still muttering under his breath because he had been forced to reveal his flying secrets to Tobo.

A huge volume of raw nastiness would be taken aloft, to

be launched either when Soulcatcher betrayed her location or our attack began to bog down.

The latter did not happen. The evaporation of the Taglian front line was a daydream come true. The second line lasted only a little while longer. The third line, evidently comprised of the best and most motivated of the Protector's troops, was more stubborn. Having spent too much time too close to Soulcatcher myself, I could imagine why the third force might have had a little extra motivation. Soulcatcher was not a thoughtful, forgiving commander.

Give her her due, though. She would not expect love or forgiveness from anyone superior to her, either. In the world where she had come of age that had been the norm. That world, of the Domination, had demanded ruthlessness and cruelty. It had forgiven neither kindness nor compassion.

The third line's stubbornness failed to withstand the precision and confidence of our men. Fainthearts began to slip away and run toward that distant treeline, where somebody appeared to be rallying survivors.

The rout had only just begun when a dome of cardinal light popped into existence in an instant, straight ahead. It faded in seconds. I was making a clumsy effort to gain altitude when a second dome of light, this time carmine, appeared and faded to my left.

There were a half dozen more flashes, each in the family of reds, before I felt confident that I was high enough and dared to divert attention from the post's controls long enough to see what Murgen had been babbling about throughout our climb.

The sorcery in progress appeared to have turned the earth a uniform black. Upon that surface something kept painting red flowers that spread from a pinpoint in an eyes' blink, almost black at the center but fading to flame yellow as the circle ended its expansion at perhaps twelve yards in diameter. From on high nothing but the sudden red chrysanthemums, blooming randomly, were readily visible. The earth looked like some bleak gameboard upon which a garden of deathflowers continue to blossom and gradually fade.

Whatever was happening, it was passive. Not coming to us. The sorcery had been in place already and was being tripped by our advancing soldiers. Who were not getting off lightly.

Soulcatcher did not make herself evident anywhere.

Way off to my left Lady and Willow vanished behind smoke as all the bamboo fireball launchers attached to their post sprayed the Taglian camp. Dozens of fires broke out down there but the red circles kept blooming amongst our soldiers.

I pushed my post forward half a mile. I told Murgen, "Saturate the wood. She's in there somewhere. Where the hell are my crows? They're never around when I need them." They had disappeared during my climb to altitude. Maybe they did not like getting too far from the surface of the earth.

There was no sign of the Unknown Shadows anywhere. But I did not expect to see signs. Tobo had sent most of the hidden folk away last night, for their own safety.

You notice strange things in times of stress. I remarked the absence of crows around the battlefield. A rather bizarre lacking which I had not witnessed before, ever. But vultures had begun to circle above the wood.

Murgen shouted something about the enemy taking heart from our misfortune. I said, "Put the fireballs along the treeline, then." Which was really my task since I had to point the Voroshk post where I wanted the fireballs to go.

Child Shukrat, better schooled in the use of the post, swept in from the east, low, laying her fire down upon the Taglian line. She wasted hardly a fireball.

Our ground advance halted. Sleepy did not withdraw but neither was she willing to face any more killing sorcery.

I would not see how bad that had been until I was back on the ground. Which was soon enough because once we exhausted our fireball supply there was nothing more Murgen and I could do from above.

I had no trouble imagining Soulcatcher over there in those woods laughing her leathers off at how she had hurt us.

The Taglians launched one uncoordinated, inept counterattack which turned disastrous when they began to run away again. Soulcatcher's sorceries did not distinguish between friend and foe, only between directions of travel.

We grounded well to the rear. I remounted my horse and went forward. Soulcatcher's sorcery had been terrible. The site where each flower of light had bloomed remained defined as a red so dark it verged on black. The black itself was fading from around the circles, trampled grass gradually becoming visible like winter wheat sprouting. But weirder crops appeared within the circles.

Men, sunken into the earth, some only ankle deep, some up to their hips and more. Frozen in the advance, still in their lines. All suits of armor no longer tenanted by even a ghost of life.

Somebody had tried opening several suits. Inside there was nothing but charred flesh and bone. A quick calculation suggested we might have lost four or five hundred men to this horror, which had taken place almost faster than it can be told.

"There's something wrong here," I said. "Soulcatcher has stopped."

"What?" Murgen asked. He was probing a deadly circle. He discovered that it was cool now and the visible surface was no thicker than a fingernail. "What's that?" Later, when we collected the dead, we learned that they had not sunk into the earth. The apparently sunken portion was not there when we dug out around them. Possibly they had melted.

"Soulcatcher stopped playing with us. She had to be controlling those circles somehow. Otherwise they would've killed her own soldiers the first time they retreated. But that isn't working anymore. What's changed? What's happened?"

Suddenly, the vultures above the wood all spiralled down rapidly, as though planning to attack something.

I said, "Let's see what Sleepy is up to."

Sleepy was sending scouts to explore the limits of the danger. So far no death flower had bloomed on our far flanks.

The vultures stopped their descent just above the treetops but continued to look more like raptors than carrion birds. One suffered an impulse to descend a little farther.

A golden-brown urine-colored strand darted up like a gigantic toad's tongue. A splatter of light surrounded the bird. It seemed to become a black cutout of a vulture. The cutout shattered into a hundred fragments. Those fluttered down like falling leaves.

The remaining vultures chose to take their business elsewhere.

Nobody but me seemed to notice what was happening.

Where were my damned ravens? I could send them to see what was happening while keeping my own sweet ass high and dry. What was the point of taking on a mythic character if I did not get to do mythic kinds of things?

Moments later Tobo and Howler were above the woods, dropping prosaic firebombs on the Taglian forces.

Lady joined us before Sleepy's scouts had found out if we could safely slide around the ends of the killing zone. She had a map she presented to the Captain. One glimpse told me my sweetie had not wasted her time aloft. She had charted the deadly circles. And a pattern was apparent. The positions of those not yet tripped were evident. Unless Soulcatcher had been aware of our airborne capacity. Then the death circles would be there solely to herd us into something far more gruesome and cruel.

Sleepy summoned her battalion commanders immediately.

69

Midway Between:
The Unanticipated

Soulcatcher's soldiers fought stubbornly for a while, along the edge of the wood, but had been too badly mauled already to last long under determined attack by our professional bloodletters.

Most of the Taglians had no desire to see their wives and children lose their husbands and fathers. Sleepy gave orders to let anyone who abandoned his weapons go.

Any Taglian economy inherited by the Prahbrindrah Drah would be better off if it was not crippled by a great slaughter of the empire's young men. It was only now recovering from the horrible losses suffered during the Shadowmaster and Kiaulune wars.

"It wasn't anywhere nearly as eloquent a victory as I'd hoped. But I'll take it," Sleepy said. "Despite our casualties. This war may have been won today."

That earned her a lot of bewildered or disbelieving looks. Soulcatcher was still out there, in a really foul temper now. More unpleasant surprises could be expected.

"But if we keep after her she'll be distracted when she reaches Taglios."

Mogaba's plans were a longshot. I said so. "And whatever sweet nothings his conscience whispered to him a couple months back, he'll be a whole lot more worried about saving Mogaba's skin once he has old enemies pounding on his door for real."

Sleepy started to say something about Aridatha Singh but thought better of it.

A carmine flash appeared on the killing ground. Using Lady's chart Tobo had triggered a booby trap by bombarding it from the Howler's flying carpet.

Sleepy told Runmust Singh, "After Tobo's done I want you to march some prisoners back and forth through there. I don't want any of those things left active. Some kid might wander in there and get himself killed." Like the countryside was swarming with stupid children.

I said, "I'd be more pleased if we could grab a few of those things for our own use. If Mogaba had something like that he might stand a chance of killing Soulcatcher."

Lady ruined the fun. "She'd smell it out. She created those things. There'll be safeguards so they can't be thrown back at her."

A whole lot of shouting started in the woods. Tobo and Shukrat darted that way, in case the soldiers needed help. Moments later Howler's carpet streaked back our way.

Tobo did not bother to dismount. He just announced, "They've found the Daughter of Night. She's in a cage. Soulcatcher ran off and left her."

Lady and I exchanged looks. That seemed completely unlikely. Unless the girl was bait in a truly deadly trap. Which might be. Soulcatcher had sown the field of death that had consumed our soldiers without the Unknown Shadows noticing her doing it.

70

Midway Between:
The Capture

The cage was inside a halfway collapsed tent. Several fireballs had ripped through the fabric but had failed to set it afire. I told everyone, "Be extremely careful here. If there was ever a time when Soulcatcher would try to spring something on us this would be it."

Sleepy had her henchmen push curious soldiers back. We

were already closer to the tent than Lady liked—though that had as much to do with who we expected to meet here as it had to do with concern about sorcerous deadfalls.

Nobody had yet been able to sense anything active in that line.

Lady told Tobo, "Go over everything three more times. Then check it again. Howler, you go over it, too." Of no one in particular she asked, "Where's Goblin?" When she got no answer she turned on the men who had found the tent, all of whom were in perfect health despite having taken time to scrounge souvenirs before they reported their find. "Where's the little man? The one who got away at Nijha."

Shrugs. They might not know what she was talking about. But one brave soul did say, "There's another cage under there. It's tipped over and broken. Maybe he got away."

Lady and I exchanged glances. Why would Goblin leave without the girl?

He would not.

Tobo called out, "There's no danger here."

Howler tried to concur but his voice gurgled off into a scream.

I said, "Something definitely ain't right. Tobo, send your unseen pals out to scout around. We especially need to know where Goblin and Soulcatcher are. As soon as we can. We have to keep after them."

Sleepy nodded irritated agreement.

Lady and I approached the tent warily.

Booby traps come in many forms.

As we had been warned, one broken cage was empty. The other lay on its side, door downward. One fine-looking woman lay sort of splattered all over inside, wearing not a stitch.

Lady stunned me by starting to rush forward saying something about her poor baby. I caught her arm. "Easy." The body looked, to me, like it had been posed. It would excite Soulcatcher's sense of humor for decades if she could get us to jump to our deaths over a child who had no more feeling for us than she did for the horses, cattle, and whatnot that passed through her life.

Lady paused but would not remain patient long. "What?"

"That isn't Booboo. I don't think." But that naked flesh could not be an illusion, could it? Goblin used to do that sort of thing. . . . But Tobo said nothing magical was going on.

I squatted, groaning as my knees creaked, reached through the bars and pulled dark hair away from the woman's neck, which it had concealed.

I pulled Lady down beside me. Her knees popped as badly as mine had. "Look there. I do pretty good work, don't I? You can hardly see the scars." I exaggerated. The scarring was ugly. But not all that ugly for somebody who had had her head sewn back on.

"Check the foot. Which foot got hurt? The right one, wasn't it?"

I uncovered the woman's right foot. The injury done by Goblin's booby trap, and Soulcatcher's own crude self-repairs, were immediately obvious.

"I hate her even more than I used to," Lady said. "Except for that heel and her scars she's still looking just as sleek as she did on her nineteenth birthday. What's wrong with her?"

I said, "I can't tell from here. But I'm not getting any closer till I know it's safe. Where'd Tobo and Howler go? Get them back here." This remained a potentially explosive situation, even if no sorcery was active. Soulcatcher would be in a foul temper when she regained consciousness.

Lady mused, "The child must have a low opinion of our intelligence if she thought this would fool us."

I wondered. Maybe we just showed up before the trap could be fully prepared.

When Tobo returned he told us, "Cat Sith just spotted Soulcatcher at the north edge of the woods. She has Goblin on a leash. She's rallied some soldiers and has them building earthworks." He became increasingly distracted as he stared at my sister-in-law.

Now was that not an interesting set of developments?

Sleepy blurted, "The Daughter of Night is pretending that she's the Protector?"

Tobo almost reeled back when he realized that he was lusting after a woman five hundred years his senior.

Lady, always an advocate for swift and decisive action when she had been in command, insisted, "We need to press her. Whoever's in charge. Every second she gets to pull things together will mean more casualties and difficulties for us later."

Sleepy did not disagree. It was hard to argue with the truth. She went off to restore order and resume the advance. It was weird that the Taglians, already broken twice and neither well-trained nor motivated, would be rallying. But Tobo insisted that they were doing so and he was not subject to fantasies. Of that sort.

It seemed unlikely that the Taglians would be well-armed. Most of the Taglian soldiers had thrown down their weapons the first time they fled.

Lady gripped my hand for a moment. "Think we'll ever really get to see her?"

"You begin to wonder if she's any closer, or any more real, than Khatovar, don't you?"

Willow Swan came bounding up. "Is it true? Have we caught Soulcatcher again?"

"News spreads fast," I said. "Yes. That's her. I'm pretty sure. You're welcome to join me while I examine her. To make sure." He had gotten closer to her than I ever had as her one-time physician and surgeon. He would have a better chance of spotting physical evidence that this was one of Soulcatcher's elaborate tricks. If he remembered anything at all after five years away.

I did not believe this was a trick. There was something badly wrong with my honey's little sister. I felt that before I got my close-up look.

Swan examined and grumbled. He had no happy recollections of the way Soulcatcher had used him way back when.

But he was not driven by any particular hatred of her, either.

Sleepy said, "You keep what this woman did to you firmly in mind, Willow Swan. I don't want to see it happen again. And if I do get a whiff, you can count on getting kneecapped before you score."

Swan wanted to rage and protest that there was no damned way that witch was going to get inside his head again. But he did not. He was only flesh and he recognized that that flesh was incapable of rational thought around any female who shared Soulcatcher's family blood.

His record spoke for itself.

"Then why don't we just kill her?" he asked. Wounded pride burned through his cool. "Right here. Right now. While we've got the best chance we'll ever get. End it all forever."

"We won't because we don't know what Goblin and Booboo did to her," I snapped when Lady seemed strangely reluctant to disappoint a fellow whose passion had fixed upon her originally. She would not be developing a sense of compassion at this late date, would she? Or of family? She and her sister were one another's oldest surviving enemies. "Soulcatcher won't help us more than she absolutely has to but she will help. For a while."

Lady nodded. Her sister was insane but her insanity was pragmatic.

Sister Soulcatcher showed no signs of recovering.

I did not say so but my outburst was part whistling past the graveyard. I was increasingly certain that there was something gravely wrong with Soulcatcher. I feared she might be dying. This was the thing that had claimed Sedvod. And nobody else saw it.

The others were all too excited by the prospect of having her at our mercy.

71

Midway Between:
Unpleasant Truth

Getting Soulcatcher awake and aware enough to understand and begin suffering because of her circumstances preoccupied Lady and Swan for some time. Murgen and Thai Dei, Sahra and Uncle Doj joined them. In time they meant to strong-arm Soulcatcher into assisting us but first they wanted to fatten up on a feast of gloating.

Soulcatcher did not cooperate. She remained steadfastly unaware, exactly the way Sedvod had done.

The racket of skirmishing rose and fell in the distance, never becoming intense. Our guys did not sound much more ambitious than were our enemies. I did not blame them for a disinclination to get killed when the battle's outcome had been determined already.

Riverwalker jogged into sight. "The Captain's compliments and could you all come up and help her? She has a situation. She'd like some advice."

"I'll be damned," I said. "Just when you think you've seen everything."

"What kind of situation?" Murgen asked. He was not distracted by Soulcatcher. He understood that when the word "situation" was used this way it meant that his son was about to be asked to jump into something particularly hot.

"We're having trouble coming to grips with what's left of the enemy."

I suggested, "Why not just leave them the hell alone now? They're on the run." Riverwalker ignored me.

"At about a hundred yards the soldiers start losing interest. The few who do manage to go on and get within fifty yards say they find themselves thinking how awful they are for interfering with Her and that they really ought to be helping

Her fulfill Her holy destiny. 'Her' not being defined but they assume they're thinking about the Protector because the Protector is the devil they know and the devil they thought they were supposed to be chasing."

Lady waved me closer. She murmured, "I'll handle this end. Take the carpet and posts up and bombard the Taglian command from outside spell range."

"We're almost out of fireballs again."

"So drop rocks. Or burning brush. Or anything else that will make her concentrate on staying out of the way. Every time she moves a few more of her troops will drift outside the spell. Whereupon they'll suddenly get smart and run away."

Her confident prescription suggested that this was an effect she knew of old.

I told everyone, "First thing we do is load up on arrows. We'll just drop them from higher than she can reach. From five hundred feet up they ought to be good and deadly." My gut knotted. I was talking about bombarding my own flesh and blood.

But part of me was certain that the girl would avoid personal damage. And part believed that a confrontation had been inherent in the situation from the moment Narayan Singh had snatched our baby from Lady's arms.

It did work. The girl, wearing her aunt's costume, darted around, followed by Goblin. The last few fireballs and firebombs got spent. Their infallible lack of accuracy refreshed my cynical view of our chances of catching a break.

The pair tried to fight back. Whenever a flier descended below a certain level a string of urine-colored lights flung upward. But I kept them too busy skipping out of harm's way to concentrate on their marksmanship. I could not tell which was the source of the deadly light.

I noted that the girl seemed unaware that the guy overhead in the ugly suit was her doting papa.

Our soldiers grasped the situation quickly and seized

those opportunities offered by the shifting perimeter around the Taglian forces.

The Daughter of Night was no soldier but she was quick and decisive and did have a source of advice in a man who had spent more than a century soldiering.

Goblin told her to attack, to get what use she could out of the troops she held in thrall. She did attack. Straight toward Sleepy, ignoring the missiles falling around her. Our people had no choice but to run from her while trying to weaken her from extreme rage. Anybody who got too close underwent a sudden change of heart and took up arms on behalf of the Deceiver messiah, without understanding what was happening.

Because she was indifferent to how many of her helpers perished, Booboo was able to chase around everywhere, breaking up everything before it got organized, gaining a recruit for each two or three men she lost, making it emotionally ever more difficult for our archers to hurl missiles at soldiers who had been comrades not that long before. The girl even came near recapturing Soulcatcher.

Then Tobo screwed up.

He assumed that his strength, combined with that of the Howler, would be enough to overpower an untrained girl if they came at her suddenly, from an unexpected direction. And maybe he was right. But he forget that her companion was not the Goblin he had grown up around. This Goblin was infected with wicked godhood.

That urine-colored light caught the flying carpet a glancing blow just before the Howler and Tobo cut loose with the best they had. A chunk of carpet turned into fluttering black scraps. Howler and Tobo and the rest of the carpet hurtled ahead, safe from spells but not from a brutal beating by the branches of the trees into which they plunged. The Howler got off a couple of heartfelt shrieks.

The urine-colored bar of light did the magical equivalent of jostling the mystical elbows of the young sorcerer and the

ancient one alike. Their spells did a lot of damage to Booboo's defenders. They even managed to stun their intended
targets. But because the spellcasters were bouncing around
in the branches in the woods, instead of reporting in, the rest
of us never got a chance to take advantage.

72

Midway Between:
The Rescuers

We had a standoff of sorts. We could not get at Goblin
and the Daughter of Night when they were most vulnerable. Their thugs did not know that we had lost our most
potent weapons, at least for a time. My ravens, who had
returned conveniently only when it was time for them to
become Tobo's mouthpieces, informed me that Howler and
Tobo had survived but were hurt. They were hidden in the
woods a few dozen yards from where the Daughter of Night
and Goblin, barely recovered enough to keep breathing,
were hunkered down.

I tried to let Sleepy know quietly but Sahra was too alert.
In moments she worked herself into a state that even Murgen
could not soften. "You've got to do something!" she
shrieked.

"The Daughter of Night will hear you," Murgen growled.

"You've got to get him out of there!"

"Be quiet!"

I agreed. Somebody had to do something. That somebody
might be me. But the only useful help I had was my two
raven assistants. They alternately reported Tobo unconscious or quietly delirious. They could not get reliable
orders from him. They refused to let me use them to transmit
orders to the other Unknown Shadows. Those were gather-

ing in numbers such that it was impossible not to catch glimpses of them when you turned or moved suddenly.

"We can't get close to him," Murgen told Sahra. He shook her. She was not listening. If she listened she would have to hear uncomfortable truths.

Shukrat stepped forward. She told us, "I can bring him out."

Sahra shut up. Even Sleepy stopped pulling the remains of our army back together and offered her attention for a moment.

"I'll need my own clothing back," Shukrat told us. Her accent was slight. "The enchantment won't touch me if I'm protected by my own clothing." Her use of Taglian had become conversational.

Sahra's hysteria faded immediately. I will never understand that woman. I would have bet on it getting worse.

The rest of us exchanged glances. We could not survive without Tobo. Not in this world. Not with our enemies. We had to get him out of there before the Daughter of Night discovered the opportunity that fortune had thrown down at her feet.

Shukrat said, "You've got to trust me sometime. This might be a good time to take a chance."

Maybe she was not as dumb as she put on.

Tobo trusted her.

I looked over her head to where Sleepy had resumed expostulating angrily with Iqbal Singh and an officer in badly dented Hsien style armor. She had heard. She waved a hand and nodded to indicate that the decision was up to me. I knew the Voroshk kids better than she did.

"All right," I told Shukrat. "But I go with you."

"How?"

"I'll put on Gromovol's . . ."

She was more amused than alarmed, though she *was* troubled. She was very worried about Tobo.

Because I have this obsessional thing about loyalties and

brotherhood and keeping faith with the past I sometimes
have trouble believing that other people respond as flexibly
to their situation as they do. I could not have made my peace
with such a dramatic shift in circumstances as easily as
Shukrat had.

I said, "That won't work, eh?"

"No. The clothing is created specially for each of us. Indi-
vidually." She had only that slight accent, no greater than my
own, but she did not yet possess a large vocabulary. Her
speech was simpler than it might have been. "Though it can
be adjusted by a tailor of sufficient skill. The skill takes
twenty years to learn, though."

"All right. Where's that stuff stashed? In Tobo's wagon?"
The kid had so much junk he needed his own wagon and
teamsters to haul it around. The wagon contained things as
diverse as marbles and miracles. He had been indulged all
his life and would not leave anything behind. "Let's go."

I hoped he had not left any protective spells where they
would keep us from getting at the tools we needed to save
his scruffy young butt.

73

Midway Between:
The Rescue

Fully attired in her family uniform Shukrat seemed a lot
more formidable than the cute little freckle face who
hung around with Tobo. Her apparel seemed to be alive,
seemed excited to have rejoined her. The black cloth kept
stirring around her, restlessly. She resembled an Unknown
Shadow who had chosen to let itself be seen. Her blue eyes
sparkled. I suspected she might be having fun.

I told her, "Tobo's dad and I will come along as far as we

can," although she did not seem to need reassurance. She did understand that having Murgen along meant Thai Dei would be there, too. And Thai Dei did not trust her at all.

Our sometimes odd personal entanglements did not interest Shukrat. Not that she would ever *talk* about them with an old fart like me.

Shukrat forgot that she was wearing that same outfit the day she fell into our hands. When she was not alone. She forgot that she was not invincible.

Sorcerers never lack for self-confidence. Especially young sorcerers.

Those whose self-confidence is justified live to become old sorcerers.

A platoon of elite fighters would creep along behind us, far enough back not to irritate Shukrat's pride but close enough to salvage her cute little behind if her confidence was not completely justified.

For Tobo's sake I would try to make sure she became an older sorceress, by at least one more day.

Murgen scrounged up fireball projectors for himself and Thai Dei. Uncle Doj scrounged up himself and Ash Wand and invited himself into the game. He might be older than dirt but he was still spryer than me. He and his disciples stole through the battered wood in silence so total I wondered if my hearing was going. My old bones were less cooperative so I ended up as rearguard. Today my whole body insisted on reminding me that I had been critically wounded not all that long ago. Although it did that almost every day.

I wore my Widowmaker armor. Though the Hsien reproduction was quieter than the metal original that Soulcatcher made I still seemed to be all clang and clatter.

I took One-Eye's spear along, against Lady's advice.

Shukrat's flying post trailed behind her. My ravens rode it, one offering directions, the other poised to carry news or unexpected holiday greetings to the rear.

It would be a holiday somewhere in the world. And fate offered me a glimpse of Goblin in the distance, evidently passed out, much as he had done after proferring the holiday excuse for being drunk, half a lifetime ago. I hefted the black spear.

I glimpsed the girl, too. She was moving but doing it like a drunk on the brink of passing out. I recalled another time, long ago, when a brother named Raven and I had ambushed a sorceress called Whisper on Soulcatcher's behalf. Circles of fortune. The madwoman had been our employer at the time. Now she worked for us. Or would be given the opportunity to work for us if I could keep her alive. That might be a tough assignment.

Seeing the girl and my old friend hurt. I wished I had a weapon I could use to end this here, now.

One-Eye's spear seemed to turn in my hand.

I pointed out the view to Murgen and Thai Dei. I breathed, "On the way out. After we have Tobo and Howler." I indicated their bamboo poles.

Murgen worked to keep a blank face. Thai Dei did not have to work. Thai Dei did not come equipped with facial expressions, so far as I could tell. Uncle Doj nodded. Uncle Doj was old friends with unpleasant necessity.

I told Murgen, "I'll do it if you can't." Sometimes you have to build a wall around your heart.

A few steps onward we encountered the emotional phenomenon the soldiers had reported. But with the girl stunned it did not overcome reason. I just had to concentrate on not giving myself up to love for the Daughter of Night.

I did wonder how much worse it had been when she was in control of all her faculties.

We reached Tobo without incident. Howler lay not ten feet away, miraculously silent. The gods do play amazing games.

I examined Tobo before I let anyone move him. His pulse

was strong and regular but he was covered with cuts and abrasions and had suffered a lot of broken bones. He was not going to be much use to anybody for a long time.

Shukrat whispered. "He would have been fine if he had been wearing this." She indicated her apparel. That seemed spellproof, too. As promised, she was suffering none of the effects of the Daughter of Night's emanations.

It was a struggle for the rest of us, and getting more difficult as Booboo regained her senses.

We got Tobo aboard a crude litter that we slung underneath the flying post. Howler we hoisted onto the log itself. We tied him into place. He was not badly hurt, just persistently unconscious. His rags had served him better than any armor.

He needed to find himself an alley and do some ragpicking. He needed a new outfit desperately. What he was wearing no longer came up to the standard of rags.

I told Thai Dei and Murgen to collect as many scraps of flying carpet as they could without alerting the Taglians to our presence. No telling what could be learned from them. We did not need Goblin and Booboo getting any brilliant notions about improving their mobility.

Howler chose that moment to wake up, stretch and greet the world with a good scream. I clamped an armored hand over the little bastard's mouth but I moved a beat too late.

Booboo's men started scrambling around. Goblin woke up and glared around, but in apparent confusion. Somebody eager to hurl himself into the gap between peril and the Daughter of Night smashed into the girl violently enough to knock her off her feet and leave her groggier than she was already.

The "love me" spell weakened significantly.

Half a dozen Taglian soldiers materialized. The first two stopped instantly when they got a look at me and Shukrat. Those behind them piled into them.

Doj leaped forward like a man a third his age. Ash Wand glittered in a dance of death.

More soldiers appeared. Lots more. Murgen and Thai Dei emptied the bamboo fireball projectors they carried, then drew swords and joined Doj in weaving a tapestry of steel.

Shukrat told me, "Go. Now. Just push the rheitgeistide. It will go ahead of you." In a straight line only, I discovered instantly, unless a couple of people pushed and pulled it real hard to get it going in a straight line in some other direction.

I did not have anyone to help me right away. Tobo's male relatives were busy turning the Taglian army into bite-sized bits of crow food. Shukrat was playing hard to hit with a band of Taglian archers.

When their arrows reached her she seemed to lose definition momentarily. Her cloak swirled around her, almost cloudlike. Nothing touched her.

A cloud of a thousand glittering little obsidian flakes boiled off Shukrat. Despite a breeze blowing into our faces, the cloud headed for the Taglians. In moments enemy soldiers were swearing, slapping themselves, forgetting to be bellicose toward me.

Most excellent.

I had seen One-Eye and Goblin pull similar stunts frequently over the years, usually with bees or hornets. One time one of them stirred up an army of ants to attack the other. Much of their creativity for much of their lives had gone into inventing new ways to harass one another.

I missed the little shits, aggravation and all.

It was not a good time to be a Taglian devotee of the Deceiver messiah, willing or otherwise. Tobo's family was making the blood fly.

That damned Goblin exploded like a starving vampire popping up out of his grave. He landed amongst his own soldiers. Three or four went down. Doj, Thai Dei and Murgen all got thrown around like they weighed nothing. Their swords seemed incapable of doing any harm. The fiercest blows sounded like they were slamming into a waterlogged tree trunk. And did about as much damage as they would have done to a huge old watersoaked log.

I recalled One-Eye's last hours. And was in motion already when I did, the black spear extended way out in my right hand, head starting to glow.

The Goblin thing whipped to one side fast enough to avoid getting skewered. It did suffer a cut that would have been enough to require stitches if it had been the true Goblin.

Its flesh felt tougher than an old smoke-cured ham.

The Goblin face betrayed complete astonishment, then horrible pain. The spear flashed and smoked in my hand. Goblin shrieked. For an instant I saw the real Goblin looking out of tormented eyes.

I fought for my balance and tried to get him with a truer thrust.

I did not get him at all. He flung out of there in complete terror of my weapon. His wound looked like it had gone gangrenous already.

All this took only moments. The troops I had asked to tag along behind wasted no time rushing up to help. Still down, Booboo was not radiating enough "love me" to disrupt their ability to fight. They started grabbing the rest of us and dragging us out of there.

"I can walk!" I snarled. Though I had almost no strength left. I got hold of the flying post and started walking it.

The soldiers carried Doj and Thai Dei. Murgen looped an arm over the shoulder of another fighter who had managed to get himself injured already.

This did not look good for the Ky family.

More of our men rushed up.

I leaned into the log. I tried not to worry. Behind me the skirmish got rowdy. More men came up on both sides. Fortunes shifted as the girl found strength or weakened. Evidently using the "love me" enchantment sucked the strength out of her flesh.

* * *

"I hate this kind of fight," I told Sleepy when she came over to see how the survivors were doing. She kept her back to the ranks of the dead.

Howler was up and around already. I had a whole team working on Tobo. Murgen was going to make it. He just needed time. But time had run out for Doj and Thai Dei. Soldiers live.

I kept doing what I could for Soulcatcher, too, mostly when my wife was not watching. "You can lose a lot of men without accomplishing a thing." I meant that as a subtle suggestion.

"They've realized they can't win. They've started moving north. Before we can finish surrounding them." I heard nothing in her voice expressing disappointment. "How bad is Tobo?"

"Not as bad as his uncle and Doj."

"Croaker."

"Sorry. We're out of business. Maybe for a long time. If Tobo has a bone that isn't broken I can't find it." I exaggerated only a little. The kid had a broken leg, a broken toe, a broken arm (two places), a concussion and a whole rack of crushed or broken ribs. "Unless you're willing to face Mogaba without him."

"Outnumbered by the best troops we'll face, commanded by the only intelligent commander we're likely to meet?" Meaning a general she had fought during the Kiaulune wars but never had beaten. She eyed Soulcatcher. "Counting on Howler to give us his best? I think not."

"Then we'd better fall back to Dejagore and get comfortable. Or move up to Ghoja."

"Ghoja," she decided instantly. "We want control of that river crossing. And that barrier."

"Mogaba isn't likely to come out right away. He'll want to know exactly what's going on before he commits himself to any course. Hell, he might not come out at all if we update him on what's going on with the Daughter of Night."

She agreed. "If we let him know, he might find a chance to do something beneficial to all of us. See that he gets the appropriate information."

How was I supposed to do that?

I did not ask.

I knelt beside Soulcatcher. Her breathing was ragged. She seemed to be getting weaker. I did ask, "How's Sahra?"

"She'll be all right. She's lived with this idea for a lot of years. She knows nobody gets out of here alive. Even if they don't have one of those silver badges. I'll let you know what she decides about funeral arrangements."

I grunted.

She left me with a final caution. "Just don't let her boy die. Things would get unpleasant."

74

Midway Between:
Escape Artists

Sometime during the excitement the Voroshk kids decided to run away. But before they ran they had to argue about how to manage it and who should be in charge after they succeeded and then they kept bickering until they wasted most of the time when the rest of us were diverted first by Soulcatcher and then by Booboo.

Nothing got decided completely. After sundown they surprised their guards using feeble disorientation spells. Gromovol killed several soldiers, mostly because Magadan cautioned him not to. As soon as they were loose Gromovol started looking for his flying post. Arkana and Magadan believed it was more important to find their clothing. Without that they were almost powerless. They wrote Gromovol off. They knew the Black Company well enough already to want to distance themselves from the doom taking shape in his future.

Arkana told Magadan, "We'll have to take one of those keys to their shadowgate, too. Otherwise we'll never get out of this world."

"If we get the chance, yes. But the main thing we need to do is to get away from these madmen." Even after several months Magadan still did not understand what was happening in this world. It was too alien. Nothing made any sense.

His own world had known no real war since his forbears had come to power.

Two hundred yards away Gromovol did something stupid and betrayed himself as he tried to steal a flying post. An alarm sounded. In minutes rage flooded the camp. The murdered guards had been found.

Arkana swore. "That idiot! We'd better surrender to somebody important right now. If we keep on running the soldiers who catch us won't listen to any explanations."

"Shukrat . . ."

"Shukrat's gone native. Shukrat's decided there's no way she'll ever get home so she might as well do the best she can for herself over here. It's probably because of her mother."

"What?"

"Her mother. Shukrat's been totally weird ever since the First Father put her mother aside for that woman Saltireva. Besides, she's infatuated with Tobo."

"He is gorgeous, isn't he?"

"Magadan! Well, yes. Exotic, anyway."

"I hear his mother was one of the great beauties of this world when she was younger. But his father grew up eating nothing but ugly soup." All the while they talked Magadan kept drifting away from the excitement. He had no destination in mind but no intention of giving himself up. There would be no chance like this ever again.

Arkana said, "Shukrat could be right."

"What?"

"Suppose she hasn't really gone native? Suppose she's just winning their trust? Maybe someday she'll just stroll off with one of their keys and leave this world."

"Damn."

"Shukrat won't do it. But we could adopt that strategy." It had not taken Shukrat long to get her post and clothing back. She was becoming an important part of the Black Company. Already.

"Why didn't we think of that?" Magadan grumbled.

Arkana said, "Because we're almost as stupid as Gromovol is. As blind to anything that isn't the way it was at home. Shukrat isn't bright. But she does see that this isn't home and never will be. I'm turning back. You do what you want. When the shouting stops I want them to find me right where they left me. I refused to run away. It was all that idiot Gromovol's fault."

But, darling ice princess, don't you know you never do anything alone?

The Voroshk never fully grasped the fact that the Unknown Shadows are with all of us always. If Tobo wanted he could catalog every breath they took. The hidden folk tap emotion. They learn to understand what is being said far faster than even language naturals like myself. The Voroshk could no longer speak secrets.

Sometimes misfortune likes to get into the game.

Magadan told Arkana, "You go ahead. Be friendly. Flirt. Do what Shukrat did. When you get your key come find me. I'll walk you home."

"Come back with me."

"I can't. They'll blame me for what Gromovol did."

The devil named appeared suddenly, running straight toward them, the light of campfires exaggerating the terror distorting his face. Gromovol had expected to fling open the door to freedom but had found it to be the door to hell and no one on the other side cared who he was.

Before it could all be sorted out and the troops calmed down Magadan had been killed, Gromovol had been wounded badly, and Arkana had been raped several times. She brought a broken leg and several cracked ribs into my care as well. In time I heard all the true details from my ravens, who seemed more inclined to be communicative while Tobo was out of action.

Soldiers whose friends have been murdered are not kindly people. In a Company without Lady and a female Captain no discipline would have been assessed at all. As it was, the discipline was light and directed mainly at those who had assaulted Arkana sexually. That could not be overlooked.

75

Taglios:
The Palace

Mogaba was not yet aware of the disaster that had befallen the Army of the Middle when he found the two women in his quarters. Lady he recognized. The young blonde he did not. She would, he presumed, be a sorceress, too. Fear cramped his stomach. His heartbeat doubled. But he betrayed nothing outwardly.

He had had to mask his emotions in the presence of madmen and a madwoman for decades. The madmen were gone. With luck the madwoman would follow. And he would persist.

He bowed slightly. "Lady. To what do I owe the unexpected honor?"

"To disasters. Of course."

The Great General glanced at the younger woman. She was completely exotic, like no woman he had ever seen.

Though white and blonde she did not resemble Willow Swan otherwise. There was an alien feel to her.

She must be from wherever the Black Company had hidden the last several years.

He said, "I'm sure you didn't come this far just to stand around looking cryptic."

"The Daughter of Night and the thing inside what used to be Goblin somehow overwhelmed the Protector. The girl put on Soulcatcher's leathers. She's pretending to be her. She's squandered ninety-five percent of your Middle Army. She's headed this way. We aren't in any condition to chase her. My husband thought you should know. He wants me to remind you that the Daughter of Night exists only to bring on the Year of the Skulls. I want you to know that Kina is real. Doubt any of the other gods you want but not this one. She's out there. We've seen her. And if she gets loose none of our other squabbles will mean a thing."

Mogaba did not need to be reminded that the Year of the Skulls would be an atrocity far huger than any of Soulcatcher's random cruelties. Catcher was mere Chaos. Kina was Destruction.

"We have a plan for handling the Protector. It should work as well against someone pretending to be the Protector. Possibly better." He did not ask what had become of Soulcatcher. He was content to hope that phase of his life was complete.

"The girl doesn't have Soulcatcher's finely honed powers but she does have plenty of raw talent. She's somehow surrounded herself with an aura that makes anyone within a hundred feet want to love her and do anything to please her. This has manifested itself before, in smaller ways, so I fear we can expect it to grow as she comes to understand it and exercise it."

"That isn't good. That's not good at all. That'll make sniping difficult. Any way around it?"

From the blonde's slight start, Mogaba judged Lady's,

"Not that we know of yet," to be less than honest. But in her place he would have reserved something, too. And what they had obviously was not reliable. Otherwise they would have used it themselves.

The Great General said, "Thank you for the warning. We'll make use of it. Was there anything more?" Down deep he nurtured the tiniest hope that there could be a reconciliation. A hope he knew was unrealistic. But everyone nurtured impossible dreams. Even the gods were pursuing the impossible.

Mogaba stated the facts as they had been reported to him. He made that point clear. "We aren't their friends. They just want someone else to assume part of the cost of eliminating the enemies they have to go through in order to get at us."

Ghopal Singh asked, "What about the truth of the report? Are they just trying to trick us into attacking the Protector? If they could get us to make the attempt and we were to fall at a time when they were close behind the Protector they'd reach the gates just when Taglios was falling into chaos."

Aridatha groaned. "*We* went to *them*, Ghopal. Remember me chasing halfway to the other end of the world to tell them we were going to try to get rid of the Protector? Remember me helping them take over Dejagore as a sign of good faith?"

"Circumstances have changed."

Mogaba interjected, "Ghopal, I've given this a lot of thought. I think it's true. The Protector is out of the game. Possibly only momentarily. Hell, probably. She's made unlikely comebacks before. What hurts my feelings, of course, is that those people don't consider us much worth worrying about in terms of the greater struggle."

Aridatha grumbled, "Which might not be that unreasonable when you think about it dispassionately."

Ghopal asked, "And you're equally sure that the Middle Army has been destroyed?" Even military insiders had not yet fully digested the news about the losses of Dejagore and the Southern Army that had clung to it's skirts. A lot of people were still waiting to hear how Dejagore responded to it's change of masters.

The nature of that response would have repercussions throughout the Taglian empire.

Would the return of the royals be celebrated? Or resented? The Dejagoran response was likely to set the fashion for all the cities and towns that came under the Company sway.

"I'm sure of it," Mogaba told Ghopal. "But I'm less sure of the condition of the invaders afterward. I got the distinct impression that their defeat of the Middle Army was neither cheap nor easy."

Aridatha said, "We've got to have better intelligence."

Mogaba took a moment to stifle his sarcasm before confessing, "I'm open to ideas. Any ideas."

No inspirations sprouted immediately.

Aridatha said, "We could always do something mythic. Like damning ourselves by bringing in an ally worse than our enemies. One that will devour us after it finishes doing what we brought it in to do."

Mogaba and Ghopal recognized the effort but did not get Aridatha's joke.

"It's an allusion. Or a parable. Or something," Aridatha explained. "Like all stories about Kina. The Lords of Light created her or brought her in for the demon plain war. And probably would have been better off if the rakshasas had won, ultimately."

Mogaba did have a sense of humor. He just had not brought it along tonight. "I guess you had to be there. Anyway, there's nobody we could bring in. We're on our own. So suggestions are in demand. Practical suggestions will be particularly welcome." That was something in the nature of a jest so, perhaps, he had brought part of his sense of humor.

Ghopal said, "All we can do is send out more spies and set up more remount stations so the spies can get their observations to us faster."

"And we have only one courier battalion." Mogaba sat quietly for half a minute. Then he asked, "How is our support among the priests and bourgeoisie? They've had time to think about the royals coming back. They plan to desert us?"

"We're the devil as far as they know," Ghopal replied. "The Protector has been their benefactor. And only a few of the slickest talkers can hope to benefit if we get thrown out. We worked hard to eliminate the Radisha's friends once we could no longer hide the fact that the princess was gone, not just hiding out feeling sorry for herself."

The Great General proposed, "Let's try the same strategy. Make believe we haven't lost the Protector. Aridatha. You seem to be distracted."

"I keep thinking about the girl. The Daughter of Night."

"And?"

"I saw her once. Five years ago. There's something about her. . . . Makes you want to throw her down on her back. And makes you want to worship her at the same time. Makes you feel like you should do anything you can to please her. It's scary when you step back far enough to realize what happened."

"She's all grown-up that way." Mogaba explained what Lady had told of events to the south. "That girl got hundreds of men killed. We'll have to assassinate her remotely somehow. See if some mechanical engine can be contrived."

"I have a question," Ghopal said.

"Go."

"What's that thing you're fiddling with? You've been playing with it ever since you got here."

"Oh. Some kind of snail shell. They're all over the Palace. Nobody knows where they come from. Nobody's ever actually seen one crawling around. They're sort of relaxing when you roll them around in your fingers."

Both Singhs eyed the Great General as though thinking his behavior was distinctly odd.

Ghopal said, "Regarding the Daughter of Night. We

might consider poison. There're some talented poisoners in Chor Bagan, the thieves' market."

The years had changed Mogaba. He did not immediately reject the suggestion as unworthy of men of honor.

76

The Taglian Territories: Another Origin Story

I suggested, "How about a standoff weapon we can launch from outside her influence? Hell, if we take the logs and carpets up high enough we can just keep dropping rocks till we get her." There was some optimism. We did not have even one carpet since Booboo knocked Howler and Tobo down. What we did have was bits and pieces of half a dozen carpets that Howler had been working on when nothing else took up his time.

Lady glared at me so intensely I began to wonder how soon I would start melting.

Killing Booboo was not yet on her list of options. Her emotions were engaged much more deeply than mine, though the problem of the girl was a torment to me, too.

My entanglement was more with the idea of the child than with the specific daughter.

Lady *wanted* to fool herself into believing there might be some way that Booboo could be redeemed.

"You're wasting time," the Prahbrindrah Drah said. The collapse of Soulcatcher's Middle Army had brought him to life. Suddenly, he believed his restoration was just a matter of marching to Taglios and yelling, "I'm back!" He had leaped into the embrace of self-delusion.

There was a lot of that going around.

Murgen joined the conference as the Prince began to

bicker with Sleepy about her plans, a situation guaranteed
not to persist for long. Sleepy would let him know who was
running the show. Murgen announced, "I just finished reading a really long message from Baladitya. Who is well and
loving every minute of his new life, thank you very much,
Sleepy. Which he did not fail to point out several times."

I asked, "What're you doing getting mail from that old
goofball?"

"He wasn't writing to me. He doesn't know me. The message was intended for Tobo."

Sleepy, who was thoroughly cranky because nothing was
going the way she wanted, grumped, "I'm sure you're going
to share every exciting detail with us, too, even though what
we all need is some sleep."

"Since you insist." Murgen grinned. He had no particular
job assignment while he was recuperating so he could do
just about anything he pleased. "His letter mostly concerned
the prisoners Shivetya is holding up there. The First Father
and Gromovol's dad. Who Shivetya took in originally just to
protect them from the shadows. Of which there are hardly
any left anymore. Them and the Voroshk have almost wiped
each other out. Sorry." He patted Shukrat's shoulder. Nobody
missed that gesture. Murgen approved of Tobo's girlfriend—
if that was what she was.

I wondered what he was doing bringing Shukrat to a staff
meeting.

Sahra, of course, bristled like a hedge hog. There were no
eligible Nyueng Bao girls anywhere within two hundred
miles and she had married a foreigner, Murgen, for love herself, against the will of most of her family, but what did that
have to do with today?

Sahra could restrain herself most of the time, these days.
In public. If Murgen was around to calm her and remind her
that Tobo was not a four-year-old anymore. But she was
under tremendous additional strain now, with all her family
dead or wounded. She had not yet pulled herself together

well enough to make decisions about funeral arrangements for her brother and Uncle Doj.

He restrained her now, with just a gentle touch.

"You got a point to make?" Sleepy said. "Or can I get back to work figuring out how to get us through this on terms that suit our needs?"

Swan muttered something about the little bit needing a good dose of man to relax her. Sleepy snarled. Swan grumbled, "Did I volunteer? I don't think so. Not recently. So don't fuck with me."

Hurriedly, Murgen told us, "Guys, Shivetya came up with another Kina origin cycle. He got this one from the Voroshk. Evidently they don't mind talking history if they're bored. In this version Kina's husband put her to sleep. When she kept acting up after she won the demon plain war for the gods by sucking the blood out of all the demons. This version of the Goddess has ten arms instead of four. Her husband, known as Chevil in the world of the Voroshk, has four arms and is a lot like the Kina we know. Sometimes he's called the Destroyer, too. But sometimes he can be cajoled or seduced into going easy. Kina can't."

His audience rustled. In some stories Khadi, one of the gentler Gunni forms of Kina, had had a husband, Bhima, who also counted the Destroyer among his many names.

All Gunni Gods have bunches of names. They get a little hard for an outsider to keep straight because when they change their names they also change their attributes. It gets particularly confusing when you have two aspects of the same god getting into an ass-kicking contest with each other.

"And this Chevi has what to do with Kina's origins?" Sleepy demanded.

"Oh, he's the one who did all the mean things to her, like chopping her up and scattering the pieces all over. But she also kills him. And brings him back to life."

"Murgen. I'm considering sending you back to the Taglians for some more rework."

"All right. Chevi has more than one wife. But there used to be only one. That was Camundamari, who has several other names, naturally. Camundamari was very dark-skinned. The other gods mocked her and called her Blackie."

Interesting. Both Khadi and Kina can mean black in some Taglian usages, though "syam" is the common and conventional word.

Murgen continued, "When Chevi himself started taunting her she flew into a huge rage, tore her skin off, and turned into Ghowrhi, the Milky One. The shed skin became Kalikausiki, which filled itself up on blood sucked from demons, then became Khat-hi, the Black One."

"Kina is a skinwalker!" Suvrin cried, startling everyone. Skinwalkers were a demonic terror little known outside Suvrin's homeland. Skinwalkers killed a man, sucked out his flesh and bones, put on his skin and stole his life. The details are pretty gruesome. Skinwalker folklore strikes me as a way for ignorant people to explain radical and bizarre changes in personality. Shifts I believe are due to poorly understood diseases. Or maybe just due to getting old.

Murgen was startled by Suvrin's outburst. Which seemed excessive to me, too. "Not a skinwalker in the way you mean," Murgen said.

Was there something in Suvrin's background?

The concept of a monster able to steal someone else's identity that way is particularly grotesque. I have seen a lot of strange and ugly things. Tobo's hidden folk are only the latest on a long list. But skinwalkers are one horror that just seems too terrible to be true.

Like the gods themselves of late there have been no manifestations before reliable witnesses. We were talking ancient legends tonight. Suvrin had referenced one of the most obscure.

I said, "Believe me, Suvrin, if there were any real skinwalkers down your way you can bet the Shadowmasters would've rooted them out and used them up. What a weapon, eh?"

"I guess," Suvrin admitted. Reluctantly.

"That's wonderful," Sleepy grumped. "Ghost-story time is over, boys. Now we let Murgen finish. He is going to finish, isn't he? Because I want to get back to what this meeting is supposed to be all about." She swung a deadly finger. "Don't you even think about puking up another wisecrack, Willow."

Swan grimaced. He had live ammunition and no ready target. Then he grinned. A time would come.

I said, "Murgen?"

"There isn't much more. Baladitya says most of the high points of the mythology agree. There's more of a death goddess to her nature over there. She's always referenced as living in a cemetery."

"She does that here, doesn't she?" I asked. "When Sleepy and Lady and you, especially, talk about your nightmares, that place you go with all the bones? That could be a Gunni style cemetery."

The Gunni burn their dead to purify them before their souls line up for reassignment in the next life. But the fires are never hot enough to consume the major bones. If a burning ground is near a major river the leftovers are generally deposited there. But a lot of places are not near a major river. And some are not near a source of firewood. And some families never save up enough to buy wood that is available.

Bones pile up.

These places are not often seen by anyone but the priests who attend them, the men in yellow who revere Majayama but watch over their shoulders because Kina and her pack of pet demons supposedly lived beneath the bone piles. Even though Kina is known to be chained up under the glittering plain until the Year of the Skulls.

I said, "I've got a lot of time to think these days. One of the things I've been pondering is why there are so many different stories about Kina. And I think I've figured it out."

My ego got a boost. Even Sleepy seemed interested,

despite herself. My wife, perhaps less enthralled, suggested, "Do go on," in a tone implying that she knew there would be no stopping me anyway.

"In those days the Company . . ."

"Croaker!"

"Sorry. Just seeing if you were listening. What clued me was the fact that there isn't any uniform Gunni doctrine. There isn't much of an hierarchy amongst Gunni priests, either, except locally. There's no central arbiter of what constitutes acceptable or unacceptable dogma. Kina isn't alone in being the subject of a hundred conflicting myths. The whole pantheon is. Pick any god you want. When you travel from village to village you'll find him wearing different names, different myths, getting mixed up with other gods, and on and on and on. We see the confusion *because* we're travelers. But up until the Shadowmaster wars almost nobody in these parts ever went anywhere. Generation after generation, century after century, people were born, lived and died in the same few square miles. You only had a few gem traders and the Strangler bands moving around. Ideas didn't travel with them. So every myth gradually mutates according to local experience and prejudice. Now first the Shadowmasters and then we land in the middle of all this. . . ."

We? A glance around showed me just three other people who had not grown up in this end of the world. For a moment I felt ancient and out of place and found myself recalling an old piece of poetry that said something to the effect: "Soldiers live. And wonder why." Meaning, why am I the one, of all those who marched with the Company when I was young, who is still alive and kicking? I do not deserve it any more than any of those men. Maybe less than some.

You always feel a little guilty when you think about it. And a little glad it was somebody else, not you.

"That's it. We're travelers. That's why it all seems alien and contradictory. Wherever we are, most of us are outsiders. Even when we do belong to the majority religion." A glance around showed me that hardly any of my audience were Gunni, either. "Well, that's my piece."

"All right, then," Sleepy said. "Back to practical problems. How do we deal with the Daughter of Night and the Goblin thing?"

"That's practically the same thing as a skinwalker," Suvrin said. "Kina put him on like a suit of clothes." Suvrin had skinwalkers on the brain tonight.

"The Daughter of Night!" Sleepy snapped. "I want to hear about the Daughter of Night. Not about Kina. Not about skinwalkers. Not about old Voroshk sorcerers, not about old librarians and not about anything else. And, Lady, if you really don't want the girl killed, then come up with an idea for disarming her that's better than any idea for taking her out. Because you're the only one here letting emotion get in the way."

77

Above Ghoja:
Seeking the One Safe Place

Goblin and the girl both rode, though their mounts remained skittish and frightened and Goblin's had to be kept in blinders so that it could not see its rider. Neither animal was allowed to look back. Goblin himself wore a rag to protect his damaged but nearly healing eyes.

The handful of soldiers who joined their flight from the middle ground fell away rapidly. Driven by the "love me" spell they gave it everything they had but eventually every man drifted outside the spell's influence, then vanished immediately.

Only the two touched by Kina crossed the bridge at

Ghoja. They reached the north bank as dawn began to paint the eastern sky. It was still only the morning after the destruction of the Taglian Middle Army. They had killed several post horses but even so had not arrived ahead of rumors of the disaster to Taglian arms.

"Our enemies have been here before us," the Goblin-thing said. He wanted to be called Khadidas, Slave of Khadi. The girl simply refused to address him by that appellation. "These people have been warned and threatened but they will raise no hand against you because of who they think you are." *Not* because of who she *was*.

The Daughter of Night played Protector with a blend of arrogance and small-mindedness nothing like her aunt's but the garrison commanders found her sufficiently convincing. And she ached every second because it was clear that these unbelievers would never yield themselves to the service of the Dark Mother. She knew that they would have tried to destroy her had they known she was not her aunt. This world deserved the Year of Skulls.

The aura the girl radiated got her through her brief confrontations.

"I'm exhausted," she whined to Goblin. "I'm not used to riding."

"We can't stop here."

"I can't go on."

"You will go on. Until you are safe." The Khadidas's voice left no doubt who it believed to be in charge. "There is a holy place not many leagues further. We'll go there."

"The Grove of Doom." There was no enthusiasm in the girl's response. "I don't want to go there. I don't like that place."

"We will be stronger there."

"It'll be the first place they'll look for us. If they don't already have soldiers there waiting." She knew that was unlikely. Those people were not yet prepared to tell their soldiers that the woman inside the black leather was not the

Protector anymore, but they did have the capacity to move their game pieces from afar. They seemed able to thwart the Goddess whenever they liked.

She said, "They already know what we're going to do. Because we just talked about it."

"We're going to the Grove. I will be much stronger there." No argument would be allowed.

The Daughter of Night was no less devoted to her spiritual mother today but she did not like this creature who bore a fragment of Kina inside him. She found it difficult to articulate even to herself, but she missed Narayan. She missed him because he had loved her. And she, in her self-centered way, had loved him enough in return that now her life was one ongoing trail of loneliness and desolation . . . leading where? This new hand of the Goddess seemed incapable of any emotion but anger. And he refused flatly to indulge her in any way, or even to acknowledge her humanity.

She was a tool. That she was a living thing with wants and emotions all her own was just an annoyance, a nuisance, an inconvenience. There was an ever stronger implication that she should learn to abandon her distractive qualities. Or else.

Goblin said, "We need a place where we can be safe and our power is strong because there is much we need to do before we commence the actual rite of resurrection." By which the Daughter of Night understood him to mean bringing on the Year of the Skulls.

She became attentive despite her inclination to be rebellious. It sounded like the Khadidas was going to impart some real information at last. Hitherto, the possessed little man had done nothing more than present his bonafides, then tell her what to do. They had been together for only a few days but throughout them he had been completely unforthcoming.

She asked, "How can we possibly bring on the Year of the Skulls? Our cult has been exterminated. I doubt that there are a hundred devout believers left in the entire world."

"There will be hands enough to undertake the holy task. Narayan Singh did well in his last years. But before we bring them together we must recover the Books of the Dead."

The Daughter of Night had to pass on the cruel truth that had been used to torment her all the while she had been a captive of the Black Company. "The Books of the Dead no longer exist. The woman who commands our cruelest enemies burned them personally. Not even a scrap survived. The monster that dwells in the place of glittering stone, that prevents my mother from rising, had the ashes scattered throughout all the realms that touch upon the demon plain."

"That's true." The Khadidas grinned evilly. "But books are knowledge. The knowledge contained within the Books of the Dead is not lost. The knowledge also resides within the Goddess herself. And whatsoever there was within her that needed to be brought forth into this world she placed within me before she sent me forth."

"You know the Books of the Dead by heart?"

"I do. Which is why we must find our one safe place. The scriptures are no good locked up inside me. They must be out, in written form, to assume their full power. They must be there so that the cantor priests can sing from them continuously during the time of resurrection. Come. We must travel faster."

The Daughter of Night hurried her pace, her exhaustion pushed back briefly by the stunning implications of what she had just heard.

The holy books were not lost!

She was ashamed that she had suffered even a slight wavering of faith.

78

Midway Between:
Bad News

People began to scurry as though in near panic. I knew the signs. News had come in and it was not good. I suspected the cavalry force sent to probe the defenses at Ghoja had suffered some major misfortune.

I headed for Sleepy's tent without being summoned. By the time I ducked inside I had overheard a half dozen rumors already, not a one of them reassuring.

Generating rumors is one thing even the most inept armed force does exceedingly well.

Sleepy was heads-together with Suvrin and Runmust, Riverwalker and several brigade commanders from Hsien. Tobo was there but was goofy with painkillers. Howler and Shukrat were not present. Tobo looked a little peeved. My guess was that he had brought the bad news but could not keep himself together well enough to contribute anything beyond his report.

I had given up on him. If he wanted to cruise around on a post trying to do things while he was all busted up and in casts I was not going to nag him anymore. He had a half-crazy mom to handle that.

Sleepy glanced my way, for a second revealed extreme irritation. That turned to resignation as other former Captains let themselves in behind me. Even Willow Swan invited himself to sit in.

Sleepy did face a unique challenge. No other Captain in the Company's history has had such a cabal of ex-Captains looking over his shoulder. Even though none of us intrude, or even offer much unsolicited advice, Sleepy's particular insecurities leave her feeling like she is being judged whenever she had to Captain in front of us. And, of course, she is, though like proper old ladies we do it only behind her back.

"Since everybody but the cooks and grooms is here, I suppose I should get on. . . . No. Tobo is here. He can tell it better than I." She deferred to the kid as soon as her gaze fell upon him. I glared at her. She had no business putting him through . . .

Tobo's eyes focused. He shut them, took a cleansing breath, started talking. "The hidden folk have been tracking Goblin and Booboo the best they can, though it's hard even when we know what route they have to take." He was something less than intimidating, strapped into position aboard a Voroshk flying log, so covered with casts and splints that he was able to use only one hand. "They travel inside a fog of, for want of a better description, divine darkness and confusion. By knowing their route, though, I was able to have the Black Hounds seed the way with snail shells. . . . I got lucky. One of the hidden folk eavesdropped on an argument between Goblin and the girl." His words came in a soft, swift gush that forced his audience to stay quiet and lean forward.

Tobo paused. For effect, I would have suspected in normal circumstances. The kid liked his drama.

The boy made the grim announcement, "The thing inside Goblin knows the Books of the Dead by heart. Once the Daughter of Night transcribes them they plan to start the rites associated with initiating the Year of the Skulls."

Fox in the henhouse, oh, my, oh!

It took Sleepy several minutes to get everyone settled down. In the interim Tobo grabbed the opportunity to relax. When a measure of calm returned he said, "That's not as bad as it sounds. Remember, there're only two people involved. Should we kill either one, the resurrection fails. For the rest of our century and beyond. And, as anyone who ever worked on the Annals will tell you at great length, it takes a long time to write a book. Even if you're just copying. I saw the Books of the Dead before Sleepy destroyed them. They were huge. And the Daughter of Night will have to transcribe them error-free. So we don't exactly face an immediate crisis even though this is trouble that we never anticipated."

I jumped in. "If you got one of your critters close enough to find out all that then you probably know right where they are. We can set up some kind of ambush." Lady and Howler were supposed to have been ransacking the cobwebby cellars of their minds in an effort to recall some ancient device whereby Goblin and the girl might be distracted, disoriented, distressed and destroyed. Or just disarmed, in the case of my missus. Realist and pragmatist though she was, she nevertheless nurtured a blind bit of self-delusion wherein she would turn Booboo around. Though she would never admit that, of course.

Tobo said, "All right, Master Strategist, Architect of the Destruction of the Shadowmaster Evil, tell me how you ambush somebody you fall in love with before they get inside crossbow range."

"Kid has a point," Lady said, eyeing me expectantly.

"Your snail-shell lurker didn't fall in love with her, did it? It just hunkered down there and eavesdropped till it decided to come running to you with its gossip."

"And?"

"So the Unknown Shadows aren't affected by the Daughter of Night. Is the opposite true?"

"They couldn't do her much physical harm."

"Skryker? Black Shuck? That big old jumping duck thing? You're shitting me."

"No, really."

"Well, they really wouldn't have to, anyway, would they? They'd just need to haunt her. Keep interfering with her sleep. Driving her crazy. Jogging her elbow whenever she tries to write. Really be guilty of all the annoyances they're blamed for back in Hsien. They could piss in her inkwell. They could hide her pens. They could spill stuff on whatever she's trying to write. They could make food go bad and milk turn sour."

"They could keep her husband from performing on her

wedding night," Sleepy snapped. "You're roaming a little far
into the future, Croaker. And possibly targeting the wrong
victim. The Goblin thing is the one who has the Books of the
Dead locked up inside his gourd. He might be able to manage without the Daughter of Night. I'm pretty sure she can't
manage without him."

Points worth considering.

"Both are just ephemeral tools," Sahra announced in a
hollow, oracular voice. "Both can be replaced. In time. So
long as Kina herself persists the threat from the glittering
plain lives on."

That took all the cheer right out of the gathering.

Everybody stared at Tobo's mother, the injured boy himself included. There was a creepy feeling to her, like something had taken control of her, to speak using her mouth.

Murgen later said Sahra had looked and sounded exactly
like her grandmother, Hong Tray, when she issued her
prophecies, decades ago.

She scared the shit out of Murgen and Tobo both. They used
all the energy they could muster to insist that Sleepy's concern
about Goblin and the Daughter of Night was not yet critical.

79

The Taglian Territories:
In Motion

Sleepy reaffirmed her determination to move north. We
limped along, accommodating the injured. We encountered no direct resistance at Ghoja, though forces loyal to the
Protector had damaged the main span of the great bridge over
the Main. It took our engineers more than a week to restore
the bridge. Throughout that week the Prahbrindrah Drah and
his sister preached to the people and soldiers of Ghoja. They

managed to win the hearts and allegiance of the majority.

The Prince was quite good with people when we let him run around loose. He preached his own restoration with an evangelical passion. He won particular favor amongst old folks nostalgic for the quiet changelessness that had characterized the world of their youth—before the coming of the Shadowmasters and the Black Company.

Except for a small memorial pasture where the fighting had been bloodiest, the battlefield on the north bank, where the Company had won a signal victory in what seemed like another lifetime, was completely built over. Back then there had been a hamlet and watchtower on the south bank, beside a ford that could be crossed only half the year. Now Ghoja threatened to become a city. The bridge, begun at my suggestion ages ago, was a strategic gem both militarily and commercially. There were strong forts and big markets on both banks now.

The girl and the Goblin thing should have done more to keep us from crossing over.

We made camp twelve miles north of the bridge, in rough, bare country still not claimed by peasants. I doubt that it was good for much but pasture. Which meant it was a wasteland amongst vegetarians. But had the ground been better I doubt many farmers would have immigrated. It was too near the high holy place of the Deceivers, the Grove of Doom.

We left the Prince and his sister at Ghoja, along with many native recruits. Sleepy thought it was time the royals got a taste of independence. She was confident that they would not conspire against the Company again. They had been included in our councils often enough to know that Tobo's hidden folk would always be close by.

Ten hours after we set camp, in the middle of the night, Sleepy changed her mind. She wanted to move a little closer to Taglios, to get between the City and the Grove of Doom.

I was awake when Riverwalker brought the news, writing by lamplight and keeping an eye on our injured. Some of them had not weathered the journey well. I was concerned about Soulcatcher in particular.

The change in plan did not irritate me as deeply as it did Lady. She had to be dragged out of a deep sleep. The way she snarled and threatened great evils left me wondering if she had not begun having nightmares again.

Riverwalker murmured, whispered. "I'm getting me a head start."

"Run, River, run. You'll need every yard you can get."

Lady gave me a look that made me wonder if I should not yell at him to wait up.

We established the new camp near a dense stand of trees which, I learned, surrounded and masked a sprawling Shadowlander cemetery that hailed from the first Shadowmaster invasion of the Taglian Territories. From before the Company's arrival. Almost no one knew about that. I had not, though I had campaigned in the region. Of the entire host only Suvrin showed any interest. He thought he might have a relative or two tucked away there.

He would have plenty of opportunity to visit tombs and graves. Sleepy planned to stay put, recruiting and training and harrying the edge of the Grove of Doom while Tobo and our other casualties recuperated. The trouble with the cemetery was, time had vandalized most of the Shadowlanders' slapdash grave markers.

The Goblin-thing and the Daughter of Night settled down, too, and they really did nothing but sit. They did not begin transcribing the Books of the Dead because they had no supplies. They did not consult with Deceivers making pilgrimages into the holy grove. Those men we left alone, every future step to be dogged by Unknown Shadows so we could follow their routines once they returned to their home environments. There were not many Stranglers left alive. This way we could find out who those few were.

Handy as it is, being able to see whatever you want takes a lot of getting used to.

The Grove of Doom was always a cruel and wicked place, filled with ancient darkness. The hidden folk hated it but they endured going in for Tobo's sake.

Their devotion to the boy gets scary when I think about it too much.

Gromovol and Arkana were mending at a pace equaling Tobo's, which was amazing but not magical. Gromovol's arrogance remained undiminished by misfortune. Arkana was understandably withdrawn.

Soulcatcher worried me increasingly. Not only did she show no improvement, she seemed to be growing weaker. She was headed right down the grim trail Sedvod had blazed.

There was a lot of sentiment favoring letting her slide, and for possibly easing Gromovol along the same dark path while he was sleeping. The jury remained out on Arkana even though the hidden folk had exculpated her in all ways but calculation and manipulation. There were random moments, widely separated, when I felt sorry for the girl.

I remembered the loneliness.

I was the only one who would talk to her, excepting Gromovol. She turned her back on him every time he tried to do so. During our reluctant chats I tried to learn more about her homeworld and, especially, Khatovar. But she did not have much to say. She knew nothing. She had a full measure of youth's indifference to the past.

Shukrat shunned Arkana completely.

Shukrat was almost pathetically eager to fit in. Shukrat really wanted to belong. I have a strong feeling she did not belong before she joined us. And maybe Arkana had, which might illuminate Shukrat's spite toward her now.

80

The Taglian Territories:
In Camp

Life is never like a canal, flowing gently through a straightforward and predictable channel. It is more like a mountain brook, zigging and zagging, tearing things up, sometimes going almost dormant before taking an unexpected and turbulent turn.

I was setting out some similar proposition to Lady and Shukrat while examining Tobo to see if he dared put any weight on the broken leg. He thought he was feeling better and was getting extremely restless, which is usually a sign that the patient is, indeed, getting better but is not nearly as far advanced as he wants to believe. We were in my VIP hospital. Soulcatcher and Arkana were present as well. Shukrat was putting on a show, fussing over Tobo while making it clear that Arkana no longer existed. Lady was on her knees beside her sister's pallet, hands flat on her thighs, motionless. She had stayed that way for almost an hour. For a while I thought she was meditating. Or she had gone into some sort of trance. Now I was starting to worry.

The women looked more like mother and daughter than sisters. Poor Lady. Against the years all men campaign in vain. And of late, time has been particularly unkind to my love.

Now that we were settled and had little to do but wait for people to mend, Lady spent time with Soulcatcher every day. She could not explain it herself.

She finally came around, looked back, asked the question that tormented her. "She's dying, isn't she?"

"I think so." I admitted. "And I don't know why. It looks like the same thing that got the Voroshk kid. So I don't know how to turn it around. Howler doesn't know how, either."

Though the screaming sorcerer never had been renowned for his skills as a healer.

"Goblin must've done something to her but it isn't sorcery." I added, "Not that anybody recognizes. And it isn't any of the diseases I see in the field." In most armies more soldiers die of dysentery than fall to enemy arms. I am proud that that has never been true in my army.

Lady nodded. She resumed staring at her sister. "I wonder what it is. Something Goblin did. We'd have to wake her up to find out, wouldn't we?" After a heartbeat, "The little bastard was right there when Sedvod took sick, too. Wasn't he?"

"I'm afraid so." I passed Tobo to Shukrat. "Take it easy on him, girl. Or we'll need to get you two a separate tent."

Tobo blushed. Shukrat grinned. I turned to Arkana. "You think you're ready to take up your dancing career again?"

"Is nothing ever serious with you?"

She caught me by surprise. Frivolity was not a crime often attached to my name. "Absolutely. None of us are going to get out of this alive so we might as well grab a laugh while we can." So One-Eye used to claim. "Cranky this morning?" I leaned forward and whispered, "I would be, too. Broken bones are no fun. I know. I've had a few. But try to smile. You're through the worst of it."

She put on her best scowl. The worst of it was still inside her head. She might never recover emotionally. She had not been brought up in a place and station where it was even conceivable that such horrors could overtake her.

"Look at it this way, child. No matter how bad you think it is right now, it can always get worse. I've been in the soldier racket a long time and I promise you, that's a natural law."

"How could my life be worse than this?"

"Think about it. You could be back home. Where you'd be dead. And you would've gone through hell getting that way. Or you could be a prisoner instead of my guest. Which means that every day could be like your one bad day.

There're plenty of guys out there who think we let you off too easy. Which reminds me of another natural law. Once you're outside the circle of people who agree that you're special, you're just another human body. And that's hardly ever a good situation for a woman. You're actually better off here, where we have women running stuff, than you would be almost anywhere else."

Arkana retreated inside herself, evidently thinking that I was threatening her. I was not. I was just thinking out loud. Maundering. Old men do that.

I told her, "You need to take it out on somebody, put Gromovol's name at the head of your list."

Lady said, "She's the only connection I have left with ninety percent of my life. The only connection with my family."

The stream takes its wild turns.

"You do anything that saves her, the first thing she'll do when she gets on her feet is try to cut you off at the knees and make you dance on the stumps."

Tobo started to say something. I poked him. We had discussed this several times. His opinion was bloody-minded.

"I know. I know. But every time I turn around it seems like someone else is gone and we're getting to be more and more alien. . . ."

"I understand. I've felt completely dislocated in time since One-Eye died. There's almost nothing left of my past." The nearest thing was come-lately Murgen. Lady and I had chosen the way—and now we were refugees from our own place and time. Though why should I be surprised at this late date? That was what the Company always was: the gathering of the landless, the hopeless, the fugitive and the outcast.

I sighed. Was I about to start creating another past as an emotional crutch?

I knelt beside Lady. "I don't think she'll last more than another week. I'm having trouble getting food down her. And more keeping it there. But I've thought of something we can do to stall death. And maybe even get a sound diagnosis."

Lady turned a gaze on me so intense I shuddered, recalling ancient times, when I was a captive in the Lady's Tower at Charm and about to face the Eye of Truth. "I'm listening."

I noted that, even now, she would not touch her sister. There was a strong selfish underpinning to her emotions. She wanted to save this mad devil sister entirely for her own sake.

"We can take her to Shivetya. We know he can cure Howler. . . ."

"He says he can. Telling us what we want to hear."

What Howler wanted to hear. I had no emotion invested in the runt's well-being. I thought the world would be improved by his extermination.

Lady's tone did not support her words. A spark of hope had been struck.

I said, "Let's have Howler get another carpet put together, then we'll slip away to the glittering plain, get him fixed up and find out what Shivetya can do for Soulcatcher. Even if he can't do anything we can stash her in the ice cavern till we have time to research what's wrong with her. That ought to be a real challenge for Tobo."

That was the course I preferred. I figured that once we installed Soulcatcher in the cave of the ancients Lady would lose interest eventually. The effect on the world at large would be the same as if we had killed her right away while Lady could sustain her tether to her roots via the pretense that she would jump in and resurrect her sister one day soon.

Lady said, "I like that idea. I'll see how soon Howler can get a carpet put together."

"All right." I peeled back one of Soulcatcher's eyelids. I saw nothing promising. I got the feeling that her essence might be absent, out wandering, lost. Paybacks, Murgen might say, if that was true.

As soon as she left, Tobo said, "You're up to something besides what you told her, aren't you?"

"Me?" I shrugged. "I have some ideas. Some of them I might have to clear with the Captain."

Shukrat then said something that ruined her dumb blonde image for me. "You know the reason that Soulcatcher followed you all down here from the north is the same reason that Lady wants to save her now? I'll bet that if she really wanted to badly enough she could've killed you all just about any time she wanted."

I stared. I looked at Tobo. I stared some more.

Shukrat reddened. She murmured, "Neither one of them ever learned how to say, 'I love you.' "

I understood. It was the same thing Goblin and One-Eye had had going for all those years, at a somewhat less lethal level. When they were sober. It was the sort of thing I see all the time amongst my brethren, who cannot, or believe that they dare not, express their real feelings. I added, "Only those two don't even know they need to say it."

81

The Shadowlander Military Cemetery: Laying To Rest

Willow Swan stuck his head into the tent. "Croaker. Murgen. Anybody who's interested. Sahra's ready to do her thing with Thai Dei and Uncle Doj."

About damned time, I thought but did not say. There were moments, lately, when I wanted to have the whole damned Nyueng Bao Community lined up and spanked. They had dragged the two corpses a hundred fifty miles while they argued bitterly about what to do with them. I did manage to keep my mouth shut but kept wanting to scream, "They don't care anymore! Do *something!* They smell. Bad!"

Not the sort of thing you do with grieving relatives, of

course. Not unless you feel like you have developed a short-age of enemies.

The Nyueng Bao had prepared a pair of ghats in a prominent place near the center of the Shadowlander military cemetery. Though only a few swamp folk remained with us those survivors were gathered in cliques, according to the funeral option they believed best honored the dead.

Who would believe a funeral could become savagely political? But people can find reasons to squabble about almost anything.

Thai Dei's send-off was less controversial, of course. He had not believed in much of anything but his own honor, himself. A ritualistic passage through the purifying flame for a warrior who would not bend, troubled only a couple of conservative old-timers who thought the ceremonies too foreign. Uncle Doj was the great bone of contention.

With Doj the burning group were in dispute with the exposure group, who wanted to lay the corpse out on a high platform and leave it till its bones were clean.

This was supposed to be the proper send-off for a high priest of the Path of the Sword—though no one could say how, why or when that idea had arisen. None of the men from Hsien, some of whom had grown up in Hsien's martial arts monasteries, had heard of any such practice there. The people of Hsien buried their dead. Doj's cronies insisted that his predecessors had been exposed exactly the way they wanted to do him now.

As we filed past the ghats, each tossing on an herb packet and a folded piece of paper carrying a prayer the fire would send along with the dead, Suvrin suggested, "They might have acquired the custom when they first passed through my country. Some of the peoples back home, back then, did expose corpses that they were especially afraid would be seized by skinwalkers."

Skinwalkers again. One of those monsters no one has ever

seen, like vampires and werewolves. With all the real monsters loose in the world, seen and suffered often enough, why did so many people trouble themselves about things no reliable witness ever saw? "Wouldn't fire work just as well?"

"Burning wasn't acceptable. It isn't even in modern times, even though so many northerners have come across the Dandha Presh."

I grunted. It must have to do with religion and religion seldom makes sense to me.

"The common people, the poor, anyone that wouldn't attract a skinwalker, gets a normal burial. Just like here." He indicated the graves around us. "People who might attract a skinwalker will be exposed. So there won't be a good suit of skin to steal." He gestured. "The above-ground tombs. They must contain priests and captains who were being stored temporarily, until they could be properly exposed. Their army must have been hard-pressed. They never got back to deal with it."

Actually, I could see several fallen collections of poles with bits of rag and bone beneath that might have been exposure platforms a long time ago. "Looks like your skinwalkers never got here to take advantage, either."

That earned me a scowl.

I was not quite sure why Suvrin was Sleepy's favorite and probable designated successor. But I never understood why Murgen picked Sleepy, either. Yet he had chosen well. She had brought the Company through the Kiaulune wars and the era of the Captivity. And there had been a lot of raised eyebrows when I had chosen Murgen to become Annalist. And Murgen had managed despite never having been quite certain of his sanity.

Sleepy saw something.

Suvrin did not agree. Suvrin insisted that he was going to leave us. But I noted that he had passed up several wonderful opportunities to do so already.

As was her right, being Thai Dei's closest surviving relative, Sahra asked Murgen to join her and Tobo in placing the torches into Thai Dei's pyre. Fitting, I thought, although the old men grumbled. Murgen and Thai Dei had been as close as brothers for a long, long time.

Sahra asked no one but Tobo to help bring the fire to Doj. Even I saluted the dead swordmaster, though in life I never trusted him.

Lady leaned against me from my left. "I suppose you'll have to admit that he was trustworthy now." Mind reading.

"I don't have to admit any such thing. He just kicked off before he could screw us over."

"No fool like an old fool."

I stopped arguing. She would win every debate by dint of outliving me. I changed the subject. "You still feel like you're getting stronger?" For an age now she had been able to steal almost no supernatural power from Kina. But long ago she had been able to parasitize enough to come close to being Soulcatcher's equal. She believed Goblin's attack on the Goddess was why there was so little power left to steal.

It seemed reasonable to me that Goblin returning as Kina's tool would mean fresh power available but it had not worked that way. Not until Goblin and the girl had entered the Grove of Doom.

"It's coming. Little by little." She sounded like she did not want to wait. "I can do a few parlor tricks now." The way she thought, that might mean she was limited to destroying small villages with a single wink. "I need to get closer to see what helps."

I did not follow up. I could feel her excitement. She hid it well but if I got her going she would drive me nuts talking about stuff that was entirely beyond me.

I could do that, too, either going on with my theories about diseases or about the Company's history.

Definitely a match made in heaven.

I told her, "Soon as we're done paying our respects, how

about you see Howler? Find out if my idea gets him moving on the carpets any faster."

"If you give him what he wants now he won't have any incentive to stay with us."

"Where's he gonna run to?"

"He'll find somewhere. He always has."

And, somehow, that always ended up in our way. "Then I expect we'll push him hard to get us a couple, three carpets. And you can hang around playing apprentice while he does, sister Shukrat."

"Yech! No way! He's creepy. He stinks. And he has more hands than some of those four-armed Gunni gods."

"He's little," Tobo called from the chair we had brought along so he could rest between ceremonial stints. "Spank him."

"That's probably what he wants."

"Get somebody to carry me around and I'll go with you," Tobo told Shukrat. "I make the Howler nervous. Croaker. What'll we call him if Shivetya cures his screaming?"

"Stinky might work. Or the Stinker for formal."

The flames of the funeral pyres leapt higher. Tobo ignored me now. I let it drop, too. Time to say goodbye, old man. They never took the oath but Thai Dei and Doj were brothers in their hearts. They stories were warp and woof of the Company tapestry.

82

With the Company:
Going South

Sleepy always saw idleness as a vacuum in need of filling. No way was she going to put up with ten thousand men sitting around, maybe spending an hour or two each day training. When they were feeling particularly ambitious.

Just miles away stood a perfectly ugly wood desperately in need of clear-cutting.

You put a whole lot of people to work on a place like that, starting from the outside and working inward, making sure you get even the tiniest twigs and shoots, you can get some great bonfires burning. The evening of the second day the soldiers had one entire horizon hidden behind ramparts of smoke.

Sleepy was *daring* Goblin and the girl to come show us what they had.

I had doubts about the wisdom of that. Sleepy was not impressed enough with the fact that Goblin had a slice of Kina stuffed inside him. And Kina's bad-ass reputation was well-deserved.

But I was not the boss. I could advise but I could not make anyone listen. My worries just earned me one of Sleepy's enigmatic smiles.

"You ready to go for a fly?" Lady asked. "Howler's got a carpet ready."

"You in a hurry?"

"You told me Sileth's only got a week. That was three days ago."

"I did, didn't I? How big is that carpet?"

"Big enough."

"I mean it, hon. It's got to have room for six people."

She stared. After several seconds she said, "I don't think I'm even going to ask. Except maybe who."

"You and Soulcatcher. Howler. Gromovol. Arkana if she wants to go."

"Still playing games, Love?"

"No game. Progress. We lost the most promising one of those kids when Magadan got killed. That was a bad career move on his part. Gromovol is as useless as teats on a bull. I'd just as soon kill him. But if we give him back to those two old Voroshk demons Shivetya's got tied up down there we might score a point or two."

She frowned.

"Thought you were the master manipulator of the greatest empire. . . ." She pointed a finger. An invisible darning needle began to sew my lips together. She *was* getting the power back. "I'll just explain then, shall I?"

"There's the man I married."

Bullshit. But I was not going to argue. "We got the top two Voroshk locked up out there on the plain. They've got no home anymore, far as we know. As far as Shivetya is letting anybody know. They have no future, nowhere to go. An apparent act of kindness might add a couple of heavyweights to our ranks just when it would be handy to have them."

"You're evil."

"I try. Let me go blow in Arkana's ear."

"You do and you'll wake up in the morning wondering how long before you get your first hot flash."

Well, well. Maybe that explained some recent crankiness. Hers. Mine was caused by the iron-strapped, rock-headed obtuseness of the people who insisted on tangling my feet. That was a whole different hunk of monkey meat.

I went to blow in Arkana's ear. Verbally.

"I'm not going to give Gromovol a choice," I told Arkana. "This is a chance for me to maybe make peace with his old man. Which is the only good that can ever come of the idiot. If I keep him here he'll eventually do something stupider than anything he's done already. I've told you before, I've been in this racket a long time. When you come up with a liability as big as Gromovol you look for a way to use him. Or you kill him. I've been getting soft in my twilight years."

Her skeptical expression told me how well I had sold that fairy tale.

"You, you're special. You get choices. You can go back if you want. You can tag along for the visit and stay with us when we're done. Or you can hang around here and not go at all."

"Oh, I'll go. I can't not. I'll decide what else I need to do after we get there."

We went aloft by night, under the light of a full moon, with Lady, Soulcatcher, Gromovol and Arkana aboard Howler's new carpet. Tobo, Shukrat, Murgen and I witched along on flying posts. Despite Sleepy's objections, and Tobo's aches and pains, Tobo insisted on coming along because Shukrat was coming. So Murgen rode with me because Sahra refused to fly. The youngsters larked about us fearlessly, engaged in some dragonfly mating ritual.

Murgen and I dropped out briefly at Dejagore. Sleepy insisted we check up on Blade and his occupation force.

Drifting down toward Dejagore's citadel, I asked, "You think Sahra's been having visions or something?"

"Huh?" Murgen's thoughts had been wandering.

"This frantic mother stuff. I swear she keeps getting worse. I thought you might have noticed her having psychic seizures. Or something."

"She don't talk about it. If she does."

"What do you think?"

"I think that if she hasn't she's definitely afraid that she might start."

"Yeah?"

"When we were young she worried about turning into her mother."

"Sometimes she's damned crabby."

"She's no Gota the Troll, though. Her body doesn't hurt her enough. So now she's terrified she's going to turn into Hong Tray. Her grandmother."

"And?"

"And maybe she will. She's started to look like the old woman did. Whenever she starts cranking about it I remind her how calm and accepting Hong Tray always was. Like a solid rock in a wild river."

"Doesn't work, does it?"

"Not for a second. Well. Somebody must've smelled us coming."

We had not yet settled to the top of the citadel tower but Blade and his chief lieutenants were there to meet us. Blade called up, "We were expecting Tobo, the way the shadows were all spooked up."

"You got lucky. The kid's hurt so you get the old farts instead. Captain wants us to check up on you. So you give us a couple of good drinks, we'll tell her you're doing a kickass job, no need to even think about you guys."

"I think we can handle that."

83

Taglios:
Decision

The sharpest-eyed spy can be misdirected or deluded if you know he is watching. Having been of the Company once and having been victimized by the Company more than once, the Great General understood its policy of deception. His understanding had served him well during the Kiaulune wars, where the trickery had gotten the best of him rarely.

He and Aridatha Singh were observing large-scale close

order drills from the wall of a fortress that bestrode a hill just south of Taglios. The soldiers had begun to show some interest in improving their skills lately. The approach of a powerful enemy was a mighty motivator.

The Great General asked, "They all went?"

"I've had the report from two independent sources within the last hour. They went out right after moonrise. A flying carpet and three flying poles. They headed south. They passed close enough to Haband's tree for him to identify the Howler, Lady, Croaker, Murgen, the boy wizard and three of those white wizard children I saw when I visited. They aren't worried about us."

"There'd be more of those."

"I'm sure the rumor is true. I've had it confirmed too many times. They're dead."

The Great General refused to take anything at face value where those people were concerned. "Where would they go?"

"Maybe something's happened at Dejagore. Or farther south."

Farther south would have to be beyond the Dandha Presh. Support for the Protector had evaporated outside those territories still directly under the Great General's control, near as his agents could determine, though there had been no outbreaks of enthusiasm for the return of the royals. The mood of the empire was indifferent, excepting amongst those who could profit, one way or another.

Same as it always was, Mogaba reflected.

Mogaba played with a snail shell as he talked. Doing so seemed almost a tick anymore. But he startled Aridatha by popping his arm back suddenly, snapping the shell out as hard as he could throw. "Time for a full-scale field exercise. Let's find out how good their intelligence is with wonder boy away."

Aridatha asked a few brisk questions. These days he commanded the division that would form the left wing of Mogaba's army. It was backboned by his own City Battalions.

The Great General said, "Make all your preparations exactly as you would if we were going down there to fight. Issue appropriate rations. But prepare in a relaxed manner. We just want to see how ready we are. So we know where we need to do more work. Don't encourage questions. And from now on I want to see our spies personally when they bring in news."

Aridatha went away wondering what Mogaba really had in mind.

The Great General sent for the rest of his staff and commanders. He spent a particularly long time, in bright midday sun, conferring with his cavalry captains.

84

Beside the Cemetery:
Confusion

Willow Swan stuck his head into Sleepy's cabin, which had been built for her from the better logs harvested from the Grove of Doom. "Another contact with Mogaba's cavalry. Three miles west of the Rock Road."

This happened periodically. It was one way the Great General kept track of his enemies. The probes became more numerous when Mogaba wanted to provoke a response. Sleepy grunted, untroubled.

"I'm a little concerned," Swan told her. "This time they're pushing harder. Since we don't have any good way to get anything out of the hidden folk who didn't run off after Tobo, we don't have any idea what Mogaba is doing. We're as blind as he is."

"Is his main force maneuvering behind his cavalry screen?"

"I get that impression."

"Then he's trying to harass us into another panic." Twice

already Taglian forces had come south and demonstrated until Sleepy responded, whereupon they had retreated rapidly. Mogaba was trying to get his virgins some confidence-building experience under the stress of near-battle. No doubt he would push them a little closer this time. "Run one brigade up behind the pickets and have them make a lot of noise. Keep another brigade in camp. Everyone else can see to their normal business. I think we're due for a reaction from the Daughter of Night pretty soon."

Her campaign against the Deceiver messiah and the Goblin-thing was much like the Great General's against her.

Swan reminded her, "We have official Deceiver titles for those two now." A fact one of the hidden folk had discovered in far Asharan, of all places, just before Tobo's departure. Asharan was a small city to the southwest unlikely to have any impact on any events unless through its band of Deceivers. "Khadidas. Khadidasa."

Slave of Khadi. Or Kina. "Is that one or both of them?"

"Those are the male and female forms. One for each."

"Willow, that girl won't be called a slave by anybody. She has the same blood as her mother and aunt. Daughter of Night suits her just fine."

Swan shrugged, departed. Tobo had said that there was no love lost between the girl and the Khadidas. That, in fact, they tended to bicker. That, further, the girl had begun to appear almost disillusioned.

The Great General's cavalry continued to harass Sleepy's scouts and pickets. Skirmishes popped up everywhere. Commercial traffic dwindled on the Rock Road. Sizable troops of horse probed the brigade deployed to screen the Company force. They were mostly Vehdna. Vehdna had a tradition of being excellent horsemen. These horsemen showed well against Hsien's professional infantry. Sleepy brought the other brigade out of camp and handed the backup role off to the native recruits.

"I'm getting worried," Swan told Sleepy.

"It must be escalating. You were just concerned before."

"Exactly my point. Why is Mogaba working so hard to make us think he's working up to a straightforward attack? Why is he trying to force a response?"

"Because he wants to see what we'll do. Unless he's trying to distract us from something else. Any chance he could've made a deal with the Deceivers?"

"Narayan Singh's son is one of his cronies."

That struck a spark. "Aridatha Singh is no Deceiver! Nor is he a Deceiver stooge."

"All right. Don't get excited."

Moments later, though, it became clear that it was time for everybody to get excited about something, fast. The unexpected and deadly happened.

Mogaba's cavalry faded away. They were replaced by the infantry of Mogaba's Second Territorial division, as numerous as Sleepy's whole army. The Taglians drove straight into the defending force, hurling them back, while the cavalry began to leak around the ends of the friendly line.

Sleepy had messengers flying around and horns blaring before it became entirely clear that this time Mogaba was not just teasing. She snapped at Swan, "We have to keep them from getting inside the camp. Whatever that costs."

"I'll handle that," Swan replied, though he was no official member of the heirarchy. "I'll use the recruits. You grab anyone else you can find." He sprinted away. If Mogaba captured the camp he would gain control of the treasure that had come down off the glittering plain. That might win his war for him right here, right now.

Swan began sorting the confusion in the camp as soon as he located the Hsien sergeants in charge of training. He announced that the enemy had launched a reconnaissance in force. Some elements might try to reach the camp.

Once he had the recruits assembled facing toward the enemy, Swan sent trusted men to move the treasure into hiding inside the old Shadowlander military cemetery. And well he did, too. Mogaba's attack was much more vigorous than expected. When it reached the camp the recruits did not long withstand it. They allowed elements of Mogaba's force to get into the camp itself.

All did not go well for the Great General, though. Soon after his own division caught the attention of his enemies, a second was supposed to rush forward east of the Rock Road, to catch the disorganized troops rushing back from the Grove of Doom to help Sleepy. The commander of that force, not sure if he was being led into a clever trap himself, vacillated until his attack had no chance of attaining success. Shortly he would find himself free to pursue new career opportunities. Many lesser officers would join him.

On the extreme left Aridatha Singh launched his attack exactly on schedule. Its initial goal was to occupy the Grove of Doom. Then it was supposed to carry on southward and westward and cut the enemy's line of withdrawal. But before Aridatha's force was well into the maneuver he received a dispatch from Mogaba directing him to pull back. The enemy had collected himself. A counterattack was expected shortly. Mogaba feared that if Sleepy discovered Aridatha she would cut him off and exterminate his division. Aridatha was a novice on the battlefield.

85

The Grove of Doom:
A Big Surprise

The Daughter of Night was ready to scream with the boredom and psychic oppression of life in the Grove of Doom. Life with Narayan had not been perfect but she had understood it. Life with the Khadidas was intolerable. The possessed little man was insufferable. Every day, all day, there were lessons. Almost always about things she already knew. Unless it was philosophical stuff about how she ought to give herself up completely to the will of Kina. About how she should strive to rid herself of even the most stubborn tatters of personality and become nothing but a vessel for Kina, not the Daughter of Night anymore but the Khadidasa.

The Khadidas droned his arguments at her while she sat with arms around shins, chin on her knees, on the steps of the Deceiver temple. Visiting Deceiver pilgrims came and went, cleaning the temple. She paid no attention. She was recalling more than one other time when she had been right here with Papa Narayan. Looking back, those days seemed almost a normal family life, now.

She began to replay thoughts from times past, immediately became restless, and wondered why. She had not thought of men in that way since she had heard about Narayan's death.

Someone came down from the temple, passed by her. He set himself to fling a pail of dirty water. There was a solid thump. The bucket man made a startled little squeak and toppled backward. He fell on the steps beside the girl, looking up at his messiah from amazed eyes. She watched the light fade from them.

An arrow stood out of his chest. It had struck him through the heart. The girl did not notice the colorful markings on the shaft, which identified not only the archer's unit but the bowman as well. She started to look around. Thumps and cries surrounded her. Arrows hissed close and thumped behind her as they found her new companion. She started to dig inside, to release the "love me" effect. A blunt arrow struck her squarely in the breastbone. A second struck her lower. She pitched forward, trying to puke up her anklebones.

The first few arrows seemed not to inconvenience the Khadidas at all. But they kept coming. And coming. And then there were Taglian soldiers all over. A high officer shouted, "Cut off the heads. We'll take them with us. Leave the bodies in the boneyard. For the ravens."

Another officer strode toward the Daughter of Night. The other Taglians all deferred to him. The girl's first response was to notice that he was incredibly handsome. Then she recalled having seen him before, years ago, when she had been a captive of the Black Company. He had been brought to see Narayan. "My brother Aridatha," she gasped out. "It seems my fate is to spend life as a prisoner." She continued to clutch her stomach. A huge Shadar soldier stood over her, ready to club her at the first hint of anything untoward.

The Taglian officer was startled but only for a moment. He grasped the part about being her brother. "You're the Daughter of Night. It's my job to make sure you don't fulfill your destiny." He eyed the thing lying beside her, motionless now but not dead. In the conventional sense. He had met Goblin that night, too.

"That is the Khadidas now," she said. "Not the wizard. It's not dead. And you can't kill it. It has the Goddess in it."

The Taglian made swift gestures. Soldiers bound the Goblin thing, then stuffed it into a hemp sack—after yanking the arrows out of its flesh. "I wouldn't count on that."

"Kina is in him."

"Suppose I chop him into little pieces, Booboo? Then have my men burn the pieces at places separated by a hundred miles. I didn't know my father and I certainly don't honor what he was. But, even so, that creature murdered him."

"What did you call me?"

"Eh? You mean Booboo?"

"Yes. That. Why did you do that?" She forced herself to look away from what was happening to the martyred Deceivers as she forced her mind away from the accusation leveled against the Khadidas.

"Your mother and father and everyone in the Black Company who cares about you calls you Booboo. Because it isn't as unwieldy as 'the Daughter of Night.' Come on. Get up. I have to keep these men moving. No tricks, either. If you misbehave you'll get hurt. These men are very scared of you."

A twinge of surprise ran through the girl. They were concerned enough about her to have a pet name for her? Narayan had not dared go that far, though she knew that he had been devoted to her.

Despite Aridatha's warning she tried to turn on the "love me" effect. It would not come. She could not tell if that was because she was so rattled or because of the Khadidas. The Goblin thing had shown the ability to interfere with her before, usually when she was not conforming to the standards it set.

For an instant she hoped her captors *would* shred the Khadidas and roast the scraps in a hundred scattered trash pits. Then she forced her personal feelings aside. This was no time. This was the time to concentrate on making sure she and the Khadidas survived until they found their opportunity to begin their great work.

That that chance would come she did not doubt. Kina would find a way. Kina always did. Kina was the darkness. And the darkness always came.

The girl remained completely docile and cooperative. She could not help noticing how restless she became each time the handsome general came near her. But he was too busy to notice her. He had received orders changing his mission.

86

Beside the Cemetery:
More Confusion

There's another division out there, east of the Rock Road somewhere," Swan told Sleepy and her staff. "My impression is that it was supposed to push past and get behind us. But it suddenly turned back north. Without us taking prisoners or getting help from the hidden folk we'll never know why."

The Unknown Shadows became a hot topic. There were a few still around but they would not be bullied into helping. Tobo had not told them to help.

Tempers did not improve during the discussion. Everyone was tired, cranky and impatient. Sleepy in particular. With no solid evidence whatsoever she was beginning to believe that Mogaba had gotten the best of her yet again. And the thing was not over yet.

The Great General had not yet broken contact entirely. He seemed willing to continue skirmishing indefinitely.

Swan told everyone, "I think we did well. The casualty ratio ran in our favor, certainly."

Sleepy snapped, "But, strategically, Mogaba must be celebrating. He's pleased with what he accomplished." She had no way of knowing any such thing, of course. She knew only that she was not pleased. Mogaba had surprised her again.

She overlooked the fact that she had managed to drive off a much superior force once the fighting started, that Mogaba might have been too subtle and clever for his own good.

Willow Swan did not overlook that. He said, "Mogaba may be back. Once he understands that he did surprise us and could've rolled over us if he'd just charged in without all the maneuvering."

Heads bobbed. One brigadier noted that were he in charge

on the other side he would attack again even if he thought his enemies expected him. He would do it just to see what would happen. And to build in the minds of the attacked a belief that they had to stay alert. Keeping ready to repel an attack would grind a force down after several days.

Sahra wandered in. Late and uninterested in the discussion. To no one in particular she said, "It's started to rain."

Because that was important news that might have a serious impact on operations, Swan stepped out for a look.

The sky was overcast. The smell of rain was in the air. But it was not raining now and did not look likely to start until well after nightfall, which was only a short while away. Swan went back inside shaking his head.

That Sahra might have been speaking figuratively or metaphorically became evident a short while later, when a patrol brought in news that the Grove of Doom had been cleansed of Deceivers.

"Even of the Daughter of Night and the Goblin thing?" Sleepy demanded.

"We didn't find their bodies, Captain. And there were plenty of bodies there. All with their heads missing. Maybe those two managed to escape."

"Maybe. I wish Tobo would get the hell back here. I really hate this being blind."

"You're totally spoiled," Swan told her.

"And loving every minute of it. Tso Lien. More work for your recon people. Find out what happened. And find out if we can run anybody down. Keeping in mind that it would please Mogaba no end to lead us into a lethal trap."

"It shall be done, my Captain."

Swan sneered at Tso Lien's flowery response. The man hailed from a province where styles of speech were as important as what was being said. He was another of those fiercely competent professional officers who had wanted to shed the feudal chains of Hsien in hopes of making his fortune.

Swan wondered if the men from the Land of Unknown Shadows might not begin concentrating more on staying alive than on winning a war. Their future fortunes were in Company hands already, hidden in that cemetery.

87

Glittering Stone:
Fortress with No Name

Oh, so alert the observing eyes when Lady and I opened the shadowgate. I tossed in several unnecessary steps just for drama and confusion. Then we were moving again, flickering southward along the shielded road toward Shivetya's great wintry fastness.

The entire plain seemed a chill, grey, wintry place, lacking all glitter. The standing stones seemed old and tired and not much interested in making any effort to proclaim the glories of the past. I did not spot any new ones. Not once did the wind grow warmer than the heart of a loan shark. We saw patches of ice and snow.

Tobo suggested the plain was getting its weather from somewhere where the season was less comfortable than our own.

"You think?" I said. "With the Khatovar gate busted completely?" There was no sense of menace to the plain today. Could the shadows have become that few?

Shukrat said, "Only, it would be the heart of summertime at home, now."

I grunted. I adjusted my flying log to make more speed. The kids had no trouble keeping up. I heard Lady curse in the distance as Howler's carpet fell behind. Howler could not hurry because his conveyance nearly filled the protected area. He had to be cautious.

* * *

As we neared Shivetya's fortress, Tobo shouted, "It's safe to go up now!" He and Shukrat shot toward the sun. Or where the sun would have stood had the weather not been vile.

"Don't you dare!" Murgen barked.

"Too late, buddy. Hang on." I was rising already, though not with the derring-do of some immortal teenager. When Murgen squawked I said, "You don't like the ride, get off and walk."

In moments we had a god's-eye view of the glittering plain.

It was not a view I had seen before, nor was it one I had heard described. From a half mile up the plain resembled the floor inside the main chamber of the fortress. That did not surprise me. But the plain's boundaries did.

Each of the sixteen sectors centered on a shadowgate. Each had its own weather, season and time of day, which became obscured and confused approaching the midway points between shadowgates.

"It's like looking at the rest of the universe from inside a crystal ball," Murgen said.

"How come you never mentioned that it looks like this?"

"Because I never saw it like this. Maybe from the ghost realm you can't see this."

From up there color came to the plain. Never before had I seen so much color in the place of glittering stone.

Tobo and Shukrat shot past us, headed down, whooping with glee. I said, "Fun time is over." Howler's carpet had come into view, creeping along the line of the road down from our own world's shadowgate.

We entered the fortress through a hole in its roof. That seemed the only damage that never repaired itself. Maybe the guardian demon found a hole more useful than a dry floor. Certainly he had no cares about weather.

Although it was daytime outside, our agent on the scene, ancient Baladitya, was napping. These days he probably spent more time snoozing then he spent awake.

By the time Murgen and I set down, Shukrat was involved in a bitter argument with Nashun the Researcher and the First-Father. She and the Voroshk sorcerers used their native tongue, of course, but exact words were of no consequence. At heart the squabble was as old as humanity itself, fugheaded antiques locking horns with omniscient youth.

"Smells in here," Murgen observed.

It flat-out stank. Evidently the Voroshk were waiting for the serving staff to clean up after them. "Guess Shivetya doesn't have a sense of smell. If I was him I'd stop feeding them till they learned to take care of their chores." Baladitya, I noted, kept up his share of the housework despite tendencies toward absentmindedness and single-mindedness.

The racket raised by Shukrat and her relatives finally disrupted the copyist's snores.

Baladitya was a hairy old scarecrow desperately in need of a change of clothing. His ragged apparel was all that he had ever worn in my experience. He was almost as bad as the Howler, although less densely wrapped.

A close encounter with scissors, comb and a tub of warm water would not have been amiss, either. Tangled wisps of fine white hair floated all around his head and face. I thought bits might begin floating away, like seeds from a dandelion.

The inside of the fortress was completely creepy. I never relaxed there. It rubbed me the same way Uncle Doj always had. Wrong. Suspiciously wrong. In a quiet, unobtrusive way. A way that left me incapable of relaxing. Baladitya zeroed in on Murgen, wanting to know all about how Sleepy was doing, about how his old friend Master Santaraksita was doing, about how Tobo was. He had the Annalist bug. Also, though he had chosen his life out here for the intellectual adventure, he did miss people.

I suspect the Voroshk were not excellent company. They probably whined constantly in a language he did not understand, making no effort to communicate other than by yelling louder and slower.

I glanced upward, wondering when the others would get around to showing up. Then I strolled away a few steps, to the outer fringe of the dome of sourceless light that illuminated Baladitya's work area. I stared at the vast, indistinct bulk of the demon Shivetya.

The darkness around the devil was deeper than I recalled it, deeper than others had recorded it. The great wooden throne was equally ill-defined. The humanoid bulk nailed to the throne by means of silver daggers seemed less substantial than I remembered. I wondered if the golem became more ethereal as he gave of himself to sustain his guests.

Visitors have to eat. Shivetya sustains his guests and allies by exuding large, mushroomlike growths of manna. I recall the taste as slightly sweet and mildly spicy in that way that leaves you trying to figure out exactly what the spice might be. Just a few bites provide immense energy and boost your confidence dramatically. But nobody gets fat eating the stuff. In fact, it is a little repulsive and you do not touch it until you are hungry or hurting.

Obviously, Shivetya himself was not going to remain chubby forever, either.

I realized that big red eyes had opened. Shivetya was regarding me with more interest than I was regarding him.

The golem did not speak aloud. We believed that it could not. When it chose to communicate it did so by speaking directly inside your brain. Some found the experience no problem. I had not endured it myself, to my recollection, so cannot describe it. If Shivetya invaded my dreams during the half generation I lay enchanted in the caverns below I had no recollection of that, either. I have no memories whatsoever of that time.

Murgen and Lady do remember. Some. They will not discuss it. They prefer to let what made it into the Annals speak for itself.

It must not have been pleasant.

The shadows left Shivetya looking like he had a dog or

jackal's head, which sparked a momentary recollection of childhood idols. I guess he *was* a sort of lord of the underworld. He just did not do much recruiting.

One huge eye closed, then reopened. The demon of glittering stone showing off his sense of humor. Knowing that wink would obsess me for days.

Hands took hold of my arm. I glanced down. My sweetheart had arrived. And in this dim light she looked much younger and happier. I whispered, "You guys finally made it."

"Howler is turning into a timid little old man. He's got the idea that he might have a future."

"Let's stroll off that direction about half a mile and get lost for half an hour."

"Well. I'm certainly tempted. But I'm wondering what's gotten into you."

I pinched her behind. She squeaked and swatted my arm. I said, "Whoops!"

Both of Shivetya's eyes were turned our way now.

Lady said, "That sort of takes the edge off the moment, doesn't it?"

It did. So did several pairs of eyes watching from where the rest of the crowd were gathered. The youngsters in particular were appalled.

"Oh, well. Life's a bitch."

88

Fortress with No Name:
Recruiting Excitement

The squabbling amongst the Voroshk went on and on, seldom subsiding for long. I suspect there were several
occasions when those two old men wanted to punish the rest
of us but were held in check by Shivetya. Tobo paid them no
mind. He remained busy communing with Baladitya or the
golem. The latter seemed to be contributing to the boy's
already excessive arsenal of power.

Whenever it became too much for them, Arkana or
Shukrat would retreat to wherever I happened to be, usually
ending up seated on the floor, facing away from the family.
"They're afraid of you," Arkana explained. "They think
you're the real terror and Tobo is all for show. They think
you destroyed our world."

"I didn't destroy anything." Curious. Her accent was not
nearly as pronounced out here, when she wanted some protection.

"I know that. You know it. Even they probably know. But
they don't want it to be their fault. Inside, they're almost as
bad as Gromovol and Sedvod. For a couple of hundred years
now to be Voroshk has meant to be perfect in every way.
Without fault."

"So how come all the arguing?"

"Because Shukrat wants to stay with you. Because Sedvod died without proper rites. Because they don't want to
believe that Gromovol did so many really stupid things,
including getting Magadan killed. That'll really cause terrible Family political trouble when the news gets back home.
Magadan's father is the First Father's brother and they really
hate each other."

Evidently the surviving Voroshk preferred to pretend that

their Family still ruled in a land not wasted by murderous shadows.

"And why are they yelling at you?"

Arkana sighed. She tucked her head down in between her knees, where I could not get a good look at her expression. "I guess because I really kind of said I don't think I want to go home, either."

Arkana really used the word "really" a real lot. "Despite what happened?"

"They don't know that part yet. They don't need to know about it."

"They won't hear about it from me. But Gromovol might . . ."

"Even Gromovol isn't stupid enough to talk about it. There's no way he can talk his way out of that being his fault. By the rules of our own people. If that came out even his own father would desert him."

Wearing a somewhat dazed expression Shukrat retreated our way. Arkana moved over a few feet but otherwise did not acknowledge her existence. Neither did Shukrat deign to see Arkana. Shukrat settled on the stone floor, arms around her legs and chin upon her knees. There were tearstreaks on her cheeks.

"Well?" I said. "Do I need to go over there and spank somebody for being rude to my little girls?"

Shukrat laughed weakly. "You'd have to hit the other end. About ten thousand times. With a blacksmith's hammer."

"Just to get their attention," Arkana said. Posed as they were now the family resemblance was clear. Only when they were up and moving under the direction of their divergent characters did they seem so different.

The girls had a point. Even the destruction of their world had not been enough to shake those two old boulders loose from their dry riverbed of fixed thought.

I asked, "Arkana, are you pulled together now? Want to come translate for me?" I could use the tongue of Juniper, of course, but this would give her a chance to feel like she was useful.

She thought about that for a moment. She exchanged glances with Shukrat. Both girls looked at me.

I promised, "I'll only bully them a little."

The older Voroshk were keeping their fangs sharp by gnawing on Gromovol. If the kid had not fucked up so badly I might have felt sorry for him. He did not have the option of returning to our world. He would have to take whatever those two chose to hand out.

"You've been a little hard on my girls," I told the First Father. "Time to knock it off. Either one of you bothered to go back and see how things turned out at home?"

No response. Other than ugly looks.

"So you don't really know how things stand. . . ." An epiphany. "Arkana, sweetie. They ran away. Coming after you kids was their excuse. And when they used it up they couldn't go back. I'll bet you Shivetya hasn't been forcing them to stay here at all." I recalled that once there had been three of them. Somebody must have gone. And maybe did not live to bring back news.

Those old men were cowards? It fit.

For the first time in generations the Voroshk faced something the Family could not overwhelm as easily as stamping a mouse. And the only way some of them could deal with that was to run away.

These two would not want to go back now in case there *were* survivors.

I said, "I'll be right back." I trotted over to Tobo, interrupted, gave him the short version. "How long are you going to be? Do I have time to take a run through the Khatovar gate with those old men so we can find out what the shadows really did do over there?"

The boy's eyes went blank.

When I was about ready to slap him to get his attention back he refocused, told me, "Shivetya says that would be a huge health risk. Shivetya says you're right about the Voroshk. They did run away. Shivetya says more courageous members of the clan are still active back there. A lot of shadows are active there, too. Shivetya says the gate is growing closed. With almost every surviving shadow on that side of it. Shivetya says leave it alone. Shivetya says go ahead with your scheme. Shivetya says not to worry about Khatovar. You can't reach it. Trying will only get you killed. And it will still be there when everything else is done."

Was that Tobo speaking or was the demon using his lips? "Shivetya, I fear, contains an awful lot of stinky brown stuff. For a guy who never eats."

"You think it's unreasonable, him being a little selfish about the order things get done? Considering the scale of his contributions?"

"Humbug." I stamped back to Arkana. I wondered how anybody was supposed to murder a goddess—and survive it so the Goddess's jailer could be hustled down the dark path right behind her. "Sweetheart, tell those old farts that I want them to fly out to your homeworld with me. That I want to see what's happened there. And that I really do want to see what's left of Khatovar."

Arkana took several little sideways steps that moved her around in front of me, putting her back to Nashun and the First Father. "You really mean that?"

Softly, because that half-wit Gromovol seemed to have become interested in what was being said, I responded, "As far as they need to know, I do."

The old men did not do much faking of any reason for avoiding a trip home for a fact-finding tour. They did make it clear that they would not go.

"What do you plan to do with your lives?" I asked. "Shivetya won't let you loaf around here forever."

They suspected they were about to be sucked into something. And they were right, of course. I added, "The Company always has room for a few good men." Or bad men, as the case might be. I was not so sure about chickenshit and mediocre men—though having a couple extra sorcerers sounded worthwhile enough to make the try.

Trouble was, if I did seduce these two, how would I keep them under control?

That sounded like something Lady ought to ponder. It was the sort of question she had dealt with regularly before I stumbled into her life.

I could hear the clockwork kerchunking inside Voroshk craniums. Their thoughts were obvious. Tell Croaker anything. Tell Croaker what he wanted to hear. Get off this cruel and frightful plain. Run away. Find a place where they have not heard of the Voroshk, where they have no major wizards of their own. Set up shop there and slap together a whole new empire.

Just as the Shadowmasters had done before them.

"Tell them I'll come back after they've had a day or two to think it over."

As she retreated with me Arkana told me, "If they agree to join you they'll give you more trouble than Gromovol did."

"Really?" I chose a tone that was supposed to let her know I might not be as dumb as I looked. "How do you suppose we could keep them from doing that?"

She did have some ideas. "Do what you did to us. Make them strip naked. Take their rheitgeistiden and their *shefsepoken*. Make them stay on the ground where they're vulnerable. But promise them they'll get everything back after they show you that you can trust them. Then you stretch it out."

"I'm going to adopt you. You'd make a wonderful daughter. Hey, evil-minded future daughter number two. You heard Arkana. What do you think?"

Grudgingly, Shukrat admitted, "I think she's right."

"Excellent! Let's go ask your wicked future mother's opinion."

We found Lady reading what Baladitya was spending his final years recording, which was, more or less, Shivetya's biography. "Darling, I've decided we need to adopt these two marvellous children. They're turning out every bit as blackhearted as we ever wanted our Booboo to be."

Lady awarded me a suspicious look, decided I was fooling around but meant what I said. More or less. "Tell me about it."

I said, "Go to it, girls."

89

Beside the Cemetery:
More Confusion

Expecting the Great General to remain offensive-minded was not enough, Sleepy knew. She had to outguess him. This one time she could not let Mogaba slide around her.

She took a twinned approach to planning, setting up two distinct staffs. The first consisted of Iqbal and Runmust Singh, Riverwalker, Sahra, Willow Swan and others who had been with her since the Kiaulune wars. She even summoned Blade up from Jaicur because Blade actually knew Mogaba personally and, at one time, had been fairly close to him.

The second general staff consisted entirely of officers from Hsien. These men knew Mogaba only as a bugaboo. And they had no knowledge of the surrounding territory beyond what they could learn from maps and scouting on their own.

Sleepy hoped to find something useful in the gap between diverging visions.

She kept her cavalry busy, scouting, chasing Mogaba's scouts, skirmishing with enemy patrols, trying to locate the bulk of the Great General's forces.

Mogaba was doing the same. Both sides relied heavily on

questioning civilians passing through. Traffic on the Rock Road had slackened but had not stopped entirely.

Each staff proposed several likely enemy campaigns. Sleepy had their opposite numbers play out a counter campaign. And in the end, after two almost sleepless days, she felt no more illuminated than she had at the beginning.

So she chose to go with intuition. That had served her best during previous dances with the Great General, anyway.

90

By the Cemetery:
Still More Confusion

The Great General told his commanders, "I'm growing concerned that all this maneuvering helps them more than it does us. It's obvious that they're without mystical support. But every hour we maneuver is an hour nearer the time when they get those advantages back."

Aridatha Singh asked, "Aren't we still at a disadvantage in a direct confrontation?"

"Soldier for soldier, possibly. But we have three times as many soldiers. And they're still trying to cover a line running all the way from the Grove of Doom to this stand near their camp. That's too much to hold with ten thousand men."

No questions came. No suggestions arose. The Great General seldom solicited advice. When Mogaba gathered his captains he planned to issue instructions. Their job would be to see that those were executed.

"I'm returning to the original plan. I'll drive straight forward, in the middle, with the Second Territorial. I'll engage and hold. Singh, you advance along your previous route with your same mission. Once you're behind them form your division in battle array and advance up the Rock Road.

If the rest of us have done our jobs you'll only have to sweep up fugitives."

Mogaba rested a hand upon the shoulder of a young officer named Narenda Nath Saraswati, scion of an old aristocratic family, of the third generation of that family to serve under arms since the opening skirmishes of the Shadowmaster wars. Two days earlier Saraswati had been a regimental chief of staff with an aggressive attitude. The Great General having been disappointed by the timid performance of his remaining division, Saraswati's aggressive nature was about to earn him a chance to shine.

Mogaba said, "Narenda, as soon as I have the enemy engaged, I want you to take your whole force forward on a narrow front, along the edge of this wood." That division having been shifted to the right since the previous engagement. "Overrun their camp. That shouldn't be difficult. They appear to be holding it with raw recruits. Once you clear the camp, reform and advance so as to strike the enemy left wing, rear, and reserve. *Don't* begin your initial attack until I do have the enemy solidly engaged.

"One more thing. I want you both to leave your main standards with me. If the enemy sees those maybe they'll think I'm concentrating everything in one place."

He paused. There were no questions. All this had been planned out before. The necessity now was renewed vigor.

"I'll go in at midmorning. Behind scouts and skirmishers. Make sure your men are well-provisioned. I'll personally strangle any officer who fails to see to the welfare of his soldiers."

The Great General's attitude was well-known, if not universally applauded by his officers. Corruption was so deeply ingrained in Taglian culture that even after more than a generation of cultural collision and occasional bloody change there were still those who failed to understand that theft from the men you commanded was not an acceptable way to supplement your income.

Whatever their differences, the Black Company, the Protector, the Great General, all the northerners who gained power, strained to increase the efficiency of their regime by rooting out graft and corruption. More than anything else, that made the outsiders incredibly alien.

"Aridatha. Wait. I've had a thought. If things go well it's likely Saraswati will break the enemy before you can get into position behind them."

"I was thinking of leaving during the night and going into hiding inside the Grove of Doom."

"Good idea. What I'm thinking, then, is, you should come out in a long line so you can catch most of the fugitives running southward. I'm especially interested in catching the kind of people who go underground and five years later turn up with a whole damned new army."

"I'll do my best."

Mogaba growled. That was a promise he hated. It sounded like an excuse being put into place beforehand. Though Aridatha was never the sort to excuse his own shortcomings. He was more the sort who found good reasons why others failed.

91

By the Cemetery:
Even More Confusion

Today's the day," Sleepy told her Captains. "I can feel it." She went on to excoriate Croaker, Tobo and that bunch for taking so long. Then she began telling people what she wanted done. She started getting arguments right away. She snapped, "Mogaba is going to split his force again. For that he's going to pay. If you want to argue with me I'll accept your resignations now. There're officers who'll do what they're told and keep their mouths shut."

A few hours later the Great General appeared almost exactly where she expected him. He was spread out over a lot of ground and had a lot of banners flying. For a time she feared she might have guessed wrong and Mogaba was just going to come straight ahead and roll right over her. But he did not attack as vigorously as he should have if that was the case.

Sleepy did not press in her turn. Not right away. She did not want to make it obvious that she had not concentrated her forces, either. She engaged in skirmishing and harassing tactics but stepped back whenever Mogaba responded in any strength. He came forward both because he had to stay in contact and because Sleepy was pulling back toward the second jaw of his trap. He seemed willing to be led that way.

When the division on the far right rushed from concealment behind a low ridge, it lost all cohesion. The troops had to cover most of a mile. Their commander was more interested in striking before his foes could respond than he was in presenting a pretty picture advancing.

The men in colored armor who came out of the hidden cemetery marched in perfect order. Some carried recently manufactured fireball projects. They began slaughtering the rabble before most of the Taglians were aware that Fortune had dealt them one from the bottom of the deck. They lasted as long as they did only because there were so many of them.

By the Cemetery:
Confusion Piled Higher

They've begun to stiffen on their right," one of Mogaba's companions announced. "But they're falling back on the other wing."

"There's something wrong," Mogaba declared. "There should be more of them."

"Why don't we rush them?"

"Do sound a general advance. But at the slow cadence."

The first confused message arrived just minutes later. Narenda Nath Saraswati's division was on the run. Saraswati himself was dead. Most of the division officers had been captured or killed.

Before he could make sense of it, Mogaba heard the horns on his right and saw the different colored blocks, every soldier with his own banner on his back, advancing. A flurry of cavalrymen swept stragglers, and fugitives, and foolish resistance out of the infantry's path.

The Great General needed only a moment to understand that Sleepy was about to kidney-punch the Second Territorial with her best. "Full attack!" he ordered. "Fastest cadence!" If he got the soldiers moving forward before they recognized their peril he could use his numbers to overcome. "The little witch finally caught me." But there was still Aridatha, moving in behind. It remained to be seen who would have whom in the end.

Mogaba drove straight toward the enemy camp. If he could get inside its palisade. . . .

93

Beyond the Grove of Doom: Confusion Grows

Aridatha learned of the developing disaster from Vehdna horsemen who had been forced to flee in his direction, around the eastern end of the battlefield, because enemy skirmishers had blocked the way north already. Aridatha was able to intuit the truth from the complete confusion of the reports.

He ordered his division to form for battle.

Backboned by his own City Battalions the force was well-drilled, if not veteran. Within two hours Singh had the enemy in sight. The invaders and their traitor native allies were involved in a huge, bloody melee with all of the Taglian troops Mogaba had been able to hold together or who had not been able to run away. Evidently the invaders had not remained sufficiently concerned about Singh's division.

Aridatha's advent was close to a complete surprise. As for its effectiveness. . . . His soldiers had no experience dealing with the terror. And they all knew that their brothers in the other divisions had lost their battle already and were busily doing their dying.

The exhausted armies disentangled as the day waned. The soldiers on both sides had endured so much horror that, gradually, they just stopped trying to interfere with an enemy who seemed willing to go away without causing trouble.

But who won?

On that day arguments could have been made both ways. Final determination would be in the hands of those historians who examined the effect the battle had on Taglian society and culture. It could be a watershed or it could be nothing important, depending on what followed and how the population responded.

Beside the Cemetery:
Sorrows Gathering

Not even Sleepy had the physical or mental energy left to do anything useful. She slumped against the saddle of a dead horse, let the twilight and exhaustion wash over her. She felt no exhilaration even though she had broken the backbone of the last Taglian army and had, for the first time, been the one who held the field when the fighting ended. Mogaba, if he lived, was the one slinking away this time.

A big contributor to her mood was the fact that this accomplishment, such as it was, was as much Suvrin's responsibility as her own. Suvrin, alone, had not abandoned all thought of the third Taglian division. He had been able to move his brigade in response, feebly, when the rest of the enemy appeared. But for Suvrin's cool head, the Great General would be here, holding the field, yet again. Though the numbers of dead and dying, likely, would be much the same.

Suvrin settled beside her. He said nothing for a long time. Neither did she. For the first time in decades she wanted to hold someone, wanted to be held by someone. But she did not act upon that want.

Finally, Suvrin spoke. "Willow Swan is dead. I saw his body a while ago."

Sleepy grunted. "I have a feeling there'll be a lot of old friends to mourn once we collect the dead. I saw Iqbal and Riverwalker go down."

"No. Not Iqbal. Who'll take care of Suruvhija?" Singh's wife was not all that bright.

"The Company, Suvrin. Until she chooses to leave." And Runmust, if he had survived. It was his obligation under Shadar religious law. "She's one of our own. We take care of our own. Do we have anyone capable of handling picket duty?"

Suvrin responded with an interrogatory grunt.

"That's the Great General over there. Iron Man Mogaba. If he's still even a little bit healthy and can pull together some kind of night attack he'll be back. Maybe even if he has to do it all by himself."

Suvrin took several deep, thoughtful breaths. "We have quite a few recruits who didn't do much but hide in the cemetery. I've already shamed some of them into picking up the battlefield."

"It won't matter if they run away as long as they run toward us."

"Uhm."

"Willow? He never did. . . . Never found his dream."

"I always pictured him as your basic everyman. Just drifting wherever the tides of life took him. Showing a flash sometimes but never really getting up and grabbing the reins. He might have been a hopeless romantic, too. According to the Annals. He had a case on Lady once. And a case on the Protector, where he was much more lucky but lived to regret it. He even had it for you for a while, I think."

"We were friends. Just good friends."

Suvrin did not argue. But there was a quaver in Sleepy's voice that made him wonder if, possibly only once or twice, there had not been something to lend substance to rumor.

It was none of his business.

"I should've avoided this mess until Tobo and the others got back."

Suvrin observed, "Mogaba wouldn't have let you. So don't beat yourself up. He would've chased you hard, trying to take advantage of the fact that they were gone."

Sleepy knew that was true but truth did not alter her emotional state. A lot of people were dead. Many of them had been comrades of long standing. It was her mission to preserve them, not to waste them. She had failed.

And the full, grim scope of the tragedy remained to be revealed.

95

Fortress with No Name:
Down Below

S he looks so peaceful," Lady intoned. We stood over her
sister, in the cavern of the ancients. Soulcatcher now
filled the identical spot that Lady had occupied during the
Captivity.

I needed a moment to realize that she was being sarcastic,
repeating the inanities you hear at funerals. She was sure Soulcatcher was partially aware of what was happening. And she
could not interact with her sister in any more intimate way.

I said, "We've done what we came to do. We need to think
about getting back to the Company." Though I remained
tempted to hazard a recon run through the Khatovar gate
before it healed completely.

And I had a notion to take a gander at the dark thing that
had been toying with our lives and destinies since before we
ever heard any of her names.

"Yes," Lady said. "There's no telling what mischief Booboo and the Khadidas and Mogaba have gotten into without
Tobo and Howler there to baby-sit."

I said, "If Mogaba realizes that Sleepy's got no wizards,
he'll be all over her like a snake on shit."

"That was colorful, if nonsensical." I noted that she did
not include herself with Tobo and Howler. Yet I suspected
strongly that she was capable of sucking Kina's power like a
queen vampire nowadays. Sometimes I wondered what that
augured for the day it came time to pay up to Shivetya. She
really hated turning into something old and dumpy and grey
that looked way too much like the mother she barely remembered.

"I just remembered a Company sergeant from before your
time. A man named Elmo. He had an unusual turn of phrase."

"You are getting old."

"I spend my whole life living in the past, darling. Let's saddle up." We had come down the long stair to the cavern aboard Voroshk flying posts. What a marvellous way to deal with stairways when you are no longer twenty years old.

Lady started to pat her sister on the shoulder, an ordinary little action. "Don't!" I barked, with enough urgency to cause a couple of small ice stalactites to fall somewhere back in the depths of the cave.

"Oh. I wasn't thinking."

There were frost-encrusted old men all along the sides of the cave. No one knew who they were. Except, possibly, Baladitya. Most of them were still alive. They were, like Soulcatcher, exiles from some unsympathetic power. But a few, including way too many Company brothers from the time of the Captivity, were dead meat. And all it had taken to kill them was a thoughtless, gentle or friendly touch.

Lady pushed past me. I surveyed the local population. As ever, it seemed the open eyes all stared right at me. I met Soulcatcher's dull gaze. For no reason I understood, I winked. We were old conspirators. We went way back. I knew her before I knew her sister, in olden times of terror.

It may have been a trick of the light or of my imagination but it seemed there was a flicker of response.

When we returned up top we found the others involved in the initial stages of getting ready to leave. Howler was exulting, loudly, to all and sundry, in his new ability to remain silent. He seemed almost grateful. Being an old cynic myself I have strong notions about the true value of human gratitude. It is a currency whose worth plunges by the hour.

Though thoroughly confused, the two old Voroshk sorcerers were collecting themselves for the journey, too. Which meant that they had surrendered to Tobo's blandishments while Lady and I were down below. They had surrendered their flying posts and special clothing rather than be forced to return to their own world.

They must have gotten some really unpleasant news.

"You understand what this means?" I asked Tobo.

"Uh?" The kid was relaxing by flirting with Shukrat. I got the impression that those two might have started sneaking off into dark corners. They had developed that goofy way of looking at each other. And they could not stay away from one another.

That would not instill Sahra with great joy.

"It means we have to stash Gromovol downstairs, too. Or kill him. Which wouldn't be politic. Because there's no way I'm going to give him the opportunity to give us any more grief by letting him come back with us."

"I'll talk to Nashun and the First Father." He turned to Shukrat. "Come on, honey."

Hah. Honey.

A procession of flying posts went down to the cave of the ancients. Oh, that was *so* much easier than clambering down and up. The elderly Voroshk, in borrowed rags, rode behind Tobo and Shukrat. Gromovol rode behind Arkana. I figured she owed him one. Her cast did not cause her any problems flying. She would be out of that soon.

Gromovol whined and begged until he became an embarrassment to everyone.

I could claim I had no mercy but that would not be true. Had I been appropriately merciless, pieces of Gromovol would have gotten distributed over half a world after I made a few cutting remarks about his character and bad behavior.

I felt like one of the Voroshk now. I *looked* like one of the Voroshk. So did my beloved. The deal with the old men compelled them to refit their wondrous black costumes for us.

Those would make marvellous complements to our Widowmaker and Lifetaker armor.

Tobo and Shukrat, too, boasted the black and undefined look, Tobo having helped himself to Gromovol's outfit.

It took only minutes to inter Gromovol, not far from the frozen corpses of several men who had been my friends. His final pleas still echoed when I told Lady, "I'm going down to the bottom of this hole. I want a look at that old bitch who's been fucking up our lives for the last fifty years."

"Are you crazy?" Tobo yelled. "I wouldn't go down there. I'm nervous just being this close."

"Then go back upstairs. Shukrat. Answer a couple of technical questions for me before you leave. Please?"

The black barrier that had frustrated Blade so was back in place. It put a terrible pressure on my mind. But the flying post did not notice it at all. The post kept moving. The Voroshk costume I wore stirred slightly, enclosing me more securely within its protection.

Although I know the names now I refuse to call post and costume by their proper, clunkily cumbersome Voroshk titles.

I passed through the barrier. Lady made a funny little sound as she came through behind me, like she did when we made love.

The scene was pretty much the way it had been described by others. What seemed to be a vast, open cavern without evident bounds, illuminated by no evident light source, and that extremely feeble. All that could be seen was a huge, ugly sprawl of flesh the color of polished eggplant. It did not move, even to breathe.

Kina looked like Shivetya's homely big sister. Kina *looked* like the embodiment of all the dark attributes I had heard assigned her, under all her many names, since first I became aware of her existence. Kina looked like many dark things.

My memories of the next few minutes are completely unreliable.

Almost immediately the great hairless head turned our way. Kina's mouth was open, exposing ugly dark fangs. She seemed to have a snake or lizard tongue. I did not recall that having been reported before in any of the conflicting myths, though her tongue was supposed to be long, the better to lap up demon blood.

The eyes of the Goddess began to open.

The immensity of her will smashed at me like a tidal wave breaking. The lights went out. For me.

"Looks like you were lucky this time," Tobo told me. "Your post got you out of there."

I wanted to tell him luck had nothing to do with it. I planned it that way. I set it up with the help of his girlfriend. But I barely had energy enough to keep breathing.

I did manage to gasp, "Lady?" Had to check on my honey.

"Better off than you are. Sleeping right now. Said to tell you to just rest. Here's some Shivetya manna. It'll give you a kick in the ass. If you can keep it down."

I managed to roll my head until I could see the demon.

Shivetya was looking back at me. A white crow was strutting around on his shoulder. Not my white raven. The demon revealed a few teeth in what he might have thought was a smile. Bizarre. I did not recall him ever having moved before.

He must have seen the inside of my head. Must know I thought I had a notion about how to get to Kina.

I hoped the Goddess could not look inside my head, too.

Someday. Down the road. If I could get all the pieces to fall into place.

The white crow sneered. I believe they can do that, those birds.

Tobo understood that something was happening but did not catch on. I think my new daughters understood better than he did.

96

The Shadowgate:
Bad News, Bad News

I was outside the shadowgate gossiping with Panda Man and Spook, who were telling me that keeping an eye on the gate was the best duty they had ever endured. The work was easy and the locals were friendly. If the damned ugly spooks from the plain did not keep nagging you. . . .

Tobo and Shukrat came through.

Almost immediately Tobo let out a cry of despair. He shouted, "There's been a battle!" A moment later he shot into the air, headed north, black cloth streaming behind him. An instant later still Shukrat shot off in his wake, gaining slowly.

Panting, Lady asked, "Does that mean we should be worried?"

"That would be my guess. The little shit must've gotten something from the hidden folk."

"And it was bad enough to set him off like that." She looked as troubled as I felt.

No good could come of any battle fought while we were away.

She asked, "Aren't you going to rush off and see what happened, too?"

"Don't see the point." I jerked a thumb in the direction of the carpet, which was creaking and sagging under the weight of people we dared not trust. "There isn't anything I could do, anyway. Look at that." A ripple, a distortion in the fabric of reality, seemed to be running over the face of the earth, chasing after Tobo and Shukrat. "The hidden folk following their hero."

"Why were they here?"

"Waiting around for Tobo."

"But they should've been with Sleepy. They don't do us any good hanging around the shadowgate when . . . oh. They don't care if they do us any good."

"Exactly. What they care about is Tobo. Anything they do that benefits the rest of us they do just to please him. Which is why two-thirds of the time I don't have the two ravens that're supposed to be my permanent shoulder-ornaments and messengers and far-seeing eyes. They keep forgetting to stick with me. They wander off to find the kid. Bet you they turn up before we catch up with Sleepy, though."

"Sounds like a sucker bet to me."

After crossing the Dandha Presh I steered a course mimicking that Sleepy had followed heading north. When Lady asked why I was not heading straight north as fast as we dared push the carpet, I told her, "Because I thought I saw something I shouldn't have on the way down. I have to check on it. I'm hoping it was my imagination." But my brief conversation with the guards at the shadowgate suggested that the nightmare might be real.

She was curious but did not ask. At the speeds we could make airborne a bit of circuitous flight would not delay us much.

I found what I was seeking on the path Sleepy had taken from Gharhawnes, at almost exactly the point where she had doubled back to get behind Dejagore. By then my confederates were extremely crabby.

"There!" I told Lady, catching just a glimpse of something moving fast inside a stand of scrubby oaks.

"There what?" She had not seen.

"The Nef."

"The Nef? The Nef are in the Voroshk world. Trapped there."

"Not according to Spook and Panda Man. They say the Nef come around every night."

"All right. But how would they get through the shadow-gate?"

"I don't know." I was flying in a circle now, giving up altitude. Once down to treetop level I cruised back and forth. I spotted nothing. Nor did I find a sign when I descended lower still and began to glide between the tree trunks.

I never found a thing. Not even a hint of a thing.

People began to yell down at me.

All right. They had a point. There were things we needed to do way north of where we were now.

97

Beside the Cemetery:
Among the Dead

It had been over for more than a day but the surgeons remained hard at work. Men still lay in long rows awaiting attention, moaning, screaming, some delirious. And some dead. A burial detail walked the rows, picking up those who had gone. Too many of those had died alone amidst the hundreds, without comfort.

The glory of war.

The ultimate fear. Mine, anyway.

I checked quickly to make sure that everyone was conforming to my decrees concerning cleanliness and sepsis. A few of the wounded would stand a better chance if the surgeons and their helpers cleaved to the rules. Even when they were exhausted, as they were now, and the temptation to cut corners became overwhelming.

Beyond our wounded lay those from Mogaba's army. They were likely to get no treatment at all, except what they could manage for themselves. I was sure that our medical supplies were as strained as our medical staff was. It looked like this was a much bigger fight than I had expected. Or, at least, a more desperate encounter with more casualties than expected in a short time.

Runmust Singh on crutches took me in to see Sleepy.

She appeared disoriented. I knew that look of old, having been there myself. She was on the edge of collapse. She had not done more than catnap since the fighting started. "You can't do it all yourself, Captain. You'll be a lot more effective if you just trust the rest of us to get things done and get yourself some rest. If Mogaba comes back now you won't be able to think fast enough or straight enough to do anybody any good."

She eyed me irritably but was too exhausted to squabble. "I take it you didn't come here past the dead."

"I came through the hospital area." She knew that I would have to do that. After we talked I would, probably, go back to offer what little help an old man with a bum hand and a bad eye could.

"Then you don't yet know that there isn't anybody left for me to trust while I take a nap. Swan is dead, Croaker. Blade is dead. Iqbal Singh is dead. Riverwalker is dead. Add Pham Huu Clee, Li Wan, both the Chun brothers and your old engineers, Cletus and Loftus. There's going to be a lot of opportunity for advancement. Name a name. Almost everybody is dead or injured. Hell, even Sahra may be dead. We haven't been able to find her."

"We're back," I said. That ought to take a load off her shoulders. "Successfully, I might add. What about Suvrin?"

"Suvrin made it through. Suvrin saved the day. Suvrin and I have agreed to take turns resting as soon as we're sure Mogaba isn't coming back. Right now we're taking turns holding everything together."

Based on what I had seen and heard already the Great General would not return any time soon—unless he came on his own. His soldiers had had enough.

Mogaba would have been back already had he had any

troops he could use. Caution and procrastination were not sins you could pin on the Great General.

I heard Tobo's voice outside, overhead. He was addressing the folk of the hidden realm. Before long we would know all we wanted to know about Mogaba's current situation. In moments thousands of wraithlike things would be involved in the search for Sahra—and everyone else still missing.

The kid was taking charge.

Sleepy mumbled, "I shouldn't have engaged him till Tobo came back."

Unwittingly, I repeated comments she had heard from Suvrin already. "Mogaba wouldn't have given you a choice. He doesn't have our intelligence resources but he does make use of the tools he has. That was our failing. Not remembering that. We should've given at least the appearance of having left a sorcerer in camp."

Sleepy nodded. "Water down the creek. Which I'll thank you to remind me whenever I begin to feel sorry for myself and start picking the thing's bones to indict myself for doing things differently."

"You're a strange bird, little girl."

"What?"

"Sorry. One-Eye's been on my mind lately." I did not explain. As long as I kept my genius sealed up inside my head there was a fair chance Kina would not find out anything she would make me regret. I asked. "What about Goblin and the girl? If there was fighting in the grove . . ."

"We don't know yet. I assume Tobo will inform us. I assume everything is going to be just peachy now that Tobo is back." She was striving for sarcasm but it was not working. She did not have strength enough to speak in anything but a monotone.

"Lady and Murgen will be here in a few minutes. Let them manage the little shit while you get your rest."

* * *

I went for an excursion amongst the unburied dead, to make goodbyes. They were laid out in rows, awaiting disposal. The weather was cold and damp so putrefaction was not far advanced but there was stench enough of blood and open bowels. Flies were rare, it being the wrong season. And crows of any sort were a rarity these days. Buzzards circled but dared not come down because the welcome they received from the living tended to be discouraging.

Once someone identified one of the fallen, Taglian prisoners moved the body to the appropriate funeral procedure group. Recruits and additional prisoners were busy building ghats, burning corpses, digging graves and filling them, or erecting exposure platforms for the few whose fate it was to leave the earth that way.

A lot of corpses had been dealt with already but I could see that, despite the season, we were going to have to dig mass graves for the Taglian fallen. There would not be time to get each man a decent funeral. Although civilians who had had men serving with Mogaba had begun to show up already, hoping to reclaim their dead.

I wondered if, in some mystical fashion, new standing stones were materializing on the glittering plain, their faces crawling with golden memorial characters.

A subaltern from the Land of Unknown Shadows approached me. It was obvious he was not pleased about having been assigned to the funeral detail. He must have embarrassed himself during the fighting. The unpleasant duty would be his reward. "Sir," he said, with a salute so crisp it should have gotten his sentence commuted, "it would be a great help if you could offer me the funerary preferences of your old comrades." There was a mildly repulsive fawning edge to his otherwise businesslike demeanor.

He led me to a spot where he had isolated non-Taglians who did not hail from Hsien. My former henchmen and a couple of Nyueng Bao occupied that little square.

"Soldiers live," I murmured. Now there was only Murgen and Lady left from the farther shore of the Sea of Torments. "Bury Swan and the engineer brothers. Inside that cemetery over there. Make sure that their graves are clearly marked. I'll want to find them later in order to put up a proper memorial. They deserve more than a parting mention in the Annals." I wondered what Swan would think of lying to rest beside all those Shadowlanders. He and Blade and Cordy Mather had helped put most of them there.

I had no idea what funeral customs obtained amongst Blade's people. Neither I nor anyone else ever learned who those people actually were. "Lay the black man down in a grave near Swan. Maybe they can be buddies in the next world, too. Maybe they'll finally get to start that brewery they always wanted."

The subaltern was puzzled by that but did not comment. The soldiers of the Land of Unknown Shadows were growing accustomed to the religious absurdities of the new world. I walked on, across ground covered by the corpses of men Sleepy had recruited during the time of Captivity. Their number was disturbing. Before long she would be as isolated from her own generation as I was isolated from mine.

A great many excellent soldiers from the Land of Unknown Shadows lay upon that cold, hard ground, too. And, unsurprisingly, so did many men who had joined us recently, locally. Poorest trained, they had stood the least chance during the fighting.

I surveyed all that death and hoped Sleepy had reached a watershed here, that henceforth she would seek solutions that did not require headbutting until somebody staggered away and collapsed from concussion. Not that all this could be blamed on her. Based on information available I could fault none of her decisions. And she was a better tactician than I had been.

98

Above the Cemetery:
Mogaba Accedes

Twenty-six hours after his order to break contact Mogaba abandoned all hope of pulling together an attack that would take advantage of the enemy's despair and disarray. His own men had been too badly mauled to set aside their own despair and disarray. Only Aridatha Singh's division retained its cohesion. Its reward was the task of screening the retreating army.

Which consisted mainly of survivors of the Second Territorial. Of Saraswati's former right wing force not one man in ten could be accounted for anymore.

Enemy cavalry remained very active. The Captain seemed disinclined to let him get near her again.

A pair of billowing black shapes passed low overhead. They radiated a chilling psychic scream. Suddenly, instinctually, Mogaba knew that he was being watched by something he could not turn fast enough to catch staring. He knew that his best opportunity had ended. He summoned his latest aide-de-camp, who had been in place only a few hours. The man's several predecessors were still down there on the field. "Bring me the Deceiver prisoners."

"Sir?"

"The prisoners General Singh captured in the Grove of Doom. I want to see them." He thought he could offer them a deal. The girl could pretend to be the Protector for a while. Taglios would be less restive if the Protector appeared publicly sometime soon.

"Those prisoners were sent north, sir. Under special constraint because of the danger General Singh told us they present."

"And he was right. That was the best thing to do. We don't

want them to fall into unfriendly hands." Publicly, Mogaba insisted on treating the recent encounter as a triumph. He expected his officers to do the same.

Mogaba spent a moment considering what options he might have. It took only a minute to conclude that withdrawal toward Taglios was the best course.

Oh, but he hated that. No matter the true facts, rumor would call it a defeat and a retreat. That would cost.

The Great General considered his aide. He did not know the man well enough to be aware of his family status. "Tonjon, is it?"

"Than Jahn, sir. A remote male ancestor is reputed to have been Nyueng Bao. My family is Vehdna."

"Excellent. Perhaps you can share religious anecdotes with the enemy Captain."

"Sir?" Sounding both baffled and irked.

"I'm sending you south under a flag of truce. To arrange for an armistice. So we can collect our dead." If anything the Great General ever did won him favor with the Taglian people, it was his effort to bring back the fallen sons so their families could honor them with all the appropriate last rites.

This time would be a bitch. There was no way he was going to recover all the Taglian dead. "Find me some priests. Every kind we have." He needed advice about what to do with so many bodies, this close to home.

The Company, Mogaba was sure, would just fling their share of Taglian corpses into one big ugly hole, cover them over and forget about them.

99

By the Military Cemetery:
Missing Persons

Tobo was distraught. Murgen was distracted. He walked around bumping into things, trapped inside his own interior world. I had not seen him so lost since his Annalist days.

No trace of Sahra had surfaced, even with the Unknown Shadows hunting. So far Tobo had determined only that she had not fallen into enemy hands. The Taglians were not looking. They were unaware, even, that they ought to bear the woman a grudge.

Sahra always had had a knack for going unnoticed.

"She's dead," Lady told me. "She was hurt, she crawled in somewhere to hide, and she died there." Which was plausible enough. Several bodies had been discovered in circumstances that fit the scenario. And Sahra was not alone in being missing. Every company in the force was unable to account for someone. Most, probably, had run away or were prisoners of war. But the hidden folk kept finding others dead in places where no one had yet thought to look.

I hoped Lady's simple explanation was the correct one. I dreaded the chance that Sahra had been captured by somebody who would use her to manipulate Tobo.

The up side was that there was a paucity of villains who might be interested. Mogaba was exonerated. Soulcatcher was buried. Booboo and the Khadidas were entombed in the big fortress guarding the southern approaches to Taglios, behind a door that could not be opened by any key still within the stronghold. Others who might have tried something sly—say the Howler or the Voroshk—had perfect alibis.

So it came down to Sahra being dead and lost or lost and

wandering around in a shock so profound that she could not recall who she was or where she belonged.

Sleepy posted a huge reward for "the capture of an older Nyueng Bao woman wanted for questioning in regard to espionage against agents of the Prahbrindrah Drah." Murgen provided a description that included the shapes and locations of moles and a birthmark unfamiliar to anyone else.

"It doesn't make much sense, does it?" my darling whispered to me. "People go at the oddest times and from the oddest causes."

"Soldiers live," I murmured.

"You're turning that into a mantra."

"You feel guilty. You wonder why him and not me, then you're glad it was him and not you, then you feel guilty. Soldiers live. And wonder why."

"One soldier lives because the gods know that I still haven't gotten my fair share of loving. Put that pen away and come on over here."

"You've sure turned into a pushy broad in your old age."

"Yeah? You should've seen me four hundred years ago."

Tobo announced, "Mogaba's had the Khadidas and the Daughter of Night moved to the palace. In a remarkable coincidence the Protector was seen publicly for the first time in months only a few hours later. She was extremely angry with the Taglians and brought one of her punishments down on their heads." He grinned. "Most likely that had something to do with all the graffiti that's begun appearing. All the good old stuff. 'Water sleeps.' 'My brother unforgiven.' And even some that aren't my doing. 'You shall lie in the ashes ten thousand years, eating only wind.' I love that one."

That one caught my attention. I had heard it before, somewhere. But I had heard them all before.

"*Rajadharma*' is everywhere. Anyone who can write seems to put that one up. Then there's '*Madhuprlya*' which means 'A Friend of the Wine' and is a popular nickname for Ghopal

Singh. Seems the lord of the Greys has a taste for the grape. The one I don't get, and which seems to trouble the Greys more than '*Madhupriya*,' is, 'Thi Kim is coming.' It doesn't make sense. Everybody assumes Nyueng Bao are involved because Thi Kim is translatable only from Nyueng Bao. As 'death walk.' Except that here it's written as a proper name."

I said, "If it's used as a name or title it would more properly come through as 'Deathwalker' or 'Death Walking.' Not so? In olden times a Deathwalker was a suspected plague carrier."

"Goblin," Lady said. "It's Deceivers announcing the coming of the Khadidas. A dead man still walking around. By the grace or curse of Kina. And a plague carrier, too, if you count the religious side."

"Maybe." Tobo did not seem convinced. I did not blame him. I had a feeling it was something more sinister myself. Based on nothing whatsoever, because Lady's suggestion *ought* to be true.

I nodded in the general direction of where Sleepy should be. "She said anything about what she's planning?"

"Not unless you count her complaining about the head-butting she's been doing with our friends from the Land of Unknown Shadows. Every brigade commander is whining about needing replacements. But none of them want local recruits—because of the language problem more than because of their lack of equipment and training—but none of them wants to see their own brigade disbanded so its soldiers can fill open slots elsewhere."

But there was no choice and everyone recognized that fact. The best answer was simple enough. And Sleepy found it without consulting me.

Instead of disbanding the hardest hit units she took the one least distressed and distributed its people amongst the others, keeping whole groups together. Being with people you know and trust is critical to a soldier. She made sure the officers got better jobs whenever possible. The displaced brigade commander became her chief of staff, with the assurance that he would be given command of all the native troops we raised, however numerous they might become.

Maximum result with least distress to oversized egos. Only a few men ended up completely disappointed.

Life has turned into a preoccupation with administrative detail.

Is that what happens when you get old? You worry more about people and their interaction than you do about drama and the violence and the wicked deeds those people do?

That is us. The Black Company. Wicked deeds done dirt cheap. But by damn! You had better pony up when payment is due. Otherwise, if we must, we will come back from the grave itself to make sure our accounts are properly balanced.

I said some of that aloud one afternoon. Tobo told me, "You're mad, old man."

"As a hatter." A reflection. "Speaking of which. You know whatever happened to One-Eye's old hat?" I was going to need that disgusting flea farm one day soon. Desperately. One-Eye had told me I would but I had not listened closely enough. I *had* listened and understood that One-Eye's wondrous spear would have to be employed in ways that the little wizard had defined well back into his healthier days. But that hat had been such a commonplace, and so foul, that it had not clung to its place in my mind.

"It may be in my junk wagon," Tobo told me. "If it's not there it'll be with mom's stuff." He winced. Sahra remained missing. "We took everything of his and Nana Gota's when we left Hsien."

"I need to find it. Fairly soon."

Tobo wondered why but did not ask. What a good boy. He did say, "If I was you I'd think about getting my stuff together, ready to move." For this Annalist all the junk and paper and pens and ink and notes and whatnot can build into piles that threaten to swamp. "Sleepy would rather stay here and spend some treasure refitting and recruiting and training and getting stronger but I convinced her that won't work. Things aren't going to slow down anywhere else. Right now we have more sorcery available than ever before in the Company's history."

"I've said so myself." More than once, in jeremiads about counting too much on powers and skills not part of the traditional Company arsenal.

"Yes, you did. But you didn't say anything about it fading away."

"Sure I did."

"You *want* it to go away. And it will. Because these aren't the kind of people who're likely to be content to do what we've got them doing. So we ought to use them up while we can."

"Meaning?"

"We need to go after Taglios while we have the power to hit it hard."

Was he starting to sound just the slightest bit bigheaded? Like he might know better than the Captain what we ought to do? Was it going to be squabble on with Sleepy now that his mother was no longer around?

Might better keep an eye on our baby boy. He was overdue to outgrow all that.

I said, "You could be right."

100

Taglios:
The Palace

Ghopal Singh's report was not reassuring. "The graffiti is everywhere but we just can't catch anybody doing it. It's much worse than it was five years ago. Nowadays, with a lot of people on our side, you'd think we'd be able to come up with a clue. All we get is nonsense about ghosts and demons and things you can see only if you're not looking for them."

Mogaba steepled long fingers under his chin. "The thing

is, Ghopal, I've seen both demons and ghosts with my own eyes. When I had just become part of the Black Company one of the Company wizards had a pet demon. It later turned out to be our enemy, but that doesn't matter. It was a demon. And during the siege of Dejagore ghosts often came and went. We all saw them, though hardly anyone ever talked about them.

"Most people blamed Nyueng Bao conjurers."

Aridatha Singh observed, "The reality of demons and ghosts doesn't affect the situation. Whether spooks or clever agitators are writing these messages, the messages are there. And enough people can read that the whole population knows what's being written."

"What would you do about it?" Mogaba asked.

"Keep watching for vandals but ignore it otherwise. If the people believe we're indifferent to the criticism they won't take it seriously either."

"A notion I hoped to put forward myself," Ghopal said. "Because people in the street have no more idea than we do who's putting that stuff up. Which makes them just as nervous as it makes us."

Mogaba grimaced, "Approved, then. With this caveat. Some of those slogans don't fit the traditional mold. 'Thi Kim is coming.' We still don't know what that means."

"The Walking Death is coming," Ghopal said. "You have to think that means the Daughter of Night's companion."

"You think it's Deceiver work, then?"

"That's my guess."

"But Thi Kim is Nyueng Bao. I've never heard of any Nyueng Bao Deceivers."

Ghopal grunted. That had gotten past him.

Aridatha made a joke of it. "We'll know him when he gets here. People will start dying."

"Ha, and one more out of charity, ha," Mogaba replied. "In the meantime, we need to make a decision about our guests. We'll have a lot of trouble keeping them under control.

Especially the wizard. Goblin. Who insists on being addressed as the Khadidas. He did help cow the mob when we had the girl pretend she was the Protector. But he has no interest in our cause. He'll devour us the instant he stops seeing us as valuable to *his* cause. Which is bringing on the end of the world."

Neither of the Singhs responded. Each understood that there was more to the Great General's words than he was actually saying. That something particularly delicate would come up had been evident from the moment it had become clear that no one else would participate in the meeting.

"I'm thinking we should get rid of him. Right now. Before he gets too comfortable and sure of himself."

"And the Daughter of Night?" Aridatha asked.

"She's not much threat on her own." Meaning the Daughter of Night could be spared. If that was what Aridatha wanted. "Though my guess is, she's too set in her ways to be redeemed."

Aridatha's coloring was pale enough to betray his embarrassment. "*That* isn't what I had in mind."

Ghopal came to his rescue. Inadvertently, having failed to catch the unspoken. "How do we get close enough to do anything? She'll make us love her so much we'll want to chop off our own toes."

"There must be ways around that."

"I'd be happy to hear suggestions."

"Well, it's obvious she can't do it all the time, whenever she wants, or Aridatha couldn't have caught her."

"Unless she wanted to be caught."

Mogaba feared there might be something to that suggestion. "And that power doesn't work on weapons. Or poisons."

"Sorcery might be a possibility," Ghopal suggested. "You think anyone knows either of their true names?"

Mogaba shook his head. "I don't think even our enemies could do much there. The girl hasn't had any name but the

Daughter of Night. The Goblin thing is two creatures in one, with the Kina side ruling. The man who knew the Goblin side's secrets is dead. So we can focus on treachery and poison right away."

"I don't want to harp," Aridatha said, "but I do have to remind everybody that the girl's parents aren't that far away. And right now our prospects don't look that great."

Mogaba suspected that to be a subtle invitation to discuss his plans. He did not accept.

He did not accept because these days he no longer had any grand plan. He believed his days were numbered, as some of the graffiti insisted. "ALL THEIR DAYS ARE NUMBERED." But the things that made him Mogaba, positive and negative, compelled him to struggle on.

101

Beside the Cemetery:
Plans

Lady had been preoccupied since our visit to Shivetya's fortress. More than usual. A couple of times I walked in on her while she was practicing her sorcery. I did not ask. The answer was plain. Her ability to steal Kina's power had returned full strength just when the Khadidas had come forward to take control of Goblin.

Lady had herself locked down, under rigid control. Being someone who has crawled all over her for years, I knew she was battling hope.

She was addicted to the power.

She had given it up, not entirely of her own volition, to prevent that old horror, her first husband, the Dominator, from resurrecting himself. Then she had gone away with me, knowing there was no way she could survive, powerless, in the world she had created. But she remembered being the Lady. And as years fled by she missed that more and more. And, I think, she missed that most when misfortune led her to a close encounter with a mirror.

A personable Dejagoran youngster we knew as Mihlos Sedona made the rounds, summoning the insiders to join Tobo and the Captain. The kid was only about sixteen but had charmed himself into a job as Sleepy's personal gopher. A smile and a winning personality is worth more than genius and sour most any day.

I thought well of Sedona myself. He had remembered to invite me to the party.

The camp was in turmoil. Sleepy had ordered preparations for movement toward Taglios. Those with the necessary expertise were producing parts for artillery pieces or siege engines to be assembled once we reached the fighting zone. Those without expertise were doing the donkey work. I wondered why Sleepy was having the work done when we did not yet know if we would need the equipment. I expect she just wanted everyone kept busy.

Can a bird sneer or smirk? The white crow observed from the arm of an incomplete, mobile stone-thrower. In my eye it seemed to do both. "Long flight for you, eh? You just get in?"

The bird jumped but did not fly away.

"Be good," I told it. "I know who you are and I know where you live."

Crow laughter, a little strained. Soldiers who remembered when crows were plentiful and dangerous paused to stare.

The crow winged it toward the cemetery.

I grumbled, "I do believe our old pal Shivetya is hedging his bets."

The day was chilly but the sky was clear. The Captain seemed to think a meeting out in the fresh air would be good for everybody. I slipped around behind her headquarters tent.

Tobo spoke first. "The Great General and his henchmen plan to keep fighting, despite our advantages. Both Generals Singh think it would be better to recognize the Prahbrindrah Drah and save Taglios the damage from heavy fighting. But loyalty is a matter of pride and honor for them, too. And the Great General isn't the Protector. They consider him their friend. As long as he's still standing I'm afraid they're going to stick with him."

No surprise there. Not to mention that Ghopal Singh did not have much choice. As director of the Greys he had no friends outside the present establishment. He had committed himself to the Protectorate, not to Taglios.

Aridatha, on the other hand, and despite his participation in the recent fighting, could be considered apolitical and committed to Taglios. The job he had done was the same job that would have been demanded of him by anyone who happened to be in power.

That was the consensus. Maybe we were just making excuses. Everybody who met Aridatha liked the guy and wished him good fortune.

"Enough of that," Sleepy snapped. "The man's a paragon. The sort we all want our daughters to marry. Fine. Tobo, get on with it."

"Last night the generals decided to destroy the Khadidas. He and the Daughter of Night can't read minds but they did sense trouble. They broke out of their cells. Which means one of them has more power than they've been showing. They're hiding somewhere in the abandoned part of the Palace. The Greys and the Palace Guard haven't found them yet. The Khadidas did something that distorted reality around them. Even the hidden folk lost them. They haven't been able to find them again. Not long after their disappearance somebody raided the kitchen. They stole a lot of food. Then somebody broke into the offices of the Inspector General of the Records and stole a shitload of paper and ink."

Murgen blurted, "They're going to reconstruct the Books

of the Dead!" This was the first real emotion he had shown since Sahra's disappearance.

"Evidently," Sleepy said. "Not something they can accomplish quickly but something they'll manage eventually. If we don't interfere. And we are going to interfere. Tonight the whole bunch of you are going to fly to Taglios. You're going to pull the same stunt you did in Jaicur. Using all the power you have available. I want you to capture Ghopal Singh and the Great General. Capture the girl and Goblin. Put Aridatha Singh in charge. Then hunker down. I'll start the army moving tomorrow. As soon as we're past the city gate I'll send for the Prahbrindrah Drah."

I tried to exchange glances with everyone, anyone around me. Nobody seemed interested. They all seemed embarrassed. Or something. Like maybe they thought Sleepy had turned simpleminded but it was up to somebody else to point that out to her.

I would bet you saw a lot of that around Mogaba. And a whole lot more around Soulcatcher before her forced retirement.

"It shall be done," Sleepy's proud new chief of staff intoned. Though he spoke Taglian that formula hailed from the Land of Unknown Shadows.

I miss One-Eye. One-Eye—or Goblin in his time—would have given that officious little asshole a mystic hotfoot. On the spot. Or maybe a case of fleas. The size of tumblebugs.

Those were the days. Except that those guys had not always gotten it right. They had screwed up and gotten me a few times, too.

There was a brief debate about whether or not to include the older Voroshk in the raid. The implication being that Tobo might not have what it took to keep an eye on so many people of dubious loyalty. Arkana appeared to have become one of us, but we did not yet *know* that. Arkana was the one who had advised Magadan to do whatever it took. . . . Our hold on the Howler was weaker now, too. The little sorcerer had become almost invisible since he no longer announced himself every few minutes. The senior Voroshk, of course, were trustworthy only until they figured out a way to mess us over. If that long. They did not seem much smarter than Gromovol had been.

I said only, "Don't get overconfident because everything's gone our way so far." Not only Sleepy but most of the others turned studiedly blank faces my way. "There're plenty of chances to stumble still ahead of us."

No doubt I would get an argument but I thought our path had run fairly straight and smooth lately. We might be just hours from our final accounting with the traitor Mogaba and only minutes longer from collecting Booboo and extinguishing the hope of the Deceivers. Events had had a ponderous inevitability almost since our first scares in the Land of Unknown Shadows.

"What?" But the question had been directed at Tobo, not me, by a startled Sleepy.

"We can't leave till after midnight. Lady is going to walk me through a raising of the dead. So we can find out what happened to Mom."

Sleepy wanted to argue but instantly understood that this was a battle she could not win. Tobo would do this thing Tobo's way, with Murgen's blessing. And it was not good to squabble in front of the troops.

"Don't take all night."

102

The Palace:
Better Housekeeping

The Great General picked up a snail shell, considered it. "More of these things around here all the time. But nobody ever sees a live one."

Ghopal said, "I'd bear down on my household staff if this was my place."

A distant crash echoed through the hallways. Greys and Guards had begun demolishing walls at random, to make it more difficult for the Deceivers to hide. And in areas they felt confident were clear they had masons sealing doorways and walling off entire hallways. Additionally, several self-anointed psychics and ghost hunters had joined the hunt.

Mogaba said, "You're probably right." He gestured to one of several young men who had been trailing them. That fellow snapped a slight bow and disappeared. Before long every domestic in the palace was involved in a massive housekeeping campaign. Mogaba observed, "We can't have this place looking a mess when our enemies get here."

A messenger huffed and puffed into the presence. The search had stumbled onto some corpses. From long ago. Three men wearing nothing but loincloths. They appeared to have gotten lost in the maze of the Palace, but had perished of wounds suffered earlier. The searchers were troubled because the corpses had not suffered much from vermin or normal putrefaction.

"Don't do anything with them," Mogaba said. "Don't even touch them. Just seal them up where they are." He told Ghopal, "Those would be some of the Deceivers who tried to assassinate the Liberator and the Radisha when you were still wearing diapers." He sighed. "No matter what we do to hurry this it's going to take an age."

"They do have to eat."

"Eventually, yes. We'll guard the kitchens at all times." And, he said aloud to no one, because these days it was more secure to communicate by passing notes, any food easily reached during quiet hours would be poisoned.

"Keep at it here, Ghopal. Day and night. Use as many people as we can spare." The Great General expected his enemies to come for him and he was making preparations to welcome them.

Mogaba withdrew to his own quarters. There he invested an hour in one of his hobbies before he moved on to the Protector's quarters to nap. He used her apartment now because no one ever went there. No one but the Great General dared. No one but the Great General could pass through the warding spells the Protector had left in place.

It had become his sanctuary.

Mogaba's scouts and spies had reported that Croaker and all his mob had rejoined the Company, back from wherever they had gone, with even more tools of deviltry.

The crisis could come any time now.

103

Beside the Cemetery:
Search for a Lost Soul

I had been in the neighborhood of necromantic activities before, and other high-order divining, but never any closer than I got that night. I do not plan to get that close again. If my honey wants somebody handy to save her sweet butt when she gets in trouble, I will tie a long rope to her ankle and attach the other end to a horse. If something goes sour I will swat the horse's butt.

This séance did not go well. And before it was over I got a

much uglier vision of that place of bones that had claimed so many of the dreams of Murgen and my beloved.

The smell was bad but the cold was worse. I have never felt such cold. I roasted myself beside a bonfire for hours after the summoning was over but mortal flames did little to defeat that bitter chill. It was so bad we did not undertake the Captain's raid that night or even the next and when we did we went only because Her Highness began wondering publicly if us slackers were waiting for summer weather.

Murgen, Sleepy and I were present at the summoning. No one else was invited, not even Shukrat or Suvrin or any of Sahra's friends. And it started going bad right away. Right after starting Lady raised a hand to massage her right temple. Soon afterward I began to catch fleeting, random impressions of things that were not there. The cold came first, then the smell. Before I saw anything there were several moments when my balance became very iffy.

Lady grew more and more excited as things continued to refuse to go the way she wanted. She started over twice. And when she finally did storm ahead she did not get where she wanted to go. Eventually she gave up. But not before the rest of us had gotten a good strong whiff of Kina's charnel dreams.

"I'm sorry," Lady told Tobo. "Kina keeps trying to get at me through our connection. The more power I siphon from her the more easily she can touch me."

Not good. We could have Lady turn kickass powerful—and be in thrall to the Goddess when she did.

She seemed to read my mind. She gave me a dirty look. "The bitch isn't going to get a hold on *me*."

I considered reminding her of whom we were speaking. The Mother of Deceit. Kina did not need control where she could manipulate. And she could manipulate whole populations. In her sleep. Instead, I asked, "Did we find out anything about Sahra?"

Lady's temper was not improving. "Certainly not what we would've if that old devil-sow hadn't decided to wreck our game." Her mind had been affected somehow. She seemed almost drunk. "We couldn't raise Sahra. Couldn't even touch her. Which leaves the matter's resolution ambiguous." Her speech continued slurred, she was aware of it, yet she persisted in trying to use difficult words. "I think she's dead. If she was alive Tobo and the hidden folk would've found her. Nothing hides from the Black Hounds for long."

"Soldiers live," I whispered. "It ain't right, something like that happening." But Fortune does not care. Unless Fortune gets a laugh out of human pain. "There has to be more meaning. . . ."

"You going mystical on us at this late date, Croaker?" Sleepy snapped. "You're the one who always says nothing has any meaning we don't put into it ourselves."

"Sure as shit sounds like me, don't it? Let's go work out our frustrations by kicking Mogaba's antique ass."

Sleepy gave us the once-over, unwilling to send us out while we were in so bleak a mood. We might be dangerous to ourselves.

She was no happier with us later. We did not improve, any of us. Finally, she swallowed her reservations and told us to go.

Howler had completed a large carpet capable of moving twenty passengers. Tonight it carried sixteen of those, plus freight. Amongst the sixteen were both elder Voroshk, a number of commando-trained soldiers from Hsien and Murgen. Murgen had been zombielike since Lady's failed ritual. He had overheard her saying she thought Sahra was dead.

I had urged him to stay behind but he insisted on joining us.

I should have stood fast. He could not help but be a liability.

Tobo was less distracted. He was too involved with Shukrat to be obsessed about his mother being missing. Still, he would bear watching.

Lady and I dressed up in full costume, with Voroshk apparel over the black Widowmaker and Lifetaker armor. My two ravens tagged along. Arkana flew with us, being tested. Which she understood fully.

Down below, dark things were on the move. They had been since nightfall.

Taglios never sleeps. Tonight those with reasons to be out after dark would have cause to worry about what might be lurking in the shadows. Hey, Mogaba. Look out. Darkness always comes.

We were still climbing away from camp when I eased over next to Lady. We flew knee to knee, our Voroshk apparel whipping in the breeze for twenty yards behind us. First we discussed which of our companions needed watching the closest, then we revisited the failed attempt to contact Sahra's spirit. For the twentieth time. Lady insisted, "I do believe she's out there, just as desperate to make contact with us as we were to make contact with her. But the ugly Goddess wants to keep us apart."

"Is Kina awake?"

"More than she has been for a long, long time. At least since Goblin went down there. Maybe since the days when she sensed her doom afoot and commenced her war on us ere ever we entered this country."

Ere ever? Wow. "I have a question on another subject. It's been bothering me for a long time but I've never quite been able to put the words together right."

"Artist."

"Power junkie."

"What's your question, Old Style?"

"What happened to Soulcatcher's shadows?"

Lady looked at me blankly.

"Come on. The old brain can't have slowed down that much. She was an accomplished shadowmaster. She didn't have a lot of shadows left because Tobo's pets kept picking them off. She stopped trying to use them against us. But she still had some hidden away somewhere. Saved for a rainy day."

Lady growled, "It couldn't have gotten any stormier than it did." But she was not arguing. She had her mind wrapped around the question. "My bet is that the Unknown Shadows finished them all off. There aren't any killer shadows left. If there were we'd still be hearing reports of unexplained deaths."

"Maybe." Probably. If they were out there anywhere the excitement the shadows would cause would be much greater than the numbers justified. The peoples of the Taglian territories had a long history of suffering from killer shadows.

Even so, I moved up until I was flying hip to hip with Tobo, an eventuality Shukrat found distasteful. She drifted away. Rather haughtily adolescent, I thought.

"I don't plan to take over your life." I told the boy about my concerns.

He seemed to agree that they were valid. "I'll find out if there's any reason to worry."

I fell back until I rejoined Lady.

She asked, "What did he say?"

"He'll check it out."

"You don't sound real happy about that."

"He said it the way you do when you agree with somebody just so you don't have to spend time with them fussing over something that doesn't bother you."

104

Taglios:
View from the Protector's Window

Mogaba's eyelids kept getting heavier. Twice he drifted off completely, to start awake violently, disturbed once by some clamor in the city, once by shouting down below that suggested the guards might have glimpsed the Khadidas. It was the wee hours of the morning, when even the heartbeat of the world had trouble thumping on.

They were not going to come tonight. They had not come last night, nor the night before. Maybe they were waiting for a larger moon.

Something dark blurred the glass in the window whence the Great General watched his own quarters and the best part of the Palace's northern face. Including all the significant entrances. He did not even breathe.

The Unknown Shadows could not find a way past the glass and the Protector's permanent wards. Mogaba resumed breathing. Slowly, invisible in the deep darkness of the room, he rose and glided nearer the glass, so that he would have a broader view.

They had come. Not when he had expected but exactly where. The same place their messengers had come every time. That same turret top.

He felt no particular elation. What he felt, in fact, was sorrow. All their lives, his and theirs, had come to no more than this. For a moment there was even the temptation to shout a warning. To cry out that that prideful fool who had made such a stupid choice in Dejagore so long ago had not meant any of them to come to this. But, no. It was too late. Fortune's die was cast. The cruel game had to be played to its end, no matter what anyone wanted.

105

The Palace:
The Great General's Place

Lady led the way, grim as ever when she donned the Life-taker persona. I was not pleased. Someone with more power ought to have been first down the stair. But Tobo was sure he needed to go last. Otherwise the Howler and the Voroshk might not feel motivated enough to participate. And Howler would not go first because he had to manage his carpet until everybody was off.

The stair was crowded. No one wanted to be there in that darkness, though only Lady, Murgen and I were old enough to remember when darkness was our determined foe. I tried to stay close to Lady, my foolish mind somehow afflicted with the notion that I had to protect her.

There went a joke of cosmic proportion.

We made it down the stairwell without mishap. And, despite a horrendous racket, without causing any alarm. Lady murmured, "Mogaba must be sleeping the sleep of the innocent. All that noise should've raised the dead."

"Uhn?"

"His quarters are straight ahead."

I knew that. We had rehearsed this raid before we left. In a half-ass sort of way. Which means not thoroughly enough to satisfy me.

"He's a heavy sleeper," I said. That was one of the few knocks against him before his defection. That and an intensity even his brother Nar had found oppressive. But I was speaking to the night. She was pulling ahead.

Someone generated a light, a feeble glowball that drifted above our heads. It had an alien feel so I assume one of the Voroshk was responsible. As the light grew so did a sense of relaxation, of confidence.

Maybe one of those cranky old men was not as dim as he let on.

"The light is my familiar," someone murmured in one of the dialects of Hsien. The phrase possessed the rhythm of ritual. Later I would learn that it was part of an incantation meant to repel the Unknown Shadows, those being disliked by everyone but Tobo.

The hidden realm was there, too, all around us. And so troubled that even I could feel it.

Tobo whispered, "There's something strange here. I had hundreds of the hidden folk put into the Palace. But none of them are reporting. As far as I can tell they aren't here anymore." He whispered to the creepy darkness. Things unseen moved around us, jostling us from directions we were not looking. Some of the stress oppressing me went away.

Lady beckoned soldiers forward. It was time to break into Mogaba's quarters. Though that implies more force than was needed. His door was not locked. Nor had it ever been before, according to Lady.

She and Shukrat took point. They knew their ways around. Unless clever Mogaba had rearranged his furniture.

Soldiers followed. The Voroshk and Howler crept inside. Murgen followed them. Lady and Shukrat began to argue sharply, in whispers, about who should find a lamp. Somebody stumbled into somebody else. Somebody fell down. Another somebody crashed into something. Then somebody else stated categorically, "Oh, shit!"

Arkana was just sliding into the room, a step ahead of me, when Tobo echoed those sentiments from behind me. He started to push. "Out of the way, damnit!"

A huge crash of breaking pottery. I had not known that Mogaba was a collector, though there were some marvellous craftsmen in this part of the world. . . .

A man screamed.

Before his lungs were empty other screams joined his. And fireballs leapt from small projectors. And I knew why so many men were screaming and why they were so panicky they were blowing holes through one another.

Shadows.

The old evil. Killer shadows.

Deadly shadows off the glittering plain. Shadows, the exploitation of which had given the Shadowmasters their name. Shadows of the sort Soulcatcher had used to prop up her Protectorate until the coming of Tobo's allies from the Land of Unknown Shadows.

I had the answer to the question I had addressed to Lady and Tobo.

People panicked completely. Fireballs flew everywhere, caused far more carnage than mere starving mad shadows. One of those ripped through my Voroshk cloak. The cloak seemed to whine but pulled itself together around me. A shadow hit me. My apparel repelled it, a fact I did not fail to note despite the rising chaos. It also shed the next fireball that found me.

I saw Lady hit several times, rapidly. I saw one of the Voroshk succumb to shadows.

I tried to bellow into the madness, to calm them down, but the panic had them all. Even Howler and Lady caught it.

But Shukrat did keep her wits about her. She crouched in a corner and let her cloak form a barrier impervious to fireballs and shadows alike.

Men fought to get out the door. Howler loosed a spell that flashed so brightly it blinded everyone not in Voroshk protective clothing, including the little sorcerer himself. His effort did not avail. A moment later he screamed with more enthusiasm than ever he had before his cure.

"Get out of my way!" Tobo bellowed. He hurled me aside. His father was inside that room.

Before I regained my feet the tower was creaking under the psychic mass of Tobo's unseen friends. Their battle with the invisible killers was brief but belated. And, probably, needless, because the fireballs ate shadows alive. Unknown

Shadows as well as the traditional lurkers in darkness.

I did not know if I wanted to get off the floor. It was very still in that other room now, except for Arkana crying. But I had to get up. We had to get moving. The rest of the palace was not silent anymore. An alarm had been sounded. People with sharp instruments would be coming to get us.

It was impossible to tell who was dead, who was dying, and who was only mildly injured. For a while it was too dark.

I got Tobo to provide another light. Then I started getting the fallen moved back to the tower top. Arkana and Shukrat and Tobo's hidden allies kept the Palace Guard at bay. I kept my emotions turned off while I lugged bodies. At the moment I could not afford to indulge.

"How are we going to get these posts and the carpet out of here?" I demanded. Lady, both of the elder Voroshk, Howler, Murgen were all out of action. So were most of the commandos.

"Shukrat and I can handle the carpet. You and Arkana will have to tow the posts."

"You hear that, new daughter?" Minutes earlier I had been about to slap the girl around to crack her shock. But she had solid stuff inside her. She was dragging the dead and injured now, calmer than most of the others.

"I know. I'll need something to use for tethers."

"Find it fast. I'll lug bodies."

A crossbow bolt buzzed past without doing any harm. An instant later the section of wall whence it had come was shattered rock and boiling flame.

Tobo was not in a kindly mood.

I told Arkana, "You get those posts out of here right now. All but mine." She had gotten some rope from aboard the carpet.

Good girl, Arkana. She got busy. Like Shukrat, she focused on the task at hand.

Funny, I thought, how the Company seemed to attract good women.

The Palace Guards and a surprising number of Greys responded to the alarm. And they refused to be intimidated by Tobo's violence and by Tobo's half-seen friends. Brave men, they. There are always brave and honorable men amongst one's enemies. Missiles filled the air. A few found targets.

I began to wonder if this would not be a good time to reconsider my lifelong determination never to leave Company people behind.

But I was incapable of leaving without my wife. And I needed the old Voroshk. Even if they were dead.

106

The Palace:
View from a High Place

Mogaba felt no elation as he watched the disaster unfold. In fact, he became more troubled. He could see that there would be survivors. Those people were still strong enough to hold off the Guards and Greys while they evacuated their casualites. That meant that, unless he enjoyed a gargantuan turn of luck and they were all killed by missiles before they could get away, he still faced a final battle.

He had no tricks left in his bag.

The shadows had not been completely effective. Which proved what he had suspected for some time. The enemy had a similar force at his disposal. And that force had responded in time to save some of the raiders.

He watched crossbow bolts, arrows and even javelins bounce off the creatures in the great seething black cloaks. Only one of those people got hurt.

A fireball's flare, as the big carpet backed away from the parapet, gave just enough light for Mogaba to distinguish the Lifetaker armor.

"Lady," he murmured. Awed.

That same flash must have reflected off his eyeballs or teeth, betraying him somehow. Because when he glanced at the post riders he found the one in the Widowmaker armor hurling straight at him, black cape expanding to shut out the sky.

107

Taglios:
Soldiers Live

I saw Mogaba behind the window. Rage devoured me. I drove straight at him, accelerating. And even as I did some tiny remnant of rationality wondered if what I had glimpsed was real, not my mind seeing what it wanted because I needed somebody else to hurt as much as I had begun to do.

If the Mogaba I saw was my own creation it vanished before I smashed into the window glazing.

The glass did not break. It did not yield at all. My post stopped dead. I did not. The post rebounded. I smacked into the glass. Then I bounced back. And fell. I had time for one very enthusiastic howl before I reached the end of my tether, then I was flailing around ten feet below my post.

The post kept driving forward, kept rebounding. I tried to climb back up but could get nowhere with only one reliable hand. The motion of the post got me swinging like the weight on a pendulum. One end of each swing brought me into intimate contact with the Palace wall.

The Voroshk cloak protected me well, but unconsciousness eventually came.

* * *

I was still dangling when I recovered. The ground was only a few yards below and moving slowly. I seemed to be flying along above the Rock Road, barely clearing the heads of travelers. I tried twisting so I could look up but could not manage. The tether was attached to me in the back, just above my waist. I did not have strength enough to twist around.

I did have a bit of pain when I struggled.

I lost consciousness again.

I was back in mankind's natural state, on the ground, when I wakened again. A pointy hunk of chert was trying to gouge a hole through my back. Somebody said something in one of the dialects of Hsien, then repeated himself in bad Taglian. Arkana materialized overhead, face somber. "You going to live, Pop?"

"All the aches and pain I've got, it's a sure thing. What happened?"

"You did something stupid."

"What else is new?" a second voice demanded. Sleepy's face materialized opposite Arkana. "How soon you going to get off your back, part-time? I need some help. This disaster show you guys engineered is about to put us out of business."

"Be right with you, Boss. Soon as I get my leg bones unbraided and my feet hooked back onto my ankles."

The effort of trying to get up, because I wanted to find my wife, pushed me over into the darkness again.

Rain in my face wakened me the next time. My physical pains had turned to dull aches. They had gotten something into me. Cataloging, I decided I had a lot of bruises but nothing was broken or permanently damaged.

Just when I started to make an effort to get up I floated upward. After a momentary panic I realized that I was on a litter, being moved in out of the rain. Being lifted onto the litter was what had interrupted my sleep, not those first few misty raindrops.

I got a better grip this time. I remained rational when Sleepy turned up. "How's my wife?" I asked, with only a small squeak in my voice.

"She's still alive. But her situation isn't good. Though it's better than it would've been if she hadn't been wearing the Voroshk outfit. I'd guess she might recover. If we can get Tobo to stay focused long enough to help."

I heard the unspecified offer of a job assignment in there somewhere. "What's the kid's problem?"

"His father got killed. Where were you?"

I grunted. "I was afraid of that." Maybe I had tried to shut it out. It was going to hurt.

Sleepy seemed to think we did not have time for pain.

I had begun to trust her instincts.

"You had it right, Croaker. Soldiers live. Only three people got out of that scrape unhurt. Tobo, Arkana and a very lucky soldier named Tam Do Linh. Howler, the First Father, Nashun the Researcher, Murgen and all the other soldiers, didn't. The rest of you are hurt. Tobo feels guilty. He thinks he should've done more. He thinks he should've realized it was a trap."

"I understand. What about Shukrat?"

"Bruises and abrasions and emotional distress. The Voroshk clothing took good care of her. It knew her so well it adapted faster than Lady's could. As I understand it."

"Murgen could've worn Voroshk protection." But he had refused. Damn him.

There had not been much fight in him since Sahra's disappearance.

"I want you to straighten Tobo out. We need him back. We need the Unknown Shadows. If I was in Mogaba's boots I'd have another attack force headed our way already."

"I don't think so."

"The man doesn't wait around, Croaker. His gospel is, seize the initiative."

I could only make an ass of myself arguing with a woman who had fought the Great General more years than I had known him. Who had lived in Taglios for as many years as I had, much more recently. Evidently I was just another cranky old man raising a fuss for the attention. Except when she needed something. "Then we'd better arrange for it to get really dangerous for him personally if anything happens to any of us."

I felt stupid before I finished saying that. For Mogaba there was little chance life would ever be more dangerous than it was already.

I had forgotten an early lesson. Try to reason like the enemy. Study him until you can think just like him. Until you can *become* him.

Sleepy told me, "You need to find yourself an apprentice, too. If you're going to keep getting involved in lethal stuff." *At your age* was implied—until the Captain actually said, "You're too long in the tooth to be out there right where it's happening. It's time you eased up and started passing your secrets along."

Sleepy went away, leaving me wondering. Who was I supposed to tap? I was inclined to pick her buttboy, Mihlos Sedona, except that the kid had one huge shortcoming. He was totally illiterate. And I did not have any inclination to put in all the hours needed to alter that condition.

Then the man I maybe should have been thinking of turned up on his own, voluntarily.

"Suvrin? What the hell's gotten into you? You're going to leave us most any day now."

"So perhaps I've had an epiphany. Maybe I need to learn the Annals because I've decided to face my destiny."

"Is that the fragrance of bullshit wafting on the breeze?" Being an old cynic I thought it was more likely that he thought this would somehow get him laid. But I did not suggest anything. I just accepted him, then groaned upon discovering that Sleepy's wonderfully educated young man neither

wrote nor read a single word of Taglian, which has been the
language of these Annals for the last twenty-five years.

Lady's book was the last written in another language. And
Murgen had translated and updated that, along with a couple
of my own that had not really needed any polish.

"Think you can learn to read and write Taglian?" I asked.
"You might never *need* to do either. . . ."

"Unless I want to read the Annals. The holy scriptures of
the Black Company."

"Yeah. If I go, you'll be on your own unless Sleepy makes
time or Lady recovers." I had had time enough now to put
together an act of indifference. But I was not convincing
anybody.

Suvrin stared, waiting for the punchline.

There was none, really, except that he ought to make an
effort to see that I stayed healthy long enough for him to
develop the needed skills.

Two days after Suvrin became my understudy Sleepy stage-
managed a ceremony that formalized his appointment as
Lieutenant of the Black Company and her heir-apparent.

We were outside that big, nameless hilltop stronghold which
broods over the Rock Road approach to Taglios. A large
plain had been leveled and prepared as a place where troops
could camp or could practice the close-order skills necessary for success in battle. Or as a place where forces defending the city could engage an advancing enemy.

No one bothered us there, other than small Vehdna cavalry bands made up of youths who wanted to show off their
courage. But I advised both Sleepy and Suvrin against leaving the stronghold unvanquished behind us.

Sleepy was no more interested in advice than ever before
but these days she did pretend to listen. Her own approach to
conquest had been a disaster mitigated only by the fact that a
few of us had survived.

108

Taglios:
Someone at the Door

Upon reflection, after we beat back a relief sortie by troops from Taglios, the commander of the fortress offered to surrender on terms. He wanted paroles for himself and damned near everyone who ever bore arms in the three nearest counties. Which was not all that unreasonable, I thought, considering we were going to turn all this over to the Prahbrindrah Drah as soon as the deal closed and the Prince could get his ass up here from Ghoja.

Even after all her years in the real world Sleepy retained some Vehdna notions about right and wrong that had nothing to do with the practicalities of the moment.

"Even if this Lal Mindrat is the worst human monster since the Shadowmasters themselves, you have to consider what your moral rigidity can cost the rest of us," I told Sleepy. Evidently Lal Mindrat had betrayed some of our allies during the Kiaulune wars. I had not heard of him before Sleepy started getting uppity so it could not have been a major betrayal.

A good many friends of the Company had been turned by the Protector in those days. Soulcatcher had had the power and wealth.

"Be flexible," I advised. "But treacherous when *absolutely* necessary."

She understood. With some half-ass help from Tobo and his friends, and the appropriate promises of parole and safe passage, Sleepy got our enemies to evacuate the stronghold with no more violence than occurred when Lal Mindrat came out with his lifeguard.

Thus the Captain finished her business with a minor traitor from her own era. For the time being.

* * *

Mogaba made our approach hell, at least for those of us who pulled the recon, picket and vanguard duties. Horsemen never stopped harassing our forward elements. The Voroshk girls and I went out whenever the enemy's behavior became overly obnoxious.

Eventually we reached the great South Gate of Taglios, something that had not existed in my time. These days a truly substantial wall stretched into the distance at either hand. The soldiers on the ramparts seemed much too small. The wall reared up like a vast cliff of limestone.

"Wow!" I told Sleepy. "There's been some changes made." The entrance to the city was a fortress in itself, outside the wall but attached to it. I could not tell from the ground for sure but it looked like an equally formidable structure guarded the pass-through from within.

Sleepy grunted. "Been a few since I was here. Methinks the Great General must have inveigled some appropriations out of the Protector somehow. They've added several feet to the height of the wall. And that barbican complex . . ." She shrugged.

As I remembered city politics, public works were particularly vulnerable to graft and corrupt practices. "Somebody in the treasury offices must have been blowing in the Protector's ear."

Sleepy grunted again, uninterested in my opinion. She was watching Suvrin spread the troops out facing the city, offering battle. No response was expected. No response was what he got.

I said, "They don't have to be careful of anybody's property, at least." More than the immensity of the wall itself, I was awed by the existence of a thousand-foot-wide band of empty ground lapping the wall's foot. What had it taken to get people moved off that ground? How did the state keep them off?

"In a few months there'll be grainfields and vegetable

patches as far as you can see. That grid of pathways marks the boundaries of the patches. They started that back right after Sahra and I first came to the city."

"Tobo's going to be a busy boy."

Sleepy examined our forces, left and right. They did not appear threatening against the backdrop of the wall. Nor did anyone atop that wall appear concerned.

"He will. I expect him and the girls to hit hard, with everything they have, right from the start, so people in there will be stunned by the fury of it. Is he going to be able to do it?"

"I can't guarantee you his heart'll be in it."

"What about you? Is your heart going to be in it?"

I heaved a huge sigh.

Sleepy asked, "How is she doing?"

Another major sigh. "Honestly? I'm worried. She just lays there, midway between life and death. She gets no better; she gets no worse. I'm starting to wonder how much the Kina connection has to do with all that."

It took a major effort to let that out. Because of what the Captain might consider if she grasped all the implications. And she began to see some right away.

I said, "If I can pull Tobo through his grief he may be able to find out if Kina's gained any control." I dreaded the possibility that the Dark Mother was setting my wife up as an alternate route of escape from her ancient prison. I could imagine a scenario wherein I struck the sleeping Goddess and freed Shivetya only to see the darkness return through the woman I love.

Not that it would take the Mother of Night to accomplish that. She was entirely willing to welcome in her own breed of darkness.

Aren't we all.

The Captain said, "I haven't heard a direct answer. Can I count on you to actually pay attention when the arrows start to fly?"

An old, old formula came to mind, from back when I was very young indeed. "I am a soldier." I said it first in the language I had spoken then, then repeated myself in Sleepy's own Dejagoran dialect. "I've been distracted before. I'm still alive."

"Yeah, soldiers live. You only get one mistake, Croaker."

"Go teach your granny to suck eggs." Which was a waste of colorful language. The expression had no meaning amongst these peoples.

"What's that?" Sleepy asked, pointing at something rising above the city.

"Looks like a big-ass kite."

109

Taglios:
No Excuses Accepted

Damn it! No matter how much I wanted it Mogaba refused to be stupid. Facing potential problems with an infestation of airborne wizards? Take advantage of the season's almost constant winds. Put up about ten thousand giant box kites with poisoned sharp things hanging on tails made of braided fibers almost too tough to cut.

There would be no zooming about with youthful exuberance over Taglios. Especially not after dark. Those kites would not be able to hurt us in our Voroshk clothing but they could entangle us and knock us off our posts. Whereupon whoever lost their seat would need someone else to come along and bring them out. Unless . . .

Shukrat once fixed me up with a post that would travel on its own when its master could not manage it.

I issued an order.

Just hours later Shukrat's post brought the girl herself

back virtually mummified in cord and deadly sharps that took hours to overcome. But she had cleaned away scores of kites.

I made Tobo untangle her. I was having a real problem getting him engaged with life. But Shukrat was supposed to be important to him.

She certainly thought so. Once he finished freeing her, too slowly to suit her, she popped him in the middle of the forehead with the heel of her right hand. "How about you at least pretend to be interested, Tobe?" And, moments later, "You're making me wonder just how bright I am."

Tobo was a real young man. He started to protest. I tried to warn him by shaking my head. No way was he going to break even here. Shukrat cut him off, unwilling to grant him the validity of any excuse. After that I tried not to hear what they were saying.

I mused on Shukrat's swift, nearly effortless grasp of Taglian. She had almost no accent at all, now. And she appeared equally adaptable regarding strange customs.

Arkana was having more difficulty but she was coming along marvelously, too.

Having allowed the girlfriend time to make her point, I approached Tobo. "Tobo, we need to know about what's going on behind those walls."

He did not look like he cared much.

Shukrat punched him.

I told him, "You have to let go."

He gave me one ugly look.

"You have to let go of the guilt. It wasn't your fault."

I doubted that telling him would do any good. These things never are rational. Your mind goes on chasing the irrational even when it *knows* the truth. If Tobo wanted to feel guilty about his father and mother he would find ways to do that in the face of every argument, of any bit of evidence, and of all the common sense in the universe. I know. I have suffered through that bleak season a few times myself.

I had a little of it going right then, featuring my wife.

Shukrat said, "The Great General did it, Tobe. The Taglian supreme commander. And he's inside those same walls."

There you go, girl. Appeal to the darkness within, to the stores of rage and hatred. We really needed to get those emotions cooking inside the most powerful sorcerer left in this part of the world.

110

Taglios: Misfortunes

The Unknown Shadows told Tobo that Mogaba and his cronies were hunkered down, waiting us out. They thought we might begin to fade away before long, despite our wealth.

They could be right. Though Sleepy had plenty of treasure left, many of the soldiers from Hsien had signed on for only one year in the field. I did not doubt that many would stay as long as their pay was on time but I did not doubt, either, that homesickness would begin to bleed us, too.

We cleared away kites faster than Mogaba could put new ones up. We made a few high altitude raids each night. We dropped firepots on the properties of known allies of the Protector, the Great General, and the Greys. But fire is a cruel and unruly ally. Some that we started spread way beyond their targets. Even more smoke than usual clung to the city.

A second midnight approach to the occupied portion of the palace provided us with some distinctly unwelcome news. We learned that Mogaba's efforts to seize our encampment beside the Shadowlander cemetery, while tactically disastrous for his loyalists, had not been entirely unprofitable.

Sleepy's chief of staff decided he needed a firsthand look at the Palace. For planning purposes. He was a thorough man. At Sleepy's urging he and other selected folk had been getting training using the Voroshk flying posts. We had seven available with only five regularly assigned. And Lady was not using hers these days. Sleepy hated seeing resources going to waste. Sleepy being Sleepy.

The chief of staff had Mihlos Sedona join us. Mihlos was the most competent of the part-time flyers though his only excuse for getting the opportunity was that the Captain liked him. And wanted his observations. No way was she going aloft herself.

I went along to make sure those two had somebody to bail them out if they got in trouble. I made them wear Voroshk apparel, too. If we were seen we could expect missile fire. Mogaba's people never gave up trying.

You just need one lucky break.

Mihlos Sedona had not yet realized that he was not immortal. He ventured too close to the enemy. Then we all learned how Mogaba had profited from disaster.

A fireball ripped through the darkness. The boy escaped the worst of it by hurling himself to one side. The fireball struck him a glancing blow, which, however, was enough to knock him off his post.

General Chu ignored my shout and went after Sedona. And actually managed to get close enough to get a hold on his post. As fireballs streaked in from half a dozen sources.

One struck Chu's post dead solid.

The explosion of that post was violent enough to set off the other. And the two in concert were violent enough to smash in an acre of Palace like an invisible giant's foot stomping on eggshells.

More Palace continued to cave in around the initial collapse.

A wicked wind flung me around like a rogue dandelion
seed. Once again I lost my grip and fell off my steed. While
dangling I caught rolling glimpses of flames beginning to
peek through cracks in the rubble, of panic beginning to
prowl amongst the soldiers atop the palace.

111

Taglios:
Sleepy Flew

We're going to start strapping you down, Pop," Arkana
told me as she towed me into camp. She had been on
a routine patrol kite-clearing when the explosion happened.
In rushing to see the results she almost got knocked out of
the sky by a daredevil swinging from a flying fence post.

"Just get me down. Fast. Preferably right in front of the
Captain's tent." Sleepy had to know. Now. And somebody
needed to go watch the Palace. If the whole damned thing
caved in. . . . If Mogaba and his henchmen died in the disaster. . . . If the Khadidas and the Daughter of Night escaped
in the resulting chaos. . . .

Some hearty fires were burning over there now. A strong
glow silhouetted the city wall now.

I kept having to explain as more notables reached the
Captain's tent. And I kept urging Sleepy to make whatever
move she was considering making right away. Never again
would the other side be as confused and disordered as they
must be now. She agreed but pointed out that our bunch
were not terribly well organized right now, either.

The Captain dealt with the problem of interruptions in the
most amazing fashion I could imagine. After delegating
Suvrin to begin preparing an attack, she told me, "Take me
up there. Show me what's happened."

"You?"

"Me. I'll keep my eyes closed until there's something to see. Before we leave I'll throw an old blanket over my seat so I won't get your post all wet."

I shook my head, disconsolate. "I wish Swan was still around. A straight line like that shouldn't go to waste. Let's do it."

"Wait. Suvrin." She issued more instructions. So he would have something to do in his spare time.

Her absence would slow nothing down.

"Tie yourself on good," I told Sleepy. "I might decide to do a few loops while we're up there."

She growled like a whole pack of angry rats. Made it clear that if she fell off I might as well just keep on going.

"All right. But coming home hanging underneath like a carp on a stringer is a lot better than the alternative."

"If you don't mind a little embarrassment."

"I don't mind at all if I'm alive to get red in the face." Something you learn as you get older. Or, at least, you should.

We were passing over the gateway complex when I realized that I had gone right back up without having paused to check on my wife.

Was I not a little old to feel guilty about everything? She would not be going anywhere any time soon.

It was not possible to get dangerously close to the Palace. The fires were huge now. The heat was intense, even through the Voroshk clothing. And the higher you flew the more turbulent the air became. There were no kites anywhere nearby anymore.

I figured Mogaba would give up on the kites soon. They were not doing us any harm.

Sleepy clung to the post with white knuckles. I wondered if we would need a chisel to break her grip once we got back on the ground. But she did manage to keep her voice sounding normal. "What in the world is burning? That place isn't anything but a big old stone pile."

The flames were not limited to the Palace now. Several fires were burning nearby. The entire area was crawling with people, most being gawkers who just got in the way of the soldiers, officials and volunteers actually trying to accomplish something.

"Somebody's still thinking," I told Sleepy. "They've put troops around the place." I dropped lower and moved close enough to spot Aridatha Singh out working two thin lines of soldiers, one facing outward, holding the mobs back, the other, stronger, facing inward. The latter were more heavily armed. Anyone leaving the palace was going to get a good hard look. "I hope they got those guys in place before the Khadidas and the girl got away."

"Back to the gate. If we're ever going to invade this city, now is the time."

"You found enough boats yet?"

She tensed up. She did not answer for a moment. "You figured it out."

"Logic suggests that it makes no sense to storm those walls with no more men than we have. Particularly when Taglios has almost no defenses on the river side." A point which would have occurred to the Great General, too.

"There is no easy way in," Sleepy told me. "The defenses on the river side just aren't as obvious." She proceeded to explain about log booms and chains that controlled traffic, forcing it into narrow channels well-ranged by massed artillery ashore. A barge loaded with attackers could be pounded into driftwood and fish food in minutes.

I said, "I see where this is going."

"Do you really? Will I attack by day or by night?"

"It's dark now but by the time you can get anybody to the point of attack the sun will be up."

"Take me back. I have to get things moving faster."

112

Taglios:
Under Siege

Ghopal Singh looked terrible. He had been close enough to the fire to have had his beard singed. He had blisters on both face and hands. His turban was gone. The rest of him was rags and smoke smell.

"You'll never pass inspection," Mogaba told him.

Singh's sense of humor was moribund. "We've got it controlled inside. It'll burn itself out. Out there in the city. . . . Pray for unseasonable rain."

"Good luck doesn't always work out, does it?"

Grudgingly, Singh said, "No way we could know what would happen if a fireball hit one of those flying things."

"No. Of course not. Here comes Aridatha. Like a crow. There'll be more bad news." Mogaba glanced eastward. Not even close to dawn yet. Why was this night stretching out so long? "You've got a spot of ash on your right trouser leg, Aridatha."

The commander of the City Battalions actually paused to deal with the matter before he realized that the Great General was teasing him. More or less. Aridatha said, "They're trying to take advantage of the confusion. I'm getting reports about ghosts and terrors at work around the South Gate and the river forts."

"They're really coming?" Ghopal Singh could not believe the enemy would assault Taglios with so few soldiers. He had expected them to just sit tight in hopes they could forge alliances with disaffected elements inside the wall. "Where?"

"The river," Mogaba predicted. "They've had time to scout. That's where we're the weakest."

"Maybe they just want us to think . . ."

"They can't get a strong force into place for a while yet.

When they attack from the air we'll know they're on their way and where they think they can get through."

Minutes later word came that enemy commandos were atop the wall half a mile west of the South Gate, ferried there by flying carpet. They were being reinforced rapidly. Neither the City Battalions nor the Greys had much strength in that area. The bulk of the Second Territorial was on the waterfront. The garrison of the barbican was responding to the threat as best it could.

Mogaba looked to the east. Once the light came the enemy would lose the advantage of his unseen allies. Then the city's defenders could exploit their big advantage in numbers.

Ten minutes later news came that swimmers armed with small fireball projectors had cut the chains and broken the booms at the upstream end of the city. Firebombs were falling amongst the artillery engines.

"You were right," Ghopal said, "It'll be the river."

"Possibly. Where are their wizards?" Mogaba wanted to know. He understood that the post riders need not be sorcerers. "If we don't see wizards we have to remain skeptical about their commitment to any particular attack. All I see now are diversions."

"Shall we go out there?" Aridatha asked.

"Out where? Would you care to bet that other attacks won't break out sometime soon? This is the best place for us to be. We're central." It had occurred to him that he was being watched. That the Captain's plans might hinge on his own behavior. Whatever he did might direct enemy efforts where he was not. It was what he would have done, given their resources. "We'll stay central. Let's get a tighter cordon around the parts of the Palace where the girl might be. That'll let us free up some more of these men."

Hundreds had been freed up already, because the gawkers had begun to melt away when fires elsewhere proved too fierce to contain. As soon as there was a specific defense to mount Mogaba would send reinforcements.

News came of fierce aerial attacks on the South Gate complex itself. Massive volleys of fireballs were riddling the stonework with thousands of holes. The sheer profligate expenditure of fireballs awed everyone.

"That's the point, you know," Mogaba said. "This Captain is more willing to fight than her predecessors were but when she does she rachets the level of violence as high as she can. She wants to stun her enemies so they'll be too numb to react while she overwhelms them." A glance around told Mogaba that the Captain's technique was enjoying some success right here, right now. And neither General Singh was eager for a lecture on the subject of combat psychology.

So Mogaba just noted, "And we'll be at a disadvantage until we know which probe will become the real attack."

And that, he suspected, had not yet been determined on the other side, either. She could just be trying to find out where she could get the best return for her investment. They never liked wasting their men, the Company Captains.

"At this point we'll let the district commanders respond to their own crises. We'll reinforce them only to stop a disaster. What I need from you two is regular gauges of the mood of the mob. So far they don't seem to care but we wouldn't want any unwelcome surprises."

Ghopal offered, "I'd say the masses favor us. It wasn't us who started all those fires."

Mogaba glanced eastward. There was a little color over there but he felt no elation. Ghopal had reminded him of the oppressive amount of work ahead once he suppressed the enemy's attacks. Fires would leave tens of thousands homeless and destitute in a city where a third of the population already enjoyed that distinction.

Maybe he should just walk away and leave all the problems to Sleepy.

113

Taglios:
Attack

It became clear to me that Sleepy wanted control of the South Gate itself. She was flinging people and material around everywhere and using up those of us able to fly, but when you did the numbers over half of our efforts were taking place within a half mile of the barbican. And the barbican itself had suffered immensely from above. Parts looked like slag pierced by ten thousand holes.

I had better information than Mogaba did. But I knew that the Great General would catch on soon enough. He possessed a well-honed instinct for things warlike.

How flexible was the Captain's planning? Could she shift her point of attack fast once Mogaba did catch on? I did not know. Whatever level of planning had gone into this, I had not been invited to participate. Only Suvrin had a real grasp of the whole picture. And I was not that sure about him. This Sleepy was as close as I used to be when it came to sharing her thoughts.

That seemed to go with the job. My predecessors had been the same way. Someday it would hurt us.

It was just past noon. Striking suddenly from all directions and enjoying maximum support from above and from Tobo, our troops pushed into the barbican complex. The defense seemed doomed once the assault teams got inside and got the outer gates open.

Mogaba did not respond. The streets near the gate complex did empty as civilians decided this seemed like a good time not to be visible. Bands of Taglian wounded retreated deeper into the city. Still no one came forward to reinforce or relieve the defenders of the barbican. Soldiers from

Mogaba's own Second Territorial began saying unkind things about their boss.

Something was not right here. Mogaba was way too passive. The man had to know that he had to do something before the night returned and the Company waxed far more powerful by grace of the Unknown Shadows.

Somehow, we had to be doing what Mogaba wanted us to do if he was doing nothing to prevent us from doing it.

Yeah. You can drive yourself crazy trying to work your way around all the angles of that kind of stuff.

Sleepy sent everybody but Tobo off to intensify the attack on the upriver waterfront defenses. Evidently we had gained a good foothold there, cheaply, so the Captain wanted to expand it.

I had begun to suspect that Sleepy really did have no fixed plan. Other than to seize whatever Mogaba was willing to let go.

An hour later, when loyalist troops did respond to the threat on the waterfront, the South Gate again became the focus of our attack.

I hoped she decided soon. I was worn out. And we still had hours of daylight left.

I was right in the first place. She chose the gate.

Back when the men on the walls finally broke into the gate houses a signal had gone up, to alert the Captain and Lieutenant. There were two gate houses and both had to be cleared. One had proven much more stubborn than the other. In the interim every man not engaged elsewhere gathered outside, ready to attack.

Now Sleepy signalled the advance. The officers all had orders to push through the barbican and drive straight on to the heart of the city. They had guides to show them the way. The Captain wanted the Palace captured swiftly. She believed we would face little resistance in the rest of Taglios once its

symbolic heart had fallen. Word was out already that the
Prahbrindrah Drah was on his way, to reclaim his family's
dominion.

Me, I would have had the Prince in my hip pocket first,
ready to flash in front of the mob right now. I would have
him lead the charge. But nobody asked me how I would handle things anymore.

114

Taglios:
Bad News, White Crow

Mogaba received the news about the South Gate in grim,
expressionless silence. He asked no questions, just
looked to the west to see how much daylight he had left. He
turned to Aridatha and Ghopal. The latter nodded slightly.

Once a messenger had departed, the Great General asked,
"Are they continuing their attack on the waterfront?"

Aridatha responded. "At last report they were stepping it
up."

"Send another company. Their main force will head
straight here. With all their sorcery supporting it. A counterattack down there should have an excellent chance of suc-
ceeding."

"And what should I do about the invaders?" Aridatha
asked.

"We've had that set for months. Just follow the plan. Let it
unfold."

Aridatha nodded, plainly wishing there was some way to
reduce the bloodshed. He was less pessimistic about the outcome of this conflict than was the Great General. But he
feared the price would be so crippling that victory would be
the greater evil for the city as a whole.

Mogaba told him, "I want you to return to your own head-quarters now. Continue to direct your troops from there."

"But . . ."

"If this goes badly and you're here with me when they come you'll have to pay a crueler price than necessary. Do as I say. Ghopal, you take over here. No one goes into the Palace. No one comes out. If the enemy gets this far make sure they know about the Khadidas and the Daughter of Night. I expect you to stay out of the way yourself. The best people to get the information to are the two wearing the fiery armor. Widowmaker and Lifetaker. They'll listen to you. They're the girl's natural parents. Aridatha, why are you still standing there? You have your instructions."

Ghopal asked, "What'll you be doing?"

"Readying a pair of counterattacks that'll make these strange foreign soldiers wish that they'd never left the land where they were born." The Great General projected immense confidence.

He did not feel a bit of it inside.

Nevertheless, his stride was that of an arrogant conquerer as he walked away from the Palace, a gaggle of messengers and functionaries scurrying behind him. He spun off orders as he went.

Mogaba spotted the white crow watching from a cornice stone. He beckoned. "Come down here." He patted his shoulder.

The bird did as it was bid, startling Mogaba's entourage.

The Great General asked, "Are you who I think you are?"

115

Taglios:
The Special Team

There were some tasks too important to entrust to anyone but family. The responsible captains at the South Gate were always related to Ghopal Singh, though they were officers in the City Battalions. They were all men who dared not be disloyal because their pasts were all tangled up with the Greys, the Great General, and the Protectorate.

Also, they were men who were mentally disciplined enough to retreat without running away. They were men who had prepared themselves and their followers for this day. Though, originally, they had expected the Protector herself to be entering their killing zone.

116

Taglios:
Outrageous Fortune

The passage through the barbican seemed a maze from inside, though there were only a half dozen turns. From above it did not look that bad. Until huge blocks of stone fell out of the walls, blocking the way ahead of and behind the Captain, trapping her, her staff and another dozen men.

The falling blocks initiated a train of mechanical events, the first of which was the launching of a storm of poisoned darts. Horses screamed and men cursed. And, as I sent my flying post downward to try to get the Captain out of there, burning oil sprayed from ports in the walls.

So this was how they had planned to get rid of Soulcatcher.

The heat drove me back. The black Voroshk clothing could not stand up to much of that.

Sleepy had chosen to place herself at the middle of the invading column. Which meant our forces had just been split in two.

A massive counterattack was sure to develop.

I pushed myself up beside Arkana, who was numb with the horror. "Get ahold of yourself! I want you to find Suvrin. Tell him I'll take charge on the city side. He can build steps to get the rest of the men past that mess. He can use the lumber meant for siege engines. Go on! Get going!"

Once again I did not have to whack her to bring her out of her stupor.

Once again Mogaba had dealt us one off the bottom of his deck. This time our chances of surviving did not look good.

We should have been prepared for it. He had *told* us that there were arrangements in place.

Sometimes you just do not hear what is being said.

I checked the sun before I reached the ground.

We would have to hang on for a bit longer than what inspired me with optimism.

"It won't be long," I insisted to the commanders on the ground. "We need to put ourselves into a position to hang on until nightfall. Once darkness comes . . ."

"The Unknown Shadows."

"The Hidden Realm."

Shouts. A scatter of arrows fell.

"Push a company along the wall that direction," I directed. "I want those steps under our control when the others start joining us." I had to show an optimism I did not feel. I *hoped* Suvrin would press his half of the attack.

No man could question the courage of the soldiers from Hsien. They mauled the City Battalions badly. They mauled reinforcements from the Second Territorial. Unfortunately, the City Battalions and Mogaba's Second Territorial elite

mauled them right back. It did not take long to see that
Sleepy might have taken too big a bite. The Great General
seemed to have plenty of reserves, though he was parsimo-
nious when it came to investing them.

Vigorous support from Arkana, Shukrat and Tobo kept us
from being overwhelmed.

Once Tobo woke up enough to begin thinking more than
mechanically the tide began to turn. Once he recalled that he
was good for something more than dropping rocks and firepots. Once he added his sorcerous skills to the girls' weaker
ones we got stinging insects, painful worms of fire, lemon
and lime snowflakes that pitted armor and flesh.

Nevertheless, the enemy kept us confined until darkness
came.

Darkness always comes.

117

Taglios:
Night and the City

The Great General took charge of the riverfront defenses
personally. He found morale abysmal when he arrived,
accompanied by reserves from the Second Territorial. The
long succession of military disasters had the soldiers suspecting that defeat was inevitable and that they were being
wasted in a hopeless cause.

The Great General himself led his own lifeguard in a
counterattack of such fury and finesse that the enemy soon
lost everything that it had taken them all day to capture.

The invaders got no support from above. The Great General interpreted that to mean that they were in desperate
straits at the South Gate.

There was not a lot of communication between forces.

Nobody knew what anybody else was doing, really. The best anyone could do was cling to the plans and hope the enemy did not get too much enjoyment from his advantages.

Mogaba's opponents tried reinforcing themselves with recent recruits. That did them little good. Those men entered the fighting in groups too small to make any difference.

The last attackers fled in the barges they had used to make their initial landings, drifting downriver because they did not have enough men healthy enough to row against the current. All the barges were overburdened, one so much so that it shipped water at the slightest rocking. It did not remain afloat long.

Mogaba treated himself to a long breather. He turned his mind off completely, closed his eyes, let the cold winter air chill him.

When he was calm and breathing normally again he allowed himself to return to the moment.

He could get the best of this thing yet. If he could get these men to the South Gate and get in a hard blow he might damage the enemy enough to earn his own people a fair chance of making it through the night. If he succeeded, victory would be his. *They* would not be able to survive everything he would throw at them tomorrow.

He opened his eyes.

The white crow stared at him from a perch on a broken cartwheel scarcely a foot from his face.

The crow started talking.

That bird was a much better messenger and spy than the crows he had known in earlier days.

The Great General listened for a long time. And wondered if the mind behind the bird was aware of his disloyalty.

He would not bring it up first.

The Great General dragged himself upright, ignoring the complaints of aching muscles. "Sergeant Mugwarth. Spread the word. All officers. Round up every man who can walk. We're moving up to relieve the South Gate."

The enemy's aerial advantage betrayed the trap before it could close. Mogaba left the soldiers to their work and hastened toward the Palace. He arrived as dusk began to deepen shadows. The view from that eminence included half a dozen fires still burning. Smoke and trickles of fire still attended the fallen parts of the Palace, too.

Awaiting him was the news that the enemy had reduced most of the defenses at the downriver end of the city. Their forces there had been augmented by the survivors from upriver. These outsiders were stubborn fighters.

"Send reinforcements?" Ghopal asked.

Mogaba thought a moment. Those foreigners ought to be near their limits. "Yes, actually. These are all your men here, around the Palace, aren't they?"

"I thought that would be best. Makes them all men I can trust."

"Let Aridatha's soldiers take their place. Send yours to the waterfront. And gather up any of your brothers and cousins who're still alive, I want them here."

"What? . . ."

"Do it. Quickly. Quickly. And round up all those captured fireball throwers."

"I think we used most of them up."

"That means they're some of them left. I want them all."

Darkness came. And soon after it did messages reached the Great General informing him that his enemies, inside both their footholds, were hunkering down for the night rather than pressing forward when their shadowy allies could come out to play.

The Great General refused to let the night intimidate him. By his example he inspired those around him. And it did seem that the enemy's spooks meant to do little more than yell "Boo!"

The Great General reorganized the city's defenses, shifting almost all responsibility into Aridatha Singh's hands. Then he led Ghopal Singh and the man's kinsmen, armed with fireball throwers, toward the waterfront conflict.

Ghopal asked, "What're we doing?"

"This is a false peace," Mogaba replied. "They lost their Captain this afternoon. The trap in the gate worked to perfection. They lost most of their command staff, too." He did not explain how he knew that. "They'll need to work out who's in charge and what they're going to do now. They might even decide to go away." He shivered, told himself it was the winter air.

But he knew that Croaker had survived the day. He knew the Company would not be going away. He knew the succession there had been assured and the new Captain would attempt to complete the work of the old.

118

Taglios:
A New Administration

I'm not ready to take over," Suvrin argued.

"And I'm too old to come back," I countered. "And the only other qualified person is in a coma." Lady was not, literally, in a coma, but, practically speaking, the effect was the same. She had nothing to contribute.

Suvrin grumbled under his breath.

"Sleepy picked you. She thought you could handle it. She's been giving you opportunities to get a feel for the job."

Sleepy was a big part of the problem. Her death, so sudden

and cruel, had stricken everyone. Most of us were still in a daze.

I said, "We take too much time here; we'll give the Children of the Dead too much time to think. We don't want them looking at how bad the numbers thing has gone since they've been on our side of the glittering plain."

A moment of self-loathing followed. That was exactly the sort of thinking I found repugnant in the Company's employers.

Suvrin reflected briefly. "We can't spend time grieving, can we? We have to go ahead. Or call it off."

"No decision there. Go ahead. I've tried to get messages to Aridatha Singh. He seems like a good man, willing to put Taglios first. He might be willing to spare the city some pain."

"If you can convince him that the Great General isn't going to eat us alive. The way Tobo tells it, Mogaba isn't particularly worried."

"He will be. Once we get settled in here I just might take the girls general hunting."

Suvrin still showed some of that pudgy, baby-fat look he had always had. He needed to get busy and develop the hardened, piratical look of a Captain.

He yielded to his hidden desires. "All right. I'll be the Captain. But I reserve the right to quit."

"Excellent. I'll spread the word, then I'll go smack Mogaba around." My hatred for the Great General was no longer virulent, though. It was more like a bad habit these days.

"I'm the Captain now, right? Completely in charge?"

"Yeah." Spoken with a twinge of suspicion.

"My first directive as Captain, then, is that you should stop putting yourself at risk."

"Huh? What? But . . ."

"Croaker, you're the only one left who can keep the Annals. You're the only one left who can read most of them.

You didn't finish teaching me and you haven't trained anyone else. I don't intend to lose our connection with our heritage. Not at this last stage. Therefore, henceforth, you're not going anywhere that'll put you at risk."

"You sonofabitch. You jobbed me. You can't do that."

"I'm the Captain. Sure I can. I just did. I'll have you restrained if that's what it takes."

"You won't have to." Because I buy into the whole Company mystique, like a religion. Because I cannot defy orders just because I do not like them. Ha-ha. How long would it take to find a way to weasel around this if I felt a genuine need? "But I wanted Mogaba."

"We'll catch him for you. Then you can skin him or whatever you want."

I went out and spread the word that we had a new Captain and that the officers should attend him. Then I looked for Arkana, who was off somewhere wasting a valuable part of her life sleeping.

As I stumbled around, shivering because things unseen were everywhere in the night, I realized that Suvrin, unwittingly, had given me orders of critical importance. If I kept running around, getting into the middle of everything, and I got myself killed for my trouble, more than the Annals would die with me. So would the little plan I had worked out for fulfilling our commitment to Shivetya.

I had not shared that with anyone, and would not unless I was convinced I was dying.

Words never spoken cannot be overheard by sleeping Goddesses.

119

Taglios:
Messenger

Guided and masked by the folk of the hidden realm, Arkana penetrated Aridatha Singh's headquarters undetected, flying post and all. The general was alone. He had collapsed of exhaustion an hour earlier. Solicitous subordinates had put him to bed. They had left sentries outside his door to keep him from being disturbed.

Arkana got in through an open window, lying flat upon her post. She was not especially nervous. She was confident that she could manage any trouble that came her way, at least for the moments it would take her to escape.

She had been instructed to flee at the first sign of trouble. She believed in those instructions with the fervor of a new convert.

Once inside she dismounted and turned her post so she could get away without any delay. She kept herself tethered to the post so it could drag her out even if she was not in the saddle. Even if she was unconscious. Maybe even if three guys were hanging onto her, trying to keep her from going.

She found a lamp and lit it. Then she awakened Aridatha Singh.

The general did not waken quickly. But he did so quietly and cautiously, understanding that he was in a dangerous situation. Maybe it was the Unknown Shadows. The sense of their presence was strong. Because they were all around.

Singh rose into a cross-legged sitting position. He moved slowly, keeping his hands in sight. He asked his question by expression alone.

Arkana strained to ignore his looks. She had been warned. . . . She was not an idiot like Gromovol. "The Captain wants to know if you received the Annalist's messages.

The Captain wants to know if you're ready to spare Taglios the agonies of further conflict." She enunciated carefully, having no desire to be misunderstood.

"Of course I do. But how do I get you people to go away?" He could not tell much about his visitor because of the Voroshk clothing.

"Here's an idea. You can have your soldiers lay down their arms." As one of the Voroshk that sort of statement directed at an outsider would not have troubled Arkana at all. But here, tonight, she was just another refugee and freelance. And a very young one at that, with limited confidence in herself. Maybe Croaker's confidence was misplaced.

That clever old man. He had set her up so she would risk her freedom rather than let him down.

That was a characteristic of old men. All old men in her experience, anyway.

Aridatha said, "There's little I'd like more than to end this fighting before even one more person gets hurt. But I have no control when it comes to making the choice between war and peace. I've undertaken obligations. I've given my word. Right now Taglios is in the keeping of the Great General. If *he* gives the order to stop fighting I'll do so instantly."

And he said no more. That was as clearly as he could speak. Even that much clarity troubled his conscience.

"That's your firm response, then?" Arkana's confidence had begun to swell.

"There is no other position open to me. Your Captain will understand."

"Your honor could get you killed. And there'd be no one to sing your praises." Arkana departed before Singh could figure out what that meant. He thought it sounded like something foreign that did not translate well.

Aridatha was a little less exhausted than he had been before he collapsed. But he did not fall asleep again for a long while, and not because of the potent sense of alien presence still filling his bedroom. He kept hearing the visitor's

last words and remembering his father. Narayan Singh. A
man of high honor, within his own world. Now without a
soul to sing his praises. Unless maybe his beloved Goddess
sang him lullabies within her terrible dreams.

And Narayan's murderer was still hiding somewhere
inside the remains of the Palace.

120

Taglios:
Thi Kim Was Always Here

Mogaba did not participate much in the fighting. He told
Ghopal, "The spirit is willing but this body is just too
damned old and tired. I'll just sit here and tell you what to
do." But mostly he visited with the white crow, which had
begun scouting for him despite the presence of unfriendly
ghosts. The bird could see those ghosts quite clearly, for it
warned him regularly when it was time to keep his mouth
shut.

When Mogaba suggested that the unseen things did not
seem to be helping the invaders much the crow told him that
the folk of the hidden realm were completely devoted to
making their master happy. What little they did contribute
they did in response to the will of their messiah, Tobo,
whom they worshipped almost as a god. As Thi Kim.
Which, in the canonical language of the priests who had created the Unknown Shadows, meant One Who Walks with
the Dead.

Startled, the Great General demanded, "You mean to tell
me that Thi Kim isn't Nyueng Bao?"

The title came from a language closely akin to the
Nyueng Bao of four centuries ago.

"So Deathwalker is the half-breed kid?"

Not Deathwalker. One Who Walks with the Dead.

Mogaba was too tired to wonder much about the difference. "Go find Aridatha Singh," Mogaba said. "I want to know what he's doing."

The bird was not pleased about being given orders. But it went.

Mogaba called for Ghopal immediately. He asked, "What're your feelings toward this city?" He knew but wanted to hear it from the man's own mouth.

Ghopal shrugged. "I'm not sure I understand. Like everyone who lives here I love it and I hate it."

"Our enemies have reorganized their chain of command. Right now they're resting. But they'll resume their attack while there's yet darkness enough to conceal their hidden allies. I'm sure now that our forces will survive the night with more than enough strength left to be able to counterattack tomorrow. I think we'll be able to hurt them badly when we do attack but their damned sorcerers will save them and when night comes again their allies will finish us." The Great General said all this without having seen any proof that the Unknown Shadows were capable of doing anything lethal. "And I think Taglios will suffer a great deal more destruction during that time. I believe that, eventually, both sides will be so weakened that, no matter who wins, neither will be able to restrain the religious factions, nor be able to contain the ambitions of the gang lords, priests or anyone else likely to take advantage of a state of disorder. We might even see rioting between the followers of the different major religions."

Ghopal nodded in the darkness, unseen. As chief Grey managing unofficial ambition had been his task. He had been particularly hard on criminal gangs. Mogaba had not dug for details but knew that something in Ghopal's past drove him to shatter criminal enterprises.

"What're you trying to say?" Ghopal asked.

"I'm saying that if we continue this war the way we are

now, we can win—probably—but we'll destroy Taglios in the process. And, even if we do lose, the results will be anarchy and destruction."

"And?"

"And our enemies don't care. They didn't come here for the city's benefit. They came to get you and me. And the Khadidas and the girl. Especially the Daughter of Night."

Mogaba felt Ghopal's growing suspicion.

The white crow would be back soon, too.

"I think we should walk away, Ghopal. And save Taglios the agony. The garrisons in the eastern provinces are loyal. We can continue the struggle from there."

Ghopal was not fooled. Neither did he raise the objection that they had little hope of success against an enemy seated in the capital, armed with a crew of wizards and well-supplied with funds.

Ghopal had known his commander a long time. The Great General was a stubborn warlord, imbued with no weakness whatsoever. Unless that was his secret love for his adopted city, that he had revealed several times lately. Ghopal found he had no trouble believing that the Great General could walk away rather than let Taglios be destroyed as a monument to his ego. This Mogaba was not the arrogant youngster who had held Dejagore against the worst the Shadowmasters had been able to deliver. "Where would we go?"

"Agra. Or possibly Mukhra in Ajitsthan."

"Vehdna strongholds, both. A band of heretic Shadar aren't likely to be welcomed. Particularly if the strife puts any more strain on religious tolerance."

"That could happen," Mogaba admitted. "Or it might not."

"Nor have we mentioned families." Family was extremely important to the Shadar. "I have only my brothers and cousins. But most of my brothers and cousins have wives and children."

Mogaba said, "I suppose they could stay here, cut off their beards and pretend to be people who haven't been getting much sun. Ghopal, I'm being completely unfair. I'm putting this all squarely on your shoulders. Stay and fight? Or go away and spare the city?"

As if to punctuate his remarks a mushroom of fire rose above the heart of the city. For an instant it resembled a gigantic, glowing brain. Flying shapes hurtled across its face.

Mogaba said, "That respite is over."

121

Taglios:
Sleeping Beauty

It was driving me crazy, having to hang back over friendly territory, observing an aerial assault on a cluster of buildings anchoring a defense stubbornly blocking our advance toward the Palace. We had brought the knowledge of war to this end of the world and we had taught our students too well. These Taglians refused to yield even in the face of sorcery and the Unknown Shadows.

Someone had pointed out that the troops of the City Battalions were mainly Vehdna and Shadar. Both religions assure swift access to rivers of wine and acres of eager virgins for the man who falls in battle. Though originally that only meant warriors who perished in the name of God.

I wondered what the Vehdna paradise was like for Sleepy.

We had not yet been able to identify her body. The corpses in that passage had been burned that badly.

"Why don't we go around these guys?" I wondered. And the answer was, they would not let us. They had an interlocking defense nicely laid out. The only way past was through. Or over.

Over we could do.

Over we did go, twenty insanely courageous Children of

the Dead at a time, with a Tobo so tired he was cross-eyed doing the lifting.

The Unknown Shadows supported their pal from every possible direction, sometimes so blatantly that I could see them clearly from where I hovered, doing nothing whatsoever that was useful to the cause.

I had a wife in the camp outside the city. It had been a while since I had gone to see how she was doing. That might be considered doing something useful.

So I did leave my brethren to go visit my wife. While a fight was going on. A fight that would, no doubt, be completely unique amongst all the fights ever fought, so that somebody really should be right there to record every nuance of its unique ebb and flow.

Lady remained unchanged. She lurked halfway between life and death. She kept talking to herself in her sleep. What I saw did not inspire me with hope. What I heard only confused me. Mostly it was incoherent. Such individual words as were recognizable did not fall together at all sensibly.

A few minutes of that reminded me why I always resisted visiting till I had forgotten the despair a visit inspired.

122

Taglios:
Unknown Shadows

Only two unmarried second-cousins of Ghopal chose to leave the city with the Great General and the commander of the Greys. Because they had families the rest all chose to take their chances with the invaders.

Mogaba understood. In the coming confusion scores of his allies would be finding new looks, new races to be, while the conquerers scoured the city for enemies. Many would somehow fail ever to have heard of the Greys, let alone have contributed to that organization's criminal oppressions.

"Here," Mogaba said, leading the way out onto an ancient, rickety dock. "This one will do." He indicated an eighteen-foot boat that, from its aroma, had been bringing in fish since sometime early in the last century.

Mogaba invited himself aboard. Ghopal and the others followed warily. Shadar and large bodies of water had a relationship somewhat like that between cats and bathtubs. Mogaba said, "Untie those ropes. You really *do* know how to row, don't you?" Ghopal had made the claim.

Singh grunted. "But not competitively."

To Mogaba's astonishment they stole the boat without a challenge. He was amazed that a vessel so large had been untenanted. There should have been at least one family aboard. But tonight the entire waterfront was silent and unpopulated, as though the riverside nights were too terrible to endure.

Mogaba's internal struggle waxed and waned. He reminded himself that it was fast becoming too late to change his mind, to give in to his prideful, arrogant side. That weakness had brought about these terrible end days. How different his life and the world would have been had he been able to control his interior demons during the siege of Dejagore.

He would hardly be a hated and lonely old man whose memories were all of serving faithfully and well a parade of despicable masters.

The white crow found them while they were trying to work out the mechanics of raising the boat's lateen sail. There was a good breeze blowing, capable of carrying them up the river far more swiftly than could their incompetent rowing.

The bird settled in the rigging. "What are you doing? I did not give you permission to flee. Why are you running away? No battle has been lost."

The Shadar gawked. Mogaba thumped himself on the

chest. "No. A great war has been won. Here. At last. Now I go somewhere where I will do no more harm anymore forever."

Ghopal looked from him to the crow and back, gradually gaining understanding of both. He grew increasingly agitated and afraid as he did so.

The bird was capable of a range of voices, though it was only a haunted crow. "Turn this vessel shoreward. Now. I will tolerate no disobedience."

"You hold no terror for me anymore, old whore," Mogaba replied. "You hold no power over me. I won't be your toy or cats-paw tonight or ever again."

"You have no idea how much you will regret this. I won't be imprisoned forever. You will be the first chore on my list when I return. Ghopal Singh. Turn this disgusting tub around . . . awk!"

Ghopal had whacked the bird with the flat of his oar. Flailing, losing feathers, shrieking, it flung from the rigging into the fetid, muddy river. The retiring commander of the Greys observed, "That bird has an amazingly fowl vocabulary." He grinned. Then he began digging through the bag he had carried aboard. He really needed a sip of wine. His kinsmen scowled. "Glower all you want, you magpies! I'm my own man now!"

The tenor of the bird's incessant natter changed suddenly, becoming pure corvine terror. It flapped in panic as the surface of the river lifted it up.

The rising water tilted the boat precariously. Ghopal lost his grasp on his bottle. One of his cousins took a wild swing with his oar, swatting a gallon of water out of the thing taking form. His effort had no enduring effect.

"Holy shit!" Ghopal said from flat on his back. "What the hell is that?" He was staring over Mogaba's shoulder.

A *thing* loomed against the light of fires burning in the city. A thing resembling a huge duck capable of a grin filled with wicked, glistening teeth. And the thing was not alone.

"Oh, man," one of Ghopal's cousins sighed. "They're all around us. What are they?"

Mogaba sighed himself. He did not say that the monsters were not the sort of things people saw and lived to describe.

123

Taglios:
Crow Talk

Aridatha Singh had just gotten back to sleep when fiery pain pierced the back of his right hand. He leapt up and flung his arm out. He thought his lamp had somehow spilled burning oil and feared his cot would be on fire. But the lamp was not burning.

Not fire. Something had bitten him, then. Or maybe clawed him. And he had thrown it across the room, where it was struggling feebly and making incoherent chicken noises. Those people were attacking him directly now? He shouted for the sentries.

Once light filled the room he discovered that his visitor was an albino crow. One of the men threw a blanket over the bird and wrapped it up. Another examined Aridatha's hand. "That's one ragged looking critter, General. You might want to see a physician. It might be diseased."

"Send for soap and hot water. . . . It doesn't look like the skin is broken much. . . . What is that?"

The blanket with the bird inside had begun talking.

"It's talking," the soldier said, so utterly amazed that he could do nothing but state the obvious.

"Seal the window. Close the door. Get yourselves ready to

hit it with something when we turn it loose." He recalled that one of the Company chieftains sometimes carried ravens on his shoulders. And one of those was white.

Escape was no longer an option for the bird. Aridatha directed, "Turn it loose now."

The crow looked like someone had tried to drown it, then had decided to pluck it featherless instead. It was in terrible shape.

The bedraggled beast cocked its head right, left, surveying the chamber. It made an obvious effort to put aside its anger, to collect its pride and dignity.

Aridatha did not think this was the raven he had seen with that man Croaker. This one seemed smaller, yet more substantial.

The bird studied Singh first with one eye, then with the other. Then it eyed the sentries. It seemed to be awaiting something.

"You have something to say, say it," Aridatha suggested.

"Send them out."

"I don't think so." He motioned two soldiers into positions where they would be better able to swat the crow.

"I am not accustomed to . . ."

"Nor am I in the habit of taking back chat from birds. I assume you bring a message. Deliver it. Or I'll wring your neck and go on about my business."

"I fear you will live to regret this, Aridatha Singh."

In that moment, with the bird's voice changing, Singh understood that he was in touch with the Protector. But her enemies had buried her beneath the glittering plain. Had they not? "I await your message. If it's just a threat I'll have Vasudha step on your head."

"Very well. Until the day, Aridatha Singh. Aridatha Singh, you are now my viceroy in Taglios. Mogaba and Ghopal are no more. I will instruct you as to what steps to take. . . ."

"Excuse me. The Great General and General Singh have been killed?"

"They tried to do something foolish. For their trouble the enemy's shadow creatures destroyed them. Which elevates you to . . ."

Aridatha turned his back on the crow. "Jitendra. Get that word out. I want every company to disengage. The only exception is to be where the enemy won't let them. And get the word across the lines that I'm prepared to discuss terms."

The white crow flew into a cursing rage.

"Throw the blanket on that thing again, Vasudha. We may have some use for it later but I don't want to listen to its nagging now."

"You could get you a wife if you needed that, General."

124

Taglios:
The Sandbar

Already there were stories on the street about how the Great General had sacrificed himself in order to void the strictures of all the oaths and vows binding him and his allies. Because he had wanted to spare the city further devastation by the invading rebels and outlanders. Amazing. We had just started taking charge and already people were nostalgic for the good old days of the Protectorate.

Hard to blame them, I suppose. It was a generation ago that the Prahbrindrah Drah last saw the inside of his capital city.

Let them feel however they wanted. As long as they stayed out of my way.

Tobo and I drifted above the Palace, studying the ruin. Smoke still found its way out of the rock pile. Every few hours a little more caved in. A third had collapsed already.

That third included almost all of the occupied modern sector. Maybe the abandoned parts had been constructed from sterner stuff. They had survived generations of neglect.

Even during the worst fighting Aridatha had used volunteers from the City Battalions to keep sifting the ruins for survivors to rescue and bodies to deliver to distraught relatives. He continued in that role, now reinforced by units formerly committed to the fighting. Elsewhere, whole battalions now engaged the more stubborn fires instead of invaders.

I asked Tobo, "You really think they're still in there somewhere?" I meant Booboo and Goblin.

"I know they are. The hidden folk have seen them. They just can't remember how to get to them."

"Strange as it may seem, I need them out of there alive. Without them I can't keep my promise to Shivetya."

Tobo grunted. I had not included him in my planning. In fact, the inner circle still consisted of a council of one. Me. And I intended to keep it that way. Nothing spoken, nothing betrayed.

"I think Arkana's in love." Below, the Voroshk girl had come up with another excuse to consult Aridatha Singh.

Tobo grunted again. He was better than he had been but victory had given him no satisfaction. He would be a long time getting over the loss of his mom and dad.

I asked, "Have you found any trace of Mogaba or Ghopal Singh?" Aridatha said they were dead. He claimed to have been told so by the white crow—not an entirely reliable witness.

The boy studied me before responding. "They drowned. While trying to escape upriver. By boat. Evidently the boat capsized."

"I see."

My tone made him stare at me intently. I could not see his expression, of course. The Voroshk apparel concealed that. And mine masked my features. We continued to dress up because some people did not approve of our conquest. Incidents abounded.

Mostly, though, Taglios had heaved a huge collective sigh and began getting on with the business of life. Thus far there had been almost no retribution against those who had served the displaced regime. Most people seemed of the opinion that the Greys had done more good than harm, since they had repressed criminal behavior with a ferocity greater than they had shown to enemies of the Great General and the Protector.

In general, the masses of people were entirely indifferent to who ruled Taglios and its dependencies. The who seldom touched their lives deeply, one way or another.

The human species never ceases to amaze me. I would have bet more people would have cared a lot more. But from the inside nothing is ever what it looks like from without.

RAJADHARMA graffiti continued to appear. Some folks are never satisfied. THI KIM IS HERE was turning up now, too. I had not pressed the kid on that. He did not want to talk about it.

I would let it ride even though that mystery was not yet solved to my satisfaction. There had to be more to his relationship with the Unknown Shadows than had become obvious so far.

I left the boy and circled the Palace. Our men had replaced the City Battalions on that perimeter. They made a colorful line. City troops were clearing rubble, particularly in areas where Tobo's friends believed people were trapped. A number remained alive, caught inside interior rooms that had not collapsed. Now thirst was their implacable enemy.

All was going as it should. It seemed. But I was not comfortable. I had a sense of there being a wrongness somewhere. Intuition. Based upon subconscious cues.

I drifted away from the Palace, waving in passing to Shukrat, who just had to see Tobo after having completed a courier run to the approaching Prahbrindrah Drah and

Radisha. Once out of sight I put on speed and headed for the river.

I started at the downstream end of the waterfront. I drifted upstream. The boats were out. As they would have been had the fighting still been under way. I asked a few questions of terrified fishermen, not at all sure what I might find. The current had had ample time to carry bodies and wreckage down to the delta swamps.

Or perhaps not.

There is a miles-long sandbar just off the curve of the north bank. It has been there so long that it is an island now, with grass on its flanks, brush above that and trees along its highest parts. The channel on its north side is narrow, shallow and choked with mud. An overturned boat lay in the mouth of that channel. One dead man sprawled in the mud. A dozen Taglians clad only in loincloths were trying to right the boat preparatory to dragging it off the bar. None of those men showed the least interest in the corpse. But it was obviously Shadar and they were all Gunni.

The scavengers had a definite interest in not being anywhere around when people came swooping out of the sky in a billowing black cloud. A couple jumped into the channel and swam for the north bank. Others ran into the growth on the island's spine. A few tried to make it back to the boat that had brought them. It had beached a hundred yards down the bar.

The dead Shadar appeared to have been an officer of the Greys. I discovered a second corpse underneath the boat, also Shadar. There were disturbed crows in and above the nearby trees, which was interesting because we saw so few of those birds anymore.

I made a couple of lazy passes overhead, to finish scaring the birds away, before dropping carefully through the branches.

Mogaba was recognizable only because of the unique color of the bits of skin left to him. Ghopal Singh I identified only by deduction. They had been tortured. Terribly, and for a long time. Mogaba maybe for days. His corpse was not that old.

I slid downstream behind the island and eventually rejoined my own people. I searched out Arkana. "We need to talk, adopted daughter." I jerked a thumb. Somewhere up high, in the brilliant noonday sun.

She picked up on my concern. She drove upward a thousand feet, tending south, as though we were going to check on the Prahbrindrah Drah's progress. In fact, a sizable dust cloud could be seen to the south.

"What is it?" she asked.

"I think Tobo may be out of control. Or so close to it as makes no difference. If we're not careful we might all be sorry his mother isn't here to scold him. And that Sleepy and Murgen are gone. He may be a grown man but he still needs direction." I told her what I had found on the sandbar.

"Why tell me? You don't let anybody in on anything, Pop."

"Because I've seen you making moon eyes at General Singh. And he was a partner with the Great General and Ghopal Singh. If Tobo's really unhinged he might go after Aridatha next."

"Why do you blame Tobo?"

I led her through my reasoning, which relied heavily on my assessment of the character of the Great General. "Mogaba knew Aridatha wanted to spare Taglios from the fighting. He wanted that himself. He couldn't surrender, though. And Aridatha's sense of honor wouldn't let him desert Mogaba. So Mogaba decided to arrange it so Aridatha wouldn't be encumbered. And Tobo got him."

"You didn't say why you blame Tobo."

"Because only Tobo could've known what Mogaba was doing and where he would be doing it. There was something badly wrong on the river that night. All the waterfront people felt it and ran off to hide in the city."

"All right. Suppose it's true. What're you going to do?"

"I just did it. I told you to be careful. And now I'm going to see if my wife's gotten any better since this morning."

I knew Lady would not have done so. I had begun to lose hope for her.

125

Taglios:
An Afternoon Off

I took Lady out for a picnic. With a little help from my adopted daughters. In the vain hope that some sunlight and fresh air would make a difference when even Tobo's best effort could not shake the enchantment holding her. According to the boy wizard I was supposed to consider myself lucky. If she had not been Lady, had been some ordinary person, she would have been long dead. He assured me this was not the spell that had claimed Sedvod and still gripped Soulcatcher. I could not see any obvious difference—except that Lady was getting no worse.

His best advice was to take my questions to the perpetrator once we found him.

The girls left me alone with my honey. I held her hand and rambled on about a thousand things: recollections, current affairs, hopes. I shared my suspicions and concerns about Tobo, too, which might have been dangerous since I had no idea what might be listening.

Nothing I did helped her even a little, nor did it seem to do me any good. I fought the good fight against despair.

A squeaky clean, thoroughly polished corporal from Hsien trotted up. "Captain's compliments, sir, and could you come to the Palace? They think they may have located the Khadidas and the Daughter of Night."

"Damn! Yes. I'll be there as soon as I can. Tell them not to mess with anything. Tell them to be *very* careful. Those two are extremely dangerous."

They knew that, of course. And Tobo would be right there to remind them. But repetition never hurts. Not when it helps get you through the deadly times.

Shukrat and Arkana came running. "What's up?" Shukrat asked.

As I explained I reflected on how much better the girls were getting along. They seemed to have shed the conflicts they had brought into Captivity.

As we three got Lady ready to go back to my tent I asked Arkana, "Will you want to go home someday?"

"What?"

"Home. Where you were born. The world I used to call Khatovar. Do you want to go back? I think I could make it happen."

"But it's all destroyed."

"Not really. The First Father and Nashun the Researcher said so, but that was just to excuse their cowardice."

"I'm not sure I want to believe that."

"Good. Excellent. That's the way I want my kids to be. Skeptical. That's the truth according to Shivetya. And I'm not a hundred percent sure of our demonic friend myself."

"Why didn't you ask me if I want to go?" Shukrat demanded.

"Because you don't want to go. You just want to be where Tobo is."

"That isn't exactly a secret. It isn't a crime, either. But I'm not bereft of my senses. You'll sure never see me do some die-for-love kind of thing. If you guys do go, tell me. I'll decide what I want to do then."

126

Taglios:
Royal Return

I did not make it to the Palace. Shukrat beat me there and came right back with instructions to head for the South Gate. The Prahbrindrah Drah was about to arrive and Suvrin wanted *somebody* there to greet the man we had been touting as the city's legitimate ruler.

Per instructions I rounded up a few men from the City Battalions, along with a handful of their officers, and off I went, grumbling all the way. I expected the Prince's homecoming would be a huge disappointment for him and his sister.

Taglios did not care.

I told several people to spread the word, to try to get something going.

That did very little good. The route inward from the gate was never more than sparsely populated with spectators and the rare feeble cheer we did hear came from really old people.

I hate to waste pomp and pageantry. Not that we did put much on. Aridatha got to bring out his marching band, a little late. Never would have been better. They were terrible. And not just because what passes for music here is so alien. I have spent half my life in this end of the world. I asked Singh, "Those guys practice much?"

"They've been too busy being soldiers."

Aridatha had an attitude I appreciated. Each one of his men was expected to be a soldier first, and whatever else secondarily.

Singh said, "I do have to tell you, this Prince doesn't look very impressive. I hope he's a better ruler than he is a showman."

I was no longer sure bringing the Prince back would be good for Taglios, myself. There had been big changes in the city and bigger changes in the man. They might have nothing in common anymore.

I shrugged. "He's old. If he hasn't got what Taglios needs Taglios won't have to put up with him for long."

In the old days the Prince and I had gotten along well. Until he had turned on us. As an officer in my command he had shown a hunger for learning and a lust for doing the best thing. So I told him straightaway, when we met inside the South Gate, that his first order of business, now that he was back in business, had to be the establishment of a generally acceptable line of succession. Otherwise chaos would follow his demise.

"*Rajadharma*, old buddy. Let's get the job done."

My remarks earned me a tired growl and not much more. The Prince seemed used up and worn out. His sister showed more spark but had a lot more years on her because she had not shared the stasis of the Captivity with her brother. Chances were, nowadays, that she would go first, despite being the younger.

She could not be titular ruler, anyway. When she did exercise the power, during all those years, there had been a pretense of a regency, in place until the legitimate ruler could resume control. Because the Prahbrindrah Drah was still alive somewhere. Neither custom nor law allowed a woman to rule in her own right.

Arkana came to meet me with the news. "They've definitely found the Khadidas and the Daughter of Night, Pop." She was a willing participant in that charade now and, more and more, helping herself to a job as my personal assistant. Now, if I could just teach her written Taglian. . . . I suspect the frequency with which I crossed the path of Aridatha Singh had something to do with all that. Singh, I noted, had not failed to recognize what a tasty morsel my little girl was, either, though Voroshk protective apparel seldom flattered.

Tobo remained patient enough to wait until I reached the Palace. Barely. And only out of impatient courtesy, because that was my real daughter and my former friend in there.

My real daughter. A grown woman, whom I had never seen. Arkana, known less than a year, was more daughter to me in life. And Narayan Singh was more a father to Booboo.

Aridatha was there and interested. I wondered why. Then I recalled that he had seen Booboo a few times before and those women have a way of getting under your skin without ever trying.

It did not occur to me that he might be thinking more about the Khadidas.

At first the Prince was put out by everyone's sudden loss of interest in him . . . then he got a good look at what had happened to the Palace.

He moaned aloud, a textbook cry of anguish. He managed some respectable gnashing of teeth.

Suvrin stepped in. The little pudgeball could be weasel-slick handling people when he wanted. Which might be the ideal leadership skill for the times. I turned to Arkana, gave her special instructions. She flew off to my rooms in the building we had taken for our headquarters. Once upon a time it had been a Greys barracks.

Most of the Greys have vanished. We all pretended not to notice that there are a disproportionate number of Shadar in the City Battalions, say compared to when we were duking it out with them in the streets.

Aridatha was sharing his own good fortune. Though there was less popular inclination toward vengeance than I had expected. And that little focused entirely on individuals.

The Radisha Drah also let out a disconsolate wail on discovering the state of the Palace. She and her brother remained still and silent for minutes. Then she slew the silence with another cry of pain.

I told Suvrin, "I hope they don't decide that this is all our fault and they just have to get even." I did not think they would be that stupid, after having survived what they had suffered for having turned on us before, but with royalty you never know. They think differently than real people. The real world never quite seems to reach them.

Smoke still trickled out of the ruins, here and there. While we watched a small avalanche of weakened masonry cascaded down.

The Prince observed, "The stonework must have suffered more than we thought during the earthquake."

"Hunh?" That had happened so long ago that I had forgotten it. "You're probably right. Plus the Protector never wasted a copper on maintenance while she was in charge." I approached Tobo, who continued to prance about impatiently. "Where are my treasures?"

As I asked, Arkana swooped down, black cloth popping and crackling in the wind. She carried One-Eye's spear and his ugly old hat. The hat still smelled of the ugly old man who had worn it.

"Right there where the red flag is."

Poles with colored streamers indicated points where the Unknown Shadows had detected something human under the rubble. There were just two red ribbons. The rest were black. There would be no rush to dig there. The red streamer not indicated by Tobo was the focus of frenzied activity.

I asked, "What's over there?"

"Ten to twelve people trapped in one of the treasury strong rooms. We're sending water and soup down through bamboo pipes. They'll be all right."

"Uhm." I could imagine the nightmares they would suffer for the rest of their lives. "Just hang onto that stuff," I told Arkana. I studied the stone around the base of the red-streamer pole. "Tobo, are they conscious down there?"

"I don't think so."

"I'd hate to think they're just waiting to do something obnoxious when we dig them out."

He said, "We can just leave them there. Without water they'll die."

"It's a solution." But not one that interested me. Only Booboo would really suffer. "Suvrin, may I?" When he nodded I beckoned some men who were standing around awaiting instructions. If the girl was aware I was sure we would get a dose of "love me" real quick. Which meant only people in Voroshk clothing should do the final digging.

The Khadidas and Daughter of Night had crawled into a corner of their hiding place when the collapse came. The walls had held up just enough. But they had not had time to collect food and water.

Sadly, my baby did have a lamp and supplies and did make a valiant attempt to keep right on enscribing the Books of the Dead, perhaps in hope of lending Kina enough strength to save her. She could not have had much hope otherwise.

I thought a lot about what Booboo had been through in her near quarter century. About what had been done to her and what she believed she was. The loving part of me thought it might be a priceless mercy if she was saved the cruelty of reawakening.

It never got beyond being a notion. No argument I could present would ever convince Lady that that was appropriate. She wanted a little Lady so badly.

I discovered the Radisha beside me. It was amazing how much she had aged. She even carried a cane. "It's true, you know," she said in a weary voice.

"What's that?" Though I knew what she was going to say.

"The coming of the Black Company did mean the end of Taglios. Just not the way we imagined."

"All we ever wanted was to pass on through."

She nodded, keeping her bitterness contained.

"You think we were hard on Taglios? Consider how happy the Shadowmasters must be."

"But you haven't finished with Taglios," the Prahbrindrah Drah observed, joining us. "I've just heard what happened to Lady. How is she?"

"Stable." He was another of those men who had been infatuated with my wife at one time. "And you're right. In a way. As long as people try to push us around people get hurt. But that shouldn't last much longer. We're close to where we have to go." I stepped forward, spoke to the men digging, first in the language of the Children of the Dead, then in Taglian. "We're getting close. Hold up till those of us who are protected can help. Tobo! Girls. They're almost through over here."

Not far off more interior brickwork surrendered to the seduction of gravity.

127

Taglios:
And My Baby

The soldiers created a precarious opening through which someone might wriggle. I asked for a lantern, meaning to be first inside, but Tobo seized it when it arrived. I did not argue. He was better equipped than I.

Seconds after the boy began to duckwalk a blast of urine-colored light ripped through the opening. It glanced off Tobo, hit a block of stone, scattered. It was a potent blast. Stone melted. And one stray ricochet found the Prahbrindrah Drah.

The results were ugly. And instantly fatal.

"That was it," Tobo called back, unaware of the disaster. "That's all he had. He's out of it now. Croaker, help me drag them out."

The Radisha began to wail.

The boy recognized the scope of the disaster immediately. The Taglian empire was, as of this moment, without an acceptable helmsman. Was without legitimate direction. "It'll have to wait a minute," I said. "The Prince is hurt. I want to get him to medical care right now." Maybe, just one more time, we could pretend the supreme authority was fine but staying out of sight. Soulcatcher got away with it. The Great General got away with it. Why not my own band of opportunists?

I feared there had been too many witnesses, though Suvrin and Aridatha took up the pretense immediately and the Radisha herself joined me after only a few heartbeats. She put on a creditable show of threatening me with serious unpleasantness if her brother happened to die.

Now aware that political disaster threatened, Tobo launched some glitzy distraction. To which I paid little attention because I was desperate to get the Prince out of the public eye. There was a lot of flash behind me, and changing colors playing through the ruins. A big bunch of masonry went down. And Shukrat began helping Tobo pull the Khadidas out of the ground.

Aridatha's men hauled the Prince's litter away.

The prince seen to, Arkana and I began to ease through the rubble toward the hole. I beckoned more stretcher-bearers. The thing being dragged into the light did not look dangerous. It looked like an old, worn-out version of a Goblin who was already dead.

"You want these now?" Arkana asked.

"Hang on just another minute. Get him over here, guys. On the stretcher. Easy. Easy! Tobo. Can you wake him up? Just for a second? Long enough for him to recognize me and what I'm doing?"

"Probably. If you want to risk it." There was a choke in the boy's voice. He looked at the spear and the ugly hat and wanted to believe that I had a way to reach the Goblin trapped inside the Khadidas. The Goblin who was always like an uncle to him.

"Oh, shit!" I said. "Wait! Wait!"

"What?"

"I just had an ugly thought. About how Kina might react through Lady if we drive the devil out of Goblin."

Tobo sucked in a bucket of air, released it. "I don't see how she could work that. But why take a chance? She is the Mother of Deception. Shuke, honey, do me a favor. Get the small carpet from my room. Just fold it up and bring it back. We'll use that to haul them away."

Shukrat jumped onto her post and zipped away. While he waited Tobo had an awning erected to keep potential rain off Goblin, then snaked back into the hole. He did not ask for help so I stood back with Aridatha and Arkana, insides turning over, awaiting my first glimpse of Booboo.

I asked Singh, "The fires under the rubble never go out. What the hell keeps burning?"

"Five hundred years worth of archives. Everything that belonged to the Inspector General of the Records. It'll make for interesting times when we try to put things back together."

Shukrat, the little darling, obviously knew her way around Tobo's quarters. She was back with a small, folded flying carpet before the kid himself poked his head back out of the hole. With Arkana's help she snapped the frame into position, stretched the fabric taut.

Arkana finally found nerve enough to speak to Aridatha directly, in a nonbusiness capacity. "You think it's going to rain?"

You could see she wanted to melt like a slug freshly sprinkled with salt. All that work to find the nerve to speak and something that feeble was all she could get out. When fat raindrops had begun plunking down at random intervals nearly a minute before.

She was just a kid.

They had the Khadidas on the flying carpet now. And a couple of soldiers, one Taglian and one from Hsien, had hold of a pair of ankles.

"You all right, Pop?" Arkana asked, holding onto my left arm.

"She looks just like Lady did the first time we met." In a time of terror. There was terror here, now, but of an entirely different sort.

"Then your wife must have had some filthy hygiene habits in her younger days."

"Ah, but she was eager to learn. Tobo, can you make sure Booboo doesn't wake up until I want her to?" I did not want to have to cope with her witchery. "And let's keep these two away from each other from now on. We don't need them getting their heads together."

"We don't need them, period," someone muttered. Shukrat, I realized. Shukrat did not like the way Tobo kept eyeballing the Daughter of Night.

Nor did my other adopted offspring particularly approve of the contemplative stares of Aridatha Singh.

Tobo called, "Croaker, you want to wake up yourself? Just for a minute? So you can take a look at her? See if anything's missing or broken?"

One of the city soldiers told another that everything looked just fine to him. A little soap and some clean clothes . . .

I never thought I would be a father and have to pretend not to hear such remarks.

The man was right. She was a beautiful child. Exactly like her mother. And like Lady's, most of her beauty lay right on the surface. I had to remind myself not to be taken in by what I saw or by what I wanted to feel. My emotions would not be trustworthy. They might not be my own. The Mother of Deceit had not left the game.

I knelt beside my daughter. My emotions were engaged indeed. I felt a thousand years old and utterly powerless. It took a major application of will to touch her.

Her skin felt cold.

In moments I reported, "She's got lots of bruises and

scrapes but there isn't any serious damage. Nothing permanent. She is dehydrated." She shook each time I touched her,
as though I was massaging her with pieces of ice. "She'll
recover, if we take care of her. Put her in with Lady."

Tobo said, "You'll need somebody to stay with her. Somebody who can control her."

"I will."

"I will."

Shukrat and Arkana both volunteered.

Well. Were they *that* concerned about competition from a
beat-up, unconscious woman who knew absolutely nothing
about men?

I would bet Tobo was grinning when he said, "All right,
ladies. Work yourselves out a schedule. Croaker, what do
you plan to do about Goblin?"

Suvrin seemed a little irked. Events were going forward
without consulting the new Captain of the Black Company.
But in matters concerning Booboo and the Khadidas he was
no expert.

"Stash him. I'll wait till I'm well-rested to deal with him.
Meantime, we need somebody to crawl into that hole and
collect up all of Booboo's scribblings. Somebody from
Hsien, preferably. Somebody illiterate. We'll take no chance
anybody will read that stuff. I'll take care of it. But right
now I'm going to go take a nap. I'm totally exhausted."

128

Taglios:
Another Great General

I was worried. I pranced from foot to foot like a little boy at a wedding who really needed to pee. It was another day and I still had not gotten started with Booboo and the Khadidas. Giving them and their Goddess any time at all was bound to lead to mischief.

But I had more immediate responsibilities. The fighting was over. Our obligation to the dead had to be handled now. And a huge city, with many dead of its own, had to be kept on a tight rein. Recent disasters would encourage plotters and conspirators.

The Children of the Dead knew how to put on a memorial for fallen comrades. Deep-voiced drums muttered and grumbled. Horns conjured forth the mood and gloom of a chilly, rainy morning despite a bright, cloudless winter sky. The soldiers paraded in all their brilliant colors, with all their thousands of banners. The locals were suitably impressed. We sent Sleepy off in more style than she could have hoped for while she lived. We said our good-byes to a great many people.

Then we stood back and rendered appropriate honors as Aridatha Singh directed equally large, if not nearly so dramatic, ceremonies honoring those who had fallen on behalf of the Protectorate. And when that was done we joined the local soldiers and the most important men of the city in honoring the Prahbrindrah Drah.

His funeral was the grandest I ever attended. I developed the distinct impression that all those leading men had gathered, however, to eyeball one another suspiciously rather than to mourn the passing of a ruler none had seen since they were young.

Aridatha Singh was popular with these men. Because Aridatha Singh had gathered to himself the loyalties of the survivors of the Second Territorial Division, the Greys, and the commanders of the rural garrisons nearest the city. Aridatha Singh had become the most powerful man in the Taglian Territories, despite having done little to acquire that power—except to be competent and a nice guy.

They say that when the hour comes, so will the man. Sometimes fate will even conspire to put a competent, honest man in the right place at the right time. Almost overnight the graffiti began giving Aridatha Mogaba's old title, Great General.

Now, if he could just manage to get by without antagonizing the occupiers.

I tried to keep an eye on Tobo but that was difficult with a kid so talented.

129

Taglios:
Open Tomb, Open Eyes

The hours of ceremony ground me down. I wanted to put myself away for another long nap. But I refused to give the Queen of Darkness any further respite.

"These are them," Arkana told me in perfectly colloquial bad Taglian, indicating eight bitty wooden kegs. "Eight different men took turns crawling in there and stuffing papers—and everything else they could find—into a keg. Which I had sealed up as soon as the man came out. By an illiterate cooper."

"You are a treasure indeed, daughter dear. Gentlemen, let's build us a bonfire." I had brought a couple of carts loaded with wood purchased from a wood seller whose

usual customers were people who needed firewood for
funeral ghats. I had been surprised to find he had any stock
left, considering recent events.

The gentlemen I spoke to all hailed from Hsien. They
knew only that the eight kegs contained the hopes of life of
a monster more blackhearted than the legendary Shadowmasters who had tortured the Land of Unknown Shadows.
And that was all they needed to know.

The pyre went up quickly, the kegs scattered throughout
it. A fraction of me bemoaned the fate of the latest incarnation of the Books of the Dead. I hate seeing any book
destroyed. But I did not interfere when the oil splashed and
the fireballs zipped in.

My reluctance might be Kina trying to manipulate me.

I stayed there until I was confident that my natural daughter's life's work had been consumed completely by the flames.

In some myths Hagna, god of fire, is Kina's mortal
enemy. In others, when she is in her Destroyer avatar, he is
her ally.

The more I am exposed to the Gunni pantheon the more
confused I become.

"What task now?" I wondered aloud.

Everyone but Arkana and a few curious street kids, the
near-feral ones called jengali, had moved along. A ragged,
bemused white crow had been hanging around, too, but it
had nothing to say. It had been doing a lot of sticking close
and keeping its beak shut lately.

"Time to wake somebody up, Pop. Your wife, your daughter or the Khadidas."

I surveyed the workmen clearing rubble. Most were civilians now, supervised by soldiers there just to keep them
from stealing any treasures they unearthed.

The masonry had stopped collapsing. The fires had
burned out. The popular consensus was that an all-new
palace should be erected, once the old structures had been
cleared away.

I could not imagine what treasures and surprises might surface if they did demolish and remove the whole rambling monster. No one ever knew the palace in its entirety. No one but a long-dead wizard named Smoke.

The death pyre of the Books of the Dead attracted more jengali, who wanted to take advantage of the warmth.

Shukrat glowered at Arkana. Seemed Arkana was not doing her share of Booboo watching. And Arkana did not care if Shukrat was pissed off.

I noticed a change in Lady. She did not seem to be in a sort of coma anymore. She seemed to be in a normal but deep sleep. I threw open a window. I am a firm believer in the health benefits of fresh air. The scruffy white crow appeared almost immediately. I asked, "How long has this been going on?" I had my back to Booboo. Cleaned and groomed and dressed in decent clothing she was quite the sleeping beauty. I tried not to look at her long. Seeing her still ripped at my heart.

"What?" Shukrat asked. She stuck her tongue out at Arkana.

"The snoring. Lady didn't snore before." I meant since she had fallen under the spell. Before, she had snored for as long as I had been sleeping with her. Though she refused to believe it.

Shukrat said, "She started right after we brought the Daughter of Night in. I didn't think anything about it."

"No reason you should."

Arkana nodded. "I never noticed her not snoring."

The white crow chuckled from the window sill. I asked, "Did she snore when she was a kid?"

The crow made a noise. The girls looked at me, then at the bird. No dummies, they realized right away that it was not just an albino with bad personal habits. Being sorceresses they soon understood that it was a genuine crow, too, rather than some creature whose usual form was no form, and out of sight.

"Assuming she is sleeping, she's been there a long time. You'd think she would've wakened on her own." I touched my wife gently. She did not respond. I shook her, much less tenderly. She groaned, muttered, rolled onto her side, pulled her knees up. I said, "Don't give me that stuff. It's time to get up."

The girls smiled. They felt my relief.

She *was* just sleeping now, even if that had been going on for a long time and might go on for a while more.

"Come on, woman! We've got work to do. You've had enough sleep for ten people."

"She's sure been getting my share."

Lady cracked an eyelid. At the same time she muttered something incoherent that sounded suspiciously like one of her traditional early morning threats.

I said, "All that rest hasn't improved her disposition any. I'll remember this next time she claims lack of sleep is why she's cranky."

"You want me to dump a bucket of cold water on her?" Arkana asked. She could be a presumptuous little witch.

"She does need a bath."

Lady growled again, but this time in a lame attempt to be cheerful.

I told her, "Don't even try to be nice." The way the human body works, returning from a coma in a good humor is flat impossible.

Her throat was dry and tight. After we dealt with that, she asked, "Where are we? How long was I down this time?"

I had lost track.

"Fifteen days? At least. Probably more," Shukrat said. "You were sleeping for all of us. We were all too busy."

Lady examined her surroundings. She knew she had not been here before. She could not Booboo from where she sat.

I told her, "The war is over. We won. Sort of. Aridatha Singh surrendered. We offered them good terms."

Lady grunted, mind not working swiftly. "Mogaba let him do that?"

"The Great General isn't with us anymore."

"I need to talk to you about that, Pop," Shukrat said. "I went out to that sandbar."

I signed her to silence. Something from the hidden realm would be around somewhere. I continued talking to Lady. "A lot of people aren't with us anymore. Including almost everybody who went to town with us the night you got hit. Sleepy, too, later on. In an ambush. Suvrin took over. He'll be all right. He'll grow into it. As long as we help him."

Arkana added, "Don't forget the Prince and General Chu. And Mihlos. I miss him."

"Because he panted around behind you like a horny hound dog," Shukrat sneered. "And you just led him on."

"And who went out of her way to make sure she wiggled and jiggled whenever he was around?"

"Girls?"

"What?"

"I'm just jealous. Where were you when I was Mihlos's age?"

Lady interrupted. "What else do I need to know?"

"The Palace fell down. We've occupied the city. Aridatha Singh is in charge now and gets Arkana wiggling and jiggling whenever he comes around. We don't know how the succession will work out. We captured Booboo and the Khadidas. We destroyed the Books of the Dead. Again. Booboo is right over there. If you want to see her." I extended a hand to help her rise. If she wanted. "She's pretty."

"I want. But I won't be able to stand up by myself. I don't think I'll even be able to sit up for long without help."

The crow snickered.

Lady gave the bird a long, hard look. Then she offered me its twin.

I asked, "How's your connection with Kina?"

"What do you mean, how is my connection?"

"Did I stutter? Is it still there? Is it stronger? Is it weaker?"

"Why?"

"Because I want to know. Why not answer me?"

The girls were startled. They looked like they wished they were anywhere else. But they spread out.

"She didn't take me over while I was sleeping, if that's what you're after. I did have some awful nightmares, though. It was like I was trapped inside her imagination for an age. But she ignored me. She had something on her mind." She came close to grinding her teeth with each word. She did not want to open up. "The nightmare went away a while ago."

I could understand. The only place I want to reveal myself, even a little, is here, where hardly anyone will ever notice.

"Did you have any sense of time? I'm thinking maybe something happening here changed what you were going through there."

"Sense of time? It was forever. And no time at all. Kina doesn't experience time the way we do. I don't think. She sure doesn't let it oppress her. Come on. Show me my baby. Before I collapse." She strained to get up.

Shukrat and Arkana got hold of her arms and helped her up. Arkana asked, "She always this cranky when she wakes up, Pop?"

"You're going to become part of the family, get used to it. You will if you don't take it personal." I chuckled when Lady asked me how I would like it if she stopped getting personal. "She's not bad today."

The crow hissed. Clearly, it did not care if Lady figured it out. In fact, what it said sounded like, "Sister, sister." Which was the taunt Lady had employed a few years ago, when she was looking out from behind the eyes of another crow.

Curious, the white crows. There has been one around, off and on, since the siege of Dejagore. Back then Murgen had been the mind behind the bird's eyes. Most of the time. Apparently. But was Shivetya the mind behind the crow-riding minds? Could he have had that much power to affect events outside the glittering plain?

That would explain a good deal. Maybe even Murgen's former difficulties with his place in time. But that would mean that Soulcatcher was not responsible for much of what we believed were her crimes. I was not sure I wanted it to be that way.

The bird snickered. Like it could read my mind.

Soulcatcher always had had a knack for reading me.

"We lost Murgen, too," I said as we moved into position facing one another over the unconscious girl.

"I understood that. From your having told me how many we lost. That would be everyone not wearing Voroshk clothing. Correct?"

"Except for one damned lucky soldier from Hsien who managed to be behind the right person at the right time. Lucky is now Tam Do's official nickname."

"Must be in the blood," Lady muttered, forcing herself to look at the girl. "The women of my blood are fated to spend most of their existence trapped and asleep." She rested her weight more fully on the girls, extended a hand to touch Booboo's cheek. She lapsed into the language of the Jewel Cities. "Asleep like this was the only way I ever saw my mother. She was the one they told the first Sleeping Beauty stories about. Her Prince Charming never came. My father did. And he was content with her the way she was."

Now there was a slice of horror to lug around in the back of your brain: knowing that your mother was not even aware that you had been born.

And we like to whine about how cruel the world is today.

They were giants in the olden days.

We will be giants ourselves five hundred years from now.

"So this is our baby." She stared. "Conceived on a battlefield." Her emotions were plain upon her face. Never had I seen her looking more vulnerable.

"This is our baby."

"Shall we wake her up?"

"I don't think so. Not now, anyway. Life is insane enough right now without asking for more trouble."

That did not set well. Not at all. Lady wanted to establish some kind of emotional dialog with this flesh of her flesh. For my part, I found that now I had been exposed directly, the emotional distress was fading away. I do not believe my thoughts were skewed by might-have-beens and wish-that-weres.

Lady did concede that it might not be a good plan to waken Booboo without Tobo there for backup.

She did not do anything untoward but she did have the girls breathing nervously for a while.

130

Taglios:
Khadidas

Tobo was there to help when I wakened my old friend Goblin, who had become the unwilling vessel of the Khadidas.

It was not that difficult once Tobo's controlling spells had been cancelled. Tobo shook Goblin while I stood by. And once the little shit began to stir Tobo stood by while I nagged.

The little man's eyelids snapped open. The eyes behind them were not the eyes of the hedge wizard Goblin. I was looking straight into large chips of the darkness. Those eyes seemed to want to suck me in.

The mouth of the Khadidas opened, preparing to vent some infamy or blasphemy. I interposed One-Eye's ragged old hat between Kina's slave and myself. The effect was electric. The Goblin body convulsed as though I had whacked it with a hot poker. I slapped the hat down on its head.

"Lift," I told Tobo, who had placed himself at the head of Goblin's cot, out of the Khadidas's field of vision. I held the hat in place while Tobo raised Goblin into a sitting position. "It works. Better than I hoped."

"Better than I thought it would, for sure."

"One-Eye always did underplay it when he did something right." The wicked light had left Goblin's eyes. Now he just looked empty. Not even a thousand-yard stare, there. More like nobody at home at all.

"Do the spear."

I did the spear. But, man, was I reluctant to trust the wisdom of a dead man when it came to putting that potent a tool into the hands of a devil.

I stood it up in front of Goblin, its butt between his heels. I wrapped his hands around the black shaft. Then I shoved One-Eye's filthy felt relic down onto his head even more solidly. *Then* I gripped his hands hard, squeezing them onto the silver-and-black wood.

Life began to enter his eyes.

I told Tobo, "Not as dramatic as watching a baby being born but dramatic enough." Even a dummy like me did not need a map to see that we were conjuring up the real Goblin.

A Goblin in pain so deep I was aware immediately that only Lady could begin to understand.

I settled myself on a stool. Tobo eased Goblin onto a chair with an upright back, then planted himself on the edge of the cot. Goblin kept turning from one of us to the other, tears streaming but unable to speak, however hard he tried. He reached out to Tobo in a silent plea for contact.

"Careful of that hat," I said. "I'm already thinking about nailing it to his head." And thinking about how wonderful a friend One-Eye had been, too. Because he had foreseen some possibility like this and had invested his final years in making a rescue feasible.

I choked up for a moment, thinking I never had a friend who would go that far for me. Then I recalled that Sleepy had spent fifteen years working to exhume the Captured. And now, barely five years later, all those people but Lady and I were gone. Belly up. Up in smoke. Finished.

Soldiers live.

Not once had Sleepy ever behaved like she believed that she had wasted her life. But I am sure she had thought it sometimes. Regarding some individuals.

I said, "You ought to keep at least one hand on the spear, Goblin." We had done nothing to rid him of the Khadidas. The monster had been pushed back into the pit where it had lain till it had sprung forward to seize control, but now behind feeble barriers. The monster was much stronger than Goblin. We would have to work hard to keep it suppressed.

"What're we going to do with you?" I asked. And felt a twinge of guilt. Because I had plans for him already. Plans that might change the world.

"What do you think, Goblin? You going to help us help you hang on?"

Goblin was getting some muscle control back. He managed a weak, "Yeah," as he nodded his head, too.

"I'm going to leave everything in the hands of you two gentlemen," Suvrin said. He nodded politely to Goblin. "I scarcely knew this man. And then mainly from the perspective of being the butt of practical jokes he and One-Eye played. Meaning I might not be disinterested even if I tried. What is that stuff around the bottom of that thing on his head?"

"Glue. That *thing* is a hat. You must've seen One-Eye wearing it. The old fart rigged it up with some spells, planning for something like what did happen."

"You told me."

"All right. The glue is because we don't want the hat to come off. Ever. If we could come up with a way that would leave him free to feed himself and scratch his butt we'd glue his hands to One-Eye's spear, too."

There is something about becoming Captain that takes the humor out of a man. It had gotten to Suvrin already. He never cracked a smile. He asked, "You gotten any useful information out of him? Not yet? When?"

"I don't know. He's coming around. Really. Remember, in practical terms he's been dead for six years. He's having trouble figuring out how to use his body again. Especially his tongue. Meanwhile, the Khadidas is still inside of him trying to take over again."

"And Lady?"

I was more concerned about my wife than I was about Goblin. She was acting strange. It did not seem like I knew her anymore. I had resurrected all my earlier worries about her connection with Kina. Kina was the master manipulator and planner. Kina schemed schemes ages long and many layers deep.

But Kina was slow. Very slow. Which was why she favored plots that required years to ripen. She could not handle swiftly changing fortunes.

"Lady is a puzzle right now," I confessed. "But a benign one."

Goblin made a gurgling sound. The Khadidas was working hard to keep him from talking.

Suvrin asked, "Do you know anything about the leading men of Taglios?"

"Not the current crop. Except for types. My advice would just be, don't ever turn your back on any of them. You could talk to Runmust Singh. If he survived the latest fighting." I had a feeling he might have been with Sleepy in that ambush. "Or you could just ask Aridatha to loan you a couple of advisors."

Suvrin seemed unusually amenable to consulting for a Captain of the Company.

He told me, "We need to resume our lessons. So I can study the Annals."

I responded, "We need some peace for that. Maybe a few years. We could build a new Company while we're at it."

Goblin gurgled again and nodded.

The little creature was like a puppy in some ways.

I told Suvrin, "I need to talk to Goblin a while." Once our hesitant new commander stepped out, I said, "We need to work out ways around the Khadidas's interference."

Nod.

"And that's how we'll do it, I guess. Unless it can control more than your speech." I peered at the little man. He did not respond. I realized that I had not posed a yes or no question. "Can it do that?"

No.

"All right, then. The most critical question of all. Is the Khadidas in direct contact with Kina?"

No. And yes. And a shrug. So we proceeded to play a game of a thousand questions during which I seemed to go the wrong direction, no matter where I went, making him gurgle in frustration. His best efforts to speak seldom produced more than one recognizable syllable.

Eventually, despite my density, I got it. The Khadidas could communicate with the Goddess only when it was in control of the Goblin flesh. It could not do so when it was not in control.

That made sense. Some. Though I had been cautioned to remember that the Goblin I was interviewing was actually a ghost that had not been able to leave when its body died and had been reanimated by the breath of the Goddess.

"That is exciting news, Goblin. Look, I have a plan." Difficult as it was, I dredged a form of it up from its hidden place deep down inside me, hoping the Goddess had no way of listening in. My plan depended entirely on my understanding of the Goblin I had known for so long, hoping he had not altered drastically during the past two decades. A man might change a lot in that much time—if he had to spend part of it dead and enslaved by the Mother of Deceivers.

On the surface Goblin seemed to like my plan, as I presented it. Seemed willing to participate. Even seemed enthusiastic about plunging One-Eye's spear into the blackest of hearts.

I told him, "I don't want to waste one minute I don't have to. You understand?"

Nod. Even a gurgled, "Yes!" With enthusiasm. With outright eagerness.

"I'll be back soon." I felt almost bad, not telling a dead man all of the truth.

131

Around Taglios: Aerial Recon

I found Arkana and asked if she wanted to go flying, nodding to indicate that she really did want to make a tour of the upper air. For the benefit of the curious I mentioned wanting to check rumors that troops loyal to the Protectorate were headed toward the city. One force had crossed the Main at Vehdna-Bota. Another was gathering out east, near Mukhra in Ajitsthan, where Mogaba had enjoyed considerable popularity among the tribes. Since those rumors were beginning to make a lot of people nervous nobody would be surprised that I would want to take a look.

And that is what we did while we were aloft, because it was work that had to be done. Doing the work, though, gave me time to talk to Arkana.

She replied, "I can see one big problem with your plan. Maybe. What happens to the plain and the shadowgates? You asked me if I wanted to go home. The answer is yes. I don't think to stay, though. Just to see what happened there. To bury my dead, I guess you could say. But I don't see how that could keep from complicating everything else if I had to do it first because there wouldn't be any way later."

"You're right. And I need to do what I've got to do as soon as I can. Before Kina catches on." If she had not foreseen the possibilities already. Or learned of them from Goblin. Or Shivetya. Or from Lady, who was smart enough to guess what I was thinking. Sometimes. "Particularly before my wife catches on. Or starts thinking I'm chasing around."

We were approaching the River Main, heading for Vehdna-Bota. There were pillars of smoke north of the ford, away from the small settlement. But not many.

Arkana told me, "That's not much of an army."

"Not in any hurry to get into harm's way, either, looks like. There's plenty of daylight left they could use for traveling."

Not in any hurry. When we went down for a closer look we found men scattering like startled roaches.

"Somebody covering his ass," I said. "Making a show of honoring his obligations. That bunch will never actually get to Taglios."

We went back up. We talked, not just about what had to be accomplished. Arkana seemed able to relax, now. Seemed to have made peace with the bad times. Some manage that with comparative ease. Others remain crippled for life. Those are not the sort who remain soldiers. They become ex-soldiers and get intimate with wine or poppies.

I asked about her leg.

She laughed. "I can be one of the old folks now. I can use it to predict the weather."

"It's all right otherwise?"

"Yes."

"I do good work."

"Lots of practice."

"You get that in this racket."

We flew back toward Taglios, chatting in a relaxed way, me thinking that this was what it would have been like had

Booboo grown up with her parents. Me fooling myself. Lying to myself. No child would grow up even as normal as Arkana if they had Lady for a mother and me for a father.

Maybe I had found the way. Adopt them after they have gotten through their formative years.

We were passing south of Taglios, going to scout the forces gathering in Ajitsthan, when Arkana spotted a billowing figure climbing toward us. "That's Shukrat."

"Have you two made peace? Real peace?"

"Sort of. Mainly because we've only got each other. From back home. If it wasn't for that we wouldn't even be talking. Partly it's because of family stuff. Things our parents did to each other. And partly it's us. She's too cute and too sweet and dumb as a bucket of rocks. But all she's ever had to do is make big eyes or bounce a little and look helpless."

"And you were the smart one. Always expected to figure it out for yourself."

"Yes."

"Well, you're growing up to be the prettier one, too. Shukrat's going to be all freckles and frump before long."

We slowed so Shukrat could catch up. She came up on my other side. I asked, "What's up, other daughter?"

"Croaker, I wanted to talk about what happened to those men on that island. That scares me. Really bad. I really like Tobo. A lot." I was sure she was bright red behind her facial wraps. She did blush easily. "But I don't think I want to be involved with anyone capable of doing that."

"We're all capable of that, Shukrat. Put in the right place at the right time and given a motive. It's the people around us that keep us from doing it."

"What do you mean?"

"I mean, Tobo cares about you. Probably a lot more than he's willing to admit. He's a passionate kid.

"Because he's what he is he's always had the capacity for huge evil, Shukrat. You know, nobody starts out to be a villain. Not the Shadowmasters. Not my wife or her sister. Not even the Voroshk. But being powerful can turn you villainous. Because there's nothing to stop you from doing whatever you want to do. Except for something inside you. For Tobo, for a long time, that something was his love and respect for his parents. He fought with Sahra every day but there was no way he was ever going to do something that would disappoint her. While she was alive. After she disappeared the brake on his dark side became his father. But now Murgen is gone, too. So there's only one more person whose good opinion is important enough to him to keep him from letting himself go."

Shukrat had to think about that for a while. She was nowhere as dim as Arkana claimed but there were times when it took her a while to get her mind wrapped all the way around complex issues.

"You're saying me caring about him is what will keep him from doing that stuff again?"

"Yes. I think that. But I also think you have to confront him with your knowledge and make him understand that you won't accept *any* excuses for behavior like that. Don't nag. Don't carp. State your case firmly and clearly, then shut up. Don't negotiate. You have to mark out an absolute limit he'll always know is there. And stick with it. You always have to know it's there, too."

Shukrat nodded.

While I waited to see if she got it I told Arkana, "I might turn out to be pretty good at this fatherly advice stuff."

"You're definitely long-winded enough."

"Thanks a lot."

"For the record, I think you're right. What you said to her."

"You know what she's talking about?"

"She warned me. In case I wanted to watch out for General Singh. Not long after you warned me about it. I had to go see what you were excited about, didn't I?"

The girl rose in my estimation every damned day.

* * *

The force gathering at Mukhra was much more of a threat
than that at Vehdna-Bota. It would mean major new trouble
if Aridatha, as the new Great General, was unable to sell the
concept of peace to Mogaba's old allies.

132

Taglios:
Wife and Child

Lady was sitting beside Booboo again. Or still. I pulled
up a stool opposite her. "Want me to take over for a
while? Give you a chance to get out and about and stretch
your legs? The Green Dragon Banner Company have a
wicked lamb stew going. Don't ask me where they found
sheep in this madhouse."

She lifted her face. There were tear tracks on her cheeks.
"Help me, Croaker. I can't stop thinking about how much
was taken away from me when Narayan Singh stole her.
How much that one event changed my life."

It changed all our lives. It affected everyone in this end of
this world and hundreds of thousands in at least two others.
But she was completely self-involved right now.

"Get up and get out of here," I told her. "Go get something
to eat. Go flying. It's a beautiful, cool day. There're signs
that things are going to start greening up soon. Go take it in.
I want you to get hold of yourself before I go. I don't want to
leave you here if you don't think you're all right."

"Go? Where are you going?"

"It's almost time to release the first contingent of the Children of the Dead. Some of us are going to scout the way
south and across the plain. And get the guys at the shadowgate busy collecting supplies. Why don't you come along?
It'll get your mind off things."

"No. I couldn't. There isn't anyone here who can take care of her."

Damn! Now I saw where she was vulnerable. I saw the door the darkness would use to get in. If it had not done so already.

Clever me, though. I knew how to close that door. Forever. And I had just set myself up to take care of it without interference.

"Go get some stew. Strut around. Make the soldiers hate me for being lucky enough to have you." There was a time when every man did. When every man responded to Lady the way women did to Aridatha Singh. But those days were gone. And so were all those men but me.

I glanced down at Booboo, then up at the silent white crow standing in the open window. It certainly seemed to run in the blood.

The white crow was around a lot now, but was quiet about it. So far I had not forgotten to look around before I said anything I did not want overheard. I needed to keep my fingers crossed for the future, though.

Lady dithered.

I said, "If you don't get going I'll call some guys in here and have them hold you down while I paddle you."

For a moment the Lady I love peeked out of the dark place. She flashed a smile, said, "Promise? That might be fun."

Once she left I collected Booboo's hand and indulged in a little of the same despair. The girl's fingers were cold as death. But she was breathing.

The white crow found it all amusing. "You've become sickeningly domestic, lover."

I growled something.

"Ah, I know. You were so stubborn when I had you. But it might be fun to see what happened if somebody said you weren't, after all these years."

I grumbled.

"Well, maybe not fun for you." And, after a moment, in a different, sorrowful, almost little girl voice, "It could have been something amazing."

No doubt. And fatal besides, probably.

133

Glittering Stone: A Dangerous Game

Only four of us flew south. Five if you counted that ragged-ass lazy crow riding the tip of Goblin's flying post. The little man was flying independently but his movements were limited by a tow rope and a safety harness, each of which connected him to a different companion. We told him it was for his safety while he was learning to manage the post but even dead he was smart enough to see through that. We did not want him haring off if the Khadidas regained control.

Goblin was much stronger now. He could manage most self care without assistance and many other uncomplicated tasks as well. He had a vocabulary of maybe thirty words. He could lay One-Eye's spear down for minutes at a time without risk of wakening the demon within.

We were blazing along through blue skies, cloaks streaming thirty yards behind, at an altitude low enough to panic livestock and send children running to tell skeptical parents. The girls whooped and shrieked, having a wonderful time. Whomever's turn it was not to mind Goblin soared and dove.

Spring was going to spring soon. With these kids that might become an adventurous season.

With spring would come the rainy season, too. Lots of wet and lots of ferocious weather.

I made a couple of brief side trips. The main one was a brief look at Dejagore, where life had settled into a semblance of normalcy and nobody was mourning the passing of one of the city's most famous daughters. Probably not one in a thousand people outside the garrison knew that Sleepy called Dejagore home.

The other side trips involved looking for evidence of the Nef in places where I thought I might have seen them before. I found nothing.

Since there had been no sign of those ghosts of the glittering stone, outside my own glimpses, I was pretty sure what I had seen had not been the genuine articles.

Tobo had expressed a suspicion that, had I not been imagining things, what I had seen were some of his hidden folk trying out disguises.

He believed some would do that just for the hell of it. The folklore of the Land of Unknown Shadows supported his contention. In fact, that sort of prank was a huge favorite.

So, probably, the Nef were less of a problem than I had feared. But a problem even so. Unless they *were* trapped in the Voroshk world.

Panda Man, at the shadowgate, robbed me of that foolish hope. "They're out there begging and whining every night, Captain."

"Looks like you guys have made yourselves right at home." They had built themselves a tiny hamlet, complete with women and livestock, most of both showing signs of gravidity.

"Best duty we ever had, Captain."

"Well, now is when it starts getting tough." I spun out a gaggle of orders. Then me and my daughters, my pal the white crow and my dead friend, passed through the shadowgate. Though I could see nothing I thought I could sense the pressure of the Nef inside.

The plain boasted a thousand patches of dirty snow. Old snow lay drifted against the standing stones on their west sides. The air was bitterly cold. The place was getting its weather from somewhere other than my native world. And it had an air of neglect. As though the residents had given up housekeeping and maintenance.

The neglect was less evident inside the nameless stronghold. The stench of human waste was gone. Evidently Baladitya had cleaned up after Shivetya's Voroshk guests. But there was a taint of wasted human.

"We need some light," I told the girls. Still competing with one another in some ways, both hastened to create those little will-o'-the-wisp glowing balls that seem to be the first trick any sorcerer learns.

The source of the odor was obvious instantly. Baladitya had fallen asleep at his worktable and had not yet awakened. The chill, dry air had done a lot to preserve him.

I was unhappy but not surprised. Baladitya must have been an antique when I was born.

Arkana and Shukrat made appropriate noises expressing sorrow.

"This isn't good," I muttered, staring at the copyist's remains. "I was counting on him to help me talk to Shivetya."

From somewhere in the darkness the white crow said, "Hi, there, soldier. Looking for a good time?"

Fumbling around after oil with which to refill Baladitya's empty lamps, I said, "Ah, yes. You. All is not lost. But neither is it found."

"What?" That voice was a high-pitched squeak. I wondered how she managed to produce so many of those, even when using a bird to do her talking.

"Trust." I recalled a time when anything she said scared the shit out of me. I guess familiarity does breed . . . something. I was almost comfortable with her. "Why on earth would you expect me to trust anything you say?"

It helped my courage, knowing she was buried and in a sort of undying coma.

"Shivetya won't let me lie."

Right. Call me a cynic. But I had a notion that the golem
might have been with us more than Kina had, over the years.
A notion that it would be impossible to untangle his manip-
ulations from hers. A suspicion that he might be just as
much a deceiver as she was when it came to maneuvering
toward the end of the world.

"Right, then. Got your word, do we? I'm comfortable
with that. Let's get started. Does the Goddess know we're
here? Does she know what's in my mind?"

"Her attention is elsewhere."

The girls took over filling and lighting the lamps. They
were good girls. They had learned to do for themselves. And
they watched their daddy at work with respect and awe. Or,
at least, they wondered what I was doing, talking to a crow
that looked diseased. And having the crow talk back, like it
was intelligent.

I told Arkana, "If you could read and write Taglian you'd
understand all about this because you'd be able to keep up
with the Annals."

"No thanks, Pop. Not even a good try. I said no yesterday,
I'm telling you no today, and all you're going to hear is no
again tomorrow. I'm not going to get pulled any deeper into
your mob than I already am."

Which is what Suvrin used to say. Suvrin, who started out
as a prisoner of war.

Shukrat said, "Don't even even bother to look over here."

I had not considered Shukrat. I would not. But I did think
Arkana might work out. If she would give it a chance. She
had a personality suitable to be one of the gang.

"Recruiting season over?" the crow demanded.

"For now." I peered into the darkness, trying to make out
more details of the golem. There was not enough light. But
the demon seemed to be asleep.

Or at least uninterested. Which puzzled me, since I was
there to set him free.

I shrugged. His indifference would not slow me down.

* * *

I collected Goblin. I led him well out onto the floor of Shivetya's vast hall, away from other ears. Had I brought a lamp along I would have been able to see how lovingly the floor detailed the features of the plain outside.

I reviewed for the little man. "Kina is a very slow thinker. We need to get this done before she understands that we're already here, that we intend to strike, and that we do have a weapon puissant enough to do the job." One-Eye's spear shimmered all the time here. Filaments of fire slithered over it in unpredictable patterns, excitedly. The edges of its head groaned as they sliced the air itself. It seemed to sense that it had come home.

No one could argue that the spear was not a masterpiece of a peculiar sort of art. No one could deny that in creating his masterwork One-Eye had reached a level of inspiration seen nowhere else in his long but rather pathetic life.

Many an artistic masterpiece has fallen into that same category: the sole triumph of the genius of its creator.

"Once we reach the black veil across the stairwell she'll start to realize her danger. You'll have to move fast. Get up as much speed as you can so you can drive the spear as deep as you can. The Lance of Passion wasn't potent enough. But it wasn't made for godslaying. One-Eye's spear is. You could name it Godslayer. You know. You were there during most of the years he worked on it. When we were in Hsien it became his whole career."

Goblin had been there. But that Goblin had been alive, not a ghost still trapped in the flesh it had worn in life. At least part of the time this Goblin was an agent of the very monster this Goblin was going to kill. Or maim. Or just irritate.

As the doubts began to circle round me like Tobo's hidden realm friends I kept right on talking, explaining yet again why he was the only one of us who could make the strike. And he really did find my arguments compelling. Or else his mind was made up and the hopes and wishes of others no longer mattered.

The Goblin thing climbed back aboard his flying post.

I pushed my own forward, so I could see the tip of his and make doubly sure I knew which one he was riding. "Let's go downstairs, then," I said. "I'll be right behind you. Your post is spelled to come back on its own if you're unconscious." He knew. He had been there when Shukrat fixed it to do that. "If that doesn't work I'll swoop in and grab you, drag your ass away. If you want, I even brought an extra hundred yards of line to hook onto your safety harness. We can tie it to your belt."

The little man looked at me like he thought I was trying too hard. He had been working himself up for a suicide mission, convinced that the destruction of his flesh was the only way he could rid himself of his parasite and find rest himself.

I played the whole scam by ear. I had no real idea what Goblin really wanted or what he hoped to achieve with the false life he had been given. I had not been able to guess much about him when he was alive. The only thing I knew for sure was that he was working crippled. Doing without One-Eye was, for him, like doing without one of his limbs.

And he did want to hurt Kina. That was never in doubt.

A long, difficult discussion ended up with me chagrined a bit as I finally got the message that Goblin was not deeply interested in backup that would pull him out if things went sour. He wanted backup that would make sure the job got done even if he failed.

I do not know why I had so much trouble recognizing and understanding Goblin's program. Possibly because I was concentrating on getting things to go forward exactly the way I wanted. Goblin had told me almost everything before, one time or another, when I had been focused enough to ask.

Personally uninclined toward mortal self-sacrifice, I had trouble overriding my cynical nature—particularly as regarded someone as self-indulgent as Goblin had been for so long.

Goblin brandished One-Eye's spear and told me what I had already told him but had not done. "Time to go downstairs, Croaker." He got it all out in a single, bell-tone clear sentence.

I patted myself down. Final check. Still not sure I was ready for this.

134

Taglios:
Best Served Cold

The only check on Tobo was Lady, who could not maintain her level of interest. The only check on Lady was the wonder boy. And he had other things on his mind. And altogether too much of that touched by the darkness.

No Shukrat, no Croaker, no Lady paying attention. Nights in the city lost their traditional noisome urban charm. Some people began to compare the new age to a time when the Protector had loosed her murderous shadows upon the city, for no more obvious reason than existed behind the unleashing of the horrors out there now.

The fact that there were few actual deaths went unremarked.

The Unknown Shadows enjoyed themselves greatly, tormenting the living. As did Tobo, who found himself free to do anything he wanted.

Except in his dreams.

A woman had begun to haunt those. A beautiful Nyueng Bao woman who seemed to be the embodiment of sorrow. He understood in his heart that this was his mother as she had appeared when she was young, before she had met his father. Usually she was not alone. Sometimes she was accompanied by a young, unbent Nana Gota. And sometimes by another woman, always gentle, always with a smile, forged of steel tougher than that of Uncle Doj's sword Ash Wand. This woman, who had to be his great grandmother, Hong Tray, never spoke. She communicated more with a disapproving eye than Sahra could say in a hundred words.

His vengeances were unacceptable to all these women who had created and formed him.

Tobo could not determine if he was being touched by the ghosts of his ancestors—a possibility entirely in keeping with Nyueng Bao beliefs—or if the women were the product of some conscience-stricken cellar of his mind. The darkness within him was strong enough to make him want to defy them.

None of them wanted to be avenged.

Sahra's ghost warned, "You won't just hurt yourself, darling. If you go on you'll be running into a trap. Put aside your pain. Embrace your true destiny and let it lift you up."

Hong Tray studied him with eyes like cold steel marbles, agreeing that he had come to a crossroads. That he was about to make a choice that would shape the rest of his life.

He knew, of course, that the words the ghost women spoke, and the ghosts themselves, had to be metaphors.

He had no trouble with his conscience when he was awake. So he tried to avoid sleep.

Sleep deprivation clouded his judgment even further.

The hidden folk always reported the same thing: Aridatha Singh would not leave his offices. He worked day and night, seldom doing more than catnap, as he tried to hold the Taglian world together by the weight of his own will. The struggle to maintain control ought to have beaten him down and have shredded his spirit in days. Most men would have started cutting throats to more swiftly facilitate reconstruction and assuage frustration. Aridatha just beat people down with reason and public opinion. He treated with no one in secret. He made sure the world knew when someone refused to handle the city's business publicly.

Obstructionists were becoming known. The mood of people displaced by strife and fire was not forgiving of traditional factionalism.

The unthinkable happened. Several men of high caste were beaten savagely. Shadar were seen in the crowds, encouraging the violence. No one wondered, though, and Aridatha Singh did not appear to be aware of that personally.

It was deep night but a light traffic continued to and from the City Battalions barracks containing Aridatha Singh's headquarters. A dark fog slowly gathered around the place. People grew sleepy. Shadows scampered among the shadows. For an instant, here and there, little people or little animals were visible briefly—had anyone been awake to see them.

Tobo came walking through it all, so tired his eyes were crossing, so sure of himself that he had not brought his flying post nor had he armored himself in Voroshk black. So sure of himself that he did not double-check reports from his Unknown Shadows.

He expected to walk in, complete his revenge, and be gone with no one the wiser. Aridatha Singh's fate would become a great and terrible mystery.

The hidden folk could tell him nothing about Singh's office. They could not get inside it. It was kept sealed airtight. But the sentries outside were snoring.

Tobo shoved the door. It gave way only grudgingly, swinging inward. He stepped inside, panting. Across the room three men had fallen forward onto a worktable or lay sprawled in their chairs. "Not good," Tobo muttered, unexcited by the presence of the potential witnesses.

"Not good at all," Aridatha said, lifting his face off the desktop.

Tobo just had time to catch the swish of air behind him before something hit the back of his head with force enough to crack bone. He went down into the darkness knowing he had been betrayed, that he had walked into a trap. The Unknown Shadows scattered in every direction, going mad, making Taglios a city of nightmares.

Sahra, Gota and Hong Tray all awaited Tobo on the other shore of consciousness. All three told him that this was a disaster entirely of his own devising. He could have avoided it simply by doing the right thing.

He had been warned beforehand. He had not listened.

Sahra's sorrow was deeper than ever Tobo had known it before.

135

Taglios:
The Mad Season

Lady dealt with the temptation easily for several days after Croaker departed. She kept reminding herself that all she had to do was hang on till he got back. By then the Daughter of Night would not be the Deceiver messiah anymore. She would be just plain Booboo.

Sense told Lady to be patient. But emotion knew no patience. And emotion threatened to devour her. Despite her long history, emotion had stolen control.

She broke after only four days.

Lady took a quick look into the hallway to make certain no one was likely to intervene, then settled on a stool beside her daughter's bed. She plucked the ends of strands of spells keeping the girl asleep and constrained. She worked quickly and deftly. She had been studying Booboo's bonds all those four days.

Those spells unravelled almost as if they had a will of their own.

Lady proceeded with an uncharacteristically naive haste. That part of her that had grown hard and bitter in the real world mocked her for her childishness. This was the world. Her world. The real world. There was no reason to expect any good to come her way.

Booboo's eyes snapped open with mechanical suddenness. The color was right but still they were not the family eyes. Nor were they Croaker's eyes. They were eyes colder than Lady's own in her cruelest hour. They were the eyes of a serpent, a naga, or a deity. For an instant Lady froze like a mouse caught in a snake's stare. Then she said, "I'm an incurable romantic. The essence of romance is an unshakable conviction that next time will be different." She tried to assert control while the girl was physically too weak to act.

The girl's "love me" aura had touched Lady already, so subtly that she remained unaware of it until it was too late.

Lady had not worn her Voroshk costume. There was no shelter from the storm.

A vibration developed down deep inside her, at glacial speeds. As it built she watched the power of the Goddess slowly fill the Daughter of Night. The buzz within Lady included a trace of mirth. She understood that her unpracticed maternal emotions had been discovered and manipulated, ever so subtly, for a very long time. So subtly that she had not suspected. Worse, so subtly that she was not adequately prepared to respond to any disaster.

Nevertheless, she was a woman of incredible will, having had ages to practice employing it.

There was a countermove left.

In an instant Lady made the cruelest decision of her life. She would regret it forever but knew the choice she made would leave her with the least painful long-term wounds.

The Lady of Charm had centuries of practice making terrible decisions quickly, and just as many years of practice living with the consequences.

From her belt Lady drew a memento of her brief passage as Captain of the Black Company. The dagger's pommel was a silver skull with one ruby eye. The ruby always seemed to be alive. Lady lifted the blade slowly, her gaze locked with that of the Daughter of Night. The sense of the presence of Kina grew ever stronger between them.

"I love you," Lady said, responding to a question never asked, existing only within the girl's heart. "I will love you forever. I will always love you. But I won't let you do this thing to my world."

Lady could do it, in spite of all. She had slain as dear before, when she was not yet as old as the child lying beneath her knife. And for less reason.

She felt a madness creep through her. She tried to concentrate. She could kill because she was filled with a conviction that there was no better thing she could do.

Kina and the Daughter of Night both strove to crack Lady's terrible will. But the dagger descended toward the girl's breast, its progress inexorable. The Daughter of Night quickly became the hypnotized prey, unable to believe that Lady's blade kept falling.

The tip of the knife touched cloth. It passed through, found flesh, then a rib. Lady shifted her weight so she could drive the blade between bones.

She never sensed it coming. The blow, seemingly struck to the right side of her head, was powerful enough to hurl her sideways a half dozen feet, into a wall. Darkness closed in. For an instant there was a living dream in which she saw herself trying to strangle her child instead of stabbing her.

The Daughter of Night felt fire rip across her chest as her would-be killer flung toward the wall. She screamed. But the agony that moved her was not that of her wound. It was a black explosion inside her mind, a sudden tidal wave of knifelike shards of a thousand dark dreams, of a scream harsher than ten thousand whetstones sharpening swords, of a rage so vast and red it could be called the Eater of Worlds.

That blow was violent enough to fling her upward and to one side. She came down sprawled across the still form of her birth mother. But she did not know. She was unconscious long before gravity placed and posed her.

A whiff of old death, of graveyard mold, hung in the air of the room.

136

Fortress with No Name: Godstalking

Goblin was too eager. Twice I felt compelled to yell at him to slow down. He plunged down the dark stairwell at a pace I could not match. Even wearing the Voroshk apparel the bruising impacts with the walls became too much for my nerve.

We had not yet gone as deep as the ice cavern where Soulcatcher lay when I bellowed an order to stop. Wonder of wonders, this time Goblin heard me. And listened. And responded when I told him we had to go back up.

"What?" He turned the word into a two syllable whisper from an old tomb.

"We can't do this in the dark. We'll beat ourselves unconscious before we get down there. Or at least get there too beaten up to think."

He made a sound that signified reluctant agreement. He had had a few unpleasant collisions of his own.

"We have to go get lights." Why had I overlooked something so obvious? Because I was too damned busy looking for the subtle and the sneaky, I suppose.

The stairwell was much too tight to turn the flying posts. We had to back them up. That was a slow, humbling, sometimes painful task. And things did not get much less humiliating when we did reach the top.

The girls and the white crow awaited us. In attitudes so smug they could be read even though the ladies were clad for action. Arkana swung a lantern back and forth.

For an instant I suffered an entirely irrelevant worry because I had not brought my Widowmaker costume. It seemed appropriate to the situation. But definitely not necessary.

All that armor ever was was a costume.

Now Shukrat waved a lantern back and forth. And laughed.

"Not a word," I grumped.

"Did I say anything?"

"You're thinking it, darling daughter."

She raised her lantern higher, the better to see what I was wearing. My apparel was in slow, creeping motion all around me, repairing extensive damage. "Not a word from me, old-timer. You know your Shukrat. Honors her elders to a fault. But I'm going to laugh, now. Please don't jump to conclusions and think that it's at you."

Arkana laughed harder.

Goblin made a series of noises, depleting his vocabulary fast.

"He's right. Give us those lanterns. We need to get this done." I hoped my dimwit failure to consider the need for light would not be the one little thing that got us destroyed. And that that was the last little thing I had been dumb enough to forget.

Goblin took the lantern from Shukrat. He headed down into the earth again. He was not nearly so hurried this time. Possibly his lust for revenge had begun to cool.

I took Arkana's lantern. The white crow flapped over to

the tip of my post. Before I finished telling it that traveling with me might not be a good idea. Shukrat had another lantern going and was helping Arkana get herself another lit.

The girls had been ready for us.

I bickered with them all the way down to the ice cavern. They had fun with me all the way. They refused to listen to my warnings.

The white crow decided the cave of the ancients would be a fine place to detour. I bellowed, "Don't touch anything in there! Especially don't touch yourself." I continued, mumbling, "When will I learn to keep my big damned mouth shut?" It would be a great and wonderful irony if the bird's touch was Soulcatcher's undoing, after all her lucky years.

Goblin got the hurries again. When I tried to slow him down he told me, "There's something going on with Kina! She's starting to stir."

"Shit!"

Keeping up was impossible, until we reached the black barrier. There Goblin's nerve failed him. There he froze, recalling the horror of the years he had spent on the other side.

"Goblin. We're almost there. We've got to do this. We've got to do it now." Numb as I was to things supernatural even I could sense Kina's proximity and her heightened awareness. Which must not be our fault. Her attention was focused elsewhere. "Now!" I said with more force.

Behind us the girls had begun whispering, troubled. They sensed much more than I ever could.

I told them, "You two go back upstairs now. I guarantee you that you'll be glad you did. Especially if things don't work out for us. Goblin."

He reclaimed his courage. Or maybe just found his hatred again. His face hardened. He started forward.

"Don't rush," I stage-whispered as he passed through the black barrier. "Girls, I mean it. Start running now. There *have* to be some survivors." I pushed through the terrible barrier behind Goblin, nearly messing myself with the fear. Despite what I had told the little man this was no time to be slow or tentative. Once we breached the barrier Kina knew that we had come. Her slowness would be our only ally.

Once I breached that barrier I flung myself into the ante-room area outside the entrance to Kina's prison. Goblin lined himself up to charge. I had to do several things at once: encourage him, prepare myself to weather what was about to happen and do my thankless bit to make this deicide work.

Got to keep the whole picture in mind. Got to do each thing on time, in the right order, just the way you worked it out over the last few months.

As Goblin surged forward I placed my flying post into the angle where the floor met the left-hand wall, then plastered myself against the wall above it and willed my Voroshk clothing to form a protective scab over it and me. Then, in light almost too dim for use, I found the right page in the First Father's notebook. I kept my protection open just enough to let me watch Goblin hurtle straight at Kina and, to my surprise, drive One-Eye's spear into her temple. I had expected him to go for the heart.

I completed the cantrip that would destroy Goblin's post, finished shutting me and my post in. Then I allowed myself to feel lower than snake shit because of what I was doing.

I had been hard at work justifying myself to myself for months. And had carried on. But now it was happening. And when it was over I would have to live with my deceits for-ever.

The entire universe shook. The cavern where Kina lay was big but it was confined. The stairwell was the only escape the products of that violence could find. The energy wave pounded at my protection.

I clung to the stone wall, beneath layers and layers of Voroshk material, while the universe howled and shuddered. I swore that if Kina was powerful enough to get through this I would enlist in her service myself because the only thing tougher than her would be the guys who tied her up. And they had not been seen for several millenia.

The noise began to fade. But I had trouble hearing it go. The roar had deafened me temporarily.

I hoped the girls did head back up the way I told them.

I hoped the violence did no damage elsewhere. I doubted that it would. A major earthquake had split the plain open without destroying the ice caves or doing any harm down here.

I willed the Voroshk clothing to open a crack through which I could see. If need be, if Kina *had* survived but was injured, I would push my post in there and blow it, too. And if I survived a second blast I would start hoping that I did not suffer a heart attack or starve to death while trying to climb those miles of steps.

The material protecting me had been so traumatized that it took ten minutes to respond. It twitched and shivered and crawled, moving in small surges, as it tried to heal itself.

Once I had an eyehole I discovered that there was nothing to see. Intense bright light still burned inside Kina's cell. It might have been fading but it was going slowly if it was.

It was half an hour before I could look for details without having my eyeballs hurt. Just as well. It took that long for my protective outfit to heal and relax sufficiently to allow me off the wall.

Those outfits are made smart. They take just long enough recovering to keep you from doing something stupid.

I mounted my post and moved forward, knowing, as I went, that my protection would not survive another blast soon.

At first I could find nothing. Later, after the light faded some more, I began to discover bits of what might once have been tooth or bone embedded in various surfaces. Of flesh, be it Goblin's or the Goddess's, there was no sign.

In fact, I doubted that any of the tooth and bone fragments

could have belonged to any mere mortal. The explosion had been that violent. More violent, even, than those that had destroyed the Voroshk shadowgate, that had initiated the collapse of the Palace.

Kina's destruction had somehow added vast energy to the explosion.

My post was not behaving quite right. It stuttered and was slow to respond. It must have gotten rattled around some even though I had done my best to protect it.

Once the light faded round where the Goddess had lain I saw what looked like a long black snake lying in the rubble of Kina's rock bed. It was the only nonwhite thing in the place, other than me.

I approached carefully. For all I knew that was the bone of darkness that had snuggled next to Kina's heart. And I was prepared to believe that anything I saw or experienced in this place would be illusion.

Kina was the Mother of Deceit.

One of the great powers of the Deceivers was their ability to leave you doubting everything and trusting no one.

The black thing was no snake. It was the deformed remains of One-Eye's spear. It had come through the violence with surprisingly little damage. It was just twisted and bent a little, and lightly charred on its surface. The metal inlays had been only slightly distorted by intense heat.

Man, he must have put some artful protective spells onto that thing.

I gathered the spear, went and made sure that I was securely attached to my post, then gave it the command to take me back to base point.

137

Taglios:
The Melancholy Wife

We wobbled down out of the sky like a family of mangy buzzards. My Voroshk clothing still had not healed completely. The girls were more tattered than I. The blast had caught them climbing the stairwell. They had bruises over most of their bodies.

The real miracle was how well all the posts had come through, though none remained unscathed.

The Grove of Doom rose to meet us, welcoming us like a mother greeting lost children.

Bizarre thoughts and images kept worming into my mind now. They worried me. They made me doubt that Kina was actually gone, not just in hiding.

Jokingly, Shukrat told me what I ought to be worried about was Kina's father and husband wanting to get even. I did not laugh. To me it seemed like a worthy concern.

The Grove of Doom was empty. Of humanity. But some birds had moved in already and there were a few small animals in the underbrush now.

There was no sense of grim foreboding about the place anymore.

"We did it," I sighed. "Finally. For real. No more Kina to torment the worlds."

Not having spent their lives under the threat of the Year of the Skulls, the girls were less excited.

The white crow settled on a nearby branch, divested itself of a dirty feather. "Are you sure?" The beast was having lots of fun tickling my fears. She and I seemed to be headed for a long and unpleasant relationship—unless I kept my promise to Shivetya.

I said, "If there was any place in this world where Kina's

survival would manifest itself, that would be here. This place has been almost a part of her since her cult began. And that might have been here. I don't think she could disengage herself from the Grove even if she wanted to."

"Then let's get going," Shukrat said.

Arkana sneered, "She can't wait to get her hands on Tobo again." She was not being mean-spirited. And Shukrat's counterfire included a mention of Aridatha Singh and Arkana's terminal timidity. Which did turn Arkana serious.

"Hey, Pop. What do you think Kina being gone will mean to the Daughter of Night?" Walking on eggshells. But worried by the glances she had seen Singh lay upon the girl, not entirely believing that every man reacted like that. "Is she going to turn normal?"

Shukrat showed a sudden interest, too.

"I don't know, baby doll. I worry, though. She's been connected to Kina from the second she was conceived. Seems like to her it would be about like you or me having our liver ripped out."

I was more worried about my wife. Her losing her connection to Kina would devastate her. Everything she was, in her own heart, was tied up in her being the terrible sorceress. Without Kina to leech from she would be just another middle-aged woman gone dumpy and grey.

The weather had been problematic all the way up from the shadowgate. We had had to skirt rain storms and thunderheads again and again. That had cost us more than a day.

Now, only twenty miles out, there was no evading the weather. Except by going up way high, where it was icy cold and almost impossible to breathe, then zigging back and forth between seething mountains of cloud while being tossed and taunted by turbulence. Shukrat and Arkana were dead set against getting caught aloft in a thunderstorm. Arkana told me, "Think what might happen if you got hit by lightning."

I did not think long. There was no one I wanted to see badly enough to have my post blow up between my legs. I headed for the ground. We holed up in a Gunni farming village where the locals treated us with the same cautious respect they would have shown a trio of nagas, the evil serpent people Gunni myth has living deep underground but surfacing to plague humanity on numerous occasions, always a couple, three villages away.

We did not steal any of their babies or maidens, nor their sacred cattle, nor even their sheep. I found it interesting that they were sufficiently flexible religiously to raise sheep for sale to folks like the Vehdna, who were going to gobble them right down.

The lightning quit stomping around soon after midnight. We left our hosts with coin enough to have them blessing our names. Which we never mentioned.

There was no lightning now but there was a steady, light rain. The Voroshk apparel helped, but only some. I was cold and miserable and my pet crow, now riding right in front of me in order to get under a fold of my cloak, was so far gone in the miseries that it no longer bothered to complain.

The Company barracks seemed both unnaturally quiet and abnormally alert. Armed sentries appeared everywhere. "Looks like Suvrin's worried about an attack."

"Something must have happened."

I hovered. "You girls sense anything?"

"Something definitely isn't right," Arkana said. "I don't know what."

"We'd better find out." Gone less than two weeks and everything had gone to hell?

Survin explained. I controlled myself and did not run off to see Lady before I got the whole story. Suvrin told me, "General Singh has Tobo in a cell that's isolated so the Unknown Shadows can't reach him for instructions. Singh won't let anyone visit Tobo. We do know the kid is hurt, though."

"Obviously. Or he wouldn't put up with this. He tried something stupid?"

"Oh, yes. And I don't have the horses to get him out of it."

"Now you do. If you want to bother. What about Lady?"

"We don't know what happened. Nobody was there. And I've had no reports recently. Last I heard, she was conscious but sullen and unresponsive. And the girl is worse. Your effort was successful?"

"Pretty much. Which probably explains Lady and Booboo." I did not expand. "It feels creepy around here."

"Gets more that way every night. Tobo's friends aren't happy. And they get unhappier by the hour. But Aridatha isn't intimidated."

"We'll see if we can't change that. After I see my wife." Or the person who used to be my wife.

I took Arkana with me. Just in case. "Don't say anything. Just stay in the background and cover me," I told her.

There was a guard outside my quarters but he was not there to keep anyone in. Probably not to keep anyone out, either. He was an early-warning marker for Suvrin. He and I exchanged nods. He broke Arkana's heart by failing to notice that she was an attractive young woman. I guess that was supposed to be obvious despite the Voroshk outfit.

Lady sat at a small table. She stared into nothingness. At some time she had been playing a solitaire-type card game but had lost interest long ago. The lamp beside her was almost drained of oil. Black smoke boiled off it because its wick needed trimming.

Wherever she was looking, it was plain she saw nothing but despair.

She had lost all interest in maintaining her appearance.

I laid my good hand on her right shoulder. "Darling. I'm back."

She did not respond right away. Once she did recognize

my voice she pulled away. "*You* did it," she said, more thinking out loud than actually speaking to me. "*You* did something to Kina." Only in the "you" was there any human emotion.

I glanced back at Arkana, to see if she was paying attention. This would be a critical moment. "I killed her. Just the way we contracted to do." If there was any fragment of the Goddess in her now, that ought to provoke a reaction.

It did but not the physical attempt at revenge I would have preferred. Almost.

She just started crying.

I did not remind her that she had known this day was coming. Instead, I asked, "How is Booboo? How is she taking it?"

"I don't know. I haven't seen her."

"What? Before I left we couldn't get you away from her long enough to eat."

The dam broke. The tears started. She became a woman I had not seen before, busted open like an overly ripe fruit. "I tried to kill her."

"What?" She had spoken very softly.

"I tried to kill her, Croaker! I tried to murder my own daughter! I tried, with all my will and strength, to put a dagger in her heart! And I would've done it if something hadn't knocked me out."

"I know you. So I know there was a reason other than you just thought it might be fun. What was it?"

She babbled. Years of holding everything together gave way. The floods swept all before them.

The timing matched my assault on Kina. Lady's violent reaction to Booboo could have been caused by fear leaking through from the Goddess. Booboo's own behavior would have been shaped the same way.

Lady sobbed for a long time. I held her. I feared for her. She had fallen so far. And I had been ballast almost every foot of the way down.

All my fault? Or just the spark and romance of youth's summer turning to the bleak seasons of despair of old age?

Arkana was a good daughter. She stood by patiently throughout the emotional storm. She remained there for me without intruding on my wife's black hours. After we left I thanked her profoundly.

"You think she'll be able to pull herself back together?" Arkana asked.

"I don't know. I don't know how to make her want to. If she did, I wouldn't have any worries. She's got an iron will when she wants to direct it. Right now I'm just going to try to keep on loving her and hoping something happens to sting her with a spark of hope."

"I don't know if I could stand being completely powerless, either. I might kill myself."

"Nine hundred ninety-nine people out of a thousand live their whole lives without having a millionth of your power. And they get by."

"Only because they're completely ignorant of what they're missing. Nobody mourns losing what they never had in the first place."

She had me there.

The full meaning of Lady's melancholy would be denied me forever because I was never able to experience life as she had at the opposite extreme. Whereas she knew my way of life very well indeed.

And that might be contributing to her despair as well.

138

Taglios:
The Lost Child

Booboo was worse than Lady. She was lost inside herself. She had real guards watching her. They told me
she had not done anything but stare into infinity since she
recovered consciousness. Not once had they felt any urge to
serve her or ravish her.

One guard was a Shadar who had followed Sleepy since
the Kiaulune wars. He told me, "Suruvhija Singh and her
children are taking care of her."

I felt a slight twinge. Iqbal Singh's widow. Favored by
Sleepy. But I had been unaware that the family had survived
the fighting south of Taglios. I had been too centered on my
own preoccupations to look after the welfare of Company
dependents.

The Daughter of Night was clean and well-groomed and
had been dressed carefully. She sat in a rocking chair, which
was an unusual piece of furniture in these parts. She was
aware of nothing outside the boundaries of her mind. She
drooled on her pretty white sari, which was only a shade
paler than her near-albino skin. Someone had placed a rag
where it would catch the drool.

Speaking of albinos. The white crow had managed to
arrive before me. But it was being very careful not to piss
me off these days.

It had overheard enough, here and there, to suspect that I
might have a great deal of influence on its future.

Shivetya had given us an unbelievable amount of help in
return for our promise to end his stewardship of the glittering plain. I meant to keep that promise. I try to keep all of
the Company's promises. Keeping our promises is what sep-
arates us from people like the Radisha, who try to screw us

rather than keep their word when that seems inconvenient.

I circled Booboo twice. She gave no sign she was aware of me. I knelt in front of her. Her eyes were open. Her pupils were tiny. Her eyes did not track when I moved a finger back and forth in front of them.

I backed off and considered options. Finally, I led Arkana into the hallway, told her what I wanted to try and how she could help.

We rejoined Booboo and the bird. Neither appeared to have moved a muscle.

Arkana and I separated, each moving slowly, as though hoping to drift around behind Booboo without being noticed. Once there we just waited. And waited.

It is hard to be patient when you are Arkana's age. Eventually she began to fidget. Which caused the occasional faint whisper of motion, after which she would even stop breathing for a while.

After a time so long even I began to get restless I signalled Arkana forward. Doing her absolute best to remain totally silent she dropped to her knees beside Booboo's right rocker, out of sight behind the girl's right ear but with her face so close Booboo might be able to feel the warmth of her presence. I did the same on the left. Neither of us moved till my knees were about to kill me. We tried to avoid breathing on the girl.

I nodded.

Arkana whispered, "Sosa, sosa," so softly that I could not hear her. So softly that even someone who did hear the words whispered directly into her ear would not be able to make them out.

I have no idea why she chose to say that. I leaned closer so the warmth of my presence would be a hint more obvious. I nodded.

"Sosa, sosa." No louder than before.

The skin on Booboo's neck twitched.

I smiled at Arkana, winked.

Treachery will out.

"Sosa, sosa."

Slowly, the girl began to turn her head toward Arkana, the child within unable to restrain her curiosity.

It was not that she had been faking. Just that nothing obvious was going to sneak past her palisade of despair.

I got up and drifted so she would not discover me without making a special effort.

Arkana gave me a look which asked how I had known that Booboo could be reached. I shrugged. Just intuition, I guessed. A conviction that her curiosity could be wakened if it was teased with sufficient subtlety.

But what now? How to hold her attention forcefully enough to keep her from running away again?

Soon the girl was seeing and hearing us perfectly well. But still she did not respond. Still she would not answer questions.

She had no will to live. And I could see why. At no time had there ever been anything in her life but Kina and the struggle to release the Goddess. Never had there been anything but the quest to bring on the Year of the Skulls.

Suruvhija appeared. I had not known her in the days when she and her husband joined the Company. She might have been a beauty, then, but I doubted it. She was not now. And none of her children made you want to jump in and hug them. But they were good people, if sad.

"You got her to wake up!" Suruvhija said. "That's great."

"Now we need to keep her that way. Any ideas?"

"Why?"

We all turned to the girl.

I asked, "What?"

"Why do you trouble me? Release me. I have no reason to live. There is no future. There will be no salvation and no resurrection now. There will be no age of wondrous rebirth."

She was wide awake now, but bleak, depressed. I dropped to my knees in front of her, took her hands in an effort to keep her engaged with the world outside her head.

"What does that mean? What you just said."

She seemed puzzled by the question. I spent a few minutes demonstrating my ignorance of her faith. I hoped a chance to explain might animate her.

I have not yet encountered a true believer who could resist an opportunity to expostulate upon his particular truth. Booboo was no exception, though she was a slow starter.

I did not interrupt until near the end. Until that point she did not mention anything I had not heard before, somewhere, in some version. "Excuse me," I said. "I think I missed something. The Year of the Skulls isn't the end of the world?"

Suruvhija's oldest boy, Bhijar, arrived with food and drink. I made sure Booboo got served first. She sucked down a pint of water before telling me, "Yes, it *is* the end of the world. Of *this* world, the way it is *now*. It's a *cleansing*. A time when all *evil* and *corruption* get swept away and only those souls with a *genuine* chance of redemption get left on the Wheel of Life."

I felt confused. I felt lost. I did not understand. I knew the Deceivers wanted to hasten the coming of the Year of the Skulls. That was pretty much what their cult was all about. I knew most Gunni wanted the opposite, but believed that the coming of the Year of the Skulls was inevitable. Someday. It was one of the Ages of Creation, the Fourth Age, ordained at the dawn of time. But this was the first I ever heard that there was supposed to be something on the other side. Particularly something apparently positive.

I murmured to myself, "All evil dies there an endless death." Then I asked, "You're telling me Kina's ultimate task was to clear away all the human dross so that good and righteous men can pass on to paradise?"

Exasperated by my density, she shook her head violently, then went to work trying to explain.

I whispered to Arkana, "Have them bring my wife."

I am not as dim as I pretended with my daughter that evening but I admit I never did get what she was trying to explain. However, I did realize that she truly believed that by destroying Kina I had deprived the world of any opportunity to get past its current age of sin and corruption into an age of enlightenment.

I guess Kina had been meant to devour all the demons again, only this time those would have been the devils of human kind who make life and history over into torture chambers.

The Lords of Light were going to have to take it from the top, hatching themselves a whole new scheme for worldly redemption. Assuming they were still around somewhere themselves.

Lady arrived, accompanied by Bhijar. She melted the moment she saw that Booboo was awake.

I watched, numb, as she took my place on her knees in front of the Daughter of Night. This was my wife? This clump of raw sentimentality was the woman who used to be the Lady, once able to inspire an entire empire with the terror of her name?

I did not listen. I have to admit that I was embarrassed by her behavior. Because I had not realized that there was so much sloppy emotion bottled up inside her. Around me Lady always clung to shreds of her old image . . . whenever she was not lost in her own realm of self-pity.

The whole scene seemed to amaze the Daughter of Night. She did not know what to make of it.

Suruvhija became embarrassed, too. She hustled her brood out of the room. The boys went quickly, unable to stand so much sentiment. Suruvhija herself offered me a look of commiseration before she shut the door.

I tried to tell Suruvhija I was thirsty. My throat was too dry. I went after her. I stumbled as I crossed the room. Not that that made any difference. Mental clumsiness was my real downfall.

I stepped into the corridor and called after Suruvhija, "Please bring some more drinking water. We're all still dry."

She nodded her understanding. She was embarrassed again, this time because she was alone with a man who was not her husband. I was about to say something to spare her when Arkana yelled at me.

It took me a moment to get back through the doorway.

Booboo had a rumel, a Deceiver strangling scarf, wrapped around her mother's throat. Her eyes were dark with the last ghost of Kina. Her strength was, obviously, supernatural. Arkana was having no luck breaking her hold. And that little blonde was no weakling.

I needed not die to get sent to hell. I had an instant to pick which torture I wanted to suffer for the rest of my existence.

I slapped Booboo with my bad hand. She did not let up. I punched her. She rocked. Blood gushed from her nose. She did not ease up on the yellow silk cloth. I drew the dagger that is with me all the time, that normally gets used only when I am eating. I reached out and pricked the skin right under her left eye.

And still she did not stop.

The white crow said, "This is Kina's revenge, Croaker."

Which hell?

Lady was almost gone.

I stabbed the girl in the arm.

She hardly even bled.

I stabbed again, trying for the elbow joint.

No good.

I tried to cut the tendons in her wrists.

All the while Arkana was still trying to pull her off from behind or to break her grip on the silk cloth or to cut that cloth.

I launched as violent a blow as I could manage. When that did nothing but rock the girl's head back again I lost control. As the saying goes, I saw red.

When Arkana finally stopped me I had stabbed my own

daughter more than twenty times. I had not killed her, though. Yet. But she had given up her hold on the strangling cloth.

Possibly too late. Lady was hacking and gasping, still choking. I got down and started trying to clear her windpipe. There seemed to be some damage to her larynx.

Arkana remained calm. She summoned help.

"Where did Booboo get the strangling scarf?" I asked. "She didn't have it before we went south." She had been stripped naked, scrubbed down, and dressed in new clothing. Then she had been placed in this room. So someone had brought her the rumel. A secret Deceiver. "We need to find out exactly who visited her." I did not want it to be Suruvhija, though she was instantly the logical suspect. Except for the fact that she was a woman. Hitherto, my wife and daughter had been the only women we knew to have been admitted to the secret brotherhood.

Still, this was a time of great changes. Suruvhija's sorrow and slowness of wit could be an act.

They do not call them Deceivers for nothing.

139

Taglios:
The Great General

The villain was not a Deceiver after all. He did not understand what a Deceiver was. He being Suruvhija's son Bhijar, whom Booboo had pulled in with her "love me" effect, working him only when no one else was around. She had sent him to a secret member of the Strangler brotherhood. He had gotten the killing scarf there. That had happened while we were in the air, coming home from the glittering plain.

The boy received only what punishment his mother thought was appropriate. The Deceiver who supplied the rumel, though, soon went the way of his Goddess. Along with a number of friends. There would be no mercy for Stranglers until the last was dead.

While others rooted out the truth I stayed busy with Lady and Booboo. I soon realized that I did not have the skills to save either. I summoned the best physicans from the Land of Unknown Shadows. To a man they told me what I did not want to hear.

Sorcery was the only hope for either woman. And Tobo was the only one with a command of the appropriate sorcery. Arkana and Shukrat could not help much. They knew little about the healing arts.

I told Suvrin, "Regardless of my personal motives, the boy is one of us. We can't leave him in a Taglian cell."

Suvrin had a little too much of the politician in him. Too much of the kind of mind willing to let an individual go so the rest will not be inconvenienced. He wanted to avoid a confrontation with Aridatha Singh.

I continued, "You *do* need to get into the Annals, Captain. You need to understand completely what it means to be a brother of the Black Company."

"Maybe I do. Until I do I'll run things the way I am now."

I did not argue. I had not expected any other answer. I met Shukrat outside, shook my head. She tested her sleep spell on the men Suvrin sent after me to make sure I behaved. That spell worked perfectly.

Shukrat and I went looking for the Great General.

Arkana kindly flew high cover.

We were going to bust Tobo out.

The flaw in that plan was, we did not know where Tobo was being held.

So we had to go ask Aridatha. Being more careful than

Tobo had been when it came to invading the Great General's quarters. Shukrat prepared the way with her sleep spell. It all started out so well I was hard pressed not to look on the dark side and expect a trap.

Singh was not easy to handle unconscious. At least not easy for a gimp old man and a mite of a teenage girl. Nevertheless, we got him aboard my post before he was missed, then took him way up high into the clouds, and through, into the moonlight.

I had Shukrat wake him up.

"We need to talk, Aridatha. And you need to stay calm while we do. Because it's almost a mile down to the ground."

Singh was a cool one. He collected himself. "What do you want?"

"Tobo. Where is he? I'm asking, counting on you to continue being concerned about Taglios. About what new fighting would do to the city."

Singh did not say anything.

I told him, "You're doing a good job of riding the tiger. But that tiger is going to get a chance to run wild if I end up having to drop your ass from a mile up in the sky."

He considered that, suspecting that I might not be bluffing. "You could start a new war."

"*You* could."

"The man tried to assassinate me."

"He won't do that again," Shukrat told him. "We're going to have a talk, Tobo and me. When we're done he'll stop doing stupid things forever." She did not sound like she had any doubts. She did make it sound like Tobo had a surprise coming.

I said, "To lay your mind at rest, it won't trouble me a bit if we get into a new fight with you people. I don't have much left to live for. I can burn Taglios to the ground without compunction. Unlike some, I don't love the place. It's done nothing to win my heart."

Arkana said, "If he kills you there won't be anyone to look out for the Radisha." The Radisha had become regent despite tradition because Aridatha Singh insisted. Strongly. And nobody wanted to argue with the Great General. Even out in the provinces resistance to the new order seemed to be weakening, almost as if it was just too much trouble to fight over all of this when things were going so well otherwise.

Arkana did not give a rat's ass about the Radisha's welfare. She just wanted Aridatha to survive this incident.

"Just tell us where Tobo is," I said. "Shukrat and I will bring him out." Slowly, slowly, I tilted my post forward. Timing its arrival well, a gap in the clouds appeared below, allowing the moonlight to get through and reflect off the surface of the river. We discovered that, when he could actually see how high he was, Aridatha Singh had a fear of heights. It proved to be one of those fears which evades reason's control.

We set him down on the north bank of the river. Arkana stayed with him. I wondered if she would find the nerve to betray her interest.

140

Taglios:
Brain Surgery

Before Tobo could help me with my women, I, with the help of the best physicians and surgeons among the Children of the Dead, had to bring him back from his head wound. His Taglian captors had done nothing for him. He was two-thirds of the way down the path to a lonely grave.

There were no other Nyueng Bao with the Company anymore. The handful who had reached Taglios with us had stolen away to their native swamps soon afterward.

Tobo required delicate surgery to clear a dozen dangerous bone chips off the surface of his brain. I did most of the work myself, using my fellow surgeons as my other hand. The job took twelve hours. Shukrat was there every second. Sometimes I thought the ghost of the boy's mother was looking over my shoulder.

I collapsed moments after we finished, my physical and emotional reserves utterly spent. Some kind souls saw to it that I got into a bed.

141

Taglios:
Family Matters

It had to be afternoon. Storm season thunder rocked the old Greys barracks. The roaring hiss of the deluge ate up almost all other sound. The air was cool to the point of feeling nippy. I told myself to enjoy the cool while I could. Once the rain stopped the heat would return. And the air would be damp enough to steam vegetables.

A whole different, pounding roar developed as wild winds began to slam and kick the barracks. Hail had begun to fall. Heavily. The streets would be filling with Taglian children determined to harvest the ice. Some surely would be injured by large hailstones. It happened frequently.

Shukrat came in. She did not look cheerful. Suruvhija followed her, bringing food and drink.

I asked, "How bad is it? Is it infection?"

Shukrat was puzzled for a moment. "Oh. No. Tobo is all right. He was even awake for a minute a little while ago."

So. The way she did not go on told me where the real problem lay.

When I jumped up, nearly injuring myself in my haste, she barked, "Take it easy! Getting in a dangerous hurry won't help." And, when I failed to calm myself enough to suit her, "You won't be fit to help anybody if you show up emotionally too ragged to cope."

She was right. An old man like me, in my professions, got plenty of exposure to that truth. Not only fear, but most emotion, is the mind killer. We do stupid things when we let emotion take over. Then we are forced to endure the consequences for the rest of our days.

I took deep breaths and drank cold water. I told myself I could handle even the worst news because I have been dealing with bad news all my life. "Lead on," I told Shukrat.

Soldiers live. Bad news is part of the life.

Arkana and the white crow were with Lady and Booboo when I arrived. Suruvhija had gotten there ahead of me. She slipped out right away, with a murmur of gratitude for excusing her son from the worst consequences of his actions.

It was not a good day for me physically either. I was having to use my cane.

Both of my women were lying on their backs, making no noise. I saw no immediate cue as to what the crisis might be. The crow paced back and forth on a shelf above Lady's cot. Arkana perched on a chair beside my daughter.

I went to my wife first.

Lady was breathing. Barely. And having to work extremely hard at it, gasping and fighting for every breath. I groaned. "I may have to cut her throat open below the obstruction." The operation might save her life but her vanity would be sorely tested. The results are never pretty.

I felt relieved as I turned to the girl. And guilty, because I felt so much relief.

Soldiers live.

Booboo was gone. But it had only just happened.

That ripped my guts out.

Arkana told me, "There was someone with her every minute, Pop. It was like she just didn't want to make it." She made me take the chair.

"Oh, I understand that part. She didn't have any reason to go on. We took everything that meant anything away from her. But knowing she wanted out, in here," and I tapped my temple, "doesn't do anything to stop the bleeding in here," tapping my chest. I drew a deep breath, let it go in a long sigh. "Tell Suruvhija to come back in."

Once the little Shadar woman returned, I told her, "Buy as much ice as you can get. I want to pack my daughter in ice."

I touched Booboo. She was still warmer than the surrounding air.

Shukrat asked, "What's up? What're you going to do?"

"I'm going to take her down to the ice cave." We had to go back to get the Children of the Dead back across the plain and to keep our word to Shivetya. Maybe sooner was better than later.

The white crow made a little sound, simply a device for getting my attention.

I said, "She's first in my heart. If that's what it takes to save her, then I'll put her down there with you, too."

Suruvhija was gone. I hoped she got no grief trying to buy ice. If anyone tried to keep her from getting the money I would be tempted to break some bones.

I did not reflect on what my response, as Captain, would have been toward an underling with my present attitude. The Words Immortal are: That Was Different.

The first ice arrived not much later. Booboo had chosen the perfect time and season to die. We bundled her in a quarter ton of hailstones, inside heavy blankets, which we sewed shut. Lady's flying post, slaved to Arkana's, was just able to hoist the weight.

The fly of indecision bit me. I wanted to get the girl into the safety of the cavern before nature had its way. But I did not want to be away from Tobo and my wife and run the risk of disaster here.

Shukrat assured me, "I'll damned well make sure Tobo is all right. And as soon as he's able I'll have him help Lady. If you're not back. Now go. Do what you have to do."

"Come on, Pop," Arkana told me. "Once we put on some altitude that ice isn't going to melt nearly so fast."

"Yeah. Shukrat. If anything happens . . . get more ice. Come on down. Maybe Shivetya can help."

Before we left I did have to visit Suvrin, to let him know what was going on and arrange it so he would know what to do if the fates ordained that this was the time when Croaker would not be coming back.

Even when you fly with the wind it takes a long time to get from Taglios to the fortress with no name. It seems to take forever when worry is your most intimate traveling companion. The white crow was not good for much of anything but an emergency source of provender. Arkana was a dutiful daughter, more helpful than she needed to be, but she was just too young. Most of her earnest conversation seemed so naive, or even foolish, that it became hard to recall a time when I was that age, still idealistic and hurling myself at life headlong, believing that truth and right must inevitably triumph.

I kept my opinions to myself. After everything she had suffered already Arkana did not deserve to have her surviving optimism skewered by my bitter cynicisms.

Perhaps her youthful shallowness was useful as a shield. It might help her shake off those early traumas. I have known people like that, who live only in the present moment.

142

Glittering Stone:
Bitter Desserts

Soon after we placed Booboo in the cave of the ancients, a scant few yards from her aunt, I was stricken by a series of horrible thoughts.

What got me nervous in the first place was the way the imprisoned Soulcatcher's gaze seemed to follow me everywhere as we brought the girl in and settled her, while Arkana set the stasis spells on her—as relayed to her by the white crow.

Paranoia struck deep.

Soulcatcher had control of the bird. And she knew all the ins and outs of the sorcery necessary to lock someone into the ice caverns—or to release a prisoner. She could let herself go.

The bird was not right there when that thought hit me. Else she would have known that I had realized the possibility. I covered up before it noticed.

I stood in the weak, sourceless, pale cold light and stared for a long time, without really seeing. My baby. Hard to believe.

"I never knew you, darling." A tear rolled down. I thought of all the cold, hard men I had known and wondered what they would think if they could see me now, having turned into a maudlin old man.

They might be envious of the fact that I had hung around long enough to become an old man.

The white crow came flapping in from wherever it had been, landed on my right shoulder. Wings slapped my face, stinging. "Goddamnit!" It had not taken the liberty before.

I do not know how long I wallowed in self-pity before the bird stirred me. Far longer than I realized at the time. The crow brought me back to this world of real trials and deep pain. "Arkana. We'd better head back now." My separation from Lady would be more than a week long before we reached Taglios.

It was going to be longer than that.

Arkana did not respond.

"Arkana?"

Arkana was not there.

The flying posts were not there.

Emotion is the mind killer.

In my worry about my women I had forgotten that my adopted daughter was the one Voroshk with a brain. The one who had said she was going to bide her time and pick her moment.

That moment had come and gone, it seemed. There was nobody down in that cavern but me and the scruffy white bird.

She had not been completely cruel. She took the key to the shadowgates so the gimp old man had no way to get away but she did not make him climb all the way up out of that hole. Only part of the way. She left my flying post just far enough up to give herself a few hours' head start. Just long enough that I had no chance to catch her.

Shivetya manna makes a tiresome diet, however good you feel for the first few hours after you eat. Self-pity and self-accusation make bitter desserts. And a crow haunted by your oldest and dearest enemy makes for a somewhat less than ideal partner in exile.

After the anger faded and the despair subsided I helped myself to Baladitya's writing materials and went to work on bringing the Annals up to date.

There was no time in that place so I do not know how long that took. It seemed longer than it probably was. I began to worry because nobody came to see why we had failed to return. I feared that meant there was no one who could come. The most likely someones who might not be able to come being Tobo or Lady.

But Shukrat was healthy. How come she did not show up?

With no one else there I found myself talking to the crow more and more. And more as time went by, in an effort to defeat the gathering despair.

Shivetya watched from his huge wooden throne, evidently amused by my predicament. While I was amused by Soulcatcher's.

She did have the knowledge to get herself out of the ice cavern. She just did not have the hands. And I thought that was delicious.

I was five or six sleeps into my exile when the Nef returned, first appearing inside my dreams.

143

Fortress with No Name:
Sleeping with the Demon

Soulcatcher kept reminding me that she was in touch with the demon. That, in fact, as long as she remained attached to the white crow she would be little more than Shivetya's tool. This information did not seem newsworthy or particularly important until I suffered the visit from the Washene, the Washane and the Washone.

I had not been especially sensitive to them in the past. I knew them better from description than encounter. This time around made clear why that was.

Their ugliness invaded my dreams but only as a sense of presence little more concrete than that of the Unknown Shadows. Golden glimmers of hideous beast-mask faces in the corner of dream's eye, and scattered single syllable fragments of attempted communication, were all that I recalled after I awakened, sweating and shaking and filled with undirected terror.

Shivetya's gaze, directed my way, seemed more amused than ever.

I soon learned that his amusement had limits.

I had made him a promise. He could look inside me and see that I intended to keep it. But he could also see that I meant to stall for as long as it took me to arrange my own life to my satisfaction.

He had been patient for ten thousand years. Now, suddenly, his patience began to wilt.

I became aware of it first while I was sleeping. On a night when the Nef were almost getting through, my dreams filled unexpectedly with a presence that pushed in like a whale driving through a pod of dolphins. A big, unseen thing that approached like the darkness itself but without containing a thread of evil. Just a vast, slow thing that was.

I knew what it was and understood that it was trying to make a mind-to-mind contact the way it had with others before me. But my mind had a hard shell around it. It was difficult for ideas to get through.

Good thing Goblin and One-Eye were no longer around. They could have gotten hours of joy out of a straight line like that.

A couple sleeps more, though, and my mind had become a sieve. Me and Shivetya were yukking it up like a couple of old tonk buddies. The white crow was put out because she did not have a job translating anymore. I guess the demon had the sheer mental brute force to make contact with anyone.

I learned from the golem in the way that Baladitya had learned before me. I learned by being taken inside the demon's living dream, where past was almost indistinguishable from present. Where the wondrous pageant of the plain's history, and the history of the worlds it connected, were all remembered, in as much detail as Shivetya had cared to witness at the time. There was a great deal about the Black Company. He had chosen the Company as the instrument of his escape a very long time ago, long before Kina chose Lady to become her instrument inside the enemy force and the vessel that would birth the Daughter of Night, who was the intended instrument of her own liberation. Long before any of us were the least aware of all the pitfalls we were going to encounter on our road to Khatovar. But Shivetya chose better than did Kina. The Goddess failed to look closely enough at Lady's character. Lady was too damned stubborn and selfish to be anyone's tool for long.

There were just seven of us when some inexplicable urge made me decide to retrace the Company's olden journeys. And of those seven, now there is just me.

Soldiers live.

The Black Company is in Suvrin's hands now. Such as it is. It is headed south now, according to Shivetya's dreams, satisfactorily avenged, planning to cross the glittering plain back to the Land of Unknown Shadows. There are only a handful of Taglians and Dejagorans and Sangelis left to miss our world. The Company will become a new thing in a new world. And pudgy little Suvrin will be its creator.

Never before had there been anyone of the Black Company who had survived so long that he could see how vast are the changes time will sculpt even upon a band determined to stay one with its past.

When my thoughts ranged those bleak marches Shivetya always filled my head with ripples of amusement. Because those were almost invisible changes when compared with those that *he* had witnessed in *his* time. He had seen empires, civilizations, entire races, come and go. He remembered the gods themselves, the ugly builders of the plain, and all the powers that had come into and changed his estate and then had faded away again. He even recalled a time when he was not alone in the fortress with no name, a time when his devotion to duty caused his mates to nail him to his throne so they could desert without him interfering.

At long last I began to understand what had happened to Murgen in those long ago days when he had had so much trouble clinging to his place in time. Murgen was crazy, some, and Soulcatcher was involved, some—those were the days when Soulcatcher had found her way onto the plain—and Murgen never had a clue himself what was happening but behind everything else was Shivetya, carefully setting up his path into retirement. And, of course, Shivetya does not see time like the rest of us. Unless we demand his attention right here at the vanguard he floats everywhere, everywhen, reexperiencing rather than remembering.

Gods, how I envied him! The entire histories of sixteen worlds were his to *know*. Not just to study and interpret but pretty much to *live* whenever the mood took him.

I did have a question. *The* question of supreme importance if I was going to set the demon free. He had to answer it to my satisfaction if he wanted me to fulfill our agreement.

What would happen to the glittering plain if he was no longer here to manage it?

144

Fortress with No Name:
Arkana's Tale

Shivetya was never as powerful as Kina but he was a whole hell of a lot faster on his mental feet. It had taken the sleeping Goddess years to impact the world outside and create a vast paranoia concerning the Black Company. Shivetya it took just weeks. It would not have taken that long had he not reached out for a specific someone with a mind shell thicker than mine: Shukrat.

The demon was disinclined to connect with Tobo. Tobo had been his good buddy before but Tobo's behavior recently hinted at potentially troublesome character flaws.

Shukrat finally began to get the idea that there might be a problem causing the prolonged absence of Arkana and her beloved adopted daddy. Even when she did start to worry, though, she did not want to leave Tobo. Tobo was less popular with the Children of the Dead than he was with the Unknown Shadows. The men from Hsien might not give their utmost to pull him through.

The boy's health kept suffering one setback after another complication. The fact that the army was moving would not help his recovery.

Shivetya could show me the Company's southward progress. And did regularly. But I would not look in on Lady. My wife's condition was more grim than Tobo's. There was nothing I could do about it but it upset me so I just did not go where the pain was going to get me. Sometimes the blind eye is the least terrible way of suffering what we cannot make right.

Then there was Arkana.

The little blonde had run off in accordance with her

own stated doctrine. Home to the world of the Voroshk. She used the key we had brought to enter the plain to make her exit. Because Shivetya was interested the once shattered Voroshk shadowgate was almost completely whole again.

In Arkana's homeworld the war with the shadows continued, but sporadically. The shadows had been reduced to a tenth of their original number. The Voroshk had suffered as badly. Their world had been all but destroyed. Not one in a hundred peasants had survived an invasion so enthusiastic it is almost impossible to find a shadow on the plain these days.

Shadows kill. They prefer people but will prey on anything they run into. Even things you find under rocks. People are smart enough to figure out ways to get through the night. Not much else can.

The few survivors in the Voroshk world were starving. They had lost so many draft animals they could not plant. Their livestock had all been taken, if not by the shadows then by the Voroshk themselves. The Voroshk had no intention of sharing the common suffering.

Arkana had gone, had seen, had changed her uncertain mind. This was not what she wanted. But she had waited too long to turn back.

She was seen. Family closed in fast. And deprived her of her post and clothing. She became a prisoner of her relatives, who began formulating big breeding plans immediately.

The shadowgate disaster had left the Voroshk with few women of childbearing age.

Arkana got elected to become queen ant for a whole new mob.

She would do what she had to do to survive. She would bide her time once again. Her uncles had confiscated her key to the shadowgates but were unaware what it was. And she was not talking. They were the sort of men who would abandon the disaster they had created and go coursing off in search of new worlds to conquer. So much easier than rebuilding.

It was a good thing Shivetya had power enough to will the shattered gate to heal itself, though that might imply that the nonfunctional gates had failed because of benign neglect. In fact, recalling what Tobo and Suvrin had reported concerning their explorations, all the shadowgates were crippled somehow.

Shivetya did not like anyone very much these days.

I let him know, "I have a couple of things left to do." Since my mind was no longer a mystery, he knew what already. And he did have a little patience left.

A pretty indulgent partner in crime, that old devil.

145

Glittering Stone:
Then Shukrat Came

Shukrat arrived while I was sleeping, dropping in through the hole in the roof. So entangled with Shivetya was I now that I knew she was there without noticing or paying much mind. My friend the white crow came and did the wake-up dirty deed. I sat up, rewarding the bird with some rude remark or other.

"Just trying to be helpful. You aren't leaving me much to do these days."

"Funny how being a prisoner reduces your options, isn't it? What goes around comes around and all that? But we can still be friends, can't we? Hi, cuter daughter. You finally got here."

Shukrat was exhausted but game. "So what's going on, Pop? Where's Arkana?"

"Well. Arkana got a wild hair, ran off home and now is knee-deep in shit." I explained.

Shukrat's reaction was, "Yuch!"

"Hey, you could be the most popular girl in town yourself if you give them the chance."

"They might try. They'll be sorry if they do. I didn't waste all my time with Tobo playing games. How come you know all that if she took your key and you can't go out poking around?"

"Shivetya and I have been getting to know one another. There isn't much else to do around here when you're waiting for your slower child to start wondering if you haven't maybe gotten yourself into some trouble."

"I see you did some writing, too."

"I'm running short on time, daughter," I said, revealing a secret never even shared with my wife. "I've had so much luck, for so long, that the law of averages is overdue to catch up. Any day. There's only one risk left that I'm willing to take. So I want to have all my shit in order before something happens. I want to check out knowing I did everything the Company could ask, and then some." My expectation that I do not have much time left has become an ever more powerful influence on my thinking since our return from the Land of Unknown Shadows. It has approached the level of obsession since I have been back here in the fortress with no name.

Shukrat proceeded with normal, journey-ending business while we talked, unloading her flying post. She swung down a large hemp sack that rattled as she said, "Let me get some rest, first, then we'll go rescue Scruffy Butt. Not because I give a damn what they do to her, you understand. Just as a favor to my Pop."

"I understand. I appreciate it. Maybe she can do the same for you, someday."

"Oh, yeah, that would be good."

"What's in the sack?"

She thought about being evasive, realized that there was no point. "Snail shells. Tobo didn't want me to travel unprotected. He worries about me."

"How is he?"

"He has good days and he has bad days. More bad than good. In his health and in his mind. It scares me. Nobody can tell me if he's going to make it. Or if he'll be sane if he does. I'm afraid it might all depend on his mother."

"What? Sahra turned up?"

"No. She's definitely dead. I think. But her ghost, and her mother's ghost and her grandmother's ghost, keep following him wherever he goes. Whenever his fever gets to him he sees them. And they talk to him. They nag him, he says. He doesn't like it. But my opinion is, he damned well ought to start listening to them. Because he gets these brain fevers every time he starts to do something that his mother wouldn't have liked while she was alive. Even if it's only something like forgetting to clean his teeth."

"You really believe he's being haunted by his female ancestors?"

"Doesn't matter if I do, Pop. *He* believes it. Even when he's fever-free and completely sane he'll say his mother intends to stay around until he no longer needs her guidance. Then she'll be free to join Murgen. Tobo really resents the implication that he isn't mature and his behavior is keeping her from her rest. And Sahra, apparently, is just as resentful of his immaturity, because she'd rather be somewhere besides here baby-sitting a grown man."

"Why do I get the feeling there's something more?"

"Because you're right. There is more. He thinks those women might run out of patience. He's afraid they'll just drag him along with them."

"You mean kill him?"

"No! His mother, Pop. Not kill him. Take him along. Out

of his body. The way they say his father used to do. Only they wouldn't let him come back. If that happened his body would die eventually. And before you tell me Sahra wouldn't let her baby die, you need to remember this ghost isn't the Sahra you knew. This Sahra has been on the other side for a while, running with ghosts who have been there a lot longer than she has. And at least one of those was able to see Tobo's various potential futures way back before Murgen and Sahra ever got together."

Sounded to me like Shukrat was just as much a believer as Tobo was.

"All right. Rest, little girl. I'll come up with a plan while you do."

Look at me. Manly man. Older than dirt, limping, one bad eye, short one hand, reads and writes, but a manly man for all that.

146

The Voroshk World:
Stronghold Rhuknavr

The Voroshk shadowgate was being watched from the other side. Shukrat's uncles hoped she would find her way home, too, and they were eager to obtain another breeder.

We did not work hard to avoid being discovered by the watchers. But we did come by night and Shukrat did leak some of her most unusual companions through to distract the sentries.

Tobo did not stint when he gave her Unknown Shadows to help her out in her adventures down this way. Unlike when he gave me those two wanna-be ravens that were never around and had not been seen now in months. He assigned her some of the biggest, the darkest, the smartest, that would stand by her and do what she said.

The Black Hounds darted around and over the two watchers, keeping them from flying just long enough for us to get through the shadowgate and add ourselves to the equation. Shukrat was able to put them both to sleep despite the state of high excitement the Unknown Shadows had aroused.

In moments we understood why.

"They're just kids!" I said, while undressing one. "This one can't be more than eleven or twelve."

The one Shukrat stripped was even younger. "These two are the youngest Tologev brothers. Somebody really is desperate if he's sending kids this young out alone when there're still shadows roaming around."

I thought that was just fine. The thinner the Voroshk were spread, the better.

The two boys we left behind, up in trees for their own safety. We confiscated their posts and clothing.

It was a long flight. We did not show ourselves during the day. Along the way Shukrat showed me the ruins of Khatovar. I did not feel inclined to explore. I did not have time. There were changes going on inside me. I had to hold them off until I got Arkana free.

The white crow mocked me and accused me of cheating on Lady. She refused to believe I was not. I no longer argued. She was still bitter because she had not been able to take me away from her sister.

Arkana was being held in a minor Voroshk fortress called Rhuknavr. We flew in low, to within a mile, then awaited midnight while floating high up in the tops of trees that were old when Khatovar fell. We put out a dozen shadowtraps Shukrat had crafted according to Shivetya's instructions. Once she released the Unknown Shadows, though, the traps were not necessary.

At my insistence Shukrat made doubly sure that the

Unknown Shadows clearly understood we were about to butt heads with people who had considerable experience dealing with creatures of darkness. Their advantage over the killer shadows was that they were not just driven clumps of hunger and hatred. They were cunning and wicked and able to reason, although unfortunately weak on the concept of cooperation.

I asked Shukrat, "You think we might have better luck in the daytime, after everybody inside there relaxes?"

"They're not that alert. They haven't had an incident here for a long time."

"How do you know that?"

"I just do. Now that I'm close enough to feel them." Meaning, probably, that she was hiding the whispers of the Unknown Shadows already.

"Uhm? Are you close enough for them to feel you?"

"No. Because I'm alone. And because I'm dressed. And because they aren't trying to feel for me."

"I see." If it was not our unseen associates it must be something like the way I had begun to sense Shivetya. "Bird. Pay attention." It was not my intent to waste any resource. The white crow was a valuable resource. "So where is my other baby, Shukrat? Be as exact as you can because my feathered friend needs to know how to get there to tell her that we're coming and she should be ready to go."

The crow squawked like it had just found a snake raiding its nest. It protested so vigorously that the surrounding night fell into an uneasy silence.

"Good for you nobody in these parts would recognize Taglian. What's the big squawk? You infiltrated how many places at other times?"

The crow continued to mutter something to the effect of, that was different. The difference mainly being whose idea the infiltration was. She understood that I was getting real thick with Shivetya, though, and the golem might have a great deal to say about whether or not she ever got out of the cave of the ancients. Once she got the frustration worked out she was ready to go.

I had Shukrat describe the interior of Rhuknavr the best she could. Which was not that well. She had not been there in ten years. The crow would have to locate Arkana on her own. Shukrat could not pin her down.

I said, "You just tell her we're coming and she should be ready. And, if she can manage it, she might put a sleep spell on anybody near enough to touch."

The crow left. We waited. I stared at the sky. I found this one far stranger than that of the Land of Unknown Shadows. There was no large moon here, apparently. At least none tonight nor during the nights I spent here before. But there were scores of little ones, the biggest maybe a fifth the size of my own. All the moons seemed terribly busy, scampering hither and yon. When I mentioned them to Shukrat she began telling me about her world's unique breed of astrology, which relied upon the motions of all those moons. Even after ages of study those moons still presented the occasional surprise.

"Once, when I was little, two of them banged off of each other. None of the others have moved quite the same way since. And it rained down pieces for years. Only about a hundred miles from here there's a place where a really big piece hit. I was at Junkledesag, which is over that way another eighty miles, and it was still awful. There were earthquakes and noise like the end of the world. There was a fire in the sky that took all night to fade away. It was like when one of the *rheitgeistiden* explodes, only a million times worse. It knocked a huge hole in the ground. Now the hole is kind of a lake."

The white crow dropped out of the night. "Ready."

"Easier than you expected, eh?"

The bird grunted sullenly.

"Show us the way, Fearless Feathered Explorer."

* * *

The next stage was anticlimactic. Only three or four actual Voroshk occupied Rhuknavr. In behavior so human I do not know why I did not foresee it, a small faction of survivors were concealing Arkana's return from the rest. For what little advantage controlling a viable breeder gave.

We left our posts nuzzling the fortress beside an unglazed hall-end window. The interior was too tight for flight. The crow showed the way to Arkana's chamber. There were no bars anywhere but there was a sleeping, non-Voroshk sentry slumped on a stool in the hallway. There had been a pretense that Arkana was a guest.

The girl jumped on me the moment we entered. "I knew you'd come."

"Did you?"

"I hoped you would. All right? I'm sorry. I was stupid. I just wanted . . . I had to . . . Thank you. Thank you. Thank you."

"Why not save your talking until we're out of here? The point of sending the bird ahead was so you'd be ready." The critter named flapped out the room's one small window.

She grabbed odds and ends. Not much. "I don't know where my *rheitgeistide* and *shefsepoke* are."

"We brought something for you. Let's go."

All went well until we were sliding out the window. Then a child, rubbing sleep from her eyes, wandered into the hallway, presumably disturbed by some sound. She stared for a moment, then folded, touched by a sleep spell from one of the girls.

Nothing happened immediately. But in time the child would tell somebody. Unless she had a habit of sleepwalking.

Comfortably aloft and heading south, I asked Arkana, "Are you pregnant?"

She took no offense. "No. They hadn't worked out who got to be first. Though every time I turned around somebody was trying to sneak in. Like they thought I couldn't possibly resist them. I passed out enough bruises that even Gromovol would've figured out that that kind of shit could get some-body hurt—but these guys were real optimists."

She had been hanging out with the right people to learn how to sucker a guy who thought girls ought to be easy prey. I said, "I guess we can thank some god for that small favor."

"You can thank Arkana for not putting up with their shit."

"That's my delicate flower."

Soon after sunrise Shukrat spotted seven or eight protean black dots bobbing in the air far behind us. "They're chasing us, Pop."

I checked. "We climb up a little higher, we'll be able to stay far enough ahead."

The girls agreed. But Arkana added, "There weren't that many of the Family at Rhuknavr. They must've sent for help from Junkledesag or Drasivrad. There aren't but fifteen or sixteen of the Family left alive."

I said, "Just in case they do start pressing us, do either of you have an objection to more of them getting hurt?"

Arkana gave me an unhappy look. Despite our hours aloft she was not yet fully clad in apparel taken from one of the boy sentries at the gate. Getting dressed is hard to do when you are riding one of those posts and staying out of sight by skimming the treetops. Not to mention that before she started changing she had to convince the clothing that it now belonged to her, not the boy from the shadowgate. "How do you expect to manage that, Pop?" She sounded suspicious. And rightly so.

"Same way I got Kina. But you'll have to name me names." I had the First Father's book with me. I had taught myself enough of the Voroshk language to use the codes to blow those guys out of the sky. If I knew who I was turning into a cloud of dust.

"Don't do that. Not if you don't have to."

I gave it a moment. Then, "If you can forgive them, then I can."

"They never really did anything to me."

They would have but I did not belabor the point. Both of these kids were too forgiving and too understanding for their own good. Those guys back there would have done a whole lot of ugly to both of them, given the chance. I know those kind of guys. I have been those kind of guys.

Just for my own pleasure, privately, when the girls were not paying attention, I tripped the codes that would kill Arkana's post. We were too far from Rhuknavr for me to tell if it worked. I hoped not, now. Because after I did it I remembered the sleepy little girl in the hallway.

She would haunt me for a while.

It was closer than it really needed to be, us getting through the shadowgate ahead of trouble. The key gave me some grief, probably because I was in too much of a hurry.

"Now what?" Shukrat asked once we were safe from the men and naked boys cursing us from the other side of the barrier.

I said, "I guess you two can go back to the army. I'm going to stay here. On the plain. With Shivetya. There's a job I've got to do. A promise I have to keep."

Nobody spoke again until we were close to the fortress with no name. Then Shukrat asked, "What about Lady?"

"If she's in good enough health you can bring her down here to me and I'll do what I can to help her. If she's not, leave her the fuck alone. Her main problem is she's got to heal herself."

Both girls looked at me like I was some really stinky monster that had just popped up in the middle of a bunny farm ripping the fur out of cute and tender throats.

"Look, I love my wife just one whole hell of a lot. There isn't any way I can explain it to you. But the fact is, love her is about all I can do. She's insane. By any standard but her own. And there's nothing I can do to change that. If you were familiar with the Annals you would know that."

Arkana sneered. "You don't ever give up, do you?"

She caught me off balance that time. "Actually, no. I wasn't thinking about finding somebody to keep the Annals. I was trying to clarify my relationship with my wife."

But did I know what that was myself? Even after all these years? Possibly more important, did *she* have any idea?

All that seemed to matter less and less as we drew closer to the fortress with no name.

147

Fortress with No Name: Putting the Pen Down

I stood before the golem Shivetya, basking in his mild impatience. I was impatient myself. But the distractions of the world still had their hold on me.

That part of Gunni philosophy is solidly founded. Before you can achieve more than the lowest possible order of spiritual focus you have to learn to put all worldly distractions aside. *All* of them. Right now. Never mind what. Otherwise there will always be that one more critical thing that just absolutely has to be handled before you can move forward.

My one more thing was Lady. My wife. Who continued to wobble on the brink of the abyss without ever quite slipping over. To me it was evident that the missing medicine now was any will to battle on. And the white crow agreed with me.

"Let me work on her," the bird told me. "Ten minutes and I'll have her so pissed off she'll melt mountains trying to get close enough to spank me."

"No doubt. But I like things the way they are. Except for how long it's taking."

Suvrin seemed to be taking forever making any headway coming south. Though he was covering ground much faster than we had headed north. Nobody was trying to slow him down.

I whiled my time exploring the expansive wonders of Shivetya's memories—but avoiding those including Khatovar. Khatovar was a dessert I meant to save until there were no distractions at all. Khatovar was a special treat for a time when every flavor could be savored.

Eventually, I yielded to the inevitable and sent the girls to bring Lady to me. Maybe my big pal on the wooden throne could give me a hint or two how to goose her into getting going again.

The Nef appeared almost as soon as the girls popped out of the hole in the roof. They were in a black humor, eager for a fight, and because I could not communicate with them my mood soon turned just as dark. I hunted up One-Eye's spear. If it could handle a Goddess it ought to be able to polish off three obnoxious, nagging spooks.

Shivetya stopped me. He could communicate with the Nef. He indicated that he would calm them down with an explanation of what we were doing here. His liberation would not sentence them to extinction. In fact, they were about to enter a new phase of existence. They were going to get work maintaining the glittering plain. There were scores of odd jobs and cleanups that needed special attention.

Shivetya and I were now so connected I could see the plain in my mind almost at will and the rest of the world, through his eyes, with only a little more effort. For a while I watched the girls race northward, each occasionally finding a moment to have fun flying.

I slept for a few hours. Or a week. When I awakened I picked up a lamp and walked over to the throne. I carried One-Eye's spear under my other arm, on the bad hand side. Shivetya and I stared at each other for a while.

"Is it time?" I asked. And, "You think we're ready to manage without the daggers, now? Yeah? Just one more little thing, then. I need to leave a note for my girls."

That turned into a letter. Trust the Annalist to go on and on.

A very clear thought. *Have you finished now? Are you certain you are done?*

"It's time."

My bridesmaids, the Nef, drifted in out of the darkness. They seemed more substantial than ever before. They like me just fine, now.

I am putting the pen down.

148

Glittering Stone: And the Daughters of Time

We saw lights from way out. What was that? There are no lights on the glittering plain. We climbed a thousand feet. By then the lights were gone except for what came out of the hole in the dome over the top of the demon's throne room. Before we got there that went away, too.

Then we were too busy getting Lady and Tobo through the hole to worry about anything else. *Rheitgeistiden* are trouble when their riders are not helping.

When we got to the floor we found only one oil lamp burning on that old man's—that scholar from Taglios's—worktable. Croaker left a note. And, that clever old fart, he wrote it in our language. Not very good, but good enough to understand.

I guess he did have the gift for tongues like he always said.

Arkana took the lamp and used it to fire up a couple of lanterns. We went off to look for Croaker. She said, "You know, he was always teasing us but after a while I did start feeling almost like he was my dad." We never ever talk about our real fathers. We would never get along.

"Yeah. He looked out for you. Maybe more than you know."

"You, too."

We found Croaker sitting beside the wooden throne. "Hey. He's still breathing."

"I don't think . . . Shit. Look. Those knives are all gone from the demon." Actually, they were laying all over the floor.

So just then the demon's eyes open and so do Croaker's and both of them look pretty confused and it is only then that I really understand what Croaker was trying to tell us in his letter. It was not some confused religious good-bye, he just did not have enough of the right words to tell us that he and the demon had it worked out to trade places. So Shivetya got to become a mortal for as long as Croaker's body would last and Croaker got to be a big, old, wise sea dragon swimming all around in the ocean of history. So both of them got to go to heaven. And the Nef were happy. And the plain went on. And the white crow kept bitching, riding around on the Croaker body's shoulder. And Arkana and I got in a running fight about who was going to go on keeping the Annals, because both of us hate to write.

So we take turns. When the little tramp will get away from Tobo long enough to pick up a pen and do her part.

A point she missed, probably because she is too dim to notice, is that Lady is recovering. A while ago I saw her spinning tiny fireballs. I think if there was some way she could make love to that big monster over there she would do it three times a day. Because it is from him that the power flows. It is, probably, the best and most meaningful gift he has ever given her and with it she can become anything she wants to be. Maybe even the young and beautiful and romantically sorrowful and remote Lady of Charm again.

But then he would have to turn Soulcatcher loose just to give balance to the world.

I wonder if he was right when he said a thousand years from now we might be the gods everyone remembers.

And I wonder what he might do about his daughter. His flesh daughter. I think there is no hope for her because she has no hope of her own, but I also think that if there is a hope, Pop will find it.

Suvrin is looking impatient. He wants to hitch a ride down to the Hsien shadowgate. He is not Aridatha Singh but he may have to do.

I guess it is time to go see our new world. The Abode of Ravens. The Land of Unknown Shadows. Shukrat says the names have a ring. That it sounds like home to her.

I think home is what I carry around inside me. I am a snail with the meat on the outside.

And it is Shukrat's damned turn to write. The sneaking, slacking little bimbo.

Incessant wind sweeps the plain. It murmurs on across grey stone, carrying dust from far climes to nibble eternally at the memorial pillars. There are a few shadows out there still but they are the weak and the timid and the hopelessly lost.

It is immortality of a sort.

Memory is immortality of a sort.

In the night, when the wind dies and silence rules the place of glittering stone, I remember. And they all live again.

Soldiers live. And wonder why.